D1107284

THE FURTHER ADVENTURES
OF THE FAMOUS FIVE

THE FURTHER ADVENTURES
OF THE FAMOUS FIVE

ENID BLYTON

Hodder
Children's
Books

a division of Hodder Headline Limited

This collection published in 2005
by Hodder Children's Books
Five Get Into Trouble first published in Great Britain in 1949
Five on Finniston Farm first published in Great Britain in 1960
Five are Together Again first published in Great Britain in 1962

For further information on Enid Blyton please contact
www.blyton.com

1

A Catalogue record for this book is
available from the British Library

ISBN 0 340 91188 3

Typeset by Hewer Text UK Ltd, Edinburgh
Printed and bound in Great Britain by
Clays Ltd, St Ives plc

The paper used in this book is a natural recyclable product
made from wood grown in sustainable forests.
The hard coverboard is recycled.

Hodder Children's Books
a division of Hodder Headline Limited
338 Euston Road
London NW1 3BH

CONTENTS

FIVE GET INTO TROUBLE

CONTENTS

CHAPTER ONE

Five make a holiday plan

'REALLY, QUENTIN, you are *most* difficult to cope with!' said Aunt Fanny to her husband.

The four children sat at the table, eating breakfast, and looking very interested. What had Uncle Quentin done now? Julian winked at Dick, and Anne kicked George under the table. Would Uncle Quentin explode into a temper, as he sometimes did?

Uncle Quentin held a letter in his hand, which his wife had just given back to him after she had read it. It was the letter that was causing all the trouble. Uncle Quentin frowned – and then decided not to explode. Instead he spoke quite mildly.

'Well, Fanny dear – how can I possibly be expected to remember exactly when the children's holidays come, and if they are going to be here with us or with your sister? You know I have my scientific work to do – and very important it is too, at the moment. *I* can't remember when the children's schools break up or go back!'

'You could always ask *me*,' said Aunt Fanny, exasperated. 'Really, Quentin, have you forgotten how we discussed having Julian, Dick and Anne here these Easter holidays because they all enjoy Kirrin and the sea so much at this time of the year? You said you would arrange to go off to your conferences *after* they had had their holidays – not in the very middle of them!'

5

'But they've broken up so late!' said Uncle Quentin. 'I didn't know they were going to do that.'

'Well, but you know Easter came late this year, so they broke up late,' said Aunt Fanny, with a sigh.

'Father wouldn't think of that,' said George. 'What's the matter, Mother? Does Father want to go away in the middle of our holidays, or what?'

'Yes,' said Aunt Fanny, and she stretched out her hand for the letter again. 'Let me see, he would have to go off in two days' time and I must certainly go with him. I can't possibly leave you children alone here, with nobody in the house. If Joanna were not ill it would be all right, but she won't be back for a week or two.'

Joanna was the cook. The children were all very fond of her, and had been sorry to find her missing when they had arrived for the holidays.

'We can look after ourselves,' said Dick. 'Anne is quite a good cook.'

'I can help too,' said George. Her real name was Georgina, but everyone called her George. Her mother smiled.

'Oh George, last time you boiled an egg you left it in the saucepan till it boiled dry! I don't think the others would like your cooking very much.'

'It was just that I forgot the egg was there,' said George. 'I went to fetch the clock to time it, and on the way I remembered Timmy hadn't had his dinner, and . . .'

'Yes, we know all about that,' said her mother with a laugh. 'Timmy had his dinner, but your father had to go without his tea!'

'Woof,' said Timmy from under the table, hearing his name mentioned. He licked George's foot just to remind her he was there.

6

'Well, let's get back to the subject,' said Uncle Quentin, impatiently. 'I've got to go to these conferences, that's certain. I've to read some important papers there. You needn't come with me, Fanny – you can stay and look after the children.'

'Mother doesn't need to,' said George. 'We can do something we badly wanted to do, but thought we'd have to put off till the summer hols.'

'Oh *yes*,' said Anne, at once. 'So we could! Do let's!'

'Yes – I'd like that too,' said Dick.

'Well – *what* is it?' asked Aunt Fanny. 'I'm quite in the dark. If it's anything dangerous, I shall say no. So make up your minds about that!'

'When do we *ever* do anything dangerous?' cried George.

'Plenty of times,' said her mother. 'Now, what's this plan of yours?'

'It's nothing much,' said Julian. 'It's only that all our bikes happen to be in first-class order, Aunt Fanny, and you know you gave us two small tents for Christmas – so we just thought it would be great fun sometime to go off on our bikes, taking our tents with us and do a little exploring round the countryside.'

'It's grand weather now – we could have fine fun,' said Dick. 'After all, you must have meant us to use the tents, Aunt Fanny! Here's our chance!'

'I meant you to use them in the garden, or on the beach,' said Aunt Fanny. 'Last time you went camping you had Mr Luffy with you to look after you. I don't think I like the idea of you going off by yourselves with tents.'

'Oh, Fanny, if *Julian* can't look after the others he must be a pretty feeble specimen,' said her husband, sounding

7

impatient. 'Let them go! I'd bank on Julian any time to keep the others in order and see they were all safe and sound.'

'Thanks, Uncle,' said Julian, who was not used to compliments from his uncle Quentin! He glanced round at the other children and grinned. 'Of course, it's easy to manage this little lot – though Anne sometimes is *very* difficult!'

Anne opened her mouth indignantly. She was the smallest and the only really manageable one. She caught Julian's grin – he was teasing her, of course. She grinned back. 'I promise to be easy to manage,' she said in an innocent voice to her uncle Quentin.

He looked surprised. 'Well, I must say I should have thought that George was the only difficult one to . . .' he began, but stopped when he saw his wife's warning frown. George *was* difficult, but it didn't make her any less difficult if that fact was pointed out!

'Quentin, you never know when Julian is pulling your leg or not, do you?' said his wife. 'Well – if you *really* think Julian can be put in charge – and we can let them go off on a cycling tour – with their new tents . . .'

'Hurray! It's settled then!' yelled George, and began to thump Dick on the back in joy. 'We'll go off tomorrow. We'll . . .'

'GEORGE! There's no need to shout and thump like that,' said her mother. 'You know your father doesn't like it – and now you've excited Timmy too. Lie down, Timmy – there he's off round the room like a mad thing!'

Uncle Quentin got up to go. He didn't like it when meal-times turned into pandemonium. He almost fell over the excited Timmy, and disappeared thankfully out of the room. What a household it was when the four children and the dog were there!

'Oh Aunt Fanny, can we really go off tomorrow?' asked Anne, her eyes shining. 'It *is* such lovely April weather – honestly it's as hot as July. We hardly need to take any thick clothes with us.'

'Well, if you think that, you won't go,' said Aunt Fanny, firmly. 'It may be hot and sunny today, but you can never trust April to be the same two days together. It may be pouring tomorrow, and snowing on the next day! I shall have to give you money, Julian, so that you can go to an hotel any night the weather is bad.'

The four children immediately made up their minds that the weather would never be too bad!

'Won't it be fun?' said Dick. 'We can choose our own sleeping-place every night and put our tents there. We can bike half the night if it's moonlight, and we want to!'

'Ooooh – biking in moonlight – I've never done that,' said Anne. 'It sounds super.'

'Well, it's a good thing there is something you want to do while we are away,' said Aunt Fanny. 'Dear me, I've been married all these years to Quentin, and still he makes this kind of muddle without my knowing! Well, well, we'd better get busy today, and decide what you're to take.'

Everything suddenly seemed very exciting. The four children rushed to do their morning jobs of making the beds and tidying their rooms, talking at the tops of their voices.

'Who would have thought we'd be off on our own tomorrow!' said Dick, pulling his sheets and blankets up in a heap together.

'Dick! *I'll* make your bed,' cried Anne, shocked to see it made in such a hurried way. 'You can't possibly make it like that!'

'Oh, *can't* I!' cried Dick. 'You just wait and see! And what's more I'm making Julian's like that too, so you clear off and do your own, Anne – tuck in every corner, smooth the pillow, pat the eiderdown – do what you like with your own bed, but leave me to make mine my own way! Wait till we're off on our biking tour – you won't want to bother about beds then – you'll roll up your sleeping-bag and that will be that!'

He finished his bed as he spoke, dragging on the cover all crooked, and stuffing his pyjamas under the pillow. Anne laughed and went to make her own. She was excited too. The days stretched before her, sunny, full of strange places, unknown woods, big and little hills, chattering streams, wayside picnics, biking in the moonlight – did Dick really mean that? How wizard!

They were all very busy that day, packing up into rucksacks the things they would need, folding up the tents into as small a compass as possible to tie on to their carriers, ferreting in the larder for food to take, looking out the maps they would want.

Timmy knew they were going off somewhere, and, of course, felt certain he was going too, so he was as excited as they were, barking and thumping his tail, and generally getting into everyone's way all day long. But nobody minded. Timmy was one of them, one of the 'Five', he could do almost everything but speak – it was quite unthinkable to go anywhere without dear old Timmy.

'I suppose Timothy can keep up with you all right, when you bike for miles?' Aunt Fanny asked Julian.

'Goodness yes,' said Julian. 'He never minds how far we go. I hope you won't worry about us, Aunt Fanny. You know what a good guard Timmy is.'

'Yes, I know,' said his aunt. 'I wouldn't be letting you go off like this with such an easy mind if I didn't know Timmy would be with you! He's as good as any grown-up at looking after you!'

'Woof, woof,' agreed Timmy. George laughed. 'He says he's as good as *two* grown-ups, Mother!' she said, and Timmy thumped his big tail on the floor.

'Woof, woof, *woof*,' he said. Which meant, 'Not two – but *three*!'

CHAPTER TWO

Away on their own

THEY WERE all ready the next day. Everything was neatly
packed and strapped to the bicycles, except for the rucksacks, which each child was to carry on his or her back.
The baskets held a variety of food for that day, but when it
had been eaten Julian was to buy what they needed.

'I suppose all their brakes are in order?' said Uncle
Quentin, thinking he ought to take some interest in the
proceedings, and remembering that when *he* was a boy
and had a bicycle, the brakes would never work.

'Oh Uncle Quentin, of course they're all right, ' said
Dick. 'We'd never dream of going out on our bikes if the
brakes and things weren't in order. The Highway Code is
very strict about things like that, you know – and so are
we!'

Uncle Quentin looked as if he had never even heard of
the Highway Code. It was quite likely he hadn't. He lived
in a world of his own, a world of theories and figures and
diagrams – and he was eager to get back to it! However, he
waited politely for the children to make last-minute ad-
justments, and then they were ready.

'Good-bye, Aunt Fanny! I'm afraid we shan't be able to
write to you, as you won't be able to get in touch with us to
let us know where you get fixed up. Never mind, enjoy
yourselves,' said Julian.

'Good-bye, Mother! Don't worry about us – we'll be
having a jolly good time!' called George.

12

'Good-bye, Aunt Fanny; good-bye, Uncle Quentin!'

'So long, Uncle! Aunt Fanny, we're off!'

And so they were, cycling down the lane that led away from Kirrin Cottage. Their aunt and uncle stood at the gate, waving till the little party had disappeared round the corner in the sunshine. Timmy was loping along beside George's bicycle, on his long, strong legs, overjoyed at the idea of a really good run.

'Well, we're off,' said Julian, as they rounded the corner. 'What a bit of luck, going off like this by ourselves. Good old Uncle Quentin! I'm glad he made that muddle.'

'Don't let's ride too many miles the first day – I always get so stiff if we do,' said Anne.

'We're not going to,' said Dick. 'Whenever you feel tired just say so – it doesn't matter where we stop!'

The morning was very warm. Soon the children began to feel wet with perspiration. They had sweaters on and they took them off, stuffing them in their baskets. George looked more like a boy than ever, with her short curly hair blown up by the wind. All of them wore shorts and thin jerseys except Julian, who had on jeans. He rolled up the sleeves of his jersey, and the others did the same.

They covered mile after mile, enjoying the sun and the wind. Timmy galloped beside them, untiring, his long pink tongue hanging out. He ran on the grassy edge of the road when there was one. He really was a very sensible dog!

They stopped at a tiny village called Manlington-Tovey. It had only one general store, but it sold practically everything – or seemed to! 'Hope it sells ginger beer!' said Julian. 'My tongue's hanging out like Timmy's!'

The little shop sold lemonade, orangeade, lime juice, grapefruit juice and ginger beer. It was really difficult to choose which to have. It also sold ice-creams, and soon the children were sitting drinking ginger beer and lime juice mixed, and eating delicious ices.

'Timmy must have an ice,' said George. 'He does so love them. Don't you, Timmy?'

'Woof,' said Timmy, and gulped his ice down in two big, gurgly licks.

'It's really a waste of ice-creams to give them to Timmy,' said Anne. 'He hardly has time to taste them, he gobbles them so. No, Timmy, get down. I'm going to finish up every single bit of mine, and there won't be even a lick for you!'

Timmy went off to drink from a bowl of water that the shopwoman had put down for him. He drank and he drank, then he flopped down, panting.

The children took a bottle of ginger beer each with them when they went off again. They meant to have it with their lunch. Already they were beginning to think with pleasure of eating the sandwiches put up into neat packets for them.

Anne saw some cows pulling at the grass in a meadow as they passed. 'It must be awful to be a cow and eat nothing but tasteless grass,' she called to George. 'Think what a cow misses – never tastes an egg and lettuce sandwich, never eats a chocolate eclair, never has a boiled egg – and can't even drink a glass of ginger beer! Poor cows!'

George laughed. 'You do think of silly things, Anne,' she said. 'Now you've made me want my lunch all the more – talking about egg sandwiches and ginger beer! I know Mother made us egg sandwiches – and sardine ones too.'

'It's no good,' chimed in Dick, leading the way into a

little copse, his bicycle wobbling dangerously, 'it's no good – we can't go another inch if you girls are going to jabber about food all the time. Julian, what about lunch?'

It was a lovely picnic, that first one in the copse. There were clumps of primroses all round, and from somewhere nearby came the sweet scent of hidden violets. A thrush was singing madly on a hazel tree, with two chaffinches calling 'pink-pink' every time he stopped.

'Band and decorations laid on,' said Julian, waving his hand towards the singing birds and the primroses. 'Very nice too. We just want a waiter to come and present us with a menu!'

A rabbit lolloped near, its big ears standing straight up inquiringly. 'Ah – the waiter!' said Julian, at once. 'What have you to offer us today, Bunny? A nice rabbit-pie?'

The rabbit scampered off at top speed. It had caught the smell of Timmy nearby and was panic-stricken. The children laughed, because it seemed as if it was the mention of rabbit-pie that had sent it away. Timmy stared at the disappearing rabbit, but made no move to go after it.

'Well, *Timmy*! That's the first time you've ever let a rabbit go off on its own,' said Dick. 'You *must* be hot and tired. Got anything for him to eat, George?'

'Of course,' said George. 'I made his sandwiches myself.'

And so she had! She had bought sausage meat at the butcher's and had actually made Timmy twelve sandwiches with it, all neatly cut and packed.

The others laughed. George never minded taking trouble over Timmy. He wolfed his sandwiches eagerly, and thumped his tail hard on the mossy ground. They all sat and munched happily, perfectly contented to be together out in the open air, eating a wonderful lunch.

15

Anne gave a scream. 'George! Look what you're doing! You're eating one of Timmy's sandwiches!'

'Urhh!' said George. 'I thought it tasted a bit strong. I must have given Timmy one of mine and taken his instead. Sorry, Tim!'

'Woof,' said Tim politely, and accepted another of his sandwiches.

'At the rate he eats them he wouldn't really notice if he had twenty or fifty,' remarked Julian. 'He's had all his now, hasn't he? Well, look out, everybody – he'll be after ours. Aha – the band has struck up again!'

Everyone listened to the thrush. 'Mind how you go,' sang the thrush. 'Mind how you go! Mind how you do-it, do-it, do-it!'

'Sounds like a Safety First poster,' said Dick, and settled down with his head on a cushion of moss. 'All right, old bird – we'll mind how we go – but we're going to have a bit of a snooze now, so don't play the band too loudly!'

'It *would* be a good idea to have a bit of a rest,' said Julian, yawning. 'We've done pretty well, so far. We don't want to tire ourselves out the very first day. Get off my legs, Timmy – you're frightfully heavy with all those sandwiches inside you.'

Timmy removed himself. He went to George and flumped himself down beside her, licking her face. She pushed him away.

'Don't be so licky,' she said, sleepily, 'just be on guard like a good dog, and see that nobody comes along and steals our bikes.'

Timmy knew what 'on guard' meant, of course. He sat up straight when he heard the words, and looked carefully all round, sniffing as he did so. Anyone about? No. Not a sight, sound or smell of any stranger. Timmy lay down again, one ear cocked, and one eye very slightly open. George always thought it was marvellous the way he could be asleep with one ear and eye and awake with the others. She was about to say this to Dick and Julian when she saw that they were sound asleep.

She fell asleep too. Nobody came to disturb them. A small robin hopped near inquisitively, and, with his head on one side, considered whether or not it would be a good thing to pull a few hairs out of Timmy's tail to line his new nest. The slit in Timmy's awake-eye widened a little – woe betide the robin if he tried any funny tricks on Timmy!

The robin flew off. The thrush sang a little more, and the rabbit came out again. Timmy's eye opened wide. The rabbit fled. Timmy gave a tiny snore. Was he awake or was he asleep? The rabbit wasn't going to wait and find out!

It was half past three when they all awoke one by one. Julian looked at his watch. 'It's almost tea-time!' he said, and Anne gave a little squeal.

'Oh no – why we've only just had lunch, and I'm still as full as can be!'

Julian grinned. 'It's all right. We'll go by our tummies for our meals, not by our watches, Anne. Come on, get up! We'll go without you if you don't.'

They wheeled their bicycles out of the primrose copse and mounted again. The breeze was lovely to feel on their faces. Anne gave a little groan.

'Oh dear – I feel a bit stiff already. Do you mean to go very many miles more, Ju?'

'No, not many,' said Julian. 'I thought we'd have tea

somewhere when we feel like it and then do a bit of shopping for our supper and breakfast and then hunt about for a really good place to put up our tents for the night. I found a little lake on the map, and I thought we could have a swim in it if we can find it.'

This all sounded very good indeed. George felt she could cycle for miles if a swim in a lake was at the end of it.

'That's a very nice plan of yours,' she said, approvingly. 'Very nice indeed. I think our whole tour ought to be planned round lakes – so that we can always have a swim, night and morning!'

'Woof,' said Timmy, running beside George's bicycle. 'Woof!'

'Timmy agrees too,' said George, with a laugh. 'But oh dear – I don't believe he brought his bathing-towel!'

CHAPTER THREE

A lovely day – and a lovely night

THE FIVE of them had a lovely time that evening. They had tea about half past five, and then bought what they wanted for supper and breakfast. New rolls, anchovy paste, a big round jam-tart in a cardboard box, oranges, lime juice, a fat lettuce and some ham sandwiches – it seemed a very nice assortment indeed.

'Let's hope we don't eat it all for supper, and have no breakfast left,' said George, packing the sandwiches into her basket. 'Get down, Timmy. These sandwiches are not for you. I've bought you a whacking big bone – *that* will keep you busy for hours!'

'Well, don't let him have it when we settle down for the night,' said Anne. 'He makes such a row, crunching and munching. He'd keep me awake.'

'*Nothing* would keep *me* awake tonight,' said Dick. 'I believe I could sleep through an earthquake. I'm already thinking kindly of my sleeping-bag.'

'I don't think we need to put up our tents tonight,' said Julian, looking up at the perfectly clear sky. 'I'll ask someone what the weather forecast was on the radio at six. Honestly I think we could just snuggle into our sleeping-bags and have the sky for a roof.'

'How smashing!' said Anne. 'I'd love to lie and look at the stars.'

The weather forecast was good. 'Fine and clear and mild.'

19

'Good,' said Julian. 'That will save us a lot of trouble –
we don't even need to unpack our tents. Come on – have
we got everything now? Does anyone feel as if we ought to
buy any more food?'

The baskets were all full. Nobody thought it advisable
to try and get anything more into them.

'We could get lots more in if Timmy would only carry
his own bones,' said Anne. 'Half my basket is crammed
with enormous bones for him. Why can't you rig up
something so that Timmy could carry his own food,
George? I'm sure he's clever enough.'

'Yes, he's clever enough,' said George. 'But he's much
too greedy, Anne. You know that. He'd stop and eat all
his food at once if he had to carry it. Dogs seem to be able
to eat anything at any time.'

'They're lucky,' said Dick. 'Wish I could. But I just *have*
to pause between my meals!'

'Now for the lake,' said Julian, folding up the map which
he had just been examining. 'It's only about five miles away.
It's called the Green Pool, but it looks a good bit bigger than
a pool. I could do with a bathe. I'm so hot and sticky.'

They came to the lake at about half past seven. It was in
a lovely place, and had beside it a small hut which was
obviously used in summer-time for bathers to change into
bathing-suits. Now it was locked, and curtains were drawn
across the windows.

'I suppose we can go in for a dip if we like?' said Dick
rather doubtfully. 'We shan't be trespassing or anything,
shall we?'

'No. It doesn't say anything about being private,' said
Julian. 'The water won't be very warm, you know, because
it's only mid-April! But after all, we're used to cold baths

20

every morning, and I daresay the sun has taken the chill off the lake. Come on, let's get into bathing things.'

They changed behind the bushes and then ran down to the lake. The water was certainly very cold indeed. Anne skipped in and out, and wouldn't do any more than that.

George joined the boys in a swim, and they all came out glowing and laughing. 'Brrr, that was cold!' said Dick. 'Come on, let's have a sharp run. Look at Anne – dressed already. Timmy, where are you? *You* don't mind the cold water, do you?'

They all tore up and down the little paths by the Green Pool like mad things. Anne was getting the supper ready. The sun had disappeared now, and although the evening was still very mild the radiant warmth of the day had gone. Anne was glad of her sweater.

'Good old Anne,' said Dick, when at last he and the others joined her, dressed again, with their sweaters on for warmth. 'Look, she's got the food all ready. You're fantastic, Anne. I bet if we stayed here for more than one night Anne would have made some kind of larder, and have arranged a good place to wash everything – and be looking for somewhere to keep her dusters and broom!'

'You're so *silly*, Dick,' said Anne. 'You ought to be glad I like messing about with the food and getting it ready for you. Oh TIMMY! Shoo! Get away! Look at him, he's shaken millions and millions of drops of lakewater all over the food. You ought to have dried him, George. You know how he shakes himself after a swim.'

'Sorry,' said George. 'Tim, say you're sorry. Why must you be so *violent* about everything? If I shook myself like that my ears and fingers would fly off into the air!'

It was a lovely meal, sitting there in the evening light, watching the first stars come out in the sky. The children and Timmy were all tired but happy. This was the beginning of their trip and beginnings were always lovely – the days stretched out before you endlessly, and somehow you felt certain that the sun would shine every single day!

They were not long in snuggling into their sleeping-bags when they had finished the meal. They had set them all together in a row, so that they could talk if they wanted to. Timmy was thrilled. He walked solemnly across the whole lot, and was greeted with squeals and threats.

'Timmy! How dare you! When I've had such a big supper too!'

'TIMMY! You brute! You put all your great big feet down on me at once!'

'George, you *really* might stop Timmy from walking all over us like that! I only hope he's not going to do it all night long.'

Timmy looked surprised at the shouts. He settled down beside George, after a vain attempt to get into her sleeping-bag with her. George turned her face away from his licks.

'Oh Timmy, I do love you but I wish you wouldn't make my face so wet. Julian, look at that glorious star – like a little round lamp. What is it?'

'It's not a star really – it's Venus, one of the planets,' said Julian, sleepily. 'But it's called the Evening Star. Fancy you not knowing that, George. Don't they teach you anything at your school?'

George tried to kick Julian through her sleeping-bag, but she couldn't. She gave it up and yawned so loudly that she set all the others yawning too.

Anne fell asleep first. She was the smallest and was more easily tired with long walks and rides than the others, though she always kept up with them valiantly. George gazed unblinkingly at the bright evening star for a minute and then fell asleep suddenly. Julian and Dick talked quietly for a few minutes. Timmy was quite silent. He was tired out with his miles and miles of running.

Nobody stirred at all that night, not even Timmy. He took no notice of a horde of rabbits who played not far off. He hardly pricked an ear when an owl hooted nearby. He didn't even stir when a beetle ran over his head.

But if George had woken and spoken his name Timmy would have been wide awake at once, standing over George and licking her, whining gently! George was the centre of his world, night and day.

The next day was fair and bright. It was lovely to wake up and feel the warm sun on their cheeks, and hear a thrush singing his heart out. 'It might be the very same thrush,' thought Dick, drowsily. 'He's saying, "Mind how you do-it, do-it, do-it!" just like the other one did.'

Anne sat up cautiously. She wondered if she should get up and have breakfast ready for the others – or would they want a bathe first?

Julian sat up next and yawned as he wriggled himself half out of his sleeping-bag. He grinned at Anne.

'Hallo,' he said. 'Had a good night? I feel fine this morning!'

'I feel rather stiff,' said Anne. 'But it will soon wear off. Hallo, George – you awake?'

George grunted and snuggled down farther in her sleeping-bag. Timmy pawed at her, whining. He wanted her to get up and go for a run with him.

Shut up, Timmy,' said George from the depth of her bag. 'I'm asleep!'

'I'm going for a bathe,' said Julian. 'Anyone else coming?'

'I won't,' said Anne. 'It will be too cold for me this morning. George doesn't seem to want to, either. You two boys go by yourselves. I'll have breakfast ready for you when you come back. Sorry I shan't be able to have anything hot for you to drink – but we didn't bring a kettle or anything like that.'

Julian and Dick went off to the Green Pool, still looking sleepy. Anne got out of her sleeping-bag and dressed quickly. She decided to go down to the pool with her sponge and flannel and wake herself up properly with the cold water. George was still in her sleeping-bag.

The two boys were almost at the pool. Ah, now they could see it between the trees, shining a bright emerald green. It looked very inviting indeed.

They suddenly saw a bicycle standing beside a tree. They looked at it in astonishment. It wasn't one of theirs. It must belong to someone else.

Then they heard splashings from the pool, and they hurried down to it. Was someone else bathing?

A boy was in the pool, his golden head shining wet and smooth in the morning sun. He was swimming powerfully across the pool, leaving long ripples behind him as he went. He suddenly saw Dick and Julian, and swam over to them.

'Hallo,' he said, wading out of the water. 'You come for a swim too? Nice pool of mine, isn't it?'

'What do you mean? It isn't really your pool, is it?' said Julian.

'Well, it belongs to my father, Thurlow Kent,' said the boy.

Both Julian and Dick had heard of Thurlow Kent, one of the richest men in the country. Julian looked doubtfully at the boy.

'If it's a private pool we won't use it,' he said.

'Oh come on!' cried the boy, and splashed cold water all over them. 'Race you to the other side!'

And off all three of them went, cleaving the green waters with their strong brown arms – what a fine beginning to a sunny day!

CHAPTER FOUR

Richard

ANNE WAS astonished to find three boys in the Green Pool instead of two. She stood by the water with her sponge and flannel, staring. Who was the third boy?

The three came back to the side of the pool where Anne stood. She looked at the strange boy shyly. He was not much older than she was, and not as big as Julian or Dick, but he was sturdily made, and had laughing blue eyes she liked. He smoothed back his dripping hair.

'This your sister?' he said to Julian and Dick. 'Hallo there!'

'Hallo,' said Anne and smiled. 'What's your name?'

'Richard,' he said. 'Richard Kent. What's yours?'

'Anne,' said Anne. 'We're on a biking tour.'

The boys had had no time to introduce themselves. They were still panting from their swim.

'I'm Julian and he's Dick, my brother,' said Julian, out of breath. 'I say – I hope we're not trespassing on your land as well as on your water!'

Richard grinned. 'Well, you are as a matter of fact. But I give you free permission! You can borrow my pool and my land as much as you like!'

'Oh thanks,' said Anne. 'I suppose it's your father's property? It didn't say "Private" or anything, so we didn't know. Would you like to come and have breakfast with us? If you'll dress with the others they'll bring you to where we camped last night.'

27

She sponged her face and washed her hands in the pool, hearing the boys chattering behind the bushes where they had left their clothes. Then she sped back to their sleeping-place, meaning to tidy up the bags they had slept in, and put out breakfast neatly. But George was still fast asleep in her bag, her head showing at the top with its mass of short curls that made her look like a boy.

'George! Do wake up. Somebody's coming to breakfast,' said Anne, shaking her.

George shrugged away crossly, not believing her. It was just a trick to make her get up and help with the breakfast! Anne left her. All right – let her be found in her sleeping-bag if she liked!

She began to unpack the food and set it out neatly. What a good thing they had brought two extra bottles of lime juice. Now they could offer Richard one.

The three boys came up, their wet hair plastered down. Richard spotted George in the bag as Timmy came over to meet him. He fondled Timmy who, smelling that other dogs had been round Richard at home, sniffed him over with great interest.

'Who's that still asleep?' asked Richard.

'That's George,' said Anne. 'Too sleepy to wake up! Come on – I've got breakfast ready. Would you like to start off with rolls and anchovy and lettuce? And there's lime juice if you want it.'

George heard Richard's voice, as he sat talking with the others and was astonished. Who was that? She sat up, blinking, her hair tousled and short. Richard honestly thought she was a boy. She looked like one and she was called George!

'Top of the morning to you, George,' he said. 'Hope I'm not eating your share of the breakfast.'

'Who are you?' demanded George. The boys told her.

'I live about three miles away,' said the boy. 'I biked over here this morning for a swim. I say – that reminds me – I'd better bring my bike up here and put it where I can see it. I've had two stolen already through not having them under my eye.'

He shot off to get his bike. George took the opportunity of getting out of her sleeping-bag and rushed off to dress. She was back before Richard was, eating her breakfast. He wheeled his bicycle as he came.

'Got it all right,' he said, and flung it down beside him. 'Don't want to have to tell my father this one's gone, like the others. He's pretty fierce.'

'My father's a bit fierce too,' said George.

'Does he whip you?' asked Richard, giving Timmy a nice little titbit of roll and anchovy paste.

'Of course not,' said George. 'He's just got a temper, that's all.'

'Mine's got tempers and rages and furies, and if anyone offends him or does him a wrong he's like an elephant – never forgets,' said Richard. 'He's made plenty of enemies in his lifetime. Sometimes he's had his life threatened, and he's had to take a bodyguard about with him.'

This all sounded extremely thrilling. Dick half-wished he had a father like that. It would be nice to talk to the other boys at school about his father's 'bodyguard'.

'What's his bodyguard like?' asked Anne, full of curiosity.

'Oh, they vary. But they're all big hefty fellows – they look like ruffians, and probably are,' said Richard, enjoying the interest the others were taking in him. 'One he had last year was awful – he had the thickest lips you ever saw, and such a big nose that when you saw him sideways you really thought he'd put a false one on just for fun.'

'Gracious!' said Anne. 'He sounds horrible. Has your father still got him?'

'No. He did something that annoyed Dad – I don't know what – and after a perfectly furious row my father chucked him out,' said Richard. 'That was the end of *him*. Jolly good thing too. I hated him. He used to kick the dogs around terribly.'

'*Oh*! What a beast!' said George, horrified. She put her arm round Timmy as if she was afraid somebody might suddenly kick him around too.

Julian and Dick wondered whether to believe all this. They came to the conclusion that the tales Richard told were very much exaggerated, and they listened with amusement, but not with such horror as the two girls, who hung on every word that Richard said.

'Where's your father now?' said Anne. 'Has he got a special bodyguard this very moment?'

'Rather! He's in America this week, but he's flying home soon – plus bodyguard,' said Richard, drinking the last of his lime juice from the bottle. 'Ummm, that's good. I say, aren't you lucky to be allowed to go off alone like this on your bikes and sleep where you like. My mother never will let *me* – she's always afraid something will happen to me.'

'Perhaps you'd better have a bodyguard too,' suggested Julian, slyly.

'I'd soon give him the slip,' said Richard. 'As a matter of fact I *have* got a kind of a bodyguard.'

'Who? Where?' asked Anne, looking all round as if she expected some enormous ruffian suddenly to appear.

'Well – he's supposed to be my holiday tutor,' said Richard, tickling Timmy round the ears. 'He's called Lomax and he's pretty awful. I'm supposed to tell him every time I go out – just as if I was a kid like Anne here.'

Anne was indignant. 'I don't have to tell anybody when I want to go off on my own,' she said.

'Actually I don't think we'd be allowed to rush off completely on our own unless we had old Timmy,' said Dick, honestly. 'He's better than any ruffianly bodyguard or holiday tutor. I wonder *you* don't have a dog.'

'Oh, I've got about five,' said Richard, airily.

'What are their names?' asked George, disbelievingly.

'Er – Bunter, Biscuit, Brownie, Bones – and er – Bonzo,' said Richard, with a grin.

'Silly names,' said George, scornfully. 'Fancy calling a dog *Biscuit*. You must be cracked.'

'You shut up,' said Richard, with a sudden scowl. 'I don't stand people telling me I'm cracked.'

'Well, you'll have to stand *me* telling you,' said George. 'I do think it's cracked to call a dog, a nice, decent dog, by a name like *Biscuit*!'

'I'll fight you then,' said Richard, surprisingly, and stood up. 'Come on – you stand up.'

George leapt to her feet. Julian shot out a hand and pulled her down again.

'None of that,' he said to Richard. 'You ought to be ashamed of yourself.'

'Why?' flared out Richard, whose face had gone very red. Evidently he and his father shared the same fierceness of temper!

'Well, you don't fight *girls*,' said Julian, scornfully. 'Or do you? Correct me if I'm wrong.'

Richard stared at him in amazement. 'What do you mean?' he said. 'Girls? Of course I don't fight girls. No decent boy hits a girl – but it's this boy here I want to fight – what do you call him? – George.'

To his great surprise Julian, Dick and Anne roared with laughter. Timmy barked madly too, pleased at the sudden ending of the quarrel. Only George looked mutinous and cross.

'What's up now?' asked Richard, aggressively. 'What's all the fun and games about?'

'Richard, George isn't a boy – she's a *girl*,' explained Dick at last. 'My goodness – she was just about to accept your challenge and fight you, too – two fierce little fox-terriers having a scrap!'

Richard's mouth fell open in even greater astonishment. He blushed redder than ever. He looked sheepishly at George.

'Are you *really* a girl?' he said. 'You behave so like a boy – and you look like one too. Sorry, George. Is your name *really* George?'

'No, Georgina,' said George, thawing a little at Richard's awkward apology, and pleased that he had honestly thought her a boy. She did so badly want to be a boy and not a girl.

'Good thing I *didn't* fight you,' said Richard, fervently. 'I should have knocked you flat!'

'Well, I like *that*!' said George, flaring up all over again. Julian pushed her back with his hand.

'Now shut up, you two, and don't behave like idiots. Where's the map? It's time we had a squint at it and decided what we are going to do for today – how far we're going to ride, and where we're making for by the evening.'

Fortunately George and Richard both gave in with a good grace. Soon all six heads – Timmy's too – were bent over the map. Julian made his decision.

'We'll make for Middlecombe Woods – see, there they are on the map. That's decided then – it'll be a jolly nice ride.'

It might be a nice ride – but it was going to be something very much more than that!

CHAPTER FIVE

Six instead of five

'LOOK HERE,' said Richard, when they had tidied up everything, buried their bits of litter, and looked to see that no one had got a puncture in a tyre. 'Look here, I've got an aunt who lives in the direction of those woods – if I can get my mother to say I can come with you, will you let me? I can go and see my aunt on the way, then.'

Julian looked at Richard doubtfully. He wasn't very sure if Richard really *would* go and ask permission.

'Well – if you aren't too long about it,' he said. 'Of course we don't mind you coming with us. We can drop you at your aunt's on the way.'

'I'll go straight off now and ask my mother,' said Richard, eagerly, and he ran for his bicycle. 'I'll meet you at Croker's Corner – you saw it on the map. That will save time, because then I shan't have to come back here – it's not much farther than my home.'

'Right,' said Julian. 'I've got to adjust my brakes, and that will take ten minutes or so. You'll have time to go home and ask permission, and join us later. We'll wait for you; at least we'll wait for ten minutes, at Croker's Corner. If you don't turn up we'll know you didn't get permission. Tell your mother we'll have you safely at your aunt's.'

Richard shot off on his bicycle, looking excited. Anne began to clear up, and George helped her. Timmy got in everyone's way, sniffing about for dropped crumbs.

'Anyone would think he was half-starved!' said Anne.

'He had a lot more breakfast than I had. Timmy, if you walk through my legs again I'll tie you up!'

Julian adjusted his brakes with Dick's help. In about fifteen minutes they were ready to set off. They had planned where to stop to buy food for their lunch, and although the journey to Middlecombe Woods was a longer trip than they had made the day before, they felt able to cope with more miles on the second day. Timmy was eager to set off too. He was a big dog, and enjoyed all the exercise he was getting.

'It'll take a bit of your fat off,' said Dick to Timmy. 'We don't like fat dogs, you know. They waddle and they puff.'

'Dick! Timmy's *never* been fat!' said George, indignantly, and then stopped as she saw Dick's grin. He was pulling her leg as usual. She kicked herself. Why did she always rise like that, when Dick teased her through Timmy? She gave him a friendly punch.

They all mounted their bicycles. Timmy ran ahead, pleased. They came to a lane and rode down it, avoiding the ruts. They came out into a road. It was not a main road, for the children didn't like those; they were too full of traffic and dust. They liked the shady lanes or the country roads where they met only a few carts or a farmer's car.

'Now, don't let's miss Croker's Corner,' said Julian. 'It should be along this way somewhere, according to the map. George, if you get into ruts like that you'll be thrown off.'

'All right, I know that!' said George. 'I only got into one because Timmy swerved across my wheel. He's after a rabbit or something. Timmy! Don't get left behind, you idiot.'

Timmy bounded reluctantly after the little party. Exercise was wonderful, but it did mean leaving a lot of marvellous wayside smells unsniffed at. It was a dreadful waste of smells, Timmy thought.

They came to Croker's Corner sooner than they thought. The signpost proclaimed the name – and there, leaning against the post, sitting on his bicycle was Richard, beaming at them.

'You've been jolly quick, getting back home and then on to here,' said Julian. 'What did your mother say?'

'She didn't mind a bit so long as I was with *you*,' said Richard. 'I can go to my aunt's for the night, she said.'

'Haven't you brought pyjamas or anything with you?' asked Dick.

'There are always spare ones at my aunt's,' explained Richard. 'Hurray – it will be marvellous to be out on my own all day with you – no Mr Lomax to bother me with this and that. Come on!'

They all cycled on together. Richard would keep trying to ride three abreast, and Julian had to warn him that cyclists were not allowed to do that. 'I don't care!' sang Richard, who seemed in very high spirits. 'Who is there to stop us, anyway?'

'*I* shall stop you,' said Julian, and Richard ceased grinning at once. Julian could sound very stern when he liked. Dick winked at George, and she winked back. They had both come to the conclusion that Richard was very spoilt and liked his own way. Well, he wouldn't get it if he came up against old Julian!

They stopped at eleven for ice-creams and drinks. Richard seemed to have a lot of money. He insisted on buying ice-creams for all of them, even Timmy.

Once again they bought food for their lunch – new bread, farmhouse butter, cream cheese, crisp lettuce, fat red radishes and a bunch of spring onions. Richard bought a magnificent chocolate cake he saw in a first-class cake-shop.

'Gracious! That must have cost you a fortune!' said Anne. 'How are we going to carry it?'

'Woof,' said Timmy longingly.

'No, I certainly shan't let *you* carry it,' said Anne. 'Oh dear, we'll have to cut it in half, I think, and two people can share the carrying. It's such an enormous cake.'

On they went again, getting into the real country now, with villages few and far between. A farm here and there showed up on the hillsides, with cows and sheep and fowls. It was a peaceful, quiet scene, with the sun spilling down over everything, and the blue April sky above, patched with great white cotton-wool clouds.

'This is grand,' said Richard. 'I say, doesn't Timmy *ever* get tired? He's panting like anything now.'

'Yes, I think we ought to find somewhere for our lunch,' said Julian, looking at his watch. 'We've done a very good run this morning. Of course a lot of the way has been downhill. This afternoon we'll probably be slower, because we'll be getting into hilly country.'

They found a spot to picnic in. They chose the sunny side of a hedge, looking downhill into a small valley. Sheep and lambs were in the field they sat in. The lambs were very inquisitive, and one came right up to Anne and bleated.

'Do you want a bit of my bread?' asked Anne, and held it out to the lamb. Timmy watched indignantly. Fancy handing out food to those silly little creatures! He growled a little, and George shushed him.

Soon all the lambs were crowding round, quite unafraid, and one even tried to put its little front legs up on to George's shoulders! That was too much for Timmy! He gave such a sudden, fierce growl that all the lambs shot off at once.

'Oh, don't be so jealous, Timmy,' said George. 'Take this sandwich and behave yourself. Now you've frightened away the lambs, and they won't come back.'

They all ate the food and then drank their lime juice and ginger beer. The sun was very hot. Soon they would all be burnt brown – and it was only April. How marvellous! Julian thought lazily that they were really lucky to have such weather – it would be awful to have to bike along all day in the pouring rain.

Once again the children snoozed in the afternoon sun, Richard too, and the little lambs skipped nearer and nearer. One actually leapt on to Julian as he slept, and he sat upright with a jerk. 'Timmy!' he began, 'if you leap on me again like that I'll . . .'

But it wasn't Timmy, it was a lamb! Julian laughed to himself. He sat for a few minutes and watched the little white creatures playing 'I'm king of the castle' with an old coop, then he lay down again.

'Are we anywhere near your aunt's house?' Julian asked Richard, when they once more mounted their bicycles.

'If we're anywhere near Great Giddings, we shall soon be there,' said Richard, riding without holding his handlebars and almost ending up in the ditch. 'I didn't notice it on the map.'

Julian tried to remember. 'Yes, we should be at Great Giddings round about tea-time, say five o'clock or thereabouts. We'll leave you at your aunt's house for tea if you like.'

'Oh no, thank you,' said Richard, quickly. 'I'd much rather have tea with *you*. I *do* wish I could come on this tour with you. I suppose I couldn't possibly? You could telephone my mother.'

'Don't be an ass,' said Julian. 'You can have tea with us if you like but we drop you at your aunt's as arranged, see? No nonsense about that.'

They came to Great Giddings at about ten past five. Although it was called Great it was really very small. There was a little tea-place that said 'Home-made cakes and jams', so they went there for tea.

The woman who kept it was a plump, cheerful soul, fond of children. She guessed she would make very little out of the tea she served to five healthy children – but that didn't matter! She set to work to cut three big plates of

FIVE GET INTO TROUBLE

well-buttered slices of bread, put out apricot jam, rasp-
berry, and strawberry, and a selection of home-made buns
that made the children's mouths water.

She knew Richard quite well, because he had sometimes
been to her cottage with his aunt.

'I suppose you'll be going to stay with her tonight?' she
said to Richard, and he nodded, his mouth full of ginger
cake. It was a lovely tea. Anne felt as if she wouldn't be
able to eat any supper at all that night! Even Timmy
seemed to have satisfied his enormous appetite.

'I think we ought to pay you double price for our
gorgeous tea,' said Julian, but the woman wouldn't hear
of it. No, no – it was lovely to see them all enjoying her
cakes; she didn't want double price!

'Some people are so *awfully* nice and generous,' said
Anne, as they mounted their bicycles to ride off again.
'You just can't help liking them. I do hope I can cook like
that when I grow up.'

'If you do, Julian and I will always live with you and not
dream of getting married!' said Dick, promptly, and they
all laughed.

'Now for Richard's aunt,' said Julian. 'Do you know
where the house is, Richard?'

'Yes, that's it over there,' said Richard, and rode up to a
gate. 'Well, thanks awfully for your company. I hope I'll
see you again soon! I have a feeling I shall! Good-bye!'

He rode up the drive and disappeared. 'What a sudden
good-bye!' said George, puzzled. 'Isn't he *odd*?'

CHAPTER SIX

Odd happenings

THEY ALL thought it really was a little odd to disappear so suddenly like that, with just a casual good-bye. Julian wondered if he ought to have gone with him and delivered him safely on the door-step.

'Don't be an ass, Julian,' said Dick, scornfully. 'What *do* you think can happen to him from the front gate to the front door!'

'Nothing, of course. It's just that I don't trust that young fellow,' said Julian. 'You know I really wasn't sure he had asked his mother if he could come with us, to tell you the truth.'

'I thought that too,' said Anne. 'He did get to Croker's Corner so very quickly, didn't he? And he had quite a long way to go really, and he had to find his mother, and talk to her, and all that.'

'Yes, I've half a mind to pop up to the aunt's house and see if she expected him,' said Julian. But on second thoughts he didn't go. He would feel so silly if the aunt was there with Richard, and all was well – they would think that he and the others ought to be asked in.

So, after debating the matter for a few minutes they all rode off again. They wanted to get to Middlecombe Woods fairly soon, because there were no villages between Great Giddings and Middlecombe, so they would have to find the woods and then go on to find a farmhouse somewhere to buy food for supper and breakfast. They hadn't been able to buy any in the shops at Great Giddings because it was early closing day, and they hadn't liked to ask the tea-shop woman to sell them anything. They felt they had taken quite enough of her food already!

They came to Middlecombe Woods, and found a very fine place to camp in for the night. It was in a little dell, set with primroses and violets, a perfectly hidden place, secure from all prying eyes, and surely unknown even to tramps.

'This is glorious,' said Anne. 'We must be miles away from anywhere: I hope we can find some farmhouse or something that will sell us food, though! I know we don't feel hungry now, but we shall!'

'I think I've got a puncture, blow it,' said Dick, looking at his back tyre. 'It's a slow one, fortunately. But I think I won't risk coming along to look for farmhouses till I've mended it.'

'Right,' said Julian. 'And Anne needn't come either. She looks a bit tired. George and I will go. We won't take our bikes. It's easier to walk through the woods. We may be an hour or so, but don't worry, Timmy will know the way back all right, so we shan't lose you!'

Julian and George set off on foot, with Timmy following. Timmy too was tired, but nothing would have made him stay behind with Anne and Dick. He must go with his beloved George!

Anne put her bicycle carefully into the middle of a bush. You never knew when a tramp might be about, watching to steal something! It didn't matter when Timmy was there, because he would growl if a tramp came within a mile of them. Dick called out that he would mend his puncture now. He had found the hole already, where a small nail had gone in.

She sat near to Dick, watching him. She was glad to rest. She wondered if the others had found a farmhouse yet.

Dick worked steadily at mending the puncture. They had been there together about half an hour when they heard sounds.

Dick lifted his head and listened. 'Can you hear something?' he said to Anne. She nodded.

'Yes. Somebody's shouting. I wonder why!'

They both listened again. Then they distinctly heard yells. 'Help! Julian! Where are you? Help!'

They shot to their feet. Who was calling Julian for help? It wasn't George's voice. The yells grew louder, to panic-stricken shrieks.

'JULIAN! Dick!'

'Why, it must be Richard,' said Dick, amazed. 'What in the world does he want? What's happened?'

Anne was pale. She didn't like sudden happenings like this. 'Shall we – shall we go and find him?' she said.

There was a crashing not far off, as if somebody was making his way through the undergrowth. It was rather dark among the trees, and Anne and Dick could see nothing at first. Dick yelled loudly.

'Hey! Is that you, Richard! We're here!'

The crashing noise redoubled. 'I'm coming!' squealed Richard. 'Wait for me, wait for me!'

They waited. Soon they saw Richard coming, stumbling as fast as he could between the trees. 'Here we are,' called Dick. 'Whatever's the matter?'

Richard staggered towards them. He looked frightened out of his life. 'They're after me,' he panted. 'You must save me. I want Timmy. He'll bite them.'

'*Who*'s after you?' asked Dick, amazed.

'Where's Timmy? Where's Julian?' cried Richard, looking round in despair.

'They've gone to a farmhouse to get some food,' said
Dick. 'They'll be back soon, Richard. Whatever's the
matter? Are you mad? You look awful.'

The boy took no notice of the questions. 'Where has
Julian gone? I want Timmy. Tell me the way they went. I
can't stay here. They'll catch me!'

'They went along there,' said Dick, showing Richard
the path. 'You can just see the tracks of their feet. Richard,
whatever is . . .?'

But Richard was gone! He fled down the path at top
speed, calling at the top of his voice, 'Julian! Timmy!'

Anne and Dick stared at one another in surprise. What had happened to Richard? Why wasn't he at his aunt's house? He must be mad!

'It's no good going after him,' said Dick. 'We shall only lose the way and not be able to find this place again – and the others will miss us and go hunting and get lost too! What *is* the matter with Richard?'

'He kept saying somebody was after him – *they* were after him!' said Anne. 'He's got some bee in his bonnet about something.'

'Bats in the belfry,' said Dick. 'Mad, dippy, daft! Well, he'll give Julian and George a shock when he runs into them – if he does! The odds are he will miss them altogether.'

'I'm going to climb this tree and see if I can see anything of Richard or the others,' said Anne. 'It's tall, and it's easy to climb. You finish mending your puncture. I should just love to know what happens to Richard.'

Dick went back to his bicycle, puzzled. Anne climbed the tree. She climbed well, and was soon at the top. She gazed out over the countryside. There was an expanse of fields on one side, and woods stretched away on the other. She looked over the darkening fields, trying to see if a farmhouse was anywhere near. But she could see nothing.

Dick was just finishing his puncture when he heard another noise in the woods. Was it that idiot of a Richard coming back? He listened.

The noise came nearer. It wasn't a crashing noise, like Richard had made. It was a stealthy noise as if people were gradually closing in. Dick didn't much like it. Who was coming? Or perhaps – *what* was coming? Was it some wild animal – perhaps a badger and its mate? The boy stood listening.

A silence came. No more movements. No more rustling. Had he imagined it all? He wished Anne and the others were near him. It was eerie, standing there in the darkening wood, waiting and watching.

He decided that he had imagined it all. He thought it would be a very good idea if he turned on his bicycle lamp, then the light would soon dispel his silly ideas! He fumbled about for it on the front of his handlebars. He switched it on and a very comforting little glow at once spread a circle of light in the little dell.

Dick was just about to call up to Anne to tell her his absurd fears when the noises came again! There was absolutely no mistake about them this time.

A brilliant light suddeningly pierced through the trees and fell on Dick. He blinked.

'Ah, so there you are, you little misery!' said a harsh voice, and someone came striding over to the dell. Somebody else followed behind.

'What do you mean?' asked Dick, amazed. He could not see who the men were because of the brilliant torch-light in his eyes.

'We've been chasing you for miles, haven't we? And you thought you'd get away. But we'd got you all the time!' said the voice.

'I don't understand this,' said Dick, putting on a bold voice. 'Who are you?'

'You know very well who we are,' said the voice. 'Didn't you run away screaming as soon as you saw Rooky? He went one way after you, and we went another – and we soon got you, didn't we? Now, you come along with us, my pretty!'

All this explained one thing clearly to Dick – that it was

46

Richard they had been after, for some reason or other –
and they thought *he* was Richard!

'I'm not the boy you're looking for,' he said. 'You'll get
into trouble if you touch *me*!'

'What's your name, then?' asked the first man.

Dick told him.

'Oh, so you're Dick – and isn't Dick short for Richard?
You can't fool us with that baby-talk,' said the first man.
'You're the Richard we want, all right. Richard Kent,
see?'

'I'm *not* Richard Kent!' shouted Dick, as he felt the
man's hand clutching his arm suddenly. 'You take your
hands off me. You wait till the police hear of this!'

'They *won't* hear of it,' said the man. 'They won't hear
anything at all! Come on – and don't struggle or shout or
you'll be sorry. Once you're at Owl's Dene we'll deal
properly with you!'

Anne was sitting absolutely petrified up in the tree. She
couldn't move or speak. She tried to call to poor Dick, but
her tongue wouldn't say a word. She had to sit there and
hear her brother being dragged away by two strange
ruffians. She almost fell out of the tree in fright, and
she heard him shouting and yelling when he was dragged
away. She could hear the sound of crashing for a long
time.

She began to cry. She didn't dare to climb down because
she was trembling so much she was afraid she would lose
her hold and fall.

She must wait for George and Julian to come back.
Suppose they didn't? Suppose they had been caught too?
She would be all by herself in the tree all night long. Anne
sobbed up in the tree-top, holding on tightly.

The stars came out above her head, and she saw the very bright one again.

And then she heard the sound of footsteps and voices. She stiffened up in the tree. Who was it this time? Oh let it be Julian and George and Timmy; let it be Julian, George and Timmy!

CHAPTER SEVEN

Richard tells an alarming tale

JULIAN AND George had managed to find a little farmhouse tucked away in a hollow. A trio of dogs set up a terrific barking as they drew near. Timmy growled and the hair rose up on his neck. George put her hand on his collar.

'I won't go any nearer with Timmy,' she said. 'I don't want him to be set on by three dogs at once!'

So Julian went down to the farmhouse by himself. The dogs made such a noise and looked so fierce that he paused in the farmyard. He was not in the least afraid of dogs, but these looked most unpleasant, especially one big mongrel whose teeth were bared in a very threatening manner.

A voice called out to him. 'Clear off, you! We don't want no strangers here. When strangers come our eggs and hens go too!'

'Good evening,' called Julian, politely. 'We are four children camping out in the woods for the night. Could you let us have any food? I'll pay well for it.'

There was a pause. The man pulled his head in at the window he was shouting from, and was evidently speaking to someone inside.

He stuck it out again. 'I told you, we don't hold with strangers here, never did. We've only got plain bread and butter, and we can give you some hard-boiled eggs and milk and a bit of ham. That's all.'

'That'll do fine,' called Julian, cheerily. 'Just what we'd like. Shall I come and get it?'

'Not unless you want to be torn to pieces by those dogs,' came back the voice. 'You wait there. I'll be out when the eggs are done.'

'Blow,' said Julian, walking back to George. 'That means we'll have to kick our heels here for a while. What an unpleasant fellow! I don't think much of his place, do you?'

George agreed with him. It was ill-kept, the barn was falling to bits, rusty bits of machinery lay here and there in the thick grass. The three dogs kept up a continual barking and howling, but they did not come any nearer. George still kept her hand firmly on Timmy. He was bristling all over!

'What a lonely place to live in,' said Julian. 'No house within miles, I should think. No telephone. I wonder what they'd do if somebody was ill or had an accident and needed help.'

'I hope they'll hurry up with that food,' said George, getting impatient. 'It'll be dark soon. I'm getting hungry too.'

At last somebody came out of the tumbledown farm-house. It was a bearded man, stooping and old, with long untidy hair and a pronounced limp. He had a grim and ugly face. Neither Julian nor George liked him.

'Here you are,' he said, waving his three dogs away behind him. 'Get back, you!' He aimed a kick at the nearest dog, and it yelped with pain.

'Oh don't!' said George. 'You hurt him.'

'He's my dog, isn't he?' said the man, angrily. 'You mind your own business!' He kicked out at another dog and scowled at George.

51

'What about the food?' said Julian, holding out his hand, anxious to be gone before trouble came between Timmy and the other dogs. 'George, take Timmy back a bit. He's upsetting the dogs.'

'Well, I like that!' said George. 'It's those other dogs that are upsetting *him*!'

She dragged Timmy back a few yards, and he stood there with all his hackles up on his neck, growling in a horrible way.

Julian took the food which was done up carelessly in old brown paper. 'Thanks,' he said. 'How much?'

'Five pounds,' said the old man, surprisingly.

'Don't be silly,' said Julian. He looked quickly at the food. 'I'll give you a pound for it, and that's more than it's worth. There's hardly any ham.'

'I said five pounds,' said the man, sullenly. Julian looked at him. 'He must be mad!' he thought. He held out the food to the ugly old fellow.

'Well, take it back,' he said. 'I haven't got five pounds to give you for food. A pound is the most I can spare. Good night.'

The old man pushed the food back, and held out his other hand in silence. Julian fished in his pocket and brought out a pound coin. He placed it in the man's dirty hand, wondering why on earth the fellow had asked him for such a ridiculous sum before. The man put the money in his pocket.

'Clear off,' he said, suddenly, in a growling voice. 'We don't want strangers here, stealing our goods. I'll set my dogs on you if you come again!'

Julian turned to go, half-afraid that the extraordinary old man *would* set his dogs on him. The fellow stood there in the half-dark, yelling abuse at Julian and George as they made their way out of the farmyard.

'Well! We'll never go *there* again!' said George, furious at their treatment. 'He's mad as a hatter.'

'Yes. And I don't much fancy his food, either,' said Julian. 'Still, it's all we'll get tonight!'

They followed Timmy back to the woods. They were glad they had him, because otherwise they might have missed the way. But Timmy knew it. Once he had been along a certain route Timmy always knew it again. He ran on now, sniffing here and there, occasionally waiting for the others to catch him up.

Then he stiffened and growled softly. George put her hand on his collar. Somebody must be coming.

Somebody *was* coming! It was Richard on his way to find them. He was still shouting and yelling, and the noise he made had already come to Timmy's sharp ears. It soon came to Julian's, and George's too, as they stood there waiting.

'Julian! Where are you? Where's Timmy? I want Timmy! They're after me, I tell you; they're after me.'

'Listen – it sounds like *Richard*,' said Julian, startled. 'What in the world is he doing here? – and yelling like that too! Come on, we must find out. Something's happened. I hope Dick and Anne are all right.'

They ran up the path as fast as they could in the twilight. Soon they met Richard, who had now stopped shouting, and was stumbling along, half-sobbing.

'Richard! What's up?' cried Julian. Richard ran to him and flung himself against him. Timmy did not go to him, but stood there in surprise. George stared through the twilight, puzzled. What in the world had happened?

'Julian! Oh Julian! I'm scared stiff,' panted Richard, hanging on to Julian's arm.

'Pull yourself together,' said Julian, in the calm voice that had made a good effect on Richard. 'I bet you're just making a silly fuss. What's happened? Did you find your aunt was out or something? And come racing after us?'

'My aunt's away,' said Richard, speaking in a calmer voice. 'She . . .'

'*Away*!' said Julian, in surprise. 'But didn't your mother know that when she said you could . . .?'

'I didn't ask my mother's permission to come,' cried Richard. 'I didn't even go back home when you thought I did! I just biked straight to Croker's Corner and waited for you. I wanted to come with you, you see and I knew my mother wouldn't let me.'

This was said with a great air of bravado. Julian was disgusted.

'I'm ashamed of you,' he said. 'Telling us lies like that!'

'I didn't know my aunt was away,' said Richard, all his sudden cockiness gone when he heard Julian's scornful voice. 'I thought she'd be there and I was going to tell her to telephone my mother and say I'd gone for a trip with *you*. Then I thought I'd come biking after you and – and . . .'

'And tell us your aunt was away, and could you come with us?' finished Julian, still scornfully. 'A deceitful and ridiculous plan. I'd have sent you back at once; you might have known that.'

'Yes, I know. But I might have had a whole night camping out with you,' said Richard, in a small voice. 'I've never done things like that. I . . .'

'What I want to know is, what were you scared of when

54

you came rushing along, yelling and crying,' said Julian, impatiently.

'Oh Julian – it was horrible,' said Richard, and he suddenly clutched Julian's arm again. 'You see, I biked down back to my aunt's gate and out into the lane and I was just going along the way to Middlecombe Woods when a car met me. And I saw who was in the car!'

'Well, *who*?' said Julian, feeling as if he could shake Richard.

'It was – it was Rooky!' said Richard, in a trembling voice.

'Who's he?' said Julian, and George gave an impatient click. Would Richard never tell his story properly?

'Don't you remember? I told you about him. He was the fellow with thick lips and a huge nose that my father had for a bodyguard last year and he chucked him out,' said Richard. 'He always swore he'd have his revenge on my father – and on me too because I told tales about him to Dad and it was because of that he was sacked. So when I caught sight of him in the car I was terrified!'

'I *see*,' said Julian, seeing light. 'What happened then?'

'Rooky recognised me, and turned the car round and chased me on my bike,' said Richard, beginning to tremble again as he remembered that alarming ride. 'I pedalled for all I was worth and when I got to Middlecombe Woods I rode into the path there, hoping the car couldn't follow. It couldn't, of course – but the men leapt out – there were three of them, two I didn't know – and they chased me on foot. I pedalled and pedalled, and then I ran into a tree or something and fell off. I chucked my bike into a bush, and ran into the thick undergrowth to hide.'

'Go on,' said Julian, as Richard paused. 'What next?'

'The men split up then – Rooky went one way to find me, and the other two went another way. I waited till I thought they were gone, then I crept out and tore down the path again, hoping to find you. I wanted Timmy, you see, I thought he'd go for the men.'

Timmy growled. He certainly would have gone for them!

'Two of the men must have been hiding, waiting to hear me start up again,' went on Richard. 'And as soon as I began to run, they chased after me. I put them off the trail, though – I dodged and hid and hid and dodged – and then I came to Dick! He was mending a puncture. But you weren't with him – and it was you and Timmy I wanted – I knew the men would soon be catching me up, you see, so I tore on and on – and at last I found you. I've never been so glad in my life.'

It was a most extraordinary story – but Julian hardly paused to think about it. An alarming thought had come into his head. What about Dick and Anne? What would have happened to them if the men had suddenly come across them?

'Quick!' he said to George. 'We must get back to the others! Hurry!'

CHAPTER EIGHT

What's the best thing to do?

STUMBLING THROUGH the dark wood, Julian and George hurried as best they could. Timmy hurried too, knowing that something was worrying both his friends. Richard followed behind, half-crying again. He really had been very much afraid.

They came at last to the little dell where they had planned to spend the night. It was quite dark. Julian called loudly:

'Dick! Anne! Where are you?'

George had made her way to where she had hidden her bicycle. She fumbled for the lamp and switched it on. She took it off and flashed it round the dell. There was Dick's bicycle, with the puncture repair outfit on the ground beside it – but no Dick, and no Anne! What had happened?

'Anne!' yelled Julian, in alarm. 'Dick! Come here! We're back!'

And then a small trembling voice came down from the tree-top overhead.

'Oh Julian! Oh Julian! I'm here.'

'It's Anne!' yelled Julian, his heart leaping in relief. 'Anne, where are you?'

'Up in this tree,' called back Anne, in a stronger voice. 'Oh Ju, I've been so frightened, I didn't dare climb down in case I fell. Dick . . .'

'Where *is* Dick?' demanded Julian.

57

A sob came down to him. 'Two horrible men came – and they've taken him away. They thought he was Richard!'

Anne's voice became a wail. Julian felt that he must get her down from the tree so that she could be with them and be comforted. He spoke to George.

'Shine that lamp up here. I'm going up to fetch Anne.'

George silently shone the light of the lamp on the tree. Julian went up like a cat. He came to Anne who was still clinging tightly to a branch.

'Anne, I'll help you down. Come on, now – you can't fall. I'm just below you. I'll guide your feet to the right branches.'

Anne was only too glad to be helped down. She was cold and miserable, and she longed to be with the others. Slowly she came down, with Julian's help, and he lifted her to the ground.

She clung to him, and he put his arm round his young sister. 'It's all right, Anne. I'm with you now. And here's George too – and old Timmy.'

'Who's *that*?' said Anne, suddenly seeing Richard in the shadows.

'Only Richard. He's behaved badly,' said Julian, grimly. 'It's all because of him and his idiotic behaviour that this has happened. Now, tell us slowly and carefully about Dick and the two men, Anne.'

Anne told him, not missing out anything at all. Timmy stood near her, licking her hand all the time. That was very comforting indeed! Timmy always knew when anyone was in trouble. Anne felt very much better when she had Julian's arm round her, and Timmy's tongue licking her!

'It's quite clear what's happened,' said Julian, when Anne had finished her alarming tale. 'This man Rooky recognised Richard, and he and the other two came after him, seeing a chance to kidnap him, and so get even with his father. Rooky was the only one who knew Richard, and he wasn't the man who caught Dick. The *others* got him – and they didn't know he wasn't Richard – and of course, hearing that his name was Dick they jumped to the conclusion that he was Richard – because Dick is short for Richard.'

'But Dick *told* them he wasn't Richard Kent,' said Anne, earnestly.

'Of course, but they thought he wasn't telling the truth,' said Julian. 'And they've taken him off. What did you say was the name of the place they were going to?'

'It sounded like Owl's Dene,' said Anne. 'Can we go there, Julian? If you told the men Dick was Dick and not Richard, they'd let him go, wouldn't they?'

'Oh yes,' said Julian. 'In any case, as soon as that fellow Rooky sets eyes on him he'll know there's a mistake been made. I think we can get old Dick away all right.'

A voice came out of the shadows nearby. 'What about *me*? Will you take me home first? *I* don't want to run into Rooky again.'

'I'm certainly not going to waste time taking *you* home,' said Julian, coldly. 'If it hadn't been for you and your tomfoolery we wouldn't have run into this trouble. You'll have to come with us. I'm going to find Dick first.'

'But I *can't* come with you – I'm afraid of Rooky!' wailed Richard.

'Well, stay here then,' said Julian, determined to teach Richard a lesson.

That was even worse. Richard howled loudly. 'Don't leave me here! Don't!'

'Now look here, if you come with us, you can always be dropped at a house somewhere, or at a police station and get yourself taken home somehow,' said Julian, exasperated. 'You're old enough to look after yourself. I'm fed up with you.'

Anne was sorry for Richard, although he had brought all this trouble on them. She knew how dreadful it was to feel really frightened. She put out a hand and touched him kindly.

'Richard! Don't be a baby. Julian will see that you're all right. He's just feeling cross with you now, but he'll soon get over it.'

'Don't you be too sure about that!' said Julian to Anne, pretending to be sterner than he really felt. 'What Richard wants is a jolly good hiding. He's untruthful and deceitful and an absolute baby!'

WHAT'S THE BEST THING TO DO?

'Give me another chance,' almost wept poor Richard, who had never in his life been spoken to like this before. He tried to hate Julian for saying such things to him – but oddly enough he couldn't. He only respected and admired him all the more.

Julian said no more to Richard. He really thought the boy was too feeble for words. It was a nuisance that they had him with them. He would be no help at all – simply a tiresome nuisance.

'What are we going to do, Julian?' asked George, who had been very silent. She was fond of Dick, and was very worried about him. Where was Owl's Dene? How could they possibly find it in the night? And what about those awful men? How would they treat Julian if he demanded Dick back at once? Julian was fearless and straightforward – but the men wouldn't like him any the better for that.

'Well now, what *are* we going to do?' repeated Julian, and he fell silent.

'It's no good going back to that farm, and asking for help, is it?' said George, after a pause.

'Not a bit of good,' said Julian, at once. 'That old man wouldn't help anyone! And there's no telephone laid on, as we saw. No, that farm's no good. What a pity!'

'Where's the map?' said George, a sudden idea coming into her head. 'Would Owl's Dene be named on it, do you think?'

'Not if it's a house,' said Julian. 'Only places are named there. You'd want a frightfully big map to show every house.'

'Well, anyway – let's look at the map and see if it shows any more farms or villages,' said George, who felt as if she must *do* something, even if it was only looking at a map. Julian produced the map and unfolded it. He and the girls bent over it, by the light of the bicycle lamp, and Richard peered over their shoulders. Even Timmy tried to look, forcing his head under their arms.

'Get away, Tim,' said Julian. 'Look, here's where we are – Middlecombe Woods – see? My word, we *are* in a lonely spot! There isn't a village for miles!'

Certainly no village was marked. The countryside was shown, hilly and wooded, with a stream here and there, and third-class roads now and again – but no village, no church, no bridge even was marked anywhere.

Anne gave a sudden exclamation and pointed to the contour of a hill on the map. 'Look, see what that hill's called?'

'Owl's Hill,' read out Julian. 'Yes, I see what you're getting at, Anne. If a house was built on that hill it might be called Owl's Dene, because of the name of the hill. What's more, a building *is* marked there! It hasn't a name, of course. It might be a farmhouse, an old ruin – or a big house of some kind.'

'*I* think it's very likely that's where Owl's Dene is,' said George. 'I bet it's that very house. Let's take our bikes and go.'

A huge sigh from Richard attracted their attention. '*Now* what's the matter with you?' said Julian.

'Nothing. I'm hungry, that's all,' said Richard.

The others suddenly realised that they too were hungry. In fact, *terribly* hungry! It was a long, long time since tea.

Julian remembered the food he and George had

brought from the farm. Should they have it now or should they eat some on their way to Owl's Hill?

'Better eat as we go,' said Julian. 'Every minute we waste means a minute of worry for Dick.'

'I wonder what they'd do with him, if Rooky sees him and says he's not me, not the boy they want,' said Richard, suddenly.

'Set him free, I should think,' said George. 'Ruffians like that would probably turn him loose in a deserted countryside and not care tuppence if he found his way home or not. We've absolutely *got* to find out what's happened – whether he's at Owl's Dene, or been set free, or what.'

'I can't come with you,' suddenly wailed Richard.

'Why?' demanded Julian.

'Because I haven't got my bike,' said Richard, dolefully. 'I chucked it away, you remember – and goodness knows where it is. I'd never find it again.'

'He can have Dick's,' said Anne. 'There it is, over there – with the puncture mended too.'

'Oh yes,' said Richard, relieved. 'For one frightful moment I thought I'd have to be left behind.'

Julian secretly wished he *could* be left behind. Richard was more trouble than he was worth!

'Yes, you can take Dick's bike,' he said. 'But no idiotic behaviour with it, mind – no riding without handlebars, or any tricks like that. It's Dick's bike, not yours.'

Richard said nothing. Julian was always ticking him off. He supposed he deserved it – but it wasn't at all pleasant. He pulled at Dick's bike, and found the lamp was missing. Dick, of course, had taken it off. He hunted round for it and found it on the ground. Dick had let it fall, and the switch had turned itself off when the lamp hit the ground. When Richard pressed the switch down the lamp came on again. Good!

'Now, come on,' said Julian, fetching his bicycle too. 'I'll hand out food to eat as we go. We must try to find our way to Owl's Hill as quick as ever we can!'

CHAPTER NINE

Moonlight adventure

THE FOUR of them rode carefully down the rough, wood-land path. They were glad when they came out into a lane. Julian stopped for a moment to take his bearings.

'Now, according to the map, we ought to go to the right here then take the left at the fork some way down, and then circle a hill by the road at the bottom, and then ride a mile or two in a little valley till we come to the foot of Owl's Hill.'

'If we meet anyone we could ask them about Owl's Dene,' said Anne, hopefully.

'We shan't meet anyone out at night in this district!' said Julian. 'For one thing it's far from any village, and there will be no farmer, no policeman, no traveller for miles! We can't hope to meet anyone.'

The moon was up, and the sky cleared as they rode down the lane. It was soon as bright as day!

'We could switch off our lamps and save the batteries,' said Julian. 'We can see quite well now we're out of the woods and in the moonlight. Rather weird, isn't it?'

'I always think moonlight's strange, because although it shines so brightly on everything, you can never see much *colour* anywhere,' said Anne. She switched off her lamp too. She glanced down at Timmy.

'Switch off your head-lamps, Timmy!' she said, which made Richard give a sudden giggle. Julian smiled. It was nice to hear Anne being cheerful again.

'Timmy's eyes *are* rather like head-lamps, aren't they?' said Richard. 'I say – what about that food, Julian?'

'Right,' said Julian, and he fished in his basket. But it was very difficult to get it out with one hand, and try to hand it to the others.

'Better stop for a few minutes, after all,' he said at last. 'I've already dropped a hard-boiled egg, I think! Come on let's stack our bikes by the side of the road for three minutes, and gulp down something just to satisfy us for now.'

Richard was only too pleased. The girls were so hungry that they too thought it a good idea. They leapt off their bicycles in the moonlit road and went to the little copse at the side. It was a pine-copse, and the ground below was littered with dry brown pine-needles.

'Let's squat here for a minute or two,' said Julian. 'I say, what's that over there?'

Everyone looked. 'It's a tumbledown hut or something,' said George, and she went nearer to see. 'Yes, that's all – some old cottage fallen to bits. There's only part of the walls left. Rather an eerie little place.'

They went to sit down under the pine-trees. Julian shared out the food. Timmy got his bit too, though not so much as he would have liked! They sat there in the pine shadows, munching hungrily as fast as they could.

'I say, can anyone hear what I hear?' said Julian, raising his head. 'It sounds like a car!'

They all listened. Julian was right. A car *was* purring quietly through the countryside! What a bit of luck!

'If only it comes this way!' said Julian. 'We could stop it and ask it for help. It could take us to the nearest police station at any rate!'

They left their food in the little copse and went to the roadside. They could see no head-lights shining anywhere, but they could still hear the noise of the car.

'Very quiet engine,' said Julian. 'Probably a powerful car. It hasn't got its head-lights on because of the bright moonlight.'

'It's coming nearer,' said George. 'It's coming down this lane. Yes – it is!'

So it was. The noise of the engine came nearer, and nearer. The children got ready to leap out into the road to stop the car.

And then the noise of the engine died away suddenly. The moon shone down on a big streamlined car that had stopped a little way down the lane. It had no lights at all, not even side-lights. Julian put out his hand to stop the others from rushing into the road and shouting.

'Wait,' he said. 'This is just a bit strange!'

They waited, keeping in the shadows. The car had stopped not far from the tumbledown hut. A door opened on the off-side. A man got out and rushed across the road to the shadow of the hedge there. He seemed to be carrying a bundle of some kind.

A low whistle sounded. The call of an owl came back. 'An answering signal!' thought Julian, intensely curious about all this. 'I wonder what's happening?'

'Keep absolutely quiet,' he breathed to the others. 'George, look after Timmy – don't let him growl.'

But Timmy knew when he had to be quiet. He didn't even give a whine. He stood like a statue, ears pricked, eyes watching the lane.

Nothing happened for a while. Julian moved very cautiously to the shelter of another tree, from where he could see better.

He could see the tumbledown shack. He saw a shadow moving towards it from some trees beyond. He saw a man waiting – the man from the car probably. Who were they? What in the world could they be doing here at this time of night?

The man from the trees came at last to the man from the car. There was a rapid interchange of words, but Julian could not hear what they were. He was sure that the men had no idea at all that he and the other children were near. He cautiously crept to yet another tree, and peered from the shadows to try and see what was happening.

'Don't be long,' he heard one man say. 'Don't bring your things to the car. Stuff them down the well.'

Julian could not see properly what the man was doing, but he thought he must be changing his clothes. Yes, now he was putting on the others – probably from the bundle the first man had brought from the car. Julian was more

and more curious. What a funny business! Who was the
second man? A refugee? A spy?

The man who had changed his clothes now picked up
his discarded ones and went to the back of the shack. He
came back without them, and followed the first man
across the lane to the waiting car.

Even before the door had closed, the engine was purring, and the car was away! It passed by the pine-copse
where the children were watching, and they all shrank
back as it raced by. Before it had gone very far it was
travelling very fast indeed.

Julian joined the others. 'Well, what do you make of all
that?' he said. 'Funny business, isn't it? I watched a man
changing his clothes – goodness knows why. He's left them
somewhere at the back of the shack – down a well, I think
I heard them say. Shall we see?'

'Yes, let's,' said George, puzzled. 'I say, did you see the
number on the car. I only managed to spot the letters –
KMF.'

'I saw the numbers,' said Anne. '102. And it was a black
Bentley.'

'Yes. Black Bentley, KMF 102,' said Richard. 'Up to
some funny business, I'll be bound!'

They made their way to the ruined shack, and pushed
through overgrown weeds and bushes into the backyard.
There was a broken-down well there, most of its brick
work missing.

It was covered by an old wooden lid. Julian removed it.
It was still heavy, though rotten with age. He peered down
the well, but there was nothing at all to be seen. It was far
too deep to see to the bottom by the light of a bicycle
lamp.

69

'Not much to be seen *there*,' said Julian, replacing the lid. 'I expect it *was* his clothes he threw down. Wonder why he changed them?'

'Do you think he could be an escaped prisoner?' said Anne, suddenly. 'He'd have to change his prison clothes, wouldn't he? – that would be the most important thing for him to do. Is there a prison near here?'

Nobody knew. 'Don't remember noticing one on the map,' said Julian. 'No, somehow I don't think the man was an escaped prisoner – more likely a spy dropped down in this desolate countryside, and supplied with clothes – or perhaps a deserter from the army. That's even *more* likely!'

'Well, whatever he is I don't like it and I'm jolly glad the car's gone with the prisoner or deserter or spy,' said Anne. 'What a curious thing that we should just be nearby when this happened! The men would never, never guess there were four children and a dog watching just a few yards away.'

'Lucky for us they *didn't* know,' said Julian. 'They wouldn't have been at all pleased! Now come on, we've wasted enough time. Let's get back to our food. I hope Timmy hasn't eaten it all. We left it on the ground.'

Timmy hadn't eaten even a crumb. He was sitting patiently by the food, occasionally sniffing at it. All that bread and ham and eggs waiting there and nobody to eat it!

'Good dog,' said George. 'You're very, very trust-worthy, Timmy. You shall have a big bit of bread and ham for your reward.'

Timmy gulped it down in one mouthful, but there was no more for him to have. The others only just had enough for themselves, and ate every crumb. They rose to their feet in a very few minutes and went to get their bicycles.

'Now for Owl's Hill again,' said Julian. 'And let's hope we don't come across any more peculiar happenings to-night. We've had quite enough.'

CHAPTER TEN

Owl's Dene on Owl's Hill

OFF THEY went again, cycling fast in the brilliant moon-light. Even when the moon went behind a cloud it was still light enough to ride without lights. They rode for what seemed like miles, and then came to a steep hill.

'Is this Owl's Hill?' said Anne, as they dismounted to walk up it. It was too steep to ride.

'Yes,' said Julian. 'At least, I think so – unless we've come quite wrong. But I don't think we have. Now the thing is, shall we find Owl's Dene at the top or not? And how shall we know it *is* Owl's Dene!'

'We could ring the bell and ask,' said Anne.

Julian laughed. That was so like Anne. 'Maybe we'll have to do that!' he said. 'But we'll scout round a bit first.'

They pushed their bicycles up the steep road. Hedges bordered each side, and fields lay beyond. There were no animals in them that the children could see – no horses, sheep or cows.

'Look!' said Anne, suddenly. 'I can see a building – at least, I'm sure I can see chimneys!'

They looked where she pointed. Yes, certainly they were chimneys – tall, brick chimneys that looked old.

'Looks like an Elizabethan mansion, with chimneys like that,' said Julian. He paused and took a good look. 'It must be a big place. We ought to come to a drive or something soon.'

They pushed on with their bicycles. Gradually the house

came into view. It was more like a mansion, and in the moonlight it looked old, rather grand and very beautiful.

'There are the gates,' said Julian, thankfully. He was tired of pushing his bicycle up the hill. 'They're shut. Hope they're not locked!'

As they drew near to the great, wrought-iron gates, they slowly opened. The children paused in surprise. Why were they opening? Not for them, that was certain!

Then they heard the sound of a car in the distance. Of course, that was what the gates were opening for. The car, however, was not coming up the hill – it was coming down the drive on the other side of the gates.

'Get out of sight, quickly,' said Julian. 'We don't want to be seen yet.'

They crouched down in the ditch with their bicycles as a car came slowly out of the open gates. Julian gave an exclamation and nudged George.

'See that? It's the black Bentley again – KMF 102!'

'How mysterious!' said George, surprised. 'What's it doing rushing about the country at night and picking up stray men! Taking them to this place too. I wonder if it *is* Owl's Dene.'

The car went by and disappeared round a bend in the hill. The children came out of the ditch with Timmy and their bicycles.

'Let's walk cautiously up to the gates,' said Julian. 'They're still open. Funny how they opened when the car came. I never saw anyone by them!'

They walked boldly up to the open gates.

'Look!' said Julian, pointing up to the great brick posts from which the gates were hung. They all looked, and exclaimed at the name shining there.

'Well! So it *is* Owl's Dene, after all!'

'There's the name in brass letters – Owl's Dene! We've found it!'

'Come on,' said Julian, wheeling his bicycle through the gateway. 'We'll go in and snoop round. We might be lucky enough to find old Dick somewhere about.'

They all went through the gates – and then Anne clutched Julian in fright. She pointed silently behind them.

The gates were closing again! But nobody was there to shut them. They closed silently and smoothly all by themselves. There was something very weird about that.

'Who's shutting them?' whispered Anne, in a scared voice.

'I think it must be done by machinery,' whispered back Julian. 'Probably worked from the house. Let's go back and see if we can find any machinery that works them.'

They left their bicycles by the side of the drive and walked back to the gates. Julian looked for a handle or latch to open them. But there was none.

He pulled at the gates. They did not budge. It was quite impossible to open them. They had been shut and locked by some kind of machinery, and nothing and nobody could open them but that special machinery.

'Blow!' said Julian, and he sounded so angry that the others looked at him in surprise.

'Well, don't you see? – we're locked in! We're as much prisoners here as Dick is, if he's here too. We can't get out through the gates, and if you take a look you'll see a high wall running round the property from the gates – and I don't mind betting it goes the *whole* way round. We can't get out even if we want to.'

They went back thoughtfully to their bicycles. 'Better

wheel them a little way into the trees and leave them,' said Julian. 'They hinder us too much now. We'll leave them and go snooping quietly round the house. Hope there are no dogs.'

They left their bicycles well hidden among the trees at the side of the wide drive. The drive was not at all well-kept. It was mossy and weeds grew all over it. It was bare only where the wheels of cars had passed.

'Shall we walk up the drive or keep to the side?' asked George.

'Keep to the side,' said Julian. 'We should easily be seen in the moonlight, walking up the drive.'

So they kept to the side, in the shadows of the trees. They followed the curves of the long drive until the house itself came into sight.

It really was very big indeed. It was built in the shape of the letter E with the middle stroke missing. There was a courtyard in front, overgrown with weeds. A low wall, about knee high, ran round the courtyard.

There was a light in a room on the top floor, and another one on the ground floor. Otherwise from that side the house was dark.

'Let's walk quietly round it,' said Julian, in a low voice. 'Goodness – what's that?'

It was a weird and terrible screech that made them all jump in alarm. Anne clutched Julian in fright.

They stood and listened.

Something came down silently and brushed George's hair. She almost screamed, but before she could, that terrible screech came again, and she put out her hand to quieten Timmy, who was amazed and scared.

'What is it, Ju!' whispered George. 'Something touched me then. Before I could see what it was it was gone.'

'Listen, it's all right,' whispered back Julian. 'It's only an owl – a screech-owl!'

'Good gracious – so it was,' breathed back George, in great relief. 'What an ass I was not to think of it. It's a barn-owl- a screech-owl out hunting. Anne, were you scared?'

'I should just think I was!' said Anne, letting go her hold on Julian's arm.

'So was I,' said Richard, whose teeth were still chattering with fear. 'I nearly ran for my life! I would have too, if I could have got my legs to work – but they were glued to the ground!'

The owl screeched again, a little farther away, and another one answered it. A third one screeched, and the night was really made hideous with the unearthly calls.

'I'd rather have a brown owl any day, calling To-whooo-oo-oo,' said George. 'That's a nice noise. But this screeching is frightful.'

'No wonder it's called Owl's Hill,' said Julian. 'Perhaps it's always been a haunt of the screech-owls.'

The four children and Timmy began to walk quietly round the house, keeping to the shadows as much as they could. Everywhere was dark at the back except two long windows. They were leaded windows, and curtains were pulled across them. Julian tried to see through the cracks.

He found a place where two curtains didn't quite meet. He put his eye to the crack and looked in.

'It's the kitchen,' he told the others. 'An enormous place – lit with one big oil-lamp. All the rest of the room is in shadow. There's a great fire-place at the end, with a few logs burning in it.'

'Anyone there?' asked George, trying to see through the crack too. Julian moved aside and let her take her turn.

'No one that I can see,' he said. George gave an exclamation as she looked, and Julian pushed her aside to look in again.

He saw a man walking into the room – a funny, dwarf-like fellow, with a hunched back that seemed to force his head on one side. He had a very evil face. Behind him came a woman – thin, drab and the picture of misery.

The man flung himself into a chair and began to fill a pipe. The woman took a kettle off the fire and went to fill hot-water bottles in a corner.

'She must be the cook,' thought Julian. 'What a misery she looks! I wonder what the man is – man-of-all-work, I suppose. What an evil face he's got!'

The woman spoke timidly to the man in the chair.

Julian, of course, could not hear a word from outside the window. The man answered her roughly banging on the arm of the chair as he spoke.

The woman seemed to be pleading with him about something. The man flew into a rage, picked up a poker and threatened the woman with it. Julian watched in horror. Poor woman! No wonder she looked miserable if that was the sort of thing that kept happening.

However, the man did nothing with the poker except brandish it in temper, and he soon replaced it, and settled down in his chair again. The woman said no more at all, but went on filling the bottles. Julian wondered who they were for.

He told the others what he had seen. They didn't like it at all. If the people in the kitchen behaved like that whatever would those in the other part of the house be like?

They left the kitchen windows and went on round the house. They came to a lower room, lit inside. But there the curtains were tightly drawn, and there was no crack to look through.

They looked up to the one room high up that was lit. Surely Dick must be there? Perhaps he was locked up in the attic, all by himself? How they wished they knew!

Dared they throw up a stone? They wondered if they should try. There didn't seem any way at all of getting into the house. The front door was well and truly shut. There was a side door also tightly shut and locked, because they had tried it. Not a single window seemed to be open.

'I think I *will* throw up a stone,' said Julian at last. 'I feel sure Dick's up there, if he has been taken here – and you're certain you heard the men say "Owl's Dene", aren't you, Anne?'

'Quite certain,' said Anne. 'Do throw a stone, Julian. I'm getting so worried about poor Dick.'

Julian felt about on the ground for a stone. He found one embedded in the moss that was everywhere. He balanced it in his hand. Then up went the stone, but fell just short of the window. Julian got another. Up it went – and hit the glass of the window with a sharp crack. Somebody came to the pane at once.

Was it Dick? Everyone strained their eyes to see – but the window was too far up. Julian threw up another stone, and that hit the window too.

'I think it *is* Dick,' said Anne. 'Oh dear – no it isn't after all. Can't *you* see, Julian?'

But the person at the window, whoever he was, had now disappeared. The children felt a bit uncomfortable. Suppose it hadn't been Dick? Suppose it had been someone else who had now disappeared from the room to go and look for them?

'Let's get away from this part of the house,' whispered Julian. 'Get round to the other side.'

They made their way round quietly – and Richard suddenly pulled at Julian's arm. 'Look!' he said. 'There's a window open! Can't we get in there?'

CHAPTER ELEVEN

Trapped!

JULIAN LOOKED at the casement window. The moonlight shone on it. It certainly was a little ajar. 'How did we miss that when we went round before?' he wondered. He hesitated a little. Should they try to get in or not? Wouldn't it be better to rap on the back door and get that miserable-looking woman to answer it and tell them what they wanted to know?

On the other hand there was that evil-looking hunchback there. Julian didn't like the look of him at all. No, on the whole it might be better to creep in at the window, see if it was Dick upstairs, set him free, and then all escape through the same open window. Nobody would know. The bird would have flown, and everything would be all right.

Julian went to the window. He put a leg up and there he was astride the window. He held out a hand to Anne. 'Come on, I'll give you a hand,' he said, and pulled her up beside him. He lifted her down on the floor inside.

Then George came, and then Richard. George was just leaning out to encourage Timmy to jump in through the window too, when something happened!

A powerful torchlight went on, and its beam shone right across the room into the dazzled eyes of the four children! They stood there, blinking in alarm. What was this?

Then Anne heard the voice of one of the men who had captured Dick. 'Well, well, well – a crowd of young burglars!'

80

The voice changed suddenly to anger. 'How *dare* you break in here! I'll hand you over to the police.'

From outside Timmy growled fiercely. He jumped up at the window and almost succeeded in leaping through. The man grasped what was happening at once, and went to the open window. He shut it with a bang. Now Timmy couldn't get in!

'Let my dog in!' said George, angrily, and stupidly tried to open the window again. The man brought his torch down sharply on her hand and she cried out in pain.

'That's what happens to boys who go against my wishes,' said the man, whilst poor George nursed her bruised hand.

'Look here,' began Julian, fiercely, 'what do you think you're doing? We're not burglars – and what's more we'd be very, very glad if you'd hand us over to the police!'

'Oh, you would, would you?' said the man. He went to the door of the room and yelled out in a tremendous voice: 'Aggie! AGGIE! Bring a lamp here at once.'

There was an answering shout from the kitchen, and almost immediately the light of a lamp appeared shining down the passage outside. It grew brighter, and the miserable-looking woman came in with a big oil-lamp. She stared in amazement at the little group of children. She seemed about to say something when the man gave her a rough push.

'Get out. And keep your mouth shut. Do you hear me?'

The woman scuttled out like a frightened hen. The man looked round at the children in the light of the lamp. The room was very barely furnished and appeared to be a sitting-room of some kind.

'So you don't mind being given up to the police?' said

the man. 'That's very interesting. You think they'd approve of you breaking into my house?'

'I tell you, we *didn't* break in,' said Julian, determined to get that clear, at any rate. 'We came here because we had reason to believe that you've got my brother locked up somewhere in this house – and it's all a mistake. You've got the wrong boy.'

Richard didn't like this at all. He was terribly afraid of being locked up in place of Dick! He kept behind the others as much as possible.

The man looked hard at Julian. He seemed to be thinking. 'We haven't a boy here at all,' he said at last. 'I really don't know what you mean. You don't suggest that I go about the countryside picking boys up and making them prisoners, do you?'

'I don't know what you do,' said Julian. 'All I know is this – you captured Dick, my brother, this evening in Middlecombe Woods, thinking he was Richard Kent – well, he's not, he's my brother Dick. And if you don't set him free at once, I'll tell the police what we know.'

'And dear me – *how* do you know all this?' asked the man. 'Were you there when he was captured, as you call it?'

'One of us was,' said Julian bluntly. 'In the tree overhead. That's how we know.'

There was a silence. The man took out a cigarette and lighted it. 'Well, you're quite mistaken,' he said. 'We've no boy held prisoner here. The thing is ridiculous. Now it's very, very late – would you like to bed down here for the night and get off in the morning? I don't like to send a parcel of kids out into the middle of the night. There's no telephone here, or I'd ring your home.'

Julian hesitated. He felt certain Dick was in the house.

If he said he would stay for the night he might be able to find out if Dick was really there or not. He could quite well see that the man didn't want them tearing off to the police. There was something at Owl's Dene that was secret and sinister.

'We'll stay,' he said at last. 'Our people are away – they won't worry.'

He had forgotten about Richard for the moment. His people certainly *would* worry! Still, there was nothing to do about it. The first thing was to find Dick. Surely the men would be mad to hold him a prisoner once they were certain he wasn't the boy. Perhaps Rooky, the ruffian who knew Richard, hadn't yet arrived – hadn't seen Dick? That must be the reason that this man wanted them to stay the night. Of course, he'd wait till Rooky came, and when Rooky said, 'No, he's not the boy we want!' they'd let Dick go. They'd have to!

The man called for Aggie again. She came at once.

'These kids are lost,' said the man to her. 'I've said I'll put them up for the night. Get one of the rooms ready – just put down mattresses and blankets, that's all. Give them some food if they want it.'

Aggie was evidently tremendously astonished. Julian guessed that she was not used to this man being kind to lost children. He shouted at her.

'Well, don't stand dithering there. Get on with the job. Take these kids with you.'

Aggie beckoned to the four children. George hung back. 'What about my dog?' she said. 'He's still outside, whining. I can't go to bed without him.'

'You'll have to,' said the man, roughly. 'I won't have him in the house at any price, and that's flat.'

84

'He'll attack anyone he meets,' said George.

'He won't meet anyone out there,' said the man. 'By the way, how did you get in through the gates?'

'A car came out just as we got there and we slipped in before the gates closed,' said Julian. 'How do the gates shut? By machinery?'

'Mind your own business,' said the man, and went down the passage in the opposite direction.

'Pleasant, kindly fellow,' said Julian to George.

'Oh, a sweet nature,' answered George. The woman stared at them both in surprise. She didn't seem to realise that they meant the opposite to what they said! She led the way upstairs.

She came to a big room with a carpet on the floor, a small bed in a corner, and one or two chairs. There was no other furniture.

'I'll get some mattresses and put them down for you,' she said.

'I'll help you,' offered Julian, thinking it would be a good idea to see round a bit.

'All right,' said the woman. 'You others stay here.'

She went off with Julian. They went to a cupboard and the woman tugged at two big mattresses. Julian helped her. She seemed rather touched by his help.

'Well, thank you,' she said. 'They're pretty heavy.'

'Don't expect you have many children here, to stay, do you?' asked Julian.

'Well, it's funny that you should come just after . . .' the woman began. Then she stopped and bit her lip, looking anxiously up and down the passage.

'Just after what?' asked Julian. 'Just after the other boy came, do you mean?'

'Sh!' said the woman, looking scared to death. 'Whatever do you know about *that*? You shouldn't have said that. Mr Perton will skin me alive if he knew you'd said that. He'd be sure I'd told you. Forget about it.'

'That's the boy who's locked up in one of the attics at the top of the house isn't it?' said Julian, helping her to carry one of the mattresses to the big bedroom. She dropped her end in the greatest alarm.

'Now! Do you want to get me into terrible trouble – and yourselves too? Do you want Mr Perton to tell old Hunchy to whip you all? You don't know that man! He's wicked.'

'When's Rooky coming?' asked Julian, bent on astonishing the woman, hoping to scare her into one admission after another. This was too much for her altogether. She stood there shaking at the knees, staring at Julian as if she couldn't believe her ears.

TRAPPED!

'What do you know about Rooky?' she whispered. 'Is he coming here? Don't tell me he's coming here!'

'Why? Don't you like him?' asked Julian. He put a hand on her shoulder. 'Why are you so frightened and upset? What's the matter? Tell me. I might be able to help you.'

'Rooky's bad,' said the woman. 'I thought he was in prison. Don't tell me he's out again. Don't tell me he's coming here.'

She was so frightened that she wouldn't say a word more. She began to cry, and Julian hadn't the heart to press her with any more questions. In silence he helped her to drag the mattresses into the other room.

'I'll get you some food,' said the poor woman, sniffing miserably. 'You'll find blankets in that cupboard over there if you want to lie down.'

She disappeared. Julian told the others in whispers what he had been able to find out. 'We'll see if we can find Dick as soon as things are quiet in the house,' he said. 'This is a bad house – a house of secrets, of strange comings and goings. I shall slip out of our room and see what I can find out later on. I think that man – Mr Perton is his name – is really waiting for Rooky to come and see if Dick is Richard or not. When he finds he isn't I've no doubt he'll set him free – and us too.'

'What about *me*?' said Richard. 'Once he sees me, I'm done for. I'm the boy he wants. He hates my father and he hates me too. He'll kidnap me, take me somewhere, and ask an enormous ransom for me, just to punish us!'

'Well, we must do something to prevent him seeing you,' said Julian. 'But I don't see why he *should* see you – it's only Dick he'll want to see. He won't be interested in what he thinks are Dick's brothers and sisters! Now for

87

goodness' sake don't start to howl again, or honestly I'll give you up to Rooky myself! You really are a frightful little coward – haven't you any courage at all!'

'All this has come about because of your silly lies and deceit,' said George, quite fiercely. 'It's all because of you that our trip is spoilt, that Dick's locked up and poor Timmy's outside without me.'

Richard looked quite taken aback. He shrank into a corner and didn't say another word. He was very miserable. Nobody liked him, nobody believed him, nobody trusted him. Richard felt very, very small indeed.

CHAPTER TWELVE

Julian looks round

THE WOMAN brought them some food. It was only bread and butter and jam, with some hot coffee to drink. The four children were not really hungry, but they were very thirsty, and they drank the coffee eagerly.

George opened the window and called softly down to Timmy. 'Tim! Here's something for you!'

Timmy was down there all right, watching and waiting. He knew where George was. He had howled and whined for some time, but now he was quiet.

George was quite determined to get him indoors if she could. She gave him all her bread and jam, dropping it down bit by bit, and listening to him wolfing it up. Anyway, old Timmy would know she was thinking of him!

'Listen,' said Julian, coming in from the passage outside, where he had stood listening for a while. 'I think it would be a good idea if we put out this light, and settled down on the mattresses. But I shall make up a lump on mine to look like me, so that if anyones comes they'll think I'm there on the mattress. But I shan't be.'

'Where will you be, then?' asked Anne. 'Don't leave us!'

'I shall be hiding outside in that cupboard,' said Julian. 'I've a sort of feeling that our pleasant host, Mr Perton, will come along presently to look us in – and I've no intention of being locked in! I think he'll flash a torch into the room, see that we're all four safely asleep on the mattresses, and then quietly lock the door. Well, *I* shall be able to unlock it when I come back from the cupboard outside and we shan't be prisoners at all!'

'Oh, that really is a good idea,' said Anne, cuddling herself up in a blanket. 'You'd better go and get into the cupboard now, Julian, before we're locked up for the night!'

Julian blew out the lamp. He tiptoed to the door and opened it. He left it ajar. He went into the passage and fumbled his way to where he knew the cupboard should be. Ah, there it was. He pulled the handle and the door opened silently. He slipped inside and left the door open just a crack, so that he would be able to see if anyone came along the wide passage.

He waited there about twenty minutes. The cupboard smelt musty, and it was very boring standing there doing absolutely nothing.

Then, through the crack in the door, he suddenly noticed that a light was coming. Ah, somebody was about!

He peered through the crack. He saw Mr Perton coming quietly along the corridor with a little oil-lamp held in his hand. He went to the door of the children's bedroom and pushed it a little. Julian watched him, hardly daring to breathe.

Would he notice that the figure on one of the mattresses was only a lump made of a blanket rolled up and covered by another blanket? Julian fervently hoped that he wouldn't. All his plans would be spoilt if so.

Mr Perton held the lamp high in his hand and looked cautiously into the room. He saw four huddled-up shapes lying on the mattresses – four children – he thought.

They were obviously asleep. Softly, Mr Perton closed the door, and just as softly locked it. Julian watched anxiously to see if he pocketed the key or not. No – he hadn't! He had left it in the lock. Oh good!

The man went away again, treading softly. He did not go downstairs, but disappeared into a room some way down on the right. Julian heard the door shut with a click. Then he heard another click. The man evidently believed in locking himself in. Perhaps he didn't trust his other comrade, wherever he was – or Hunchy or the woman.

Julian waited a while and then crept out of the cupboard. He stole up to Mr Perton's room and looked through the keyhole to see if the room was in darkness or not. It was! Was Mr Perton snoring? Not that Julian could hear.

However Julian was not going to wait till he heard Mr Perton snore. He was going to find Dick – and he was pretty certain that the first place to look was in that attic upstairs!

'I bet Mr Perton was up there with Dick and heard me throwing stones at the window,' thought Julian. 'Then he slipped down and opened that window to trap us into getting in there, and we fell neatly into the trap! He must have been waiting inside the room for us. I don't like Mr Perton – too full of bright ideas!'

He was half-way up the flight of stairs that led to the attics now – going very carefully and slowly, afraid of making the stairs creak loudly. They did creak – and at every creak poor Julian stopped and listened to see if anyone had heard!

There was a long passage at the top turning at both ends into the side-wings. Julian stood still and debated – now which way ought he to go? Where exactly was that lit window? It was somewhere along this long passage, he

91

was certain. Well, he'd go along the doors and see if a light shone out through the keyhole, or under the door anywhere.

Door after door was ajar. Julian peeped round each, making out bare dark attics, or box-rooms with rubbish in. Then he came to a door that was closed. He peered through the keyhole. No light came from inside the room.

Julian knocked gently. A voice came at once – Dick's voice. 'Who's there?'

'Sh! It's me – Julian,' whispered Julian. 'Are you all right, Dick?'

There came the creak of a bed, then the pattering of feet across a bare floor. Dick's voice came through the door, muffled and cautious.

'Julian! How did you get here? This is marvellous! Can you unlock the door and let me out?'

Julian had already felt for a key – but there was none. Mr Perton had taken *that* key, at any rate!

'No. The key's gone,' he said. 'Dick, what did they do to you?'

'Nothing much. They dragged me off to the car and shoved me in,' said Dick, through the door. 'The man called Rooky wasn't there. The others waited for him for some time, then drove off. They thought he might have gone off to see someone they meant to visit. So I haven't seen him. He's coming tomorrow morning. What a shock for him when he finds I'm not Richard!'

'Richard's here too,' whispered Julian. 'I wish he wasn't – because if Rooky happens to see him he'll be kidnapped, I'm sure! The only hope is that Rooky will only see *you* – and as the other men think we're all one family, they may let us all go. Did you come straight here in the car, Dick?'

'Yes,' said Dick. 'The gates opened like magic when we got here, but I couldn't see anybody. I was shoved up here and locked in. One of the men came to tell me all the things Rooky was going to do to me when he saw me – and then he suddenly went downstairs and hasn't come back again.'

'Oh, I bet that was when we chucked stones up at your window,' said Julian at once. 'Didn't you hear them?'

'Yes, so that was the crack I heard! The man with me went across to the window at once and he must have seen you. Now, what about *you*, Ju? How on earth did you get here? Are you all really here? I suppose that was Timmy I heard howling outside.'

Julian quickly told him all his tale from the time he and George had met the howling Richard to the moment he had slipped up the stairs to find Dick.

93

There was a silence when he had finished his tale. Then Dick's voice came through the crack.

'Not much good making any plans, Julian. If things go all right, we'll be out of here by the morning, when Rooky finds I'm not the boy he wants. If things go wrong at least we're all together, and we can make plans then. I wonder what his mother will think when Richard doesn't get home tonight.'

'Probably think he's gone off to the aunt's,' said Julian. 'I should think he's a very unreliable person. Blow him! It was all because of him we got into this fix.'

'I expect the men will have some cock-and-bull story tomorrow morning, about why they got hold of you, when they find you're not Richard,' went on Julian. 'They'll probably say you threw stones at their car or something, and they took you in hand – or found you hurt and brought you here to help you! Anyway, whatever they say, we won't make much fuss about it. We'll go quietly – and then we'll get things moving! I don't know what's going on here, but it's something fishy. The police ought to look into it, I'm certain.'

'Listen, that's Timmy again,' said Dick. 'Howling like anything for George, I suppose. You'd better go, Julian, in case he wakes up one of the men and they come out and find you here. Good night. I'm awfully glad you're near! Thanks awfully for coming to find me.'

'Good night,' said Julian, and went back along the corridor, walking over the patches of moonlight, looking fearfully into the dark shadows in case Mr Perton or somebody else was waiting for him!

But nobody was about. Timmy's howling died down. There was a deep silence in the house. Julian went down the stairs to the floor on which the bedroom was where the others lay asleep. He paused outside it. Should he do any further exploring? It really was such a chance!

He decided that he would. Mr Perton was fast asleep, he hoped. He thought probably Hunchy and the woman had gone to bed too. He wondered where the other man was, who had brought Dick to Owl's Dene. He hadn't seen him at all. Perhaps he had gone out in that black Bentley they had seen going out of the gate.

Julian went down to the ground floor. A brilliant thought had just occurred to him. Couldn't he undo the front door and get the others down, and send them out, free? He himself couldn't escape, because it would mean leaving Dick alone.

Then he gave up the idea. 'No,' he thought. 'For one thing George and Anne would refuse to go without me – and even if they agreed to get out of the front door, and go down the drive to the gates, how would they undo them? They're worked by some machinery from the house.'

So his brilliant idea came to nothing. He decided to look into all the rooms on the ground floor. He looked into the kitchen first. The fire was almost out. The moonlight came through the cracks of the curtains and lit up the dark silent room. Hunchy and the woman had evidently retired somewhere.

There was nothing of interest in the kitchen. Julian went into the room opposite. It was a dining-room, with a long polished table, candlesticks on the walls and mantelpiece, and the remains of a wood fire. Nothing of interest there either.

The boy went into another room. Was it a workroom, or what? There was a radio there, and a big desk. There was a stand with a curious instrument of some kind that had a stout wheel-like handle. Julian suddenly wondered if it would open the gates! Yes, that was what it was for. He saw a label attached to it. Left Gate. Right Gate. Both Gates.

'That's what it is – the machinery for opening either or both of the gates. If only I could get Dick out of that room I'd get us all out of this place in no time!' said Julian. He twisted the handle – what would happen?

CHAPTER THIRTEEN

Strange secret

A CURIOUS groaning, whining noise began, as some kind of strong machinery was set working. Julian hurriedly turned the handle back. If it was going to make all that noise, he wasn't going to try his hand at opening the gates! It would bring Mr Perton out of his room in a rush!

'Most ingenious, whatever it is,' thought the boy, examining it as well as he could in the moonlight that streamed through the window. He looked round the room again. A noise came to his ears and he stood still.

'It's somebody snoring,' he thought. 'I'd better not mess about here any more! Where are they sleeping? Somewhere not far from here, that's certain.'

He tiptoed cautiously into the next room and looked inside it. It was a lounge, but there was nobody there at all. He couldn't hear the snoring there either.

He was puzzled. There didn't seem to be any other room nearby where people could sleep. He went back to the workroom or study. Yes, now he could hear that noise again – and it *was* somebody snoring! Somebody quite near – and yet not near enough to hear properly, or to see. Most peculiar.

Julian walked softly round the room, trying to find a place where the snoring sounded loudest of all. Yes, by this bookcase that reached to the ceiling. That was where the snoring sounded most of all. Was there a room behind this wall, next to the workroom? Julian went out to investigate. But there was no room behind the study at all – only the wall of the corridor, as far as he could see. It was more and more mysterious.

He went back to the study again, and over to the bookcase. Yes, there it was again. *Somebody* was asleep and snoring not far off – but WHERE?

Julian began to examine the bookcase. It was full of books jammed tightly together – novels, biographies, reference books – all higgledy-piggledy. He removed some from a shelf and examined the bookcase behind. It was of solid wood.

He put back the books and examined the big book-case again. It was a very solid affair. Julian looked carefully at the books, shining in the moonlight. One shelf of books looked different from the others – less tidy – the books not so jammed together. Why should just one shelf be different?

Julian quietly took the books from that shelf. Behind them was the solid wood again. Julian put his hand at the back and felt about. A knob was hidden in a corner. A knob! Whatever was that there for?

Cautiously Julian turned the knob this way and that. Nothing happened. Then he pressed it. Still nothing happened. He pulled it – and it slid out a good six inches.

Then the whole of the back of that particular shelf slid quietly downwards, and left an opening big enough for somebody to squeeze through! Julian held his breath. A sliding panel! What was behind it?

A dim flickering light came from the space behind. Julian waited till his eyes were used to it after the bright moonlight. He was trembling with excitement. The snoring now sounded so loud that Julian felt as if the snorer must be almost within hand's reach!

Then gradually he made out a tiny room, with a small narrow bed, a table and a shelf on which a few articles could dimly be made out. A candle was burning in a corner. On the bed was the snorer. Julian could not see what he was like, except that he looked big and burly as he lay there, snoring peacefully.

'What a find!' thought Julian. 'A secret hiding-place – a place to hide all kinds of people, I suppose, who have enough money to pay for such a safe hole. This fellow ought to have been warned not to snore! He gave himself away.'

The boy did not dare to stay there any longer, looking into that curious secret room. It must be built in a space between the wall of the study and the wall of the corridor – probably a very old hiding-place made when the house was built.

Julian felt for the knob. He pushed it back into place, and the panel slid up again, as noiselessly as before. It was evidently kept in good working order!

The snoring was muffled again now. Julian replaced the books, hoping that they were more or less as he had found them.

He felt very thrilled. He had found one of the secrets of Owl's Dene, at any rate. The police would be *very* interested to hear about that secret hole – and perhaps they would be even more interested to hear about the person inside it!

It was absolutely essential now that he and the others should escape. Would it be all right if he went without Dick? No, if the men suspected any dirty work on his part – discovered that he knew of the secret hole, for instance – they might harm Dick. Regretfully Julian decided that

99

there must be no escape for him unless everyone, including Dick, could come too.

He didn't explore any more. He suddenly felt very tired indeed and crept softly upstairs. He felt as if he simply must lie down and think. He was too tired to do anything else.

He went to the bedroom. The key was still in the lock outside. He went into the room and shut the door. Mr Perton would find the door unlocked the next morning, but probably he would think he hadn't turned the key properly. Julian lay down on the mattress beside Richard. All the others were fast asleep.

He meant to think out all his problems – but no sooner had he closed his eyes than he was fast asleep. He didn't hear Timmy howling outside once more. He didn't hear the screech-owl that made the night hideous on the hill. He didn't see the moon slide down the sky.

It was not Mr Perton who awoke the children next morning, but the woman. She came into the room and called to them.

'If you want breakfast you'd better come down and have it!'

They all sat up in a hurry, wondering where in the world they were. 'Hallo!' said Julian, blinking sleepily. 'Breakfast, did you say? It sounds good. Is there anywhere we can wash?'

'You can wash down in the kitchen,' said the woman, sullenly. 'I'm not cleaning any bathroom up after you!'

'Leave the door unlocked for us to get out!' said Julian, innocently. 'Mr Perton locked it last night.'

'So he said,' answered the woman, 'but he *hadn't* locked it! It wasn't locked when I tried the door this morning.

Aha! You didn't know that, did you? You'd have been wandering all over the house, I suppose, if you'd guessed that.'

'Probably we should,' agreed Julian, winking at the others. They knew that he had meant to go and find Dick in the night, and snoop round a bit – but they didn't know all he had discovered. He hadn't had the heart to wake them and tell them the night before.

'Don't you be too long,' said the woman, and went out of the door, leaving it open.

'I hope she's taken some breakfast up to poor old Dick,' said Julian, in a low voice. The others came close to him.

'Ju, did you find Dick last night?' whispered Anne. He nodded. Then, very quickly and quietly he told them all he had discovered – where Dick was, and then how he had heard the snoring, and discovered the secret panel, the hidden room, and the man who slept so soundly there, not knowing that Julian had seen him.

'Julian! How thrilling!' said George. 'Whoever would have thought of all that?'

'Oh yes, and I discovered the machinery that opens the gates too,' said Julian. It's in the same room. But come on, if we don't go down to the kitchen that woman will be after us again. I hope Hunchy won't be there, I don't like him.'

Hunchy, however, *was* there, finishing his breakfast at a small table. He scowled at the children, but they took absolutely no notice of him.

'You've been a long time,' grumbled the woman. 'There's the sink over there, if you want to wash, and I've put a towel out for you. You look pretty dirty, all of you.'

'We are,' said Julian, cheerfully. 'We could have done with a bath last night – but we didn't exactly get much of a welcome, you know.'

When they had washed they went to a big scrubbed table. There was no cloth on it. The woman had put out some bread and butter and some boiled eggs and a jug of steaming hot cocoa. They all sat down and began to help themselves. Julian talked cheerfully, winking at the others to make them do the same. He wasn't going to let the hunchback think they were scared or worried in any way.

'Shut up, you,' said Hunchy, suddenly. Julian took no notice. He went on talking, and George backed him up valiantly, though Anne and Richard were too scared, after hearing the hunchback's furious voice.

'Did you hear what I said?' suddenly yelled Hunchy, and got up from the little table where he had been sitting. 'Hold your tongues, all of you! Coming into my kitchen and making all that row! Hold your tongues!'

Julian rose too. 'I don't take orders from you whoever you are,' he said, and he sounded just like a grown-up. 'You hold your tongue – or else be civil.'

'Oh, don't talk to him like that, don't,' begged the woman, anxiously. 'He's got such a temper – he'll take a stick to you!'

'I'd take a stick to *him* – except that I don't hit fellows smaller than myself,' said Julian.

What would have happened if Mr Perton hadn't appeared in the kitchen at that moment nobody knew! He stalked in and glared round, sensing that there was a row going on.

'You losing your temper again, Hunchy?' he said. 'Keep it till it's needed. I'll ask you to produce it sometime today possibly – if these kids don't behave themselves!' He looked round at the children with a grim expression. Then he glanced at the woman.

'Rooky's coming soon,' he told her. 'And one or two others. Get a meal – a good one. Keep these children in here, Hunchy, and keep an eye on them. I may want them later.'

He went out. The woman was trembling. 'Rooky's coming,' she half-whispered to Hunchy.

'Get on with your work, woman,' said the dwarf. 'Go out and get the vegetables in yourself – I've got to keep an eye on these kids.'

The poor woman scuttled about. Anne was sorry for her. She went over to her. 'Shall I clear away and wash up for you?' she asked. 'You're going to be busy and I've nothing to do.'

'We'll all help,' said Julian. The woman gave him an astonished and grateful glance. It was plain that she was not used to good manners or politeness of any sort.

'Yah!' said Hunchy, sneeringly. 'You won't get round *me* with your smarmy ways!'

Nobody took the slightest notice of him. All the children began to clear away the breakfast things, and Anne and George stacked them in the sink, and began to wash them.

'Yah!' said Hunchy again.

'And yah to you,' said Julian, pleasantly, which made the others laugh, and Hunchy scowl till his eyes disappeared under his brows!

CHAPTER FOURTEEN

Rooky is very angry

ABOUT AN hour later there was a curious grinding, groaning noise that turned to a whining. Richard, Anne and George jumped violently. But Julian knew what it was.

'The gates are being opened,' he told them, and they remembered how he had described the machinery that opened the gates – the curious wheel-like handle, labelled 'Left Gate. Right Gate. Both Gates'.

'How do *you* know that?' asked Hunchy at once, surprised and suspicious.

'Oh, I'm a good guesser,' replied Julian airily. 'Correct me if I'm wrong, but I couldn't help thinking the gates were being opened, and I'm guessing it's Rooky that's coming through them!'

'You're so sharp you'll cut yourself one day,' grumbled Hunchy, going to the door.

'So my mother told me when I was two years old,' said Julian, and the others giggled. If there was any answering back to be done, Julian could always do it!

They all went to the window. George opened it. Timmy was there, sitting just outside. George had begged the woman to let him in, but she wouldn't. She had thrown him some scraps, and told George there was a pond he could drink from, but beyond that she wouldn't go.

'Timmy,' called George, as she heard the sound of a car purring quietly up the drive, 'Timmy, stay there. Don't move!'

She was afraid that Timmy might perhaps run round to the front door, and go for anyone who jumped out of the car. Timmy looked up at her inquiringly. He was puzzled about this whole affair. Why wasn't he allowed inside the house with George? He knew there were some people who didn't welcome dogs into their houses – but George never went to those houses. It was a puzzle to him, too, to understand why she didn't come out to him.

Still, she was there, leaning out of the window; he could hear her voice; he could even lick her hand if he stood up on his hind legs against the wall.

'You shut that window and come inside,' said Hunchy, maliciously. He took quite a pleasure in seeing that George was upset at being separated from Timmy.

'Here comes the car,' said Julian. They all looked at it – and then glanced at each other. KMF 102 – of course!

The black Bentley swept by the kitchen windows and up to the front door. Three men got out. Richard crouched back, his face going pale.

Julian glanced round at him raising his eyebrows, mutely asking him if he recognised one of the men as Rooky. Richard nodded miserably. He was very frightened now.

The whining, groaning noise came again. The gates were being shut. Voices came from the hall, then the men went into one of the rooms, and there was the sound of a door being shut.

Julian wondered if he could slip out of the room unnoticed and go up to see if Dick was all right. He sidled to the door, thinking that Hunchy was engrossed in cleaning an array of dirty shoes. But his grating voice sounded at once.

'Where you going? If you don't obey orders I'll tell Mr Perton – and won't you be sorry!'

'There's quite a lot of people in this house going to be sorry for themselves soon,' said Julian, in an irritatingly cheerful voice. 'You be careful, Hunchy.'

Hunchy lost his temper suddenly and threw the shoe-brush he was using straight at Julian. Julian caught it deftly and threw it up on the high mantelpiece.

'Thanks,' he said. 'Like to throw another?'

'Oh don't,' said the woman, beseechingly. 'You don't know what he's like when he's in a real temper. Don't!'

The door of the room that the men had gone into opened, and somebody went upstairs. 'To fetch Dick,' thought Julian at once. He stood and listened.

Hunchy got another shoe-brush and went on polishing, muttering angrily under his breath. The woman went on preparing some food. The others listened with Julian. They too guessed that the man had gone to fetch Dick to show him to Rooky.

Footsteps came down the stairs again – two lots this time. Yes, Dick must be with the man, they could hear his voice.

'Let go my arm! I can come without being dragged!' they heard him say indignantly. Good old Dick! He wasn't going to be dragged about without making a strong protest.

He was taken into the room where the other three men were waiting. Then a loud voice was heard.

'He's not the boy! Fools, you've got the wrong boy!'

Hunchy and the woman heard the words too. They gaped at one another. Something had gone wrong. They went to the door and stood there silently. The children just

stood behind them. Julian edged Richard away very gradually.

'Rub some soot over your hair,' he whispered. 'Make it as black as you can, Richard. If the men come out here to see us, they're not likely to recognise you so easily if your hair's black. Go on, quick, while the others aren't paying attention.'

Julian was pointing to the inside of the grate, where black soot hung. Richard put his trembling hands into it and covered them with it. Then he rubbed the soot over his yellow hair.

'More,' whispered Julian. 'Much more! Go on. I'll stand in front of you so that the others can't see what you're doing.'

Richard rubbed soot even more wildly over his hair. Julian nodded. Yes, it looked black enough now. Richard looked quite different. Julian hoped Anne and George would be sensible enough not to exclaim when they saw him.

There was evidently some sharp argument going on in the room off the hall. Voices were raised, but not many words could be made out from where the children stood at the kitchen door. Dick's voice could be heard too. It suddenly sounded quite clearly.

'I TOLD you you'd made a mistake. Now you just let me go, see!'

Hunchy suddenly pushed everyone roughly away from the door – except poor Richard who was standing over in a dark corner, shaking with fright!

'They're coming,' he hissed. 'Get away from the door.'

Everyone obeyed. Hunchy took up a shoe-brush again,

the woman went to peel potatoes, the children turned over the pages of some old magazines they had found.

Footsteps came to the kitchen door. It was flung open. Mr Perton was there – and behind him another man. No mistaking who *he* was!

Thick-lipped, with an enormous nose – yes, he was the ruffian Rooky, once bodyguard to Richard's father, the man who hated Richard because he had told tales on him and who had been sent off in disgrace by the boy's father.

Richard cowered back in his corner, hiding behind the others. Anne and George had given him astonished stares when they had noticed his hair, but neither of them had said a word. Hunchy and the woman didn't seem to have noticed any change in him.

Dick was with the two men. He waved to the others. Julian grinned. Good old Dick!

Rooky glanced at all four children. His eyes rested for a moment on Richard, and then glanced away. He hadn't recognised him!

'Well, Mr Perton,' said Julian. 'I'm glad to see you've got my brother down from the room you locked him up in last night. I imagine that means he can come with us now. Why you brought him here as you did, and made him a prisoner last night I can't imagine.'

'Now look here,' said Mr Perton, in quite a different voice from the one he had used to them before, 'now look here, quite frankly we made a mistake. You don't need to know why or how – that's none of your business. This isn't the boy we wanted.'

'We *told* you he was our brother,' said Anne.

'Quite,' said Mr Perton, politely. 'I am sorry I disbelieved you. These things happen. Now, we want to make you all a handsome present for any inconvenience you have suffered – er – ten pounds for you to spend on ice-creams and so on. You can go whenever you like.'

'And don't try and tell any fairy stories to anyone,' said Rooky suddenly, in a threatening voice. 'See? We made a mistake – but we're not having it talked about. If you say anything silly, we shall say that we found this boy lost in the woods, took pity on him and brought him here for the night – and that you kids were – found trespassing in the grounds. You understand?'

'I understand perfectly,' said Julian, in a cool rather scornful voice. 'Well, I take it we can all go now, then?'

'Yes,' said Mr Perton. He put his hand into his pocket and took out some pound coins. He handed two to each of the children. They glanced at Julian to see if they were to take them or not. Not one of them felt willing to accept Mr Perton's money. But they knew they must take them if Julian did.

Julian accepted the two coins handed to him, and pocketed them without a word of thanks. The others did the same. Richard kept his head down well all the time, hoping that the two men would not notice how his knees were shaking. He was really terrified of Rooky.

'Now clear out,' said Rooky when the ten pounds had been divided. 'Forget all this – or you'll be very sorry.'

He opened the door that led into the garden. The children trooped out silently, Richard well in their midst. Timmy was waiting for them. He gave a loud bark of welcome and flung himself on George, fawning on her, licking every bit of her he could reach. He looked back at the kitchen door and gave a questioning growl as if to say, 'Do you want me to go for anyone in there?'

'No,' said George. 'You come with us, Timmy. We'll get out of here as quickly as we can.'

'Give me your pound coins, quick,' said Julian in a low voice, when they had rounded a corner and were out of sight of the windows. They all handed them to him wonderingly. What was he going to do with them?

The woman had come out to watch them go. Julian beckoned to her. She came hesitatingly down the garden. 'For you,' said Julian, putting the coins into her hand. 'We don't want them.'

The woman took them, amazed. Her eyes filled with tears. 'Why, it's a fortune – no, no, you take them back. You're kind, though – so kind.'

Julian turned away, leaving the astonished and delighted woman standing staring after them. He hurried after the others.

'That was a very, very good idea of yours,' said Anne, warmly, and the others agreed. All of them had been sorry for the poor woman.

'Come on,' said Julian. 'We don't want to miss the opening of the gates! Listen, can you hear the groaning noise back at the house. Somebody has set the machinery working that opens the gates. Thank goodness we're free – and Richard too. That *was* a bit of luck!'

'Yes, I was so scared Rooky would recognise me, even though my hair was sooted black,' said Richard, who was now looking much more cheerful. 'Oh look, we can see the end of the drive now, and the gates are wide open. We're free!'

'We'll get our bikes,' said Julian. 'I know where we left them. You can ride on my crossbar Richard, because we're a bike short. Dick must have his bike back now – you remember you borrowed it? Look, here they are.'

They mounted their bicycles and began to cycle down the drive – and then Anne gave a scream.

'Julian! Look, look – the gates are closing again. Quick, quick – we'll be left inside!'

Everyone saw in horror that the gates were actually closing, very slowly. They pedalled as fast as they could – but it was no use. By the time they got there the two great gates were fast shut. No amount of shaking would open them. And just as they were so very nearly out!

CHAPTER FIFTEEN

Prisoners

THEY ALL flung themselves down on the grass verge and groaned.

'What have they done that for, just as we were going out?' said Dick. 'Was it a mistake, do you think? I mean – did they think we'd had time to go out, or what?'

'Well, if it was a mistake, it's easy to put right,' said Julian. 'I'll just cycle back to the house and tell them they shut the gates too soon.'

'Yes, you do that,' said George. 'We'll wait here.'

But before Julian could even mount his bicycle there came the sound of the car purring down the long drive. All the children jumped to their feet. Richard ran behind a bush in panic. He was terrified of having to face Rooky again.

The car drew up by the children and stopped. 'Yes, they're still here,' said Mr Perton's voice, as he got out of the car. Rooky got out too. They came over to the children.

Rooky ran his eyes over them. 'Where's that other boy?' he asked quickly.

'I can't imagine,' said Julian, coolly. 'Dear me, I wonder if he had time to cycle out of the gateway. Why did you shut the gates so soon, Mr Perton?'

Rooky had caught sight of Richard's shivering figure behind the bush. He strode over to him and yanked him out. He looked at him closely. Then he pulled him over to Mr Perton.

'Yes, I thought so – *this* is the boy we want! He's sooted

his hair or something, and that's why I didn't recognise him. But when he'd gone I felt sure there was something familiar about him – that's why I wanted another look.' He shook poor Richard like a dog shaking a rat.

'Well, what do you want to do about it?' asked Mr Perton, rather gloomily.

'Hold him, of course,' said Rooky. 'I'll get back at his father now – he'll have to pay a very large sum of money for his horrible son! That'll be useful, won't it? And I can pay this kid out for some of the lies he told his father about me. Nasty little rat.'

He shook Richard again. Julian stepped forward, white and furious.

'Now you stop that,' he said. 'Let the boy go. Haven't you done enough already – keeping my brother locked up for nothing – holding us all for the night – and now you talk about kidnapping! Haven't you just come out of prison? Do you want to go back there?'

Rooky dropped Richard and lunged out at Julian. With a snarl Timmy flung himself between them and bit the man's hand. Rooky let out a howl of rage and nursed his injured hand. He yelled at Julian.

'Call that dog to heel. Do you hear?'

'I'll call him to heel all right – if you talk sense,' said Julian, still white with rage. 'You're going to let us all go, here and now. Go back and open these gates.'

Timmy growled terrifyingly, and both Rooky and Mr Perton took some hurried steps backwards. Rooky picked up a very big stone.

'If you dare to throw that I'll set my dog on you again!' shouted George, in sudden fear. Mr Perton knocked the stone out of Rooky's hand.

'Don't be a fool,' he said. 'That dog could make mincemeat of us – great ugly brute. Look at his teeth. For goodness' sake let the kids go, Rooky.'

'Not till we've finished our plans,' said Rooky fiercely, still nursing his hand. 'Keep them all prisoners here! We shan't be long before our jobs are done. And what's more I'm going to take that little rat there off with me when I go! Ha! I'll teach him a few things – and his father too.'

Timmy growled again. He was straining at George's hand. She had him firmly by the collar. Richard trembled when he heard Rooky's threats about him. Tears ran down his face.

'Yes, you can howl all you like,' said Rooky, scowling at him. 'You wait till I get you! Miserable little coward, you never did have any spunk, you just ran round telling tales and misbehaving yourself whenever you could.'

'Look, Rooky, you'd better come up to the house and have that hand seen to,' said Mr Perton. 'It's bleeding badly. You ought to wash it and put some stuff on it – you know a dog's bite is dangerous. Come on. You can deal with these kids afterwards.'

Rooky allowed himself to be led back to the car. He shook his unhurt fist at the children as they watched silently.

'Interfering brats! Little . . .'

But the rest of his pleasant words were lost in the purring of the car's engine. Mr Perton backed a little, turned the car, and it disappeared up the drive. The five children sat themselves down on the grass verge. Richard began to sob out loud.

'Do shut up, Richard,' said George. 'Rooky was right when he said you were a little coward, with no spunk. So you are. Anne's much pluckier than you are. I wish to goodness we had never met you.'

Richard rubbed his hands over his eyes. They were sooty, and made his face look most peculiar with streaks of black soot mixed with his tears. He looked very woebegone indeed.

'I'm sorry,' he sniffed. 'I know you don't believe me – but I really am. I've always been a bit of a coward – I can't help it.'

'Yes you can,' said Julian, scornfully. 'Anybody can help being a coward. Cowardice is just thinking of your own miserable skin instead of somebody else's. Why, even little Anne is more worried about us than she is about herself – and that makes her brave. She couldn't be a coward if she tried.'

This was a completely new idea to Richard. He tried to wipe his face dry. 'I'll try to be like you,' he said, in a muffled voice. 'You're all so decent. I've never had friends like you before. Honestly, I won't let you down again.'

'Well, we'll see,' said Julian, doubtfully. 'It would certainly be a surprise if you turned into a hero all of a sudden – a very *nice* surprise, of course – but in the meantime it would be a help if you stopped howling for a bit and let us talk.'

Richard subsided. He really looked very peculiar with his soot-streaked face. Julian turned to the others.

'This is maddening!' he said. 'Just as we so nearly got out. I suppose they'll shut us up in some room and keep us there till they've finished whatever this "job" is. I imagine the "job" consists of getting that hidden fellow away in safety – the one I saw in the secret room.'

'Won't Richard's parents report his disappearance to the police?' said George, fondling Timmy, who wouldn't stop licking her now he had got her again.

'Yes, they will. But what good will that do? The police won't have the faintest notion where he is,' said Julian. 'Nobody knows where we are, either, come to that, but Aunt Fanny won't worry yet, because she knows we're off on a cycling tour, and wouldn't be writing to her anyway.'

'Do you think those men will really take me off with them when they go?' asked Richard.

'Well, we'll hope we shall have managed to escape before that,' said Julian, not liking to say yes, certainly Richard would be whisked away!

'How *can* we escape?' asked Anne. 'We'd never get over those high walls. And I don't expect anyone ever comes by here – right at the top of this deserted hill. No tradesman would ever call.'

'What about the postman?' asked Dick.

'They probably arrange to fetch their post each day,' said Julian. 'I don't expect they want anyone coming here at all. Or, there may be a letter-box outside the gate. I never thought of that!'

They went to see. But although they craned their necks to see each side, there didn't seem to be any letter-box at all for the postman to slip letters in. So the faint hope that had risen in their minds, that they might catch the postman and give him a message, vanished at once.

'Hallo, here's the woman – Aggie, or whatever her name is,' said George, suddenly, as Timmy growled. They all turned their heads. Aggie was coming down the drive in a hurry – could she be going out? Would the gates open for her?

Their hopes died as she came near. 'Oh, there you are! I've come with a message. You can do one of two things – you can stay out in the grounds all day, and not put foot

119

into the house at all – or you can come into the house and be locked up in one of the rooms.'

She looked round cautiously and lowered her voice. 'I'm sorry you didn't get out; right down upset I am. It's bad enough for an old woman like me, being cooped up here with Hunchy, but it's not right to keep children in this place. You're nice children too.'

'Thanks,' said Julian. 'Now, seeing that you think we're so nice – tell us, is there any way we can get out besides going through these gates?'

'No. No way at all,' said the woman. 'It's like a prison, once those gates are shut. Nobody's allowed in, and you're only allowed out if it suits Mr Perton and the others. So don't try to escape – it's hopeless.'

Nobody said anything to that. Aggie glanced over her shoulder as if she feared somebody might be listening – Hunchy perhaps – and went on in a low voice.

'Mr Perton said I wasn't to give you much food. And he said Hunchy's to put down food for the dog with poison in it, so don't you let him eat any but what I give you myself.'

'The brute,' cried George, and she held Timmy close against her. 'Did you hear that, Timmy? It's a pity you didn't bite Mr Perton too!'

'Sh!' said the woman, afraid. 'I didn't mean to tell you all this, you know that – but you're kind, and you gave me all that money. Right down nice you are. Now you listen to me – you'd better say you'd rather keep out here in the grounds, because if you're locked up I wouldn't dare to bring you much food in case Rooky came in and saw it. But if you stay out here it's easier. I can give you plenty.'

'Thank you very much,' said Julian, and the others nodded too. 'In any case we'd rather be out here. I suppose Mr Perton is afraid we'd stumble on some of his strange secrets in the house if we had the free run there! All right, tell him we'll be in the grounds. What about our food? How shall we manage about that? We don't want to get you into trouble, but we're very hungry for our meals, and we really could do with a good dinner today.'

'I'll manage it for you,' said Aggie, and she actually smiled. 'But mind what I say now – don't you let that dog eat anything Hunchy puts down for him! It'll be poisoned.'

A voice shouted from the house. Aggie jerked her head up and listened. 'That's Hunchy,' she said. 'I must go.'

She hurried back up the drive. 'Well, well, well,' said Julian, 'so they thought they'd poison old Timmy, did they? They'll have to think again, old fellow, won't they?'

'Woof,' said Timmy, gravely, and didn't even wag his tail!

CHAPTER SIXTEEN

Aggie – and Hunchy

'I FEEL as if I want some exercise,' said George, when Aggie had gone. 'Let's explore the grounds. You never know what we might find!'

They got up, glad of something to do to take their minds off their surprising problems. Really, who would have thought yesterday, when they were happily cycling along sunny country roads, that they would be held prisoner like this today? You just never knew what would happen. It made life exciting, of course, but it did spoil a cycling tour!

They found absolutely nothing of interest in the grounds except a couple of cows, a large number of hens, and a brood of young ducklings. Evidently even the milkman didn't need to call at Owl's Dene! It was quite self-contained.

'I expect that black Bentley goes down each day to some town or other, to collect letters, and to buy meat, or fish,' said George. 'Otherwise Owl's Dene could keep itself going for months on end if necessary without any contact with the outside world. I expect they've got stacks and stacks of tinned food.'

'It's weird to find a place like this, tucked away on a deserted hill, forgotten by everyone – guarding goodness knows what secrets,' said Dick. 'I'd love to know who that man was you saw in the secret room, Julian – the snorer!'

'Someone who doesn't want to be seen even by Hunchy

or Aggie,' said Julian. 'Someone the police would dearly love to see, I expect!'

'I *wish* we could get out of here,' said George, longingly. 'I hate the place. It's got such a nasty "feel" about it. And I hate the thought of somebody trying to poison Timmy.'

'Don't worry, he won't be poisoned,' said Dick. 'We-won't let him be. He can have half *our* food, can't you, Timmy, old fellow?'

Timmy agreed. He woofed and wagged his tail. He wouldn't leave George's side that morning, but stuck to her like a leech.

'Well, we've been all round the grounds and there's nothing much to see,' said Julian, when they had come back near the house. 'I suppose Hunchy sees to the milking and feeds the poultry and brings in the vegetables. Aggie has to manage the house. I say – look – there's Hunchy now. He's putting down food for Timmy!'

Hunchy was making signs to them. 'Here's the dog's dinner!' he yelled.

'Don't say a word, George,' said Julian in a low voice. 'We'll pretend to let Timmy eat it, but we'll really throw it away somewhere – and he'll be frightfully astonished when Timmy is still all-alive-o tomorrow morning!'

Hunchy disappeared in the direction of the cowshed, carrying a pail. Anne gave a little giggle.

'I know what we'll pretend! We'll pretend that Timmy ate half and didn't like the rest so we gave it to the hens and ducks!'

'And Hunchy will be frightfully upset because he'll think they'll die and he'll get into a row,' said George. 'Serve him right! Come on, let's get the food now.'

She ran to pick up the big bowl of food. Timmy sniffed

at it and turned away. It was obvious that he wouldn't have fancied it much even if George had allowed him to have it. Timmy was a very sensible dog.

'Quick, get that spade, Ju, and dig a hole before Hunchy comes back,' said George, and Julian set to work grinning. It didn't take him more than a minute to dig a large hole in the soft earth of a bed. George emptied all the food into the hole, wiped the bowl round with a handful of leaves and watched Julian filling in the earth. Now no animals could get at the poisoned food.

'Let's go to the hen-run now, and when we see Hunchy we'll wave to him,' said Julian. 'He'll ask us what we've been doing. Come on. He deserves to have a shock.'

They went to the hen-house, and stood looking through the wire surrounding the hen-run. As Hunchy came along they turned and waved to him. George pretended to scrape some scraps out of the dog's bowl into the run. Hunchy stared hard. Then he ran towards her, shouting.

'Don't do that, don't do that!'

'What's the matter?' asked George, innocently, pretending to push some scraps through the wire. 'Can't I give the hens some scraps?'

'Is that the bowl I put the dog's food down in?' asked Hunchy, sharply.

'Yes,' said George.

'And he didn't eat all the food – so you're giving it to my hens!' shouted Hunchy in a rage, and snatched the bowl out of George's hands. She pretended to be very angry.

'Don't! Why shouldn't your hens have scraps from the dog's bowl? The food you gave Timmy looked very nice – can't the hens have some?'

Hunchy looked into the hen-run with a groan. The hens

were pecking about near the children for all the world as if they were eating something just thrown to them. Hunchy felt sure they would all be dead by the next day – and then, what trouble he would get into!

He glared at George. 'Idiot of a boy! Giving my hens that food! You deserve a good whipping.'

He thought George was a boy, of course. The others looked on with interest. It served Hunchy right to get into a panic over his hens, after trying to poison dear old Timmy.

Hunchy didn't seem to know what to do. Eventually he took a stiff brush from a nearby shed and went into the hen-run. He had evidently decided to sweep the whole place in case any poisoned bits of food were still left about. He swept laboriously and the children watched him, pleased that he should punish himself in this way.

'I've never seen anyone bother to sweep a hen-run before,' said Dick, in a loud and interested voice.

'Nor have I,' said George at once. 'He must be very anxious to bring his hens up properly.'

'It's jolly hard work, I should think,' said Julian. 'Glad I haven't got to do it. Pity to sweep up all the bits of food, though. An awful waste.'

Everyone agreed heartily to this.

'Funny he should be so upset about my giving the hens any scraps of the food he put down for Timmy,' said George. 'I mean, it seems a bit *suspicious*.'

'It does rather,' agreed Dick. 'But then perhaps he's a suspicious character.'

Hunchy could hear all this quite plainly. The children meant him to, of course. He stopped his sweeping and scowled evilly at them.

'Clear off, you little pests,' he said, and raised his broom as if to rush at the children with it.

'He looks like an angry hen,' said Anne, joining in.

'He's just going to cluck,' put in Richard, and the others laughed. Hunchy ran to open the gate of the hen-run, red with anger.

'Of course, it's just struck me – he *might* have put poison into Timmy's bowl of food,' said Julian, loudly. 'That's why he's so upset about his hens. Dear, dear, how true the old proverb is – he that digs a pit shall fall into it himself!'

The mention of poison stopped Hunchy's rush at once. He flung the broom into the shed, and made off for the house without another word.

'Well, we gave him a bit more than he bargained for,' said Julian.

'And you needn't worry, hens,' said Anne, putting her face to the wire-netting of the run. 'You're not poisoned – and we wouldn't *dream* of harming you!'

'Aggie's calling us,' said Richard. 'Look, perhaps she's got some food for us.'

'I hope so,' said Dick. 'I'm getting very hungry. It's funny that grown-ups never seem to get as hungry as children. I do pity them.'

'Why? Do you *like* being hungry?' said Anne as they walked over to the house.

'Yes, if I know there's a good meal in the offing,' said Dick. 'Otherwise it wouldn't be at all funny. Oh goodness – is this all that Aggie has provided?'

On the window-sill was a loaf of stale-looking bread and a piece of very hard yellow cheese. Nothing else at all. Hunchy was there, grinning.

'Aggie says that's your dinner,' he said, and sat himself

down at the table to spoon out enormous helpings of a very savoury stew.

'A little revenge for our behaviour by the hen-run,' murmured Julian softly. 'Well, well, I thought better than this of Aggie. I wonder where she is.'

She came out of the kitchen door at that moment, carrying a washing-basket that appeared to be full of clothes. 'I'll just hang these out, Hunchy, and I'll be back,' she called to him. She turned to the children and gave them a broad wink.

'There's your dinner on the window-sill,' she said. 'Get it and take it somewhere to eat. Hunchy and I don't want you round the kitchen.'

She suddenly smiled and nodded her head down towards the washing-basket. The children understood immediately. Their real dinner was in there!

They snatched the bread and cheese from the sill and followed her. She set down the basket under a tree, where it was well-hidden from the house. A clothes-line stretched there. 'I'll be out afterwards to hang my washing,' she said, and with another smile that changed her whole face, she went back to the house.

'Good old Aggie,' said Julian, lifting up the top cloth in the basket. 'My word, just look here!'

CHAPTER SEVENTEEN

Julian has a bright idea

AGGIE HAD managed to pack knives, forks, spoons, plates and mugs into the bottom of the basket. There were two big bottles of milk. There was a large meat-pie with delicious looking pastry on top, and a collection of buns, biscuits and oranges. There were also some home-made sweets. Aggie had certainly been very generous!

All the things were quickly whipped out of the basket. The children carried them behind the bushes, sat down and proceeded to eat a first-rate dinner. Timmy got his share of the meat-pie and biscuits. He also gobbled up a large part of the hard yellow cheese.

'Now we'd better rinse everything under that garden tap over there, and then pack them neatly into the bottom of the basket again,' said Julian. 'We don't want to get Aggie into any sort of trouble for her kindness.'

The dishes were soon rinsed and packed back into the basket. The clothes were drawn over them – nothing could be seen!

Aggie came outside to them in about half an hour. The children went to her and spoke in low voices.

'Thanks, Aggie, that was super!'

'You *are* a brick. We did enjoy it!'

'I bet Hunchy didn't enjoy his dinner as much as *we* did!'

'Sh!' said Aggie, half-pleased and half-scared. 'You never know when Hunchy's listening. He's got ears like a hare! Listen, I'll be coming out to get the eggs from the hen-run at tea-time. I'll have a basket with me for the eggs – and I shall have your tea in it. I'll leave your tea in the hen-house when I get the eggs. You can fetch it when I've gone.'

'You're a wonder, Aggie!' said Julian, admiringly. 'You really are.'

Aggie looked pleased. It was plain that nobody had said a kind or admiring word to her for years and years. She was a poor, miserable, scared old woman – but she was quite enjoying this little secret. She was pleased at getting the better of Hunchy too. Perhaps she felt it was some slight revenge for all the years he had ill-treated her.

She hung out some of the clothes in the basket, left one in to cover the dinner things, and then went back into the house.

'Poor old thing,' said Dick. 'What a life!'

'Yes, *I* shouldn't like to be cooped up here for years and years with ruffians like Perton and Rooky,' said Julian.

'It looks as if we shall be if we don't hurry up and think of some plan of escape,' said Dick.

'Yes. We'd better think hard again,' said Julian. 'Come over to those trees there. We can sit on the grass under them and talk without being overheard anywhere.'

'Look, Hunchy is polishing the black Bentley,' said George. 'I'll just pass near him with Timmy, and let Timmy growl. He'll see Timmy's all alive and kicking then.'

So she took Timmy near the Bentley, and of course he growled horribly when he came upon Hunchy. Hunchy promptly got into the car and shut the door. George grinned.

'Hallo!' she said. 'Going off for a ride? Can Timmy and I come with you?'

She made as if she was going to open the door, and Hunchy yelled loudly: 'Don't you let that dog in here! I've seen Rooky's hand – one finger's very bad indeed. I don't want that dog going for *me*.'

'Do take me for a ride with you, Hunchy,' persisted George. 'Timmy loves cars.'

'Go away,' said Hunchy, hanging on to the doorhandle for dear life. 'I've got to get this car cleaned up for Mr Perton this evening. You let me get out and finish the job.'

George laughed and went off to join the others.

'Well, he can see Timmy's all-alive-o,' said Dick, with a grin. 'Good thing too. We'd find ourselves in a much bigger fix if we hadn't got old Timmy to protect us.'

They went over to the clump of trees and sat down.

'What was it that Hunchy said about the car?' asked Julian. George told him. Julian looked thoughtful. Anne knew that look – it meant that Julian was thinking of a plan! She prodded him.

'Ju! You've got a plan, haven't you? What is it?'

'Well, I'm only just wondering about something,' said Julian, slowly. 'That car – and the fact that Mr Perton is going out in it tonight – which means he will go out through those gates . . .'

'What of it?' said Dick. 'Thinking of going with him?'

'Well, yes, I was,' said Julian, surprisingly. 'You see, if he's not going till dark, I think I could probably get into the boot and hide there till the car stops somewhere, and then I could open the boot, get out, and go off for help!'

Everyone looked at him in silence. Anne's eyes gleamed. 'Oh Julian! It's a brilliant plan.'

'It sounds jolly good,' said Dick.

'The only thing is – I don't like being left here without Julian,' said Anne, suddenly feeling scared. 'Everything's all right if Julian's here.'

'*I* could go,' said Dick.

'Or I could,' said George, 'only there wouldn't be room for Timmy too.'

'The boot looks pretty big from outside,' said Julian. 'I wish I could take Anne with me. Then I'd know she was safe. You others would be all right so long as you had Timmy.'

They discussed the matter thoroughly. They dropped it towards tea-time when they saw Aggie coming out with a basket to collect the eggs. She made a sign to them not to come over to her. Possibly someone was watching. They stayed where they were, and watched her go into the hen-house. She remained there a short time, and then came out with a basketful of new-laid eggs. She walked to the house without looking at the children again.

'I'll go and see if she's left anything in the hen-house,' said Dick, and went over to it. He soon appeared again, grinning. His pockets bulged!

Aggie had left about two dozen potted-meat sand-wiches, a big slab of cherry cake and a bottle of milk. The children went under the bushes and Dick unloaded his pockets. 'She even left a bone for old Tim,' he said.

'I suppose it's all right,' said George doubtfully. Julian smelt it.

'Perfectly fresh,' he said. 'No poison here at all! Any-way, Aggie wouldn't play a dirty trick like that. Come on, let's tuck in.'

They were very bored after tea, so Julian arranged some

132

races and some jumping competitions. Timmy, of course, would have won them all if he had been counted as a proper competitor. But he wasn't. He went in for everything, though, and barked so excitedly that Mr Perton came to a window and yelled to him to stop.

'Sorry!' yelled back George. 'Timmy's so full of beans today, you see!'

'Mr Perton will be wondering why,' said Julian, with a grin. 'He'll be rowing Hunchy for not getting on with the poison job.'

When it began to grow dark the children went cautiously to the car. Hunchy had finished working on it. Quietly Julian opened the boot and looked inside. He gave an exclamation of disappointment.

'It's only a small one! I can't get in there, I'm afraid. Nor can you, Dick.'

'I'll go then,' said Anne, in a small voice.

'Certainly not,' said Julian.

'Well – *I'll* go,' said Richard, surprisingly. 'I could just about squash in there.'

'*You!*' said Dick. 'You'd be scared stiff.'

Richard was silent for a moment. 'Yes, I should,' he admitted. 'But I'm still ready to go. I'll do my very best if you'd like me to try. After all, it's me or nobody. You won't let Anne go and there's not enough room for George and Timmy and not enough for either you or Julian, Dick.'

Everyone was astonished. It didn't seem a bit like Richard to offer to do an unselfish or courageous action. Julian felt very doubtful.

'Well, this is a serious thing, you know, Richard,' he said. 'I mean, if you're going to do it, you've got to do it properly – go right through with it, not get frightened in the middle and begin howling, so that the men hear you and examine the boot.'

'I know,' said Richard. 'I think I can do it all right. I do wish you'd trust me a bit.'

'I can't understand your offering to do a difficult thing like that,' said Julian. 'It doesn't seem a bit like you – you've not shown yourself to be at all plucky *so* far!'

'Julian, I think *I* understand,' said Anne suddenly, and she pulled at her brother's sleeve. 'He's thinking of *our* skins this time, not of his own – or at least he's trying to. Let's give him a chance to show he's got a bit of courage.'

'I only just want a chance,' said Richard in a small voice.

'All right,' said Julian. 'You shall have it. It'll be a very pleasant surprise if you take your chance and do something helpful!'

'Tell me exactly what I've got to do,' said Richard, trying to keep his voice from trembling.

'Well, once you're in the boot we'll have to shut you in. Goodness knows how long you'll have to wait there in the dark,' said Julian. 'I warn you it will be jolly stuffy and uncomfortable. When the car goes off it will be more uncomfortable still.'

'Poor Richard,' said Anne.

'As soon as the car stops anywhere and you hear the men get out, wait a minute to give them time to get out of sight and hearing – and then scramble out of the boot yourself and go straight to the nearest police station,' said Julian. 'Tell your story *quickly*, give this address – Owl's Dene, Owl's Hill, some miles from Middlecombe Woods – and the police will do the rest. Got all that?'

'Yes,' said Richard.

'Do you still want to go, now you know what you're in for?' asked Dick.

'Yes,' said Richard again. He was surprised by a warm hug from Anne.

'Richard, you're nice – and I didn't think you were!' said Anne.

He then got a thump on the back from Julian. 'Well, Richard, pull this off and you'll wipe out all the silly things you've done! Now, what about getting into the boot immediately? We don't know when the men will be coming out.'

'Yes. I'll get in now,' said Richard, feeling remarkably brave after Anne's hug and Julian's thump. Julian opened the boot. He examined the inside of the boot-cover. 'I don't believe Richard could open it from the inside,' he said. 'No, he couldn't. We mustn't close it tight, then – I'll have to wedge it a bit open with a stick or something. That will give him a little air, and he'll be able to push the boot open when he wants to. Where's a stick?'

Dick found one. Richard got into the boot and curled himself up. There wasn't very much room even for him! He looked extremely cramped. Julian shut the boot and wedged it with a stick so that there was a crack of half an inch all round.

Dick gave him a sharp nudge. 'Quick, someone's coming!'

135

CHAPTER EIGHTEEN

Hunt for Richard!

MR PERTON could be seen standing at the front door, outlined in the light from the lamp in the hall. He was talking to Rooky, who, apparently, was not going out. It seemed as if only Mr Perton was leaving in the car.

'Good luck, Richard,' Julian whispered, as he and the others melted into the shadows on the other side of the drive. They stood there in the darkness, watching Mr Perton walk over to the car. He got in and slammed the door. Thank goodness he hadn't wanted to put anything in the boot!

The engine started up and the car purred away down the drive. At the same time there came the grating sound of the gate machinery being used.

'Gates are opening for him,' muttered Dick. They heard the car go right down the drive and out of the gateway without stopping. It hooted as it went, evidently a signal to the house. The gates had been opened just at the right moment. They were now being shut, judging by the grinding noise going on.

The front door closed. The children stood in silence for a minute or two, thinking of Richard shut up in the boot.

'I'd never have thought it of him,' said George.

'No, but you just simply never know what is in anybody,' said Julian thoughtfully. 'I suppose even the worst coward, the most despicable crook, the most dishonest rogue *can* find some good thing in himself if he wants to badly enough.'

136

'Yes, it's the "wanting-to" that must be so rare, though,' said Dick. 'Look, there's Aggie at the kitchen-door. She's calling us in.'

They went to her. 'You can come in now,' she said. 'I can't give you much supper, I'm afraid, because Hunchy will be here – but I'll put some cake up in your room, under the blankets.'

They went into the kitchen. It was pleasant with a log-fire and the mellow light from an oil-lamp. Hunchy was at the far end doing something with a rag and polish. He gave the children one of his familiar scowls. 'Take that dog out and leave him out,' he ordered.

'No,' said George.

'Then I'll tell Rooky,' said Hunchy. Neither he nor Aggie seemed to notice that there were only four children, not five.

'Well, if Rooky comes here I've no doubt Timmy will bite his other hand,' said George. 'Anyway, won't he be surprised to find Timmy still alive and kicking?'

Nothing more was said about Timmy. Aggie silently put the remains of a plum-pie on the table. 'There's your supper,' she said.

There was a very small piece each. As they were finishing, Hunchy went out. Aggie spoke in a whisper.

'I heard the radio at six o'clock. There was a police message about one of you – called Richard. His mother reported him missing and the police put it out on the radio.'

'Did they really?' said Dick. 'I say, they'll soon be here then!'

'But do they know where you are?' asked Aggie, surprised. Dick shook his head.

'Not yet – but I expect we'll soon be traced here.'

Aggie looked doubtful. 'Nobody's ever been traced here yet – nor ever will be, it's my belief. The police did come once, looking for somebody, and Mr Perton let them in, all polite-like. They hunted everywhere for the person they said they wanted, but they couldn't find him.'

Julian nudged Dick. He thought *he* knew where the police might have found him – in the little secret room behind that sliding panel.

'Funny thing,' said Julian. 'I haven't seen a telephone here. Don't they have one?'

'No,' said Aggie. 'No phone, no gas, no electricity, no water laid on, no nothing. Only just secrets and signs and comings and goings and threats and . . .'

She broke off as Hunchy came back, and went to the big fire-place, where a kettle was slung over the burning logs. Hunchy looked around at the children.

'Rooky wants the one of you that's called Richard,' he said, with a horrible smile. 'Says he wants to teach him a few lessons.'

All the four felt extremely thankful that Richard was not there. They felt sure he wouldn't have liked the lessons that Rooky wanted to teach him.

They looked round at one another and then all round the room. 'Richard? Where *is* Richard?'

'What do you mean – where's Richard?' said Hunchy, in a snarling voice that made Timmy growl. 'One of you is Richard – that's all I know.'

'Why – there were five children – now there's only four!' said Aggie, in sudden astonishment. 'I've only just noticed. Is Richard the missing one?'

'Dear me, *where's* Richard gone?' said Julian, pretending to be surprised. He called him. 'Richard! Hey, Richard, where are you?'

Hunchy looked angry. 'Now, none of your tricks. One of you is Richard. Which one?'

'Not one of us is,' answered Dick. 'Gracious, where *can* Richard be? Do you suppose we've left him in the grounds, Ju?'

'Must have,' said Julian. He went to the kitchen window and swung it wide open. 'RICHARD!' he roared. 'You're wanted, RICHARD!'

But no Richard answered or appeared, of course. He was miles away in the boot of the black Bentley!

There came the sound of angry footsteps in the hall and the kitchen door was flung open. Rooky stood there, scowling, his hand done up in a big bandage. With a delighted bark Timmy leapt forward. George caught him just in time.

'That dog! Didn't I say he was to be poisoned?' shouted Rooky, furiously. 'Why haven't you brought that boy to me, Hunchy?'

Hunchy looked afraid. 'He doesn't seem to be here,' he answered sullenly. 'Unless one of these here children is him, sir.'

Rooky glanced over them. 'No, he's not one of them. Where is Richard?' he demanded of Julian.

'I've just been yelling for him,' said Julian, with an air of amazement. 'Funny thing. He was out in the grounds all day with us, and now we're indoors, he just isn't here. Shall I go and hunt in the grounds?'

'I'll shout for him again,' said Dick, going to the window. 'RICHARD!'

'Shut up!' said Rooky. '*I'll* go and find him. Where's my torch? Get it, Aggie. And when I find him, he'll be sorry for himself, very, very sorry!'

'I'll come too,' said Hunchy. 'You go one way and I'll go another.'

'Get Ben and Fred too,' ordered Rooky. Hunchy departed to fetch Ben and Fred, whoever they were. The children supposed they must be the other men who had arrived with Rooky the night before.

Rooky went out of the kitchen door with his powerful torch. Anne shivered. She was very, very glad that Richard couldn't be found, however hard the men looked for him. Soon there came the sound of other voices in the grounds, as the four men separated into two parties, and began to search every metre.

'Where is he, the poor boy?' whispered Aggie.

HUNT FOR RICHARD!

'I don't know,' said Julian, truthfully. He wasn't going to give any secrets away to Aggie, even though she seemed really friendly to them.

She went out of the room and the children clustered together, speaking in low voices.

'I *say*, what a blessing it was Richard that went off in the Bentley and not one of *us*,' whispered George.

'My word, yes – I didn't like the look on Rooky's face when he came into the kitchen just now,' said Julian.

'Well, Richard's got a little reward for trying to be brave,' said Anne. 'He's missed some ill-treatment from Rooky!'

Julian glanced at a clock in the kitchen. 'Look, it's almost nine. There's a radio on that shelf. Let's put it on and see if there's a message about Richard.'

He switched it on and twiddled the knob till he got the right station. After a minute or two of news, there came the message they wanted to hear.

'Missing from home since Wednesday, Richard Thurlow Kent, a boy of twelve, well-built, fair hair, blue eyes, wearing grey shorts and grey jersey. Probably on a bicycle.'

So the message went on, ending with a police telephone number that could be called. There was of course no message about Julian and the others. They were relieved. 'That means that Mother won't be worrying,' said George. 'But it also means that unless Richard can get help nobody can possibly find out we're here – if we're not missed we can't be searched for, and I don't really want to be here much longer.'

141

Nobody did, of course. All their hopes were now on Richard. He seemed rather a broken reed to rely on – but you never knew! He just might be successful in escaping unseen from the boot and getting to a police station.

After about an hour Rooky and the others came in, all in a furious temper. Rooky turned on Julian.

'What's happened to that boy? You must know.'

'Gr-r-r-r-r,' said Timmy at once. Rooky beckoned to Julian to come into the hall. He shut the kitchen door and shouted at Julian again.

'Well, you heard what I said – where's that boy?'

'Isn't he out in the grounds?' said Julian, putting on a very perturbed look. 'Good gracious, what *can* have happened to him? I assure you he was with us all day. Aggie will tell you that – and Hunchy too.'

'They've already told me,' said Rooky. 'He's not in the grounds. We've gone over every metre. Where is he?'

'Well, would he be somewhere in the house, then?' suggested Julian, innocently.

'How can he be?' raged Rooky. 'The front door's been closed and locked all day except when Perton went out. And Hunchy and Aggie swear he didn't come into the kitchen.'

'It's an absolute mystery,' said Julian. 'Shall I hunt all over the house? The others can help me. Maybe the dog will smell him out.'

'I'm not having that dog out of the kitchen,' said Rooky. 'Or any of *you*, either! I believe that boy's about somewhere, laughing up his sleeve at us all – and I believe you know where he is too!'

'I don't,' said Julian. 'And that's the truth.'

'When I *do* find him, I'll . . . I'll . . .' Rooky broke off, quite unable to think of anything bad enough to do to poor Richard.

He went to join the others, still muttering. Julian went thankfully back to the kitchen. He was very glad Richard was well out of the way. It was pure chance that he had gone – but what a very good thing! Where was Richard now? What was he doing? Was he still in the boot of the car? How Julian wished he knew!

CHAPTER NINETEEN

Richard has his own adventure

RICHARD HAD been having a much too exciting time. He had gone with the car, of course, crouching in the boot at the back, with a box of tools digging into him, and a can of petrol smelling horribly nearby, making him feel sick.

Through the gates went the car, and down the hill. It went at a good pace, and once stopped very suddenly. It had gone round a corner and almost collided with a stationary lorry, so that Mr Perton had put the brake on in a hurry. Poor Richard was terrified. He bumped his head hard on the back of the boot and gave a groan.

He sat curled up, feeling sick and scared. He began to wish he had not tried to be a hero and get help. Being any kind of a hero was difficult – but this was a dreadful way of being heroic.

The car went on for some miles; Richard had no idea where it was going. At first he heard no other traffic at all – then he heard the sound of many wheels on the road, and knew he must be getting near a town. Once they must have gone by a railway station or railway line because Richard could distinctly hear the noise of a train, and then a loud hooting.

The car stopped at last. Richard listened intently. Was it stopping just for traffic lights – or was Mr Perton getting out? If so, that was his chance to escape!

He heard the car door slam. Ah, Mr Perton was out of the car then. Richard pressed hard at the cover of the boot. Julian had wedged it rather tightly, but it gave at last, and the lid of the boot opened. It fell back with rather a noise.

Richard looked out cautiously. He was in a dark street. A few people were walking on the pavement opposite. A lamp-post was some way away. Could he get out now – or would Mr Perton be about and see him?

He stretched out a leg to slide from the boot and jump to the ground – but he had been huddled up in an awkward position for so long that he was too stiff to move. Cramp caught him and he felt miserably uncomfortable as he tried to straighten himself out.

Instead of jumping out and taking to his heels at once, poor Richard had to go very slowly indeed. His legs and arms would *not* move quickly. He sat for a half-minute on the open boot-lid, trying to make up his mind to jump down.

And then he heard Mr Perton's voice! He was running down the steps of the house outside which he had parked the car. Richard was horrified. It hadn't dawned on him that he would come back so quickly.

He tried to jump from the boot-cover, and fell sprawling to the ground. Mr Perton heard him, and, thinking someone was trying to steal something from his car he rushed up to the boot.

Richard scrambled up just in time to get away from his outstretched hand. He ran to the other side of the road as fast as he could, hoping that his stiff, cramped legs wouldn't let him down. Mr Perton tore after him.

'Hey, you, stop! What are you doing in my car?' shouted Mr Perton. Richard dodged a passer-by and tore on, panic-stricken. He mustn't be caught; he mustn't be caught!

Mr Perton caught up with him just under the lamp-post. He grabbed Richard's collar and swung him round roughly. 'You let me go!' yelled Richard, and kicked Mr Perton's ankles so hard that he almost fell over.

Mr Perton recognised him! 'Good gracious – it's you!' he cried. 'The boy Rooky wants! What are you doing here? How did you . . .?'

But with a last despairing struggle, Richard was off again, leaving his coat in Mr Perton's hands! His legs were feeling better now, and he could run faster.

He tore round the corner, colliding with another boy. He was off and away before the boy could even call out. Mr Perton also tore round the corner and collided with the same boy – who, however, was a bit quicker than before, and clutched Mr Perton by the coat, in a real rage at being so nearly knocked over again.

By the time Mr Perton had got himself free from the angry boy, Richard was out of sight. Mr Perton raced to the corner of the road, and looked up and down the poorly lit road. He gave an exclamation of anger.

'Lost him! Little pest – how did he get here? Could he have been at the back of the car? Ah, surely that's him over there!'

It was. Richard had hidden in a garden, but was now being driven out by the barking of a dog. In despair he tore out of the gate and began running again. Mr Perton tore after him.

Round another corner, panting hard. Round yet another, hoping that no passer-by would clutch at him and stop him. Poor Richard! He didn't feel at all heroic, and didn't enjoy it a bit either.

He stumbled round the next corner and came into the

main street of the town – and there, opposite, was a lamp that had a very welcome word shining on the glass.

POLICE

Thankfully Richard stumbled up the steps and pushed open the police station door. He almost fell inside. There was a kind of waiting-room there with a policeman sitting at a table. He looked up in astonishment as Richard came in in such a hurry.

'Now then, what's all this?' he asked the boy.

Richard looked fearfully back at the door, expecting Mr Perton to come in at any moment. But he didn't. The door remained shut. Mr Perton was not going to visit any police station if he could help it – especially with Richard pouring out a most peculiar story!

Richard was panting so much that he couldn't say a word at first. Then it all came out. The policeman listened in amazement, and very soon stopped Richard's tale, and called a big burly man in, who proved to be a most important police inspector.

He made Richard tell his tale slowly and as clearly as he could. The boy was now feeling much better – in fact he was feeling quite proud of himself! To think he'd done it – escaped in the boot of the car, got out, managed to get away from Mr Perton, and arrive safely at the police station. Marvellous!

'Where's this Owl's Dene?' demanded the Inspector, and the constable nearby answered.

'Must be that old place on Owl's Hill, sir. You remember we once went there on some kind of police business, but it seemed to be all right. Run by a hunch-back and his sister for some man who is often away abroad – Perton, I think the name was.'

'That's right!' cried Richard. 'It was Mr Perton's car I came here in – a black Bentley.'

'Know the number?' said the Inspector, sharply.

'KMF 102,' said Richard at once.

'Good lad,' said the Inspector. He picked up a telephone and gave a few curt instructions for a police car to try to trace the Bentley immediately.

'So you're Richard Thurlow Kent,' he said. 'Your mother is very upset and anxious about you. I'll see that she is telephoned straight away. You'd better be taken home now in a police car.'

'Oh but, sir, can't I go with you to Owl's Dene when you drive up there?' said Richard, deeply disappointed. 'You'll be going there, won't you? – because of all the others – Anne, Dick, George and Julian.'

'We'll be going all right,' said the Inspector, grimly. 'But you won't be with us. You've had enough adventures. You can go home and go to bed. You've done well to escape and come here. Quite the hero!'

Richard couldn't help feeling pleased – but how he wished he could race off to Owl's Dene with the police. What a marvellous thing it would be to march in with them and show Julian how well he had managed his part of the affair! Perhaps Julian would think better of him then.

The Inspector, however, was not having any boys in the cars that were to go to Owl's Dene, and Richard was taken off by the young constable, and told to wait till a car came to take him home.

The telephone rang, and the Inspector answered it. 'No trace of the Bentley? Right. Thanks.'

149

He spoke to the young constable. 'Didn't think they'd get him. He's probably raced back to Owl's Dene to warn the others.'

'We'll get there soon after!' said the constable with a grin. 'Our Wolseley's pretty well as fast as a Bentley!'

Mr Perton had indeed raced off, as soon as he saw Richard stumbling up the police station steps. He had gone back to his car at top speed, jumped in, slammed the door and raced away as fast as he could, feeling certain that the police would be on the look-out for KMF 102 immediately.

He tore dangerously round the corners, and hooted madly, making everyone leap out of the way. He was soon out in the country, and there he put on terrific speed, his powerful headlights picking out the dark country lanes for half a mile ahead.

As he came to the hill on which Owl's Dene stood, he hooted loudly. He wanted the gates opened quickly! Just as he got up to them they opened. Someone had heard his hooting signal – good! He raced up the drive and stopped at the front door. It opened as he jumped out. Rooky stood there, and two other men with him, all looking anxious.

'What's up, Perton? Why are you back so quickly?' called Rooky. 'Anything wrong?'

Mr Perton ran up the steps, shut the door and faced the three men in the hall.

'Do you know what's happened? That boy, Richard Kent, was in the car when I went out! See? Hidden in the back or in the boot, or somewhere! Didn't you miss him?'

'Yes,' said Rooky. 'Of course we missed him. Did you let him get away, Perton?'

'Well, seeing that I didn't know he was in hiding, and had to leave the car to go in and see Ted, it was easy for him to get away!' said Mr Perton. 'He ran like a hare. I nearly grabbed him once, but he wriggled out of his coat. And as he ended up finally in the police station I decided to give up the chase and come back to warn you.'

'The police will be out here then, before you can say Jack Robinson,' shouted Rooky. 'You're a fool, Perton – you ought to have got that boy. There's our ransom gone west – and I was so glad to be able to get my hands on the little brute.'

'It's no good crying over spilt milk,' said Perton. 'What about Weston? Suppose the police find *him*. They're looking for him all right – the papers have been full of only two things the last couple of days – Disappearance of Richard Thurlow Kent and Escape from Prison of Solomon Weston! And we're mixed up with both these. Do you want to be shoved back into prison again, Rooky? You've only just come out, you know. What are we going to do?'

'We must think,' said Rooky, in a panic-stricken voice. 'Come in this room here. We must *think*.'

CHAPTER TWENTY

The secret room

THE FOUR children had heard the car come racing up the drive, and had heard Mr Perton's arrival. Julian went to the kitchen door, eager to find out what he could. If Mr Perton was back, then either Richard had played his part well, and had escaped – or he had been discovered, and had been brought back.

He heard every word of the excited talk out in the hall. Good, good good! – Richard had got away – and was even now telling his tale to the police. It surely wouldn't be very long before the police arrived at Owl's Dene then – and what surprising things they would find there!

He tiptoed out into the hall when he heard the men go into the room nearby. What were their plans! He hoped they would not vent their rage on him or the others. It was true they had Timmy, but in a real emergency Rooky would probably think nothing of shooting the dog straightaway.

Julian didn't at all like what he heard from the room where the men talked over their plans.

'I'm going to bang all those kids' heads together as hard as I can, to start with,' growled Rooky. 'That big boy – what's his name? – Julian or something – must have planned Richard Kent's escape – I'll give him a real good thrashing, the interfering little beast.'

'What about the sparklers, Rooky?' said another man's voice. 'We'd better put them in a safe hiding-place before the police arrive. We'll have to hurry.'

'Oh, it'll be some time before they find they can't open that gate,' said Rooky. 'And it'll take a little more time before they climb that wall. We'll have time to put the sparklers into the room with Weston. If *he's* safe there, they'll be safe too.'

'Sparklers!' thought Julian, excited. 'Those are diamonds – so they've got a haul of diamonds hidden somewhere. Whatever next?'

'Get them,' ordered Mr Perton. 'Take them to the secret room – and be quick about it, Rooky. The police may be here at any minute now.'

'We'll spin some tale about that kid Richard and his friends,' said the voice of a fourth man. 'We'll say they were caught trespassing, the lot of them, and kept here as a little punishment. Actually, if there's time, I think it would be best to let the rest of them go. After all – they don't *know* anything. They can't give away any secrets.'

Rooky didn't want to let them go. He had grim plans for them, but the others argued him over. 'All right,' he said sullenly. 'Let them go, then – if there's time! You take them down to the gate, Perton, and shove them out before the police arrive. They'll probably set off thankfully and get lost in the dark. So much the better.'

'You get the sparklers then, and see to them,' said Mr Perton, and Julian heard him getting up from his chair. The boy darted back to the kitchen.

It looked as if there would be nothing for it but to let themselves be led down to the gates and shoved out, and Julian decided that if that happened they would wait at the gateway till the police arrived. They wouldn't get lost in the dark, as Rooky hoped!

153

Mr Perton came into the kitchen. His eyes swept over the four children. Timmy growled.

'So you made a little plan, did you, and hid Richard in the car?' he said. 'Well, for that we're going to turn you all out into the night and you'll probably lose yourselves for days in the deserted countryside round here and I hope you do!'

Nobody said anything. Mr Perton aimed a blow at Julian, who ducked. Timmy sprang at the man, but George had hold of his collar, and he just missed snapping Mr Perton's arm in two!

'If that dog had stayed here a day longer I'd have shot him,' said Mr Perton, fiercely. 'Come on, all of you, get a move on.'

'Good-bye, Aggie,' said Anne. Aggie and Hunchy watched them go out of the kitchen door into the dark garden. Aggie looked very scared indeed. Hunchy spat after them and said something rude.

But, when they were half-way down the drive, there came the sound of cars roaring at top speed up the hill to the gates of Owl's Dene! Two cars, fast and powerful, with brilliant headlights. Police cars, without a doubt! Mr Perton stopped. Then he shoved the children roughly back towards the house. It was too late to set them free and hope they would lose themselves.

'You look out for Rooky,' he said to them. 'He goes mad when he's frightened – and he's going to be frightened now, with the police hammering at the gates!'

Julian and the others cautiously edged into the kitchen. They weren't going to risk meeting Rooky if they could help it. Nobody was there at all, not even Hunchy or Aggie. Mr Perton went through to the hall.

'Have you put those sparklers away?' he called, and a voice answered him: 'Yes. Weston's got them with him. They're O.K. Did you get the kids out in time?'

'No – and the police are at the gates already,' growled Mr Perton.

A howl came from someone – probably Rooky. 'The police – already! If I had that kid Richard here I'd skin him alive. Wait till I've burnt a few letters I don't want found – then I'll go and get hold of the other kids. I'm going to put somebody through it for this, and I don't care who.'

'Don't be foolish, Rooky,' said Mr Perton's voice. 'Do you want to get yourself into trouble again through your violent temper? Leave the kids alone.'

Julian listened to all this and felt very uneasy indeed. He ought to hide the others. Even Timmy would be no protection if Rooky had a gun. But where could he hide them?

'Rooky will search the whole house from top to bottom if he loses his temper much more, and really makes up his mind to revenge himself on us,' thought Julian. 'What a pity there isn't another secret room – we could hide there and be safe!'

But even if there was one he didn't know of it. He heard Rooky go upstairs with the others. Now, if he and the other children were going to hide somewhere in safety, this was their chance. But WHERE could they hide?

An idea came to Julian – was it a brilliant one, or wasn't it? He couldn't make up his mind at first. Then he decided that brilliant or not they had got to try it.

He spoke to the others. 'We've got to hide. Rooky isn't safe when he's in a temper.'

'Where shall we hide?' said Anne, fearfully.

'In the secret room!' said Julian. They all gaped at him in amazement.

'But – but somebody else is already hidden there – you told us you saw him last night,' said George at last.

'I know. That can't be helped. He's the last person to give us away, if we share his hiding-place – he wouldn't want to be found himself!' said Julian. 'It will be a frightful squash, because the secret room is very, very small – but it's the safest place I can think of.'

'Timmy will have to come too,' said George firmly. Julian nodded.

'Of course. We may need him to protect us against the hidden man!' he said. 'He may be pretty wild at us all invading his hiding-place. We don't want to have him calling Rooky. We'll be all right once we're in the room, because Timmy will keep him quiet. And once we're in he won't call out because we'll tell him the police are here!'

'Fine,' said Dick. 'Let's go. Is the coast clear?'

'Yes. They're all upstairs for some reason or other,' said Julian. 'Probably destroying things they don't want found. Come on.'

Hunchy and Aggie were still not to be seen. They had probably heard what the scare was about and were hidden away themselves! Julian led the way quietly to the little study.

They stared at the big, solid wooden bookcase that stretched from floor to ceiling. Julian went quickly to one shelf and emptied out the books. He felt for the knob.

There it was! He pulled it out, and the back panel of the shelf slid noiselessly downwards, leaving the large hole there, like a window into the secret room.

The children gasped. How strange! How very extraordinary! They blinked through the hole and saw the small room behind, lit by a little candle. They saw the hidden man too – and he saw them! He looked at them in the very greatest astonishment.

'Who are you?' he said, in a threatening voice. 'Who told you to open the panel? Where're Rooky and Perton?'

'We're coming through to join you,' said Julian quietly. 'Don't make a noise.'

He shoved George up first. She slid through the narrow opening sideways and landed feet-first on the floor. Timmy followed immediately, pushed through by Julian.

The man was up on his feet now, angry and surprised. He was a big burly fellow, with very small close-set eyes and a cruel mouth.

'Now look here,' he began in a loud voice. 'I won't have this. Where's Perton? Hey, Per . . .'

'If you say another word I'll set my dog on you,' said

George, at a sign from Julian. Timmy growled so fero-
ciously that the man shrank back at once.

'I – I . . .' he began. Timmy growled again and bared all
his magnificent teeth in a snarl. The man climbed up on
the narrow bed and subsided, looking astonished and
furious. Dick went through the opening next, then Anne.
By that time the small room was uncomfortably crowded.

'I say,' said Julian, suddenly remembering something, 'I
shall have to stay outside the room – because the books
have got to be put back, otherwise Rooky will notice the
shelf is empty and guess we're hiding in the secret room.
Then we'll be at his mercy.'

'Oh Ju, you must come in with us,' said Anne, frightened.

'I can't, Anne. I must shut the panel and put the books
back,' said Julian. 'I can't risk your being discovered till
the police have safely caught that madman Rooky! I shall
be all right, don't you worry.'

'The police?' whispered the man in the secret room, his
eyes almost falling out of his head. 'Are the police here?'

'At the gates,' answered Julian. 'So keep quiet if you
don't want them on top of you at once!'

He pushed the knob. The panel slid back into place
without a sound. Julian replaced the books on the shelf as
fast as he could. Then he darted out of the study, so that
the men would not even guess what he had been up to. He
was very thankful that Rooky had kept away long enough
for him to carry out his plan.

Where should he hide himself? How long would it take
the police to get over the wall, or break down the great
gates? Surely they would soon be here?

There came the sound of footsteps running down the

stairs. It was Rooky. He caught sight of Julian at once. 'Ah – there you are! Where are the others? I'll show you what . . .'

Rooky carried a whip in his hand and looked quite crazy. Julian was afraid. He darted back into the study and locked the door. Rooky began to hammer at it. Then such a crash came on the door that Julian guessed he was smashing it down with one of the hall chairs. The door would be down in a moment!

CHAPTER TWENTY-ONE

A very exciting finish!

JULIAN WAS a courageous boy, but just at that minute he felt very scared indeed. And what must the children hidden in the secret room beyond be thinking? Poor Anne must be feeling terrified at Rooky's shouts and the crashing on the door.

And then a really marvellous idea came to Julian. Why, oh why hadn't he thought of it before? He could open the gates himself for the police to come in! He knew how to do it – and there was the wheel nearby in the corner, that set the gate machinery working! Once he had the gates open it would not be more than a few minutes, surely, before the police were hammering at the front door.

Julian ran to the wheel-like handle. He turned it strongly. A grinding, whining noise came at once, as the machinery went into action.

Rooky was still crashing at the door with the heavy chair. Already he had broken in one panel of it. But when he suddenly heard the groaning of the machinery that opened the gates, he stopped in panic. The gates were being opened! The police would soon be there – he would be caught!

He forgot the beautiful stories he had arranged to tell, forgot the plans that he and the others had made, forgot everything except that he must hide. He flung down the chair and fled.

Julian sat down in the nearest chair, his heart beating as

if he had just been running a race. The gates were open – Rooky had fled – the police would soon be there! And, even as he sat thinking this, there came the sound of powerful cars roaring up the wide drive. Then the engines stopped, and car doors were thrown open.

Someone began to hammer at the front door. 'Open in the name of the law!' cried a loud voice, and then came another hammering.

Nobody opened the door. Julian unlocked the half-broken door of the study he was in, and peered cautiously into the hall. No one seemed to be about.

He raced to the front door, pulled back the bolts, and undid the heavy chain, afraid each moment that some of the men would come to punch him away. But they didn't.

The door was pushed open by the police, who swarmed in immediately. There were eight of them, and they looked surprised to see a boy there.

'Which boy's this?' said the Inspector.

'Julian, sir,' said Julian. 'I'm glad you've come. Things were getting pretty hot.'

'Where are the men?' asked the Inspector, walking right in.

'I don't know,' said Julian.

'Find them,' ordered the Inspector, and his men fanned out up the hall. But before they could go into any room, a cool voice called to them from the end of the corridor.

'May I ask what all this is?'

It was Mr Perton, looking as calm as could be, smoking a cigarette. He stood at the door of his sitting-room, seeming quite unperturbed. 'Since when has a man's house been broken into for no reason at all?'

'Where are the rest of you?' demanded the Inspector.

'In here, Inspector,' drawled Mr Perton. 'We were having a little conference, and heard the hammering at the door. Apparently you got in somehow. I'm afraid you'll get into trouble for this.'

The Inspector advanced to the room where Mr Perton stood. He glanced into it.

'Aha – our friend Rooky, I see,' he said, genially. 'Only a day or two out of prison, Rooky, and you're mixed up in trouble again. Where's Weston?'

'I don't know what you mean,' said Rooky, sullenly. 'How should I know where he is? He was in prison last time I knew anything about him.'

'Yes. But he escaped,' said the Inspector. 'Somebody helped him, Rooky. Somebody planned his escape for him – friends of yours – and somebody knows where the diamonds are that he stole and hid. I've a guess that you're going to share them with him in return for getting your friends to help him. Where is Weston, Rooky?'

'I tell you I don't *know*,' repeated Rooky. 'Not here, if that's what you're getting at. You can search the whole house from top to bottom, if you like. Perton won't mind. Will you, Perton? Look for the sparklers, too, if you want to. I don't know anything about them.'

'Perton, we've suspected you for a long time,' said the Inspector, turning to Mr Perton, who was still calmly smoking his cigarette. 'We think you're at the bottom of all these prison escapes – that's why you bought this lonely old house, isn't it? – so that you could work from it undisturbed? You arrange the escapes, you arrange for a change of clothes, you arrange for a safe hiding-place till the man can get out of the country.'

'Utter nonsense,' said Mr Perton.

A VERY EXCITING FINISH!

'And you only help criminals who have been known to do a clever robbery and hide the stuff before they're caught,' went on the Inspector, in a grim voice. 'So you know you'll make plenty of profit on your deals, Perton. Weston is here all right – and so are the diamonds. Where are they?'

'They're not here,' said Perton. 'You're at liberty to look and see. You won't get anything out of *me*, Inspector. I'm innocent.'

Julian had listened to all this in amazement. Why, they had fallen into the very middle of a nest of thieves and rogues! Well, *he* knew where Weston was – and the diamonds too! He stepped forward.

'Tell your story later, son,' said the Inspector. 'We've things to do now.'

'Well, sir, I can save you a lot of time,' said Julian. 'I know where the hidden prisoner is – and the diamonds too!'

Rooky leapt to his feet with a howl. Mr Perton looked at Julian hard. The other men glanced uneasily at one another.

'You don't know anything!' shouted Rooky. 'You only came here yesterday.'

The Inspector regarded Julian gravely. He liked this boy with the quiet manners and honest eyes.

'Do you mean what you say?' he asked.

'Oh yes,' said Julian. 'Come with me, sir.'

He turned and went out of the room. Everyone crowded after him – police, Rooky and the others, but three of the policemen quietly placed themselves at the back.

Julian led them to the study. Rooky's face went purple, but Perton gave him a sharp nudge and he said nothing.

Julian went to the bookcase and swept a whole shelf of books out at once.

Rooky gave a terrific yell and leapt at Julian. 'Stop that! What are you doing?'

Two policemen were on the infuriated Rooky at once. They dragged him back. Julian pulled out the knob and the panel slid noiselessly downwards, leaving a wide space in the wall behind.

From the secret room four faces gazed out – the faces of three children – and a man. Timmy was there too, but he was on the floor. For a few moments nobody said a single word. The ones in the hidden room were so surprised to see such a crowd of policemen looking in at them – and the ones in the study were filled with amazement to see so many children in the tiny room!

'WELL!' said the Inspector. 'Well, I'm blessed! And if that isn't Weston himself, large as life and twice as natural!'

Rooky began to struggle with the policemen. He seemed absolutely infuriated with Julian.

'That boy!' he muttered. 'Let me get at him. That boy!'

'Got the diamonds there, Weston?' asked the Inspector, cheerfully. 'May as well hand them over.' Weston was very pale indeed. He made no move at all. Dick reached under the narrow bed and pulled out a bag. 'Here they are,' he said, with a grin. 'Jolly good lot they feel – heavy as anything! Can we come out now, Ju?'

All three were helped out by policemen. Weston was handcuffed before he was brought out. Rooky found that he also had handcuffs on all of a sudden, and to Mr Perton's angry surprise he heard a click at his own wrists too!

'A very, very nice little haul,' said the Inspector, in his most genial voice, as he looked inside the bag. 'What happened to your prison clothes, Weston? That's a nice suit you've got on – but you weren't wearing that when you left prison.'

'I can tell you where they are,' said Julian, remembering. Everyone stared in amazement, except George and Anne, who also knew, of course.

'They're stuffed down a well belonging to an old tumble-down shack in a lane between here and Middlecombe Woods,' said Julian. 'I could easily find it for you any time.'

Mr Perton stared at Julian as if he couldn't believe his ears. 'How do you know that?' he asked roughly. 'You can't know a thing like that!'

'I do know it,' said Julian. 'And what's more you took him a new suit of clothes, and arrived at the shack in your black Bentley, didn't you – KMF 102? I saw it.'

'That's got you, Perton,' said the Inspector, with a pleased smile. 'That's put you on the spot, hasn't it? Good boy, this – notices a whole lot of interesting things. I shouldn't be surprised if he joins the police force some day. We could do with people like him!'

Perton spat out his cigarette and stamped on it viciously, as if he wished he was stamping on Julian. Those children! If that idiot Rooky hadn't spotted Richard Kent and gone after him, none of this would have happened. Weston would have been safely hidden, the diamonds sold, Weston could have been sent abroad, and he, Perton, would have made a fortune. Now a pack of children had spoilt everything.

'Any other people in the house?' the Inspector asked Julian. 'You appear to be the one who knows more than anybody else, my boy – so perhaps you can tell me that.'

'Yes – Aggie and Hunchy,' said Julian, promptly. 'But don't be hard on Aggie, sir – she was awfully good to us, and she's terrified of Hunchy.'

'We'll remember what you say,' promised the Inspector. 'Search the house, men. Bring along Aggie and Hunchy too. We'll want them for witnesses, anyway. Leave two men on guard here. The rest of us will go.'

It needed the black Bentley as well as the two police cars to take everyone down the drive and on to the next town! The children's bicycles had to be left behind, as they could not be got on the cars anywhere. As it was, it was a terrific squash.

'You going home tonight?' the Inspector asked Julian. 'We'll run you back. What about your parents? Won't they be worried by all this?'

'They're away,' explained Julian. 'And we were on a cycling tour. So they don't know. There's really nowhere we can go for the night.'

But there was! There was a message awaiting the Inspector to say that Mrs Thurlow Kent would be very pleased indeed if Julian and the others would spend the night with Richard. She wanted to hear about their extraordinary adventures.

'Right,' said Julian. 'That settles that. We'll go there – and anyway, I want to bang old Richard on the back. He turned out quite a hero after all!'

'You'll have to stay around for a few days,' said the Inspector. 'We'll want you, I expect – you've a very fine tale to tell, and you've been a great help.'

'We'll stay around then,' said Julian. 'And if you could manage to have our bikes collected, sir, I'd be very grateful.'

Richard was at the front door to meet them all,

although by now it was very late indeed. He was dressed in clean clothes and looked very spruce beside the dirty, bedraggled company of children that he went to greet.

'I wish I'd been in at the last!' he cried. 'I was sent off home, and I was wild. Mother – and Dad – here are the children I went off with.'

Mr Thurlow Kent had just come back from America. He shook hands with all of them. 'Come along in,' he said. 'We've got a fine spread for you – you must be ravenous!'

'Tell me what happened, tell me at once,' demanded Richard.

'We simply *must* have a bath first,' protested Julian. 'We're filthy.'

'Well, you can tell me while you're having a bath,' said Richard. 'I can't wait to hear!'

It was lovely to have hot baths and to be given clean clothes. George was solemnly handed out shorts like the boys, and the others grinned to see that both Mr and Mrs Kent thought she was a boy. George, of course, grinned too, and didn't say a word.

'I was very angry with Richard when I heard what he had done,' said Mr Kent, when they were all sitting at table, eating hungrily. 'I'm ashamed of him.'

Richard looked downcast at once. He gazed beseech-ingly at Julian.

'Yes – Richard made a fool of himself,' said Julian. 'And landed us all into trouble. He wants taking in hand, sir.'

Richard looked even more downcast. He went very red, and looked at the table-cloth.

'But,' said Julian, 'he more than made up for his silliness, sir – he offered to squash himself into the boot of the car, and escape that way, and go and warn the police. That took some doing, believe me! I think quite a bit of Richard now!'

He leaned over and gave the boy a pat on the back. Dick and the others followed it up with thumps, and Timmy woofed in his deepest voice.

Richard was now red with pleasure. 'Thanks,' he said, awkwardly. 'I'll remember this.'

'See you do, my boy!' said his father. 'It might all have ended very differently!'

'But it didn't,' said Anne happily. 'It ended like this. We can all breathe again!'

'Till the next time,' said Dick, with a grin. 'What do *you* say, Timmy, old boy?'

'Woof,' said Timmy, of course, and thumped his tail on the floor. 'WOOF!'

FIVE ON FINNISTON FARM

CONTENTS

CHAPTER ONE

The Five are all together again

'PHEW!' SAID Julian, mopping his wet forehead. 'What a day! Let's go and live at the equator – it would be cool compared to this!'

He stood leaning on his bicycle, out of breath with a long steep ride up a hill. Dick grinned at him. 'You're out of training, Ju!' he said. 'Let's sit down for a bit and look at the view. We're pretty high up!'

They leaned their bicycles against a nearby gate and sat down, their backs against the lower bars. Below them spread the Dorset countryside, shimmering in the heat of the day, the distance almost lost in a blue haze. A small breeze came wandering round, and Julian sighed in relief.

'I'd never have come on this biking trip if I'd guessed it was going to be as hot as this!' he said. 'Good thing Anne didn't come – she'd have given up the first day.'

'George wouldn't have minded,' said Dick. 'She's game enough for anything.'

'Good old Georgina,' said Julian, shutting his eyes. 'I'll be glad to see the girls again. Fun to be on our own of course – but things always seem to happen when the four of us are together.'

'*Five*, you mean,' said Dick, tipping his cap over his eyes. 'Don't forget old Timmy. What a dog! Never knew one that had such a wet lick as Tim. I say – won't it be fun to meet them all! Don't let's forget the time, Julian. Hey,

175

wake up, stupid! If we go to sleep now we won't be in time to meet the girls' bus.'

Julian was almost asleep. Dick looked at him and laughed. Then he looked at his watch, and did a little calculating. It was half past two.

'Let's see now – Anne and George will be on the bus that stops at Finniston Church at five past three,' he thought. 'Finniston is about a mile away, down this hill. I'll give old Julian fifteen minutes to have a nap – and hope to goodness I don't fall asleep myself!'

He felt his own eyes closing after a minute, and got up at once to walk about. The two girls and Tim *must* be met, because they would have suitcases with them, which the boys planned to wheel along on their bicycles.

The Five were going to stay at a place called Finniston Farm, set on a hill above the little village of Finniston. None of them had been there before, nor even heard of it.

THE FIVE ARE ALL TOGETHER AGAIN

It had all come about because George's mother had heard from an old school friend, who had told her that she was taking paying guests at her farmhouse – and had asked her to recommend visitors to her. George had promptly said she would like to go there with her cousins in the summer holidays.

'Hope it's a good place!' thought Dick, gazing down into the valley, where cornfields waved in the little breeze. 'Anyway, we shall only be there for two weeks – and it *will* be fun to be together again.'

He looked at his watch. 'Time to go!' He gave Julian a push. 'Hey – wake up!'

''Nother ten minutes,' muttered Julian, trying to turn over, as if he were in bed. He rolled against the gate-bars and fell on to the hard dry earth below. He sat up in surprise. 'Gosh – I thought I was in bed!' he said. 'I could have gone on sleeping for hours.'

'Well, it's time to go and meet that bus,' said Dick. 'I've had to walk about all the time you were a sleep, I was so afraid I'd go off myself. Come on Julian – we really must go!'

They rode down the hill, going cautiously round the sharp corners, remembering how many times they had met herds of cows, wide farm carts, tractors and the like, on their way through this great farming county. Ah – there was the village, at the bottom of the hill. It looked old and peaceful and half-asleep.

'Thank goodness it sells ginger beer and ice-creams!' said Dick, seeing a small shop with a big sign in the window. 'I feel as if I want to hang out my tongue, like Timmy does, I'm so thirsty!'

'Let's find the church and the bus stop,' said Julian. 'I

saw a spire as we rode down the hill, but it disappeared when we got near the bottom.'

'There's the bus!' said Dick, as he heard the noise of wheels rumbling along in the distance. 'Look, here it comes. We'll follow it.'

'There's Anne in it – and George, look!' shouted Julian. 'We're here exactly on time! Hey, George!'

The bus came to a stop by the old church, and out jumped Anne and George, each with a suitcase – and out leapt old Timmy too, his tongue hanging down, very glad to be out of the hot, jerky, smelly bus.

'There are the boys!' shouted George, and waved wildly as the bus went off again. 'Julian! Dick! I'm so glad you're here to meet us!'

The two boys rode up, and jumped off their bikes, while Timmy leapt round them, barking madly. They thumped the girls on their backs, and grinned at them. 'Just the same old couple!' said Dick. 'You've got a spot on your chin, George, and why on *earth* have you tied your hair into a ponytail, Anne?'

'You're not very polite, Dick,' said George, bumping him with her suitcase. 'I can't think why Anne and I looked forward so much to seeing you again. Here, take my suitcase – haven't you any manners?'

'Plenty,' said Dick, and grabbed the case. 'I just can't get over Anne's new hair-do. I don't like it, Anne – do you, Ju? Ponytail! A donkey tail would suit you better Anne!'

'It's all right – it's just because the back of my neck was so hot,' said Anne, shaking her hair free in a hurry. She hated her brothers to find fault with her. Julian gave her arm a squeeze.

'Nice to see you both,' he said. 'What about some ginger

beer and ice-cream? There's a shop over there that sells them. And I've a sudden longing for nice juicy plums!'

'You haven't said a word to Timmy yet,' said George, half offended. 'He's been trotting round you and licking your hands – and he's so dreadfully hot and thirsty!'

'Shake paws, Tim,' said Dick, and Timmy politely put up his right paw. He shook hands with Julian too and then promptly went mad, careering about and almost knocking over a small boy on a bicycle.

'Come on, Tim – want an ice-cream?' said Dick, laying his hand on the big dog's head. 'Hark at him panting, George – I bet he wishes he could unzip his hairy coat and take it off! Don't you Tim?'

'Woof!' said Tim, and slapped his tail against Dick's legs.

They all trooped into the ice-cream shop. It was half dairy, half baker's. A small girl of about ten came to serve them.

'Mum's lying down,' she said. 'What can I get you? Ice-creams, I suppose? That's what everyone wants today.'

'You supposed right,' said Julian. 'A large one each, please – five in all – and four bottles of ginger pop as well.'

'*Five* ice-creams – do you want one for that dog, then?' said the girl in surprise, looking at Timmy.

'Woof,' he said at once.

'There you are,' said Dick, 'he said yes!'

Soon the Five were eating their cold ice-creams, Timmy licking his from a saucer. Before he had had many licks, the ice-cream slid from the saucer, and Timmy chased it all the way round the shop, as it slid away from his vigorous licks. The little girl watched him, fascinated.

'I must apologise for his manners,' said Julian, so-

179

lemnly. 'He hasn't been very well brought up.' He at once had a glare from George, and grinned. He opened his bottle of ginger beer. 'Nice and cold,' he said. 'Here's a happy fortnight to us all!' He drank half the glass at top speed, and set it down with a great sigh.

'Well, blessings on the person who invented ice-cream, ginger pop and the rest!' he said. 'I'd rather invent things like that any day than rockets and bombs. Ha – I feel better now. What about you others? Do you feel like going to find the farm?'

'Whose farm?' asked the little girl, coming out from behind the counter to pick up Timmy's saucer. Timmy gave her a large, wet and loving lick as she bent down.

'Ooooh!' she said, pushing him away. 'He licked all down my face!'

'Probably thought you were an ice-cream,' said Dick, giving her his hanky to wipe her cheek. 'The farm we want is called Finniston Farm. Do you know it?'

'Oh *yes*,' said the little girl. 'You go down the village street, right to the end, and turn up the lane there – up to the right. The farmhouse is at the top of the lane. Are you staying with the Philpots?'

'Yes. Do you know them?' asked Julian, getting out some money to pay the bill.

'I know the twins there,' said the girl. 'The two Harries. At least, I don't know them *well* – nobody does. They're just wrapped up in each other, they never make any friends. You look out for their old great-grandad – *he's* a one he is! He once fought a mad bull and knocked it out! And his *voice* – you can hear it for miles! I was real scared of going near the farm when I was little. But Mrs Philpot, she's nice. You'll like her. The twins are very good to her – and to their dad, too – work like farm hands all the holidays. You won't know t'other from which, they're so alike!'

'Why did you call them the two Harries?' asked Anne, curiously.

'Oh, because they've both . . .' began the child, and then broke off as a plump woman came bustling into the shop.

'Janie – you go and see to the baby for me – I'll see to the shop now. Run along!'

Away went the small girl, scuttling through the door.

'Little gasbag she is!' said her mother. 'Anything more you want?'

'No thanks,' said Julian, getting up. 'We must go. We're to stay at Finniston Farm, so we may be seeing you again soon. We liked the ice-creams!'

'Oh – so you're going there, are you?' said the plump woman. 'I wonder how you'll get on with the Harries! And keep out of Grandad's way – he's over eighty, but he can still give a mighty good thumping to anyone who crosses him!'

The Five went out into the hot sun again. Julian grinned round at the others. 'Well – shall we go and find the nice Mrs Philpot – the unfriendly Harries, whoever they might be – and the fearsome great-grandad? Sounds interesting, doesn't it?'

CHAPTER TWO

Finniston Farm

THE FOUR children, with Timmy trotting beside them, walked down the hot, dusty village street until they came to the end, and then saw the lane turning off to the right, just as the little girl had told them.

'Wait a minute,' said Anne, stopping at a curious little shop at the end of the village street. 'Look – here's an interesting shop – it sells antiques. Look at those old horse-brasses – I'd like to get one or two of those. And just see those lovely old prints!'

'Oh *no* – not now, Anne,' said Julian, with a groan. 'This awful craze of yours for second-hand shops has been going on too long! Horse-brasses! You've got stacks of them already! If you think we're going to go into that dark, smelly little shop and . . .'

'Oh, I'm not going in *now*,' said Anne, hurriedly. 'But it does look rather exciting. I'll come by myself sometime and browse round.' She glanced at the name on the shop front. 'William Finniston – how funny to have the same name as the village! I wonder if . . .'

'Oh come *on*,' said George impatiently, and Timmy tugged at her skirt. Anne gave one backward glance at the fascinating little shop window, and hurried after the others, making up her mind to slip down to the shop one day when she was alone.

They all went up the little winding lane, where red poppy-heads jigged about in the breeze, and after a while

183

they came in sight of the farmhouse. It was a big one, three storeys high, with whitewashed walls, and the rather small windows belonging to the age in which it was built. Old-fashioned red and white roses rambled over the porch, and the old wooden door stood wide open.

The Five stood on the scrubbed stone entrance, looking into the dim hall. An old wooden chest stood there, and a carved chair. A rather threadbare rug lay on the stone floor, and a grandfather clock ticked slowly and loudly.

Somewhere a dog barked, and Timmy at once barked back. 'WOOF, WOOF!'

'Be quiet, Timmy,' said George sharply, afraid that a horde of farm dogs might come rushing out. She looked for a bell or a knocker, but couldn't see either. Then Dick spotted a beautiful wrought-iron handle hanging down from the roof of the porch. Could it be a bell?

He pulled it, and at once a bell jangled very loudly somewhere in the depths of the farmhouse, making them all jump. They stood in silence, waiting for someone to come. Then they heard footsteps and two children came up the hallway.

They were *exactly* alike! The most twinny twins I've ever seen, thought Anne, in amazement. Julian smiled his friendliest smile. 'Good afternoon – I – er – I hope you're expecting us.'

The twins stared at him without a smile. They nodded together. 'Come this way,' they both said, and marched back down the hall. The four stared at one another in surprise.

'Why so stiff and haughty?' whispered Dick, putting on a face exactly like the twins.' Anne giggled. They all followed the twins, who were dressed exactly alike in navy jeans and navy shirts. They went right down the long hall, passed a stairway, round a dark corner, and into an enormous kitchen, which was obviously used as a sitting room as well.

'The Kirrins, Mother!' said the twins, together, and at once disappeared through another door, shoulder to shoulder. The children found themselves facing a pleasant-looking woman standing by a table, her hands white with flour. She smiled, and then gave a little laugh.

'Oh, my dears! I didn't expect you quite so soon! Do forgive my not being able to shake hands with you – but I was just making scones for your tea. I'm so pleased to see you. Did you have a good journey here?'

It was nice to hear her welcoming voice and see her wide smile. The Five warmed to her at once. Julian put down the suitcase he was carrying and looked round the room.

'What a lovely old place!' he said. 'You carry on with your scone-making, Mrs Philpot – we'll look after ourselves. Just tell us where to go. It's nice of you to have us.'

'I'm glad to,' said Mrs Philpot. 'I expect your aunt told you the farm's not doing too well, and she kindly said she'd send you here for two weeks. I've some other boarders too – an American and his son – so I'm pretty busy.'

'Well, you don't need to bother too much about *us*,' said Dick. 'In fact, we'll camp out under a haystack if you like – or in a barn. We're used to roughing it!'

'Well – that *might* be a help,' said Mrs Philpot, going on with her mixing. 'I've a bedroom that would do for the girls all right – but I'm afraid you boys would have to share one with the American boy – and – er – well, you mightn't like him.'

'Oh, I expect we'll get on all right,' said Julian. 'But my brother and I would certainly *prefer* to be by ourselves, Mrs Philpot. What about putting up camp beds or something in a barn? We'd love that!'

Anne looked at Mrs Philpot's kind, tired face, and felt suddenly sorry for her. How awful to *have* to have your home invaded by strangers, whether you liked them or not! She went over to her.

'You tell Georgina and me anything you'd like us to do to help,' she said. 'You know – making the beds and dusting and things like that. We're used to doing things at home, and . . .'

'I'm going to enjoy having *you*!' said Mrs Philpot, looking round at them all. 'And you won't need to help very much. The twins do a great deal – too much, I think, bless them – because they help on the farm too. Now, you go up the stairs to the very top of the house, and you'll see two bedrooms, one on each side of the landing – the left-hand one is yours, girls – the other is where the American boy is sleeping. And as for you two boys, you can slip out to the barn, and see if you'd like a couple of camp beds there. I'll get the twins to take you.'

The twins came back at this minute, and stood silently shoulder to shoulder, as alike as peas in a pod. George looked at them.

'What's your name?' she said to one twin.

'Harry!' was the answer. She turned to the other. 'And what's yours?'

'Harry!'

'But surely you don't have the same name?' exclaimed George.

'Well, you see,' explained their mother, 'we called the boy Henry, and he became Harry, of course – and we called the girl Harriet, and *she* calls herself Harry for short – so they're known as the Harries.'

'I thought they were both *boys*!' said Dick in amazement. 'I wouldn't know which is which!'

'Well, they felt they *have* to be alike,' said Mrs Philpot, 'and as Harry can't have long hair like a girl Harriet has to have shorter hair to be like Harry! I very often don't know one from the other myself.'

Dick grinned. 'Funny how some girls want to be boys!' he said, with a sly glance at George, who gave him a furious look.

'Twins, show the Kirrins up to the top bedroom,' said Mrs Philpot, 'and then take the boys out to the big barn. They can have the old camp beds, if they like the look of the barn.'

'*We* sleep out there,' said the Harries, both together, and scowled just like George.

'Well, you shouldn't,' said their mother. 'I told you to take your mattresses to the little room off the dairy.'

'It's too stuffy,' said the twins.

'Hang on – we don't want to cause trouble,' said Julian, feeling that the twins were too unfriendly for words. 'Can't *we* sleep in the room off the dairy?'

'Certainly not,' said Mrs Philpot, and sent the Harries a warning glance. 'There's room for you all in the big barn. Go on now, twins, do as I tell you, take the four up to the top bedroom, with the cases, and then out to the barn.'

The twins went to pick up the suitcases, still looking mutinous. Dick interposed himself between them and the cases. '*We'll* carry them,' he said stiffly. 'We don't want to be any more trouble to you than we can help.'

And he and Julian picked up a suitcase each, and set off after the Harries, who looked suddenly surprised. George followed with Timmy, more amused than cross. Anne went to pick up a spoon that Mrs Philpot had dropped.

'Thank you, dear,' said Mrs Philpot. 'Look – don't get upset by the twins. They're a funny pair – but good at heart. They just don't like strangers in their home, that's all. Promise you won't mind them? I do want you to be happy here.'

Anne looked at the kindly, tired face of the woman beside her, and smiled. 'We'll promise not to worry about the twins – if you'll promise not to worry about *us*!' she said. 'We can look after ourselves, you know – honestly, we're used to it. And please do tell us when you want anything done!'

She went out of the room and up the stairs. The others

were already in one of the two bedrooms at the top of the house. It was a fairly big room, white-washed, with rather a small window and boarded floors. Julian looked at the boards he was standing on. 'I say! Look at the wood this floor's made of – solid old oak, worn white with the years! This farmhouse must be very old. And look at the beams running across the walls and into the roof. Hey, twins, this is a wonderful old house!'

The twins unbent enough to nod in time together. 'Seems as if you two go by clockwork – you speak the same words at the same time, you walk in time, you nod your heads in time!' said Dick. 'But, I say – do you *ever* smile?'

The twins looked at him with dislike. Anne nudged Dick. 'Stop it, Dick! Don't tease them. Perhaps they'd show you the barn now. We'll unpack some clean things we've brought for you in our case, and come down with them when we're ready.'

'Right,' said Dick, and he and Julian went out of the room. Opposite, with its door open, was the other room, where the American boy slept. It was so very untidy that Dick couldn't help exclaiming.

'Gosh – how does he get his room into all that mess?' He and Julian went down the stairs, and Dick turned back to see if the Harries were following. He saw them standing at the top, each shaking a furious fist at the door of the American boy's room. And what a furious look on their faces, too!

Whew! thought Dick. The Harries have got some sort of grudge against him – let's hope they don't get one for us, too. 'Well – now for the barn,' he said aloud. 'Don't go so fast, Ju. Wait for the twins – they're just falling over themselves to look after us!'

CHAPTER THREE

Out in the barn

THE TWINS stalked out of the farmhouse and took the two boys round the dairy shed, and up to an enormous barn. One of them pushed open the great door.

'I *say!*' said Julian, gazing into the dark barn. 'I never saw such a great barn in all my life! It's as old as the hills – look at those beams soaring up into the roof – it reminds me of a cathedral, somehow. I wonder why they built the roof so high. What do you store in here, twins?'

'Sacks of meal,' said the Harries together, opening and shutting their mouths as one. The two boys saw a couple of camp beds in a corner of the barn.

'Look,' said Julian, 'if you really would rather sleep here alone, we'll sleep in the little room off the dairy that your mother spoke of.'

Before the twins could answer, a shrill barking came from the direction of the camp beds, and the boys saw a tiny black poodle there, standing up, quivering in every hair.

'What a tiny thing!' said Julian. 'Is he yours? What's his name?'

'Snippet,' came the answer from both at once. 'Come here, Snippet!'

At once the tiny black poodle hurled himself off the camp bed and raced over to them. He fawned on them all, barking in delight, licking everyone in turn. Dick picked him up, but the twins at once clutched Snippet themselves.

'He's OUR dog!' they said so fiercely that Dick backed away.

'All right, all right – you can have him. But be careful Tim doesn't eat him!' he said. A look of fear came over the faces of the Harries, and they turned to one another, anxiously.

'It's all right,' said Julian, hastily. 'Tim's gentle with small things. You needn't be afraid. I say – why do you have to be so *dumb*? It really wouldn't hurt you to be a bit friendly. And do let us sleep in your old room – we really don't mind.'

The twins looked at each other again, as if reading one another's thoughts, and then they turned gravely to the boys, not looking quite so unfriendly.

'We will *all* sleep here,' they said. 'We will fetch the other camp beds.' And off they marched, Snippet running excitedly at their heels.

Julian scratched his head. 'Those twins make me feel peculiar,' he said. 'I don't feel they are quite *real*. The way they act and speak together makes me feel as if they're puppets or something.'

'They're just jolly rude and unfriendly,' said Dick, bluntly. 'Oh well – they won't get in our way much. I vote we explore the farm tomorrow. It looks quite a big one – spreading out over the hill slopes everywhere. I wonder if we could get a ride on a tractor?'

At that moment a bell rang loudly from the direction of the house. 'What's that for?' said Dick. 'Tea, I hope!'

The twins came back at that moment with two more camp beds, which they proceeded to set up as far from their own as possible. Dick went to give a hand, but they waved him off, and put up the beds most efficiently and quickly by themselves.

'Tea is ready,' they said, standing up when the beds were finished, and blankets and pillows set out on them. 'We will show you where to wash.'

'Thanks,' said Dick and Julian together, and then grinned at one another. 'Better be careful,' said Julian, 'or we'll catch their habit of speaking exactly at the same moment. I say – isn't that poodle funny – look at him stalking that jackdaw!'

A black jackdaw, the nape of his neck showing grey as he ran in front of Snippet, had flown down from somewhere in the roof of the barn. As Snippet danced after him he ran behind sacks, scurried into corners and led the little dog such a dance that the two boys roared. Even the twins smiled.

'Chack!' said the jackdaw, and rose into the air. He settled himself on the middle of the poodle's back, and Snippet promptly went mad, and tore about the barn at top speed.

'Roll over, Snippet!' shouted the Harries, and Snippet at once flung himself on his back – but the jackdaw, with a triumphant 'chack' rose at once into the air, and alighted on one twin's head.

'I say, is he tame?' said Dick. 'What's his name?'

'Nosey. He's ours. He fell down a chimney and broke his wing,' said the twins. 'So we kept him till it was well and now he won't leave us.'

'Gosh!' said Dick, staring at them. 'Did you *really* say all that – or was it the jackdaw? You *can* talk properly, after all.'

Nosey pecked at the twin's ear nearest to him, and the twin gave a yell. 'Stop it, Nosey!' The jackdaw rose into the air, with a 'chack-chack-chack' that sounded very like a laugh, and disappeared somewhere in the roof.

Just then the two girls came to find the boys in the barn, sent by Mrs Philpot, who was sure they hadn't heard the bell. Timmy was with them, of course, sniffing into every corner, enjoying the farm smells everywhere. They came to the barn and looked in.

'Oh, there you are!' called Anne. 'Mrs Philpot said we . . .'

Timmy began to bark, and she stopped. He had caught sight of Snippet sniffing behind the sacks, still hunting for the cheeky jackdaw. He stood still and stared. What in the wide world was that funny little black creature? He gave another loud bark and shot over towards the poodle, who gave a terrified yelp and leapt into the arms of one of the twins.

'Take your dog away,' said both twins, fiercely, glaring at the four.

'It's all right – he won't hurt Snippet,' said George, advancing on Timmy and taking hold of his collar. 'He really won't.'

'TAKE YOUR DOG AWAY!' shouted the twins, and up in the roof somewhere the jackdaw said, 'CHACK, CHACK, CHACK!' just as fiercely.

'All right, all right,' said George, glaring as angrily as the twins. 'Come on, Tim. That poodle wouldn't be more than a mouthful for you, anyway!'

They all went back to the farmhouse in silence, Snippet having been left behind on the camp bed belonging to one of the twins. They cheered up when they came into the big, cool kitchen. Tea was now laid on the farmhouse table, a big solid affair of old, old oak. Chairs were set round and it all looked very home-like.

'Hot scones,' said George, lifting the lid of a dish. 'I

194

never thought I'd like hot scones on a summer's day, but
these look heavenly. Running with butter! Just how I like
them!'

The four looked at the home-made buns and biscuits
and the great fruit cake. They stared at the dishes of home-
made jam, and the big plate of ripe plums. Then they
looked at Mrs Philpot, sitting behind a very big teapot,
pouring out cups of tea.

'You mustn't spoil us, Mrs Philpot,' said Julian, thinking that really his hostess was doing too much. 'Please
don't let us make too much work for you!'

A loud, commanding voice suddenly made them all
jump. Sitting in a big wooden armchair near the window
was someone they hadn't seen – a burly old man with a
shock of snowy white hair and a luxuriant white beard
almost down to his waist. His eyes were startlingly bright
as he looked across at them.

'TOO MUCH WORK! What's that you say? TOO MUCH
WORK? Ha, people nowadays don't know what work is,
they don't! Grumble, grumble, GRUMBLE, asking for this
and expecting that! Pah! PAH, I say!'

'Now now, Grandad,' said Mrs Philpot, gently. 'You
just sup your tea and rest. You've been out on the farm all
day, and it's too much work for you.'

That set the old man off again. 'TOO MUCH WORK! Now
let me tell you something. When I was a young lad, I . . .
hallo, who's this?'

It was Timmy! He had been startled by the sudden
shouting of the old man, and had stood up, his hackles
rising, and a low growl down in his throat. And then a
very curious thing happened.

Timmy walked slowly over to the fierce old man, stood

195

by him – and laid his head gently on his knee! Everyone stared in astonishment, and George could hardly believe her eyes!

At first the old man took no notice. He just let Timmy stay there, and went on with his shouting. 'No one knows anything these days. They don't know a good sheep or a good bull or a good dog. They . . .'

Timmy moved his head a little, and the old man stopped again. He looked down at Timmy, and patted him on the head. 'Now *here's* a dog – a REAL dog. A dog that could be the best friend any man ever had. Ah, he reminds me of my old True, he does.'

George was staring in amazement at Timmy. 'He's never done a thing like that before,' she said.

'All dogs are like that with old Grandad,' said Mrs Philpot softly. 'Don't mind his shouting. He's like that. See – your Timmy is lying down by Grandad – now they'll both be happy. Grandad will have his tea and be nice and quiet. Don't take any notice of him now.'

Still astonished, the children ate a marvellous tea, and were soon talking eagerly to Mrs Philpot, asking her questions about the farm.

'Yes, of course you can go on the tractor. And we've an old Land Rover too – you can motor round the farm in that, if you like. Wait till my husband comes in – he'll tell you what you can do.'

Nobody saw a little black shadow come in at the door, and sidle softly over to Grandad – Snippet the poodle! He had left the barn and come to the kitchen he loved. It was only when Mrs Philpot turned round to ask the old man to have another cup of tea that she saw a very strange sight indeed. She nudged the twins, and they hurried to look.

They saw Timmy lying peacefully down on Grandad's big feet – and Snippet the poodle lying between Timmy's great front paws! Well – what an astonishing sight to be sure!

'Grandad's happy now,' said Mrs Philpot. 'Two dogs at his feet. And now, look – here's my husband! Come along in, Trevor – we're all here, the dogs as well!'

CHAPTER FOUR

Junior!

A BIG man came into the kitchen, very like the twins to look at. He stooped, and seemed tired. He didn't smile, but just nodded.

'Trevor, here are the visitors I told you about,' said Mrs Philpot. 'Look, this is Julian and . . .'

'More visitors?' said Trevor with a groan. 'Good heavens – what a crowd of children! Where's that American boy? I've got a bone to pick with him. He tried to set the tractor going by himself this morning, and . . .'

'Oh, Trevor – never mind about that now. Just wash and come and have your tea,' said Mrs Philpot. 'I've kept some of your favourite scones for you.'

'Don't want any tea,' said her husband. 'Can't stop – except for just one cup, and that I'll take in the dairy. I've got to go and see to the milking. Bob's off today.'

'We'll help, Dad!' said the twins speaking together, as usual, and they got up from the table at once.

'No – you sit down,' said their mother. 'You've been on the go from seven o'clock this morning. Sit down and finish your tea in peace.'

'I could do with your help, twins,' said their father, as he went through the door towards the dairy, 'but now your mother's got so many on her hands, she'll need you more than I do!'

'Mrs Philpot – let the twins go if they want to,' said

198

Julian at once. 'We can help, you know – we're used to helping at home.'

'And what's more, we like it,' said Anne. 'Do let us, Mrs Philpot – we'll feel much more at home then. Can't we clear away and wash up and all that, while the twins go and help with the milking?'

'YOU LET 'EM HELP!' shouted old Great-Grandad suddenly from his corner, making Timmy and Snippet leap to their feet, startled. 'WHAT ARE CHILDREN COMING TO NOWADAYS WAITED ON HAND AND FOOT? PAH!'

'Now, now, Grandad,' said poor Mrs Philpot. 'Don't you start worrying. We can manage fine.'

The old man made a loud, explosive noise, and banged his hand down on the arm of his chair. 'WHAT I SAY IS THIS . . .'

But he got no further, for the sound of footsteps could be heard in the hall, coming towards the kitchen, and loud, American voices came nearer and nearer.

'See here, Pop – I wanna come with you! This place is dead. You take me up to London with you, aw, Pop, go on, do!'

'That the Americans?' asked Dick, turning to the twins. Their faces had gone as black as thunder. They nodded. In came a burly man, looking rather odd in smart town clothes, and a fat pasty-faced boy of about eleven. The father stood at the door and looked round rubbing his hands.

'Hiya, folks! We've been over to that swell old town and picked up some fine souvenirs – my, my, they were cheap as dirt! We late for tea? Hallo, who're all these folks?'

He grinned round at Julian and the others. Julian stood up politely. 'We're four cousins,' he said. 'We've come to stay here.'

'Stay here? Where you gonna sleep, then?' demanded the boy, pulling up a chair to the table. 'This is a one-eyed place, ain't it, Pop.'

'Shut up,' said the twins together, and gave the boy such a glare that Anne stared in astonishment.

'Aw, go on, I can say what I like, can't I?' said the boy. 'Free country, isn't it? Gee, you should just see America! That's something! Mrs Philpot, I'll have a bit of that cake – looks good to me.'

'CAN'T YOU SAY PLEASE?' roared a voice from the corner. That was Great-Grandad of course! But the boy took no notice, and merely held out his plate, while Mrs Philpot cut him an enormous slice of cake.

'I'll have the same as Junior, Mrs Philpot ma'am,' said the American, and sat down at the table. He held out his plate too. 'Say, you should see the things we've bought. We've had a day, haven't we, Junior?'

'Sure, Pop,' said Junior. 'Say, can't I have an iced drink? Look here – who's going to drink hot tea on a day like this!'

'I'll get you some iced lemonade,' said Mrs Philpot, rising.

'LET HIM GET IT HIMSELF! LITTLE BRAT!' That was Great-Grandad again, of course. But the twins were already up and on their way to fetch the lemonade themselves. George caught sight of their faces as they passed her, and had a shock of surprise. Goodness – how those twins hated that boy!

'That old grand-daddy of yours must be a bit of a nuisance to you,' said the American in a low voice to Mrs Philpot. 'Always butting in, isn't he? Rude old fellow, too.'

'NOW DON'T YOU SIT THERE WHISPERING!' shouted Grandad. 'I CAN HEAR EVERY WORD!'

'Now, now, Grandad, don't upset yourself,' said poor Mrs Philpot. 'You just sit there and have a nap.'

'No. I'm going out again,' said Great-Grandad heaving himself up. 'There's some people here that fair make me ill!'

And out he went leaning on his stick, a magnificent figure with his head of snow-white hair and his long beard.

'Like someone out of the Old Testament,' said Anne to Dick. Timmy got up and followed the old man to the door, with Snippet close behind him. Junior saw Timmy at once.

'Hey! Look at that big dog!' he said. 'Who's he? I've not seen him before. Hey, you, come and have a bun.'

Timmy took not the slightest notice. George addressed Junior in an icy voice. 'That's my dog Timmy. I don't allow anyone to feed him except me.'

'Shucks!' said Junior and threw the cake down on the floor, so that it slid to Tim's feet. 'That's for you dog!'

Timmy looked down at the cake, and stood perfectly still. Then he looked at George. 'Come here, Timmy,' said George, and he walked straight to her. The cake lay on the floor half-broken into crumbs.

'My dog is not going to eat that,' said George. 'Better pick it up, hadn't you? It's made a bit of a mess on the floor.'

'Pick it up yourself,' said Junior, helping himself to another bun. 'Gee – what a glare you've got! Makes me want my sunglasses, brother!' He gave George a sudden sharp dig in the ribs, and she gasped. Timmy was beside her in a moment, growling so deeply that Junior slid out of his seat in alarm.

'Say, Pop – this dog's fierce!' he said. 'He tried to bite me!'

'He did not,' said George. 'But he *might* bite if you don't do what I said, and pick up that bun!'

'Now, now,' said Mrs Philpot, really distressed. 'Leave it – it can be swept up afterwards. Will you have another piece of cake, Mr Henning?'

It really was an embarrassing meal, and Anne longed for it to be over. Junior quietened down considerably when he saw Timmy lying down between his chair and George's, but his father made up for that by talking non-stop about the 'wunnerful' things he had bought that day. Everyone was extremely bored. The twins came back with a jug of orangeade, which they placed on the table, with two glasses, in case Mr Henning wanted some. They then disappeared.

'Where have they gone?' demanded Junior, having poured a glass of orangeade straight down his throat in a most remarkable manner. 'Gee, that was good.'

'The twins have gone to help with the milking, I expect,' said Mrs Philpot, looking suddenly very weary. Julian looked at her. She must find these meals very tiring, he thought, coping with so many people. Junior piped up at once.

'I'll go and help with the milking,' he said, and slid off his chair.

'I'd rather you didn't, Junior,' said Mrs Philpot. 'You upset the cows a bit last time, you know.'

'Aw gee – that was because I was new to it,' said Junior. Julian looked at Mr Henning, expecting him to forbid Junior to go, but he said nothing. He lit a cigarette and threw the match down on the floor.

George scowled when she saw Junior heading for the door. How dare he go out to the milking against the wishes of his hostess? She murmured a few words to Timmy, and he got up at once and ran to the door, barring it against Junior.

'Get out of my way, you,' said Junior, stopping. Timmy growled. 'Say, call him back, will you?' said Junior, turning round. No one said anything. Mrs Philpot rose and began to gather things together. It seemed to George as if she had tears in her eyes. No wonder, if this kind of thing happened every day!

As Timmy stood like a statue in the doorway, giving small threatening growls every now and again, Junior decided to give up. He dearly longed to give the dog a kick, but didn't dare to. He walked back to his father.

'Say, Pop – coming for a walk?' he said. 'Let's get out of here.'

Without a word father and son walked out of the other door. Everyone heaved a sigh of relief.

'You go and sit down and have a rest, Mrs Philpot,' said Anne. 'We'll do the washing-up. We'd love to!'

JUNIOR!

'Well – it's really kind of you,' said Mrs Philpot. 'I've been on the go all day, and twenty minutes' rest will do me good. I'm afraid Junior gets on my nerves. I do *hope* Timmy won't bite him!'

'He'll give him a nip before long,' said George cheerfully, collecting cups and saucers with Anne. 'What are you boys going to do? Go to the milking shed?'

'Yes. We've milked cows plenty of times,' said Dick. 'Nice job! I like the smell of cows. See you later, girls – and if that little pest tries any tricks, just give us a call! I'd love to rub his face into that crumby mess on the floor!'

'I'm just going to sweep it up,' said Anne. 'See you at supper-time!'

The boys went out, whistling. Mrs Philpot had disappeared. Only George, Anne and Timmy were left, for Snippet had gone out with the Harries.

'I rather wish we hadn't come,' said George, carrying out a tray to the scullery. 'It's an AWFUL lot for Mrs Philpot to do. Still – if she needs the money . . .'

'Oh well – we can help – and we'll be out most of the day,' said Anne. 'We shan't see much of Junior – little beast!'

You're wrong, Anne. You'll see far too much of him! It's a good thing Timmy's there – he's the only one that can manage people like Junior!

CHAPTER FIVE

Evening at the farm

GEORGE AND ANNE went out to find the others in the milking shed. There were plenty of cows there, swishing their tails. The milking was almost finished, and the twins were driving some of the cows back to the field.

'Hallo – how did you get on?' asked Anne.

'Fine – it was fun,' said Dick. 'My cows did better than Julian's, though – I sang to them all the time, and they loved it!'

'Silly!' said George. 'Did you have a talk with the farmer?'

'Yes – he says he's got an old Land Rover and he'll take us all over the farm tomorrow,' said Dick, pleased. '*And* we can ride on that tractor, if Bill – that's one of his farm hands – will let us. He says Bill won't have Junior on the tractor at any price – so maybe there'll be a row if he sees us on it!'

'Well, I'm all ready for a row, and so is Timmy,' said George grimly. 'Sooner or later I'm going to tell Junior a few home-truths.'

'We'd all like to do that,' said Julian. 'But let's hold our horses till a good moment comes – I don't want that nice Mrs Philpot upset – and you know, if we caused her to lose the two Americans she might suffer badly – in her pocket! I bet they pay well.'

'Well – *I* understand all that too, Ju,' said George. 'But Timmy doesn't. He's longing to have a go at Junior!'

'And how I share that feeling!' said Dick, rubbing Timmy's big head. 'What's the time? Shall we go for a walk?'

'No,' said Julian. 'My legs feel stiff with cycling up so many Dorset hills today. I vote we just stroll around a bit, not go for miles.'

The Five set off together, wandering round the farm buildings. They were all very old, some of them falling to pieces. The roofs had great Dorset tiles, made of stone, uneven and roughly shaped. They were a lovely grey, and were brilliant with lichen and moss.

'Aren't they gorgeous?' said George, stopping to look at the tiles on a small outhouse. 'Look at that lichen, did you ever see such a brilliant orange? But what a pity – half of them have gone from this roof, and someone has replaced them with horrid new tiles!'

'Maybe the Philpots sold them,' said Julian. 'Old tiles like that, brilliant with lichen, can fetch quite a bit of money – especially from Americans. There's many a barn out in America covered with old tiles from this country, moss and all. A bit of old England!'

'If I had a lovely old place like this I wouldn't sell one single tile, or one single bit of moss!' said George, quite fiercely.

'Maybe you wouldn't,' said Dick. 'But some would – if they loved their farm enough and didn't want to see it go to pieces for lack of money. Their fields would be worth more than old tiles to them!'

'I bet old Grandad wouldn't sell them if he could help it!' said Anne. 'I wonder if the American has tried to buy any of these tiles? I guess he has.'

They had an interesting time wandering round. They

found one old barn-like shed stacked with ancient cast-away junk, and Julian rummaged in it with great interest.

'Look at this giant cartwheel!' he said, peering into a dark corner. 'It's almost as tall as I am! My word – they must have made all their own wheels here in the old days – in this very shed, perhaps. And maybe their own tools too. Look at *this* old tool – what in the *world* is it?'

They gazed at the curious curved tool, still as strong and as good as it had been two or three centuries before. It was heavy and Julian thought that he wouldn't have liked to use it for more than ten minutes at a time!

'But I bet old Grandad could use it for a whole day and never get tired,' he said. 'When he was a young man, I mean. He must have been as strong as an ox, then.'

'Well, you remember what the girl at the dairy said,' put in Anne. 'She said he had once fought a bull and knocked it out. We must ask him about that. I bet he'd love to tell us.'

'He's a real old character!' said Julian. 'I like him, shouts and temper and all. Come on – it's getting lateish. We didn't ask about the evening meal. I wonder what time we ought to get back for it?'

'Half past seven,' said George. 'I asked. We'd better go back now, because we'll have to get ourselves clean – and Anne and I want to help lay the table.'

'Right. Back we go,' said Julian. 'Come on, Tim. Stop sniffing about that old rubbish. Surely you can't smell anything exciting there!'

They went back to the farmhouse, and the girls went to wash at the kitchen sink, seeing Mrs Philpot already pre-paring for supper. 'Won't be a minute!' called Anne. 'We'll do those potatoes for you, Mrs Philpot. I say, what a lovely farm this is. We've been exploring those old sheds.'

208

'Yes – they need clearing out,' said Mrs Philpot, who looked better for the rest she had had. 'But old Great-Grandad, he won't have them touched. Says he promised *his* Grandad not to let them go to anyone! But we did sell some of those lovely old grey tiles once – to an American, of course, a friend of Mr Henning's, and Grandad almost went out of his mind. Shouted day and night, poor old chap, and went about with a pitchfork in his hand all the time, daring any stranger even so much as to walk over the fields! We had such a time with him.'

'Good gracious!' said Anne, having a sudden vision of the grand old man stalking about his fields, shouting, and waving a great pitchfork.

Supper was really a very pleasant meal, for Mr Henning and Junior didn't come in. There was much talk and laughter at the table, though the twins, as usual, said hardly anything. They puzzled Anne. Why should they be *so* unfriendly? She smiled at them once or twice, but each time they turned their eyes away. Snippet lay at their feet, and Timmy lay under the table. Great-Grandad was not there, nor was Mr Philpot.

'They're both making the best of the daylight,' said Mrs Philpot. 'There's a lot to do on the farm just now.'

The children enjoyed the meat-pie that Mrs Philpot had baked, and the stewed plums and rich cream that followed. Anne suddenly yawned a very large yawn.

'Sorry!' she said. 'It just came all of a sudden. I don't know why I feel so sleepy.'

'You've set *me* off now,' said Dick, and put his hand in front of an even larger yawn. 'Well, I don't wonder we feel sleepy. Ju and I set off at dawn this morning – and I know you girls had a jolly long bus ride!'

'Well, you go to bed, all of you, as early as you like,' said Mrs Philpot. 'I expect you'll want to be up bright and early in the morning. The Harries are always up about six o'clock – they just will *not* stay in bed!'

'And what time does Junior get up?' asked George with a grin. 'Six o'clock too?'

'Oh, not before nine o'clock, usually,' said Mrs Philpot. 'Mr Henning comes down about eleven – he likes his breakfast in bed. So does Junior.'

'WHAT? You don't mean to say you take breakfast up to that lazy little pest?' said Dick, astounded. 'Why don't you go and drag him out by the ankles?'

'Well – they are guests and pay well for being here,' said Mrs Philpot.

'*I'll* take Junior his breakfast,' said George, much to everyone's astonishment. 'Timmy and I together. We'd like to. Wouldn't we, Timmy?'

Timmy made a most peculiar noise from under the table. 'That sounded like a *laugh* to me,' said Dick. 'And I'm not surprised! I'd just like to see Junior's face if you and Tim walked in on him with his breakfast!'

'Do you bet me I won't do it?' demanded George, really on the defensive now.

'Yes. I do bet you,' said Dick at once. 'I bet you my new pocket-knife you won't!'

'Taken!' said George. Mrs Philpot looked puzzled. 'No, no, my dears,' she said. 'I can't have one guest waiting on another. Though I must say those stairs are a trial to my legs, when I'm carrying up trays!'

'*I'll* take up Junior's tray *and* Mr Henning's too, if you like,' said George, in a half-kind, half-fierce voice.

'NOT Mr Henning's,' said Julian, giving George a warn-

211

ing look. 'Don't go too far, old thing. Just Junior's tray will be enough.'

'All right, all right,' said George, rather sulkily. 'Aren't Junior and Mr Henning coming in to supper?'

'Not tonight,' said Mrs Philpot, in a thankful voice. 'They're dining at some hotel in Dorchester, I think. I expect they get a bit tired of our simple farmhouse meals. I only hope they won't be too late back. Great-Grandad likes to lock up early.'

The children were really glad when the evening meal was cleared away and washed up, for they all felt heavy with sleep. The good strong air, the exciting day and the many jobs they had done had really tired them.

'Goodnight, Mrs Philpot,' they said, when everything was done. 'We're off to bed. Are the twins coming too?'

The twins actually condescended to nod. They looked

tired out. Julian wondered where Mr Philpot and old Great-Grandad were – still out working, he supposed. He yawned. Well, he was for bed – and even if he had had to sleep on the bare ground that night, he knew he would sleep well! He thought longingly of his camp bed.

They went their various ways – the twins and Julian and Dick to the big barn – the girls upstairs to the room opposite Junior's. George peeped into it. It was even untidier than before, and obviously Junior must have been eating nuts up there, for the floor was strewn with shells.

They were soon in bed – the girls together in the big, rather hard, old bed, the boys in their separate camp beds. Timmy was on George's feet, and Snippet slept first on one twin's feet, and then on the other's. He was always perfectly fair in his favours!

A crashing noise awoke the girls about two hours later, and they sat upright in bed, alarmed. Timmy began to bark. George crept to the top of the stairs, hearing Grandad's loud voice below, and then crept back to Anne.

'It's Mr Henning and Junior come back,' she said. 'Apparently old Grandad had locked up, and they crashed and banged on the knocker. My, what a to-do! Here comes Junior!' And indeed, here Junior did come, stamping up the stairs and singing loudly.

'Little pest!' said George. 'Wait till I take him his breakfast tomorrow!'

CHAPTER SIX

A little excitement for breakfast

IT WAS fun to sleep in the barn. Dick tried to keep awake for a while, and enjoy the barn smell, and the sight of the stars in the sky seen through the open door, where a cool little night breeze came wandering in.

Julian fell asleep at once, and did not even hear the crashing of the knocker at the front door of the farmhouse when the Hennings came in, or the loud voices. He awoke with a start at about one o'clock in the morning, and sat straight up in bed, his heart beating fast. What on earth was that noise he had heard?

He heard it again and laughed. 'What an ass I am! It's only an owl. Or maybe more than one. And gosh, what was that high little scream? A mouse – or a rat? Perhaps the owls are hunting in here?'

He lay still and listened. He suddenly felt a rush of cool air over his face, and stiffened. That must have been an owl's soft-feathered wings! Owls' wings made no noise, he knew. The feathers were so soft that not even a quick-eared mouse could hear an owl swooping silently down!

There came another little high-pitched squeak. The owl's doing his job well, thought Julian. What a fine hunting place for him – a barn where food stuffs are stored – overrun with mice and rats, of course. I bet this owl is worth his weight in gold to the farmer. Well, owl, do your job – but for goodness sake don't mistake my nose for a mouse! Ah – there you go again – just over my head. I saw you then – a shadow passing by!

He fell asleep once more and didn't wake until the sun streamed into the barn, lighting up hundreds of tiny motes floating in the air. Julian looked at his watch.

'Half past seven! And I meant to be up at seven. Dick! Wake up!'

Dick was so sound asleep that he didn't wake even when Julian shook him. He merely rolled over and settled down again. Julian glanced across the barn, and saw that the twins' camp beds were empty. They had stacked their pillows and bedclothes in neat piles, and disappeared silently out of the door. Without waking us! thought Julian, pulling on his socks. I wonder if I can wash at the big kitchen sink. 'Dick – *will* you wake up?' he said loudly. 'It might be TEN O'CLOCK for all you care!'

Dick heard the two shouted words and sat up at once, looking aghast. 'Ten o'clock? Oh *no*! Gosh, I must have slept all round the clock, Oh, I *say* – I didn't mean to be late for breakfast. I . . .'

'Calm down,' grinned Julian, brushing his hair. 'I only said, "It might be ten o'clock for all you care!" Actually, it's just gone half past seven.'

'Thank goodness for that,' said Dick, lying back in bed. 'Oh for ten minutes more!'

'The twins have gone already,' said Julian. 'I wonder if the girls are up. Oh, my goodness, what's that?'

Something had jabbed him sharply in the back, making him jump violently. Julian swung round, expecting it to be Junior or one of the twins playing a silly joke.

'Oh – it's *you* – Nosey the jackdaw!' he said, looking at

the cheeky bird, now perched on his pillow. 'You've got a jolly sharp beak!'

'Chack!' said the jackdaw, and flew to his shoulder. Julian felt flattered – until the jackdaw pecked his ear! 'Here – you take the bird,' he said to the unwary Dick, and handed Nosey to him. Nosey promptly pounced on the watch lying beside Dick's pillow and flew off with it. Dick gave an angry yell.

'Bring that back, you crazy bird! Don't you know a watch when you see one? He's taken my watch, Ju – goodness knows where he'll hide it!'

'He's gone into the roof,' said Julian. 'We'd better tell the twins. Perhaps they can deal with him. Now WHY doesn't he take Junior's watch – that would be a trick I should *really* applaud!'

'CHACK, CHACK, CHACK,' said Nosey, exactly as if he agreed. He had to open his beak to say 'chack' and the watch promptly fell out. It bounced on to a sack far below, and the bird swooped down to get it. Dick also swooped, and as the watch had now slipped between two sacks, he managed to get it before the jackdaw.

Nosey flew up into the roof, and 'chacked' angrily. 'Don't use such bad language,' said Dick severely, strapping on his watch. 'You ought to be ashamed of yourself!'

They went out of the barn and round to the farmhouse. There were sounds of people about, and the two boys felt quite ashamed of being so late! Breakfast was on the table, but already quite a number of people seemed to have had it!

'The girls haven't had theirs,' said Dick, looking at the places set in front of the chairs where George and Anne had sat the night before. 'But the twins have. It looks as if *everyone* has, except us four, apparently! Ah – here's Mrs Philpot. Sorry we're late. We overslept, I'm afraid.'

'That's all right!' said Mrs Philpot, smiling. 'I don't expect my visitors to be up early. Anyone can sleep late on a holiday!'

She held a tray in her hands, and set it down on the table. 'That's for Mr Henning – he'll ring when he wants his breakfast. That's Junior's tray over there. I make the coffee when they ring,' she said, and went out again.

There was cold ham for breakfast, boiled eggs and fruit. The two boys tucked in, and looked round reprovingly when the two girls came, with Timmy behind them, still sleepy-eyed. 'Overslept, I suppose?' said Dick, pretending to be shocked. 'Sit down, I'll pour you some coffee.'

'Where's Junior – not down yet, I hope?' said George anxiously. 'I haven't forgotten my bet about taking up his breakfast!'

'I say – do you think it's all right to let George take up

Junior's breakfast?' said Julian, after a pause. 'George, don't throw the tray at him or anything, will you?'

'I might,' said George, eating a boiled egg. 'Anything to get your new pocket-knife from you!'

'Well, don't go too far teasing Junior,' said Julian warningly. 'You don't want to make the Henning family walk out and leave Mrs Philpot high and dry!'

'All right, all right,' said George. 'Don't nag. I think I'll have another egg, Dick. Pass one over, please. I don't know why I'm so hungry.'

'Leave a bit of room for this ham,' said Dick, who had cut himself two good slices. 'It's out of this world! Simply too good to be true! I could eat it all day.'

The two girls tucked into their breakfast, and just as they were finishing, a bell rang very loudly in the kitchen, jangling just above their heads. They jumped violently. Mrs Philpot came into the room at once. 'That's Mr Henning's bell,' she said. 'I must make his coffee.'

'I'll take up his tray,' said Anne. 'George is going to take up Junior's.'

'Oh no – I *really* don't like you to do that,' said Mrs Philpot, distressed. Just then another bell rang. It jangled to and fro for a very long time.

'That's Junior's bell,' said Mrs Philpot. 'He always seems to think I'm quite deaf!'

'Bad-mannered little beast!' said Dick, and was pleased to find that Mrs Philpot didn't disagree!

Anne waited till Mr Henning's tray was ready, and then firmly put her hands to the sides. '*I'm* going to take it to Mr Henning,' she said in a most determined voice, and Mrs Philpot smiled gratefully and let her lift it. 'Bedroom on the left of the stairs, first floor!' she said. 'And he likes his curtains pulled, too, when his breakfast is brought.'

'And does Junior like *his* pulled as well?' inquired George, in such a sugary voice that the two boys looked round at her suspiciously. What was she up to now?

'Well – I do pull them for him,' said Mrs Philpot, 'but don't *you* pull them if you don't feel like it! Thank you very much, dear!'

Anne had already gone upstairs with Mr Henning's tray, and now George set off with Junior's. She winked at Dick. 'Get that pocket-knife ready for me!' she said, and disappeared through the door, grinning wickedly. She went carefully upstairs with Timmy close at her heels, wondering whatever George was doing with a tray!

George came to Junior's door. It was shut. She gave it a violent kick and it flew open. She entered, clattering with her feet, and set the tray down on a table with a jolt that upset the coffee. She went whistling to the windows, and pulled the curtains back across the poles so that they made a loud clattering noise.

Junior had apparently fallen asleep again, his head under the clothes. George upset a chair with a crash. That made Junior sit up, half scared. 'What's going on here?' he began. 'Can't you bring my breakfast without . . .' Then he saw that it was George in the room, not the kindly Mrs Philpot.

'Get out!' he said angrily. 'Crashing about like that! Pull the curtains across again. The sun's too strong. And look how you've spilt the coffee! Why didn't Mrs Philpot bring my breakfast? She usually does. Here – put the tray on my knees, like she does!'

George whipped the bed clothes off him, took up the tray and set it down violently on his pyjamaed knees. The hot coffee got a violent jerk and some drops fell on to his

bare arm. They were hot, and he yelled loudly. He lashed
out at George, and hit her hard on the shoulder.

That was a very great mistake. Timmy, who was at the
door watching, leapt on to the bed at once, growling. He

pulled the terrified boy on to the floor, and kept him lying there, standing over him, deep growls coming from the depths of his great body.

George took absolutely no notice. She went round the room, humming a little tune, putting this and that straight, tidying the dressing-table, not seeming to notice what Timmy was doing. She shut the door so that no one would hear Junior's howls.

'George – take this dog off me!' begged Junior. 'He'll kill me! GEORGE! I'll tell my Pop on you. I'm sorry I hit you. Oh, DO take this dog off me, PLEASE do!'

He began to weep, and George looked scornfully down at him. 'You nasty spoilt little pest,' she said. 'I've a good mind to leave you here all morning, with Timmy on guard! But this time I'll be generous to you. Come here, Tim. Leave that funny little worm there on the floor!'

Junior was still weeping. He crept into bed and wrapped the blankets round him. 'I don't want any breakfast,' he wept. 'I'll tell Pop about you. He'll get you all right.'

'Yes, you tell him,' said George, tucking him in so tightly that he couldn't move. 'You tell him – and I'll whisper into Timmy's ear that you've told tales on me – and honestly, I simply don't know what *he'll* do!'

'You are the most horrible boy I've ever met,' said Junior, knowing when he was beaten. George grinned. So he thought she was a boy, did he? Good!

'Mrs Philpot isn't going to bring up your breakfast any more,' she said. '*I'm* going to – with Timmy. See? And if you dare to ring that bell more than once each morning, you'll be sorry!'

'I don't *want* my breakfast brought up,' said Junior, in a

small voice. 'I'd rather get up and go downstairs for it. I don't *want* you to bring it.'

'Right. I'll tell Mrs Philpot,' said George. 'But if you change your mind, just tell me. I'll bring it up any morning – with Timmy!'

She went out and banged the door, Timmy trotting down the stairs in front of her, puzzled but pleased. He didn't like Junior any more than George did.

George went into the kitchen. Dick and Julian were still there. 'You've lost your bet, Dick,' said George. 'Pocket-knife, please. I not only took up his breakfast, and accidentally spilt hot coffee on him, but Timmy here pulled him out of bed and stood over him, growling. What a sight that was! Poor Junior doesn't want his breakfast in bed any more! He's coming down for it each morning.'

'Good for you, George!' said Dick, and slid his pocket-knife across the table. 'You deserve to win. Now – sit down and finish *your* breakfast and mind – I'm not betting anything else for a long, long time!'

CHAPTER SEVEN

The twins change their minds

THE TWINS, Harry and Harriet, had had their breakfast some while ago. They now came into the big kitchen, Snippet at their heels, and scowled to see the Five *still* having breakfast there. Anne was in fits of laughter over George's account of the way she dealt with Junior.

'You *should* have seen his face when I plonked the breakfast tray on his knees, and the hot coffee splashed him!' said George. 'He let out a yell that startled even old Timmy. And when he hit me, and Timmy leapt on the bed and dragged him out on to the floor, his eyes nearly fell out of his head!'

'No wonder he's decided to come down to breakfast each morning, then,' said Julian. 'He'll be scared stiff of you appearing with a breakfast tray again!'

The twins listened to this in amazement. They looked at one another, and nodded. Then they walked up to the breakfast table, and for once, only one twin spoke. Whether it was Harry or Harriet, nobody knew, for they both looked so much alike.

'What's happened?' said the twin to George. 'Why did *you* take up Junior's breakfast tray?'

'Because we were all so fed up with the way Junior – *and* his Pop – impose on your mother,' said George. 'Fancy a *boy* having breakfast in bed!'

'So old George took it into her head to take up his

223

breakfast herself, and said she'd teach him such a lesson he'd be a bit more considerate of your mother in future,' said Dick. 'What's more, I was idiotic enough to bet George she wouldn't do it – and now she's won my best pocket-knife off me – look!'

George proudly displayed the knife. The twins each gave a sudden loud laugh, which surprised the others very much. 'Well!' said Dick. 'Fancy you being able to *laugh*! You always look so fierce and unfriendly. Well, now that you've condescended to talk to us, let me tell you this – we think your mother is absolutely tops, and far from giving her more trouble, we're all going to help as much as we can. Got that?'

Both twins were smiling broadly now. They took it in turns to speak, which was really much more friendly than their usual stiff way of talking in unison.

'We hate Junior!' said one twin. 'He thinks our mother is a kind of slave, to come when he rings for her, or shouts for her.'

'His father's the same,' said the other twin. 'Wanting this and that, and sending our mother all over the place to fetch and carry for him. Why doesn't he go and stay at a hotel?'

'He doesn't because he's so set on snooping out our old things and buying them,' said the other twin. 'I know for a fact that Mother has sold him some of her own things – but she just *had* to have some money; things are so expensive, and we grow out of our clothes so quickly.'

'It *is* nice to hear you talking properly,' said Julian, clapping the twin on the back. 'And now would you mind letting us know how to tell which of you is which? I know one's a boy and one's a girl, but you both look exactly alike to me – you might be two boys!'

The twins gave sudden, mischievous grins. 'Well – don't you tell Junior, then,' said one. 'You can always tell *me* by this scar on my hand, see? Harriet hasn't any scar. I'm Harry.'

The four looked at the long thin scar on the boy's hand. 'I got that by tearing the back of my hand on barbed wire,' said Harry. 'Now you'll know us from each other! But tell us all about George and the breakfast tray, from beginning to end. Good old George. She looks just as much a boy as Harriet does.'

It was very pleasant to find the twins so friendly, after their stiff, sullen dislike. The four warmed to them – and when Mrs Philpot suddenly appeared in the kitchen to clear away breakfast, she was astounded to see her twins talking and laughing happily with the others. She stood and stared, a delighted smile on her face.

'Mother! Junior's not going to have breakfast in bed any more!' said Harry. 'Listen why!' And the story had to be told all over again. George went red. She was afraid that Mrs Philpot would be displeased. But no, she threw back her head and laughed.

'Oh, that really does me good,' she said. 'But I hope Junior doesn't tell his father, and they don't both go off in a hurry! We do need their money, you know, much as I hate having them here. Now I *must* clear away breakfast!'

'No, you mustn't. That's *our* job,' said Anne. 'Isn't it, twins?'

'YES!' said both twins together. 'We're all friends now, Mother – let them belong to the family.'

'Well, I'll go and see to the chickens, then, if you're going to clear away,' said Mrs Philpot. 'You can wash up, too, bless you!'

'Look – how would you like to go round the farm in our old Land Rover today?' said Harry to the others. 'It's the best way to see over the farm. I think Bill's got to go round this morning, and check on the fields and the stock. He'll take you, if I ask him.'

'Fine!' said Julian. 'What time?'

'In about half an hour,' said Harry. 'I'll find Bill – and when you hear a horn hooting, come on out. By the way, Bill isn't much of a talker, but if he takes to you, he'll be quite pally.'

'Right,' said Julian. 'Can Dick and I do something while the others are clearing away?'

'Gosh yes, there's ALWAYS something to do on a farm,' said Harry. 'Come on up to the chicken-houses – Harriet and I are patching them up to stop the rain leaking in.'

Julian and Dick, with Timmy behind them, immediately

went off with the twins, now as merry and friendly as before they had been dour and sullen! What a change!

'Well, thank goodness I took Junior's breakfast up to him, and put him in his place,' said George, folding up the tablecloth. 'It was apparently just the one thing that would make the twins friendly! Listen, Anne, I believe that's Junior coming.'

She slipped behind the dresser, while Anne set the chairs straight round the table. Junior came creeping in very quietly indeed, and looked round fearfully. He seemed very relieved to find only Anne there. He considered that she was *quite* harmless!

'Where's that dog?' he asked.

'What dog?' said Anne innocently. 'Snippet?'

'No – that great ugly mongrel – and that awful boy he belongs to,' said Junior, still fearful.

'Oh, you mean George, I suppose,' said Anne, amused that Junior thought George was a boy. 'Well, look over there!'

Junior saw George advancing on him from behind the dresser, gave one agonised yell and fled, fearing that she had Timmy behind her. George laughed.

'We shan't have much trouble with *him* in future,' she said. 'I just hope he doesn't say too much to his Pop!'

After a while they heard the sound of a hooter outside. 'That's the Land Rover,' said George, excited. 'Well, we've just finished the washing-up. Hang up the teacloths to dry, Anne. I'll pop these dishes into the cupboard . . .'

Soon they were out of the great kitchen door and down the passage that led to the yard. Not far off was a van-like car, the Land Rover. It was an old one, very dirty, and a bit lopsided. Dick and Julian yelled to the girls.

'Buck up! Didn't you hear us hooting?'

The girls ran to the Land Rover. Bill, the farm hand, was at the wheel. He grinned at them and nodded. Timmy greeted George as if he hadn't seen her for a year and almost knocked her down in his playfulness.

'Tim! Don't be so silly!' said George. 'Planting your

great muddy paws all over me! Where are the twins? Aren't they coming?'

'Naw,' said Bill. 'They be busy.'

They all got in, and were just about to set off when someone else appeared. 'Wait! I'm coming! Wait, I say!'

And up ran Junior, full of himself as usual. 'Jump down, Tim – go to him,' said George, in a low voice. And very willingly indeed Timmy leapt down and ran straight towards the unsuspecting Junior. He gave one loud yell, turned, and fled for his life.

'Well, that's got rid of *him*!' said Dick, with much satisfaction. 'Look at Timmy – he's laughing all over his hairy old face! You love a joke, don't you, Tim?'

It did indeed look as if Tim was laughing, for he had his mouth wide open, showing all his teeth, and his tongue was hanging out happily. He leapt back into the car.

'Sensible dog, that,' said Bill, and then relapsed into his usual silence as he started up the Land Rover with a really shattering noise. It moved off towards the fields.

How it jolted! The four clung to the sides of the van, almost bumped off their seats as the Land Rover jerked its way over field paths, up hill and down hill, jolting in and out of deep ruts, appearing to be on the point of over-turning at any minute. Anne wasn't sure that she liked it much, but the others enjoyed every minute.

'Now you'll see the farmland,' said Bill, as they came to the top of the hill. 'Look yonder! Could be the finest farm in the country, if Mr Philpot had the money!'

CHAPTER EIGHT

All round the farm

THE FIVE thoroughly enjoyed their ride over the big farm. It spread out in all directions over undulating hills, and the van swung up and down and continually lurched round corners. It stopped every now and again so that the children might see the magnificent views.

Bill told them the names of the great fields as they passed them. 'That's Oak Tree Field – that's Hangman's Copse over there – that's Tinkers' Wood Field – and that's Faraway Field – the farthest from the farm-house.'

Name after name came from his lips, and it seemed as if the sight of the fields he knew and loved suddenly set his tongue going. He told them about the stock too. 'They're the new cows over there – give good milk they do – helps a farmer no end to get money every week for milk, you know. And they're the bulls, down in that field. Fine creatures, too – cost a mint of money. But Mr Philpot, he believes in good animals. He'd rather go without a new car than buy poor stock. They're the sheep right away over there – see, dotted about on those slopes. Can't take you to see 'em today, though. You'd like Shepherd. He's been here so long, and is so old, he knows every inch of the farm!'

He relapsed into silence after his unusual spate of talk, and turned down a path that took the children back towards the farmhouse, using a different route, to show them even more fields.

There were glorious fields of corn, golden in the sun, waving in the breeze with a wonderful rustling noise. 'I could sit here for hours and look at that, and listen,' said Anne.

'Then don't you marry a farmer, if you want to do that, for a farmer's wife has no time to sit!' said Bill dryly, and was silent again.

They jolted along, shaken to the bones, but loving every minute. 'Cows, calves, sheep, lambs, bulls, dogs, ducks, chickens,' chanted Anne. 'Corn, kale, beet, cauliflower – ooh, Bill, look out!'

The van had gone at such speed into a deep rut that Anne was nearly flung out. Timmy shot through the back entrance of the van, and landed on the ground, rolling over and over. He got slowly to his feet, looking most amazed.

'Timmy! It's all right! It was only a bigger hole than usual!' shouted George. 'Buck up – jump in!'

As the Land Rover didn't stop, Timmy had to gallop after it, and enter with a flying leap from the back. Bill gave a snort of laughter, which made the wheel wobble dangerously. 'This old car's almost human,' he said. 'Just jigs about for joy on a day like this!'

And he drove headlong over a slanting path and straight down into a hollow, making poor Anne groan again. 'All very well for Bill!' she said, in Julian's ear. '*He's* got the wheel to hang on to!'

In spite of the jolting and bumping the Five enjoyed their ride round the farm immensely. 'Now, we really know what it's like!' said Julian, as the Land Rover came to a very sudden stop near the farmhouse, throwing them all on top of one another. 'My word – no wonder old

Great-Grandad and Mr and Mrs Philpot love the place. It's GRAND! Thanks awfully, Bill. We've enjoyed it tremendously! Wish *my* family had a farm like this!'

'Farm like this? Ay. It's taken centuries to grow,' said Bill. 'All the names I told you – they're centuries old too.

Nobody knows now who was hanged down in Hangman's Copse – or what tinkers came to Tinkers' Wood. But they're not forgot as long as the fields are there!'

Anne stared at Bill in wonder. Why, that was almost poetry, she thought. He turned and saw her gazing at him. He nodded at her.

'You understand all right, miss, don't you?' he said. 'There're some that don't, though. That Mr Henning, he raves about it all – but he don't understand a thing. As for that boy of his!' And to Anne's surprise he turned and spat into the ditch. 'That's what I think of *him*!'

'Oh – it's just the way he's been brought up, I expect,' said Anne. 'I've met heaps of fine American children, and . . .'

'Well, *that* one wants a hiding!' said Bill, grimly. 'And if it wasn't that Mrs Philpot begged me to keep my hands off him, he'd be black and blue, that boy! I tell you! Trying to ride on the nervy calves and chasing the hens till they're scared off egg-laying – and stoning the ducks, poor critters – and slitting sacks of seed just for the fun of seeing it dribble out and waste! Hoo, wouldn't I like to shake him till his bones rattled!'

The four listened in silence, horrified. Junior was much worse than they had thought, then. George felt very very pleased that she had taught him a lesson that morning.

'Don't you worry any more about Junior,' said Julian grimly. '*We'll* keep him in order while we're here!'

They said goodbye and walked back to the farm-house, stiff and sore from the bumpy, bone-shaking ride, but with their minds full of the lovely sloping hills, the blue distance, the waving corn, and the feel of a farmland in good heart.

'That was good,' said Julian, voicing the feelings of the others. 'Very good. I somehow feel more English for having seen those Dorset fields, surrounded by hedges, basking in the sun.'

'I like Bill,' said Anne. 'He's so – so solid and real. He *belongs* to the land, just as the land belongs to him. They're one!'

'Ah – Anne has discovered what farming really means!' said Dick. 'I say, I'm starving, but I really don't like to go and ask for anything at the farmhouse. Let's go down to the village and get buns and milk at the dairy.'

'Oh *yes*!' said Anne and George, and Timmy gave a few sharp, short barks as if he thoroughly agreed. They set off down the lane that led to the village, and soon came to the little ice-cream shop, half baker's half dairy. Janie, the small talkative girl, was there again. She smiled at them in delight.

'You're here again!' she said, in pleasure. 'Mum's made some macaroons this morning. See – all gooey and fresh!'

'Now how did you guess that we are all very partial to macaroons?' said Dick, sitting down at one of the two little tables there. 'We'll have a plateful, please.'

'What, a *whole* plateful?' exclaimed Janie. 'But there's about twenty on a plate!'

'Just about right,' said Dick. 'And an ice-cream each, please. Large. And don't forget our dog, will you?'

'Oh no, I won't,' said Janie. 'He's a very *nice* dog, isn't he? Have you noticed what lovely smiley eyes he has?'

'Well, yes, we have. We know him quite well, you see,' said Dick, amused. George looked pleased. She did so like Timmy to be praised. Timmy liked it too. He actually went up to Janie and licked her hand!

Soon they had a plateful of delicious macaroons in front

of them – and they were indeed nice, and *very* 'gooey' inside, as Janie had so rightly said. George gave Timmy one, but it was really wasted on him, because he gave one crunch, and then swallowed it! He also chased his ice-cream all over the floor again, much to Janie's delight.

'How do you like it at Mrs Philpot's?' she asked. 'Kind, isn't she?'

'Very!' said everyone together.

'We love being at the farm,' said Anne. 'We've been all over it this morning, in the Land Rover.'

'Did Bill take you?' asked Janie. 'He's my uncle. But he don't usually say much to strangers.'

'Well, he said plenty to us,' said Julian. 'He was most interesting. Does he like macaroons?'

'Oooh yes,' said Janie, rather astonished. 'Everyone likes Mum's macaroons.'

'Could he eat six, do you think?' asked Julian.

'Ooooh *yes*,' said Janie, still astonished, her blue eyes opened wide.

'Right. Put six in a bag for me,' said Julian. 'I'll give them to him in return for a great ride.'

'That's right down nice of you,' said Janie, pleased. 'My uncle's been on Finniston Farm all his life. You ought to get him to tell you about Finniston Castle before it was burnt down, and . . .'

'Finniston *Castle*!' exclaimed George, in surprise. 'We went all over the farm this morning, and saw every field – but we didn't see any ruined castle.'

'Oh no, you wouldn't *see* anything!' said Janie. 'I told you – it was burnt down. Right to the ground, ages ago. Finniston Farm belonged to it, you know. There're some pictures of it in a shop down the road. I saw them, and . . .'

'Now, Janie, Janie, how many times have I told you not to chatter to customers?' said Janie's mother, bustling in, frowning. 'That tongue of yours! Can't you learn that people don't want to hear your chatter, chatter, chatter?'

'We like talking to Janie,' said Julian, politely. 'She's most interesting. Please don't send her away.'

But Janie had fled, red-cheeked and scared. Her mother began to arrange the goods on the counter. 'Let's see now – what did you have?' she said. 'Good gracious, where have all those macaroons gone? There were at least two dozen there!'

'Er – well – we had almost twenty – and the dog helped, of course – and Janie put six in a bag for us – let's see now . . .'

'There were twenty-four on that plate,' said Janie's mother, still amazed. 'Twenty-four! I counted them!'

'And five ice-creams,' said Julian. 'How much is that altogether? Most *delicious* macaroons they were!'

Janie's mother couldn't help smiling. She totted up the bill, and Julian paid. 'Come again,' she said, 'and don't you let that little gas-bag of mine bore you!'

They set off down the street, feeling very pleased with life. Timmy kept licking his lips as if he could still taste macaroon and ice-cream! They walked to the end of the street, and came to the little lane that led up to the farm. Anne stopped.

'I'd like to go and look at the horse-brasses in this little antique shop,' she said. 'You go on. I'll come later.'

'I'll come in with you,' said George, and she turned to the little shop window. The boys walked on by themselves. 'We'll probably be helping on the farm somewhere!' shouted back Dick. 'So long!'

Just as Anne and George were going into the shop, two
people came out and almost bumped into them. One was
Mr Henning, the American, the other was a man they
hadn't seen before. 'Good morning,' Mr Henning said to
them, and went into the street with his friend. Anne and
George walked into the dark little shop.

There was an old man there, drumming on the counter,
looking quite angry. He gave the two girls such a glare that
they felt quite frightened!

'That man!' said the old man, and frowned so fiercely
that his glasses fell off. Anne helped him to find them
among the clutter of quaint old trinkets on his counter. He
fixed them on his nose again and looked sternly at the two
girls and Timmy.

'If you've come to waste my time, please go,' he said.
'I'm a busy man, children are no good to me. Just want to
nose round and touch this and that and never buy any-

237

thing! That American boy now – he's . . . ah, but you
don't know what I'm talking about, do you? I'm upset.
I'm *always* upset when people want to buy our beautiful
old things and take them away to a country they don't
belong to. Now . . .'

'It's all right, Mr Finniston,' said Anne, in her gentle
voice. 'You *are* Mr Finniston, aren't you? I just wanted to
look at those lovely old horse-brasses please. I won't
bother you for long. We're staying at Finniston Farm,
and . . .'

'Ah – at Finniston Farm, did you say?' said the old man,
his face brightening. 'Then you've met my great friend,
dear old Jonathan Philpot. My very great friend!'

'Is that Mr Philpot, the twins' father?' said George.

'No, no, no – it's old Great-Grandad! We were at school
together,' said the old man, excited. 'Ah – I could tell you
some tales of the Finnistons and the castle they once
owned. Yes, yes – I'm a descendant of the owners of that
castle, you know – the one that was burnt down. Oh, the
tales I could tell you!'

And it was just at that moment that the adventure
began – the Finniston Farm adventure that the Five were
never to forget!

CHAPTER NINE

A very interesting tale

ANNE AND GEORGE looked at the old man, fascinated, as he talked to them. He stood there behind the counter of his little, dark antique shop, surrounded by things even older than himself, a little, bent old man with only a few hairs on his head. He had a kindly, wrinkled face with eyes so hooded with drooping lids that they seemed to look out through slits.

The two girls were thrilled to hear that old Mr Finniston was actually descended from the long-ago Finnistons, who lived in Finniston Castle.

'Is that why your name's Finniston?' asked Anne. 'Tell us about the castle. We only heard about it for the first time today. But we don't even know exactly whereabouts it stood. I didn't see a single stone when we went round the farm this morning!'

'No, no, you wouldn't,' said Mr Finniston. 'It was burnt right down to the ground, you see – and through the centuries people have taken the old stones for building walls. Ah well – it was a long long time ago!'

'How long?' asked George.

'Let's see now – it was burnt down in 1192 – the twelfth century,' said Mr Finniston. 'Norman times, you know. Ever heard of the Normans? Schooling isn't what it was, I know, so maybe . . .'

'Of *course* we've heard of the Normans!' said George, indignantly. 'Every child knows them! They conquered

239

England, and the first Norman king was William the First, 1066!'

'Hmmm – that's right. You've had *some* schooling then,' said Mr Finniston. 'Well, it was a Norman castle – look, like that one in this picture, see?' And he showed them a copy of an old print. They gazed at the stone castle pictured there.

'Yes. It's a Norman castle,' said George. 'Was Finniston Castle just like that?'

'I've got a copy of an old drawing of it somewhere,' said the old fellow. 'I'll find it and show it to you sometime. A small castle, of course – but a very fine specimen. Well, well, you won't be interested in such details, I know. *How* it was burnt down, I don't know. Can't find out for certain. The story goes that it was attacked at night by the enemy, and there were traitors in the castle itself who set fire to it – and while the castle folk were fighting the fire, the enemy walked in and slew nearly all of them.'

'So the castle was no use for living in after that, I suppose,' said Anne. 'But it's strange there isn't even a stone to be seen anywhere.'

'Oh, but that's where you're wrong!' said Mr Finniston, triumphantly. 'There *are* stones from the castle – all over the farm. But only I and old Great-Grandad know where they are now! There's an old wall with some of the castle stones at the bottom – and there's a well – but no, I mustn't tell you those secrets. You might tell them to the Americans who come here and buy up all our old treasures!'

'We won't! We promise!' said both girls at once, and Timmy thumped his tail on the floor, as if he too agreed.

'Well, maybe Great-Grandad will show you one or two of the old castle stones,' said Mr Finniston. 'But I doubt it – I doubt it! I'll tell you one thing you can see at the farmhouse, though – everybody knows about it, so it's no secret. Have you seen the old kitchen door that leads out into the yard?'

'Yes. That oak door, studded with iron knobs, do you mean?' said Anne at once. 'They're quite fashionable now as front doors in ordinary houses, you know. Surely that farmhouse door isn't a real old one?'

Mr Finniston put his head into his hands and groaned as if he were in pain.

'Fashionable! FASHIONABLE! What will they do next? Surely you can't mix up that fine old door with the trashy copies you've seen in modern houses? What's the world coming to? Couldn't you *feel* that that door was real – was as old as the centuries – and once hung on great hinges in a *castle*? Don't you *know* when things are grand with the weight of years?'

'Well,' said Anne, rather out of her depth, 'I did notice the door – but you see, it's very dark just there, and we really can't see it very clearly.'

'Ah – well – most people go about with their eyes shut half the time!' said Mr Finniston. 'You have a look at that door – feel it – look at the great knocker on it. Think of the old Norman folk who hammered on the door with it, all those ages ago!'

George sighed. This kind of thing didn't interest her as much as it interested Anne. A thought suddenly struck her.

'But Mr Finniston – if the castle was built of *stone* – how was it burnt to the *ground*?' she said. 'What happened?'

'I can't find out,' said Mr Finniston sadly. 'I've been into every old library in the county, and looked up every old book of that period – and I've delved into the old records in Finniston church. As far as I can make out, the castle was stormed by enemies – and, as I said, traitors inside set fire to it at the same time. The floors fell in, and the castle was left blazing from top to bottom. The great walls fell inwards and covered the base – and the Finniston family fled. Lord Finniston was killed – but his Lady took the children and hid them – it's said she hid them in the old chapel, near the barns of the farm. Maybe she took them down a secret underground passage, leading from the dungeons to the old chapel itself.'

'An old *chapel* – is it still there?' asked Anne. 'Or was it burnt too?'

'No – it wasn't burnt. It's still standing,' said Mr Finniston. 'Old Great-Grandad will show you.' He shook his head sorrowfully. 'It's a storehouse for grain now. Sad, sad. But, mind you – it's still full of prayer!'

The girls stared at him, wondering what he meant. They began to think he must be a little mad. He stood with his head bent, saying nothing for a while. Then he looked up.

'Well, that's the story, my dears – and it's not only a story, it's history! It happened eight hundred years ago. And I'll tell you something else . . .'

'What?' asked the two girls.

'That castle had cellars – and dungeons!' said the old man. 'The fire only burnt down to the ground floor, which was made of earth flattened down, not wood, so it wouldn't burn. The cellars and dungeons can't have been destroyed – are they still there, undamaged? That's what's been in my mind all these long years. What was down in those cellars – and *is it still there*?'

He spoke in such a hollow voice that the girls felt quite scared. George recovered herself first. 'But why were the dungeons never uncovered?' she asked. 'I mean, surely someone must have thought of them and wondered about them?'

'Well, when the castle fell and the walls collapsed, any underground entrances must have been completely covered with enormously heavy stones,' said Mr Finniston, peering at them earnestly. 'The peasants and farm hands living around couldn't possibly move them, and maybe they were too scared to, anyhow. They probably lay there for years, till the wind and weather broke them up. Then they were taken to build walls and line wells. But by that time everyone had forgotten about dungeons. Might have been centuries later, you see.'

He stood and brooded for a while, and the girls waited

politely for him to go on. 'Yes – everyone forgot . . . and everyone still forgets,' he said. 'Sometimes I wake up in the night and wonder what's underground there. Bones of prisoners? Chests of money? Things stored away by the Lady of the castle? I wake up and wonder!'

Anne felt uncomfortable. Poor old man! He lived absolutely in the past! His mind had woven for him a living fantasy, a story that had no certain foundation, no real truth. She was sorry for him. She wished she could go and see the place where the old castle had once stood! It would be overgrown with grass and weeds, nettles would wave there, and poppies dance in the summer. There would probably be nothing at all to show where once a proud castle had stood, its towers high against the sky, flags flying along the battlements. She could almost hear the cries of the enemy, galloping up on horseback, and the fearful clash of swords! She shook herself and stood up straight.

'I'm as bad as this old man!' she thought. 'Imagining things! But what a *tale*! The others will love to hear it. I wonder if the American knows it.'

'Does that American, Mr Henning, know the old story?' she asked, and the old man straightened up at once.

'Not the whole of it – only what he has heard in the village!' he said. 'He comes here and pesters me. He'd like to bring in men and dig up the whole thing! I know him! He'd buy up all the farm, just for the sake of getting that castle site – if he really *knew* there was something worth having, deep under the ground where it once stood. You won't tell him what I've told you, will you? I've talked too much. I always do when someone's upset me. Ah, to think my ancestors once lived in Finniston Castle – and here I am now, a poor old man in a little antique shop that nobody comes to!'

'Well, *we've* come to it,' said Anne. 'I did want to buy some horse-brasses, but I'll come another time. You're upset now. You go and have a rest!'

They went out of the little shop, almost on tiptoe! 'My word!' said George, thrilled. 'I just can't *wait* to tell the boys! What a story – and it really sounded true, Anne, didn't it? I vote we find out where that old castle really stood, and then go and have a look round. Who knows what we might find! Come along – let's get back to the farm as quickly as we can!'

CHAPTER TEN

Quite a bit of shouting

ANNE AND GEORGE, with Timmy running in front, went
back to the farm to find the boys, but they couldn't see
them anywhere and gave up. Then they went indoors and
found Mrs Philpot shelling peas. They took over the job at
once.

'The boys are still helping to mend the hen-house,' said
Mrs Philpot. 'The Harries are pleased to have two more
pairs of hands to help them! Something always seems to
need repairing! If only we could get a few things we need
so badly – a new tractor, for instance. But they cost so
much! The barns want mending too and the hen-houses
are almost falling down!'

'I hope the harvest will be good for you,' said Anne.
'That will help, won't it?'

'Oh yes – we'll keep our fingers crossed for fine weather
from now on!' said Mrs Philpot. 'Thank goodness the
cows are such good milkers! What we should do without
our milk money, I really don't know! But there – why
should I bother you with *my* troubles when you're here for
a nice holiday!'

'You don't bother us – and we think it's awfully nice of
you to let us help,' said Anne. 'We shouldn't like it if you
didn't!'

The girls had no chance of telling the boys what old
Mr Finniston had told them, until the afternoon came.
They were up at the hen-houses with the two Harries and

246

Snippet, happily hammering and sawing. Snippet was delighted to have so many people whistling cheerily round him, and busily took bits of wood from one boy to another, under the mistaken impression that he was a great help!

Nosey the jackdaw was there too, but he wasn't nearly so popular as Snippet! He pounced on any bright nail or screw he saw, and flew off with it, heedless of the exasperated shouts that followed him.

'Blow that jackdaw!' said Julian, looking up crossly. 'He's just taken the very nail I wanted! Nosey by name and nosey by nature!'

The twins laughed. They seemed entirely different children now that they were friendly – amusing, helpful and most responsible. Julian and Dick admired them – no work was too hard, no hours were too long, if they could help their mother or father.

'We hated you coming here because we knew it would give Mother so much more work,' said Harry. 'We thought if we were beastly to you, you'd go. But you don't make more work! You help an awful lot. It's fun to have you here.'

'I hope the girls are back,' said Dick. 'I know your mother wants help with the peas – such a lot of people to shell for – let me see – counting in your great-grandad, there will be about a dozen people in to dinner. Whew! I certainly *do* hope the girls are in. Ah – here comes that nosey jackdaw again. Look out, Julian, he's after those screws. Snippet, chase him!'

Away went the tiny poodle after the cheeky jackdaw, barking in his high little voice, thoroughly enjoying having so many children round him. Nosey flew up on to the top

247

of the hen-house, and flapped his wings, chacking rude things in a very loud voice indeed.

Dinner was rather a crowded meal, for everyone was there. Great-Grandad frowned when he saw Mr Henning come in with Junior. Junior strutted to his place at table, giving George his best scowl. However, she was just as good at scowling as Junior, and Mr Henning, who happened to catch sight of her giant-size scowl, had quite a shock.

'Now, now, my boy,' he said to her. 'Why pull such an ugly face?'

Nobody told him that George was a girl. Mrs Philpot was really very much amused. She liked George, and couldn't help thinking she would have made a very good boy indeed!

'Er – Mrs Philpot – would it be all right if I bring a friend to lunch here tomorrow?' asked Mr Henning. 'He's called Durleston – Mr Durleston – and he's a great authority on antiques. He's going to give me some advice. You'll remember that you told me you had a quaint old hole in the wall in one of the bedrooms – where in the old days people used to heat embers for warming-pans, and bricks to put in between the bedsheets. I thought I . . .'

'You thought you could buy 'em, I suppose!' old Great-Grandad suddenly shouted from his place at the head of the table. He thumped on the cloth with the handle of his knife. 'Well, you ask my permission first, see? This place is still mine. I'm an old man, I'm nearly ninety, but I've still got all my wits about me. I don't like this selling of things that have been in our family for donkey's years! That I don't! And . . .'

'Now, now, Grandad, don't excite yourself,' said Mrs Philpot, in her gentle voice. 'Surely it's better to sell old things that we shall never use, in order to buy new tools, or wood to mend the barns?'

'Why can't we sell 'em to our *own* folks, then?' shouted

Great-Grandad, banging with his fork as well. 'Taking them out of the country! Part of our history, they are! Selling our birthright, that's what we're doing – for a mess of potage! That's out of the Bible, let me tell you, Mr Henning, in case you don't know.'

'SURE I KNOW,' said Mr Henning, getting up and shouting back at Great-Grandad. 'I'm not as ignorant as you seem to think. You ought to be glad that a poor, run-down, back-dated country like Britain has got anything to sell to a fine upstanding one like America! You . . .'

'That's enough, Mr Henning,' said Mrs Philpot, with such dignity that Mr Henning blushed red and sat down in a great hurry. 'Sorry, ma'am,' he said. 'But that old man, he gets under my skin; he sure does! What's gotten into him? All I want is to buy things you want to sell. You want new tractors – I want old junk and I'm willing to pay for it. That's all there is to it – buying and selling!'

'OLD JUNK!' shouted Great-Grandad again, banging with his glass now. 'Do you call that great old cart-wheel you bought OLD JUNK? Why, that's more than two hundred years old! *My* great-grandad made it – he told me so, when I was a mite of a boy. You won't find another wheel like it in England. HOO – that wheel was made before the first American was born! I tell you . . .'

'Now, now, Grandad, you know you'll feel ill if you go on like this,' said Mrs Philpot, and she got up and went to the old man, who was shaking with fury. 'You belong to old times, and you don't like the new times, and I don't blame you. But things change, you know. Calm yourself, and come with me and have a lie-down.'

Surprisingly, the old fellow allowed Mrs Philpot to lead him out of the room. The seven children had all sat silent while the shouting had been going on. Mr Philpot, looking worried, broke his habitual silence and addressed a few words to the equally worried-looking Mr Henning.

'Storm in a teacup,' he said. 'Soon blow over.'

'Hmmmm,' said Mr Henning. 'Spoilt my dinner! Selfish, ignorant, rude old man.'

'He's not,' said one of the twins, in a voice trembling with anger. 'He's . . .'

'Enough, Harry!' said his father, in such a stern voice that Harry subsided at once, but began to grind his teeth to show that he was still angry, making a most remarkable noise at the now silent table. Junior had sat as still as a mouse all the time, scared of the angry old man. Timmy had given a few small growls, and Snippet had shot straight out of the kitchen as soon as Great-Grandad had begun to shout!

Mrs Philpot came back, and sat down, looking sad and tired. Julian began to talk to her about Janie and the macaroons, and soon succeeded in making her smile. She even laughed out loud when George told her that they had six macaroons to give Bill for taking them out in the Land Rover.

'I know those macaroons,' announced Junior. 'I buy about thirty of them a week. They're just wunnerful!'

'Thirty! No wonder you're so pasty-faced, then,' said George, before she could stop herself.

'Aw shucks! Pasty-face yourself!' retorted Junior, feeling safe with his father near him.

He heard a sudden ominous growl under the table, felt hot breath on his leg, and decided to say no more. He had forgotten all about the watchful Timmy!

Julian thought it was about time to have some bright

251

conversation, and began to tell Mrs Philpot about the hen-houses and what a good job they were making of patching them to make them rain-proof. Mr Philpot listened too, nodded, and actually joined in.

'Yes – you're good with your hands, you boys. I had a look when I came by. Fine work!'

'Harriet's good, too,' said Harry at once. 'She did that corner where the rats get in. Didn't you, Harry?'

'*I* wanted to help, Pop, but they shooed me off, like I was a hen!' said Junior in an aggrieved tone. 'Seems as if they don't want me around. That makes it pretty lonely, Pop. Can't I come out with you this afternoon?'

'No,' said Pop, shortly.

'Aw, *c'mon*, Pop,' said Junior, in a whiny voice. 'Aw shucks, Pop, lemme come!'

'NO!' said Pop, exasperated. Timmy gave a growl again. He didn't like cross voices. He couldn't imagine why there was so much quarrelling here, and sat up, tense and still, until George gave him a gentle push with her toe. Then he lay down again, his head across her feet.

Everyone was glad when the meal was over, delicious though the food had been. The girls and Harriet insisted that Mrs Philpot should go and have a rest while they did all the clearing away and washing-up. 'Now, try not to be unkind to Junior this afternoon,' she said, as she went. 'He'll be all alone when his father's gone. Do let him be with you.'

Nobody answered. They hadn't the least intention of allowing Junior to be with them. 'Spoilt, bad-mannered little idiot!' thought George, clearing away with such vigour that she almost knocked Anne over.

'Julian,' she said in a low voice, catching him at the door

as he went out, 'Anne and I have something interesting to tell you. Where will you be this afternoon?'

'Up in the hen-houses, I expect,' said Julian. 'We'll watch out for you and Anne. See you in about half an hour.'

Junior had sharp ears. He heard exactly what George had said, and he was full of curiosity at once. What was this interesting thing George wanted to tell the boys? Was it a secret? All right – he'd be on hand somewhere to hear it!

And so, when the girls had finished their work, and set off to the hen-houses, Junior followed discreetly behind! He kept well out of sight until he saw George and Anne disappear into a hen-house, where the others were working – and then he crept to a corner outside and put his ear to a knot-hole in the wood. I'll get my own back now! he thought. *I'll* make them smart for leaving me out of things! Just see if I don't!

CHAPTER ELEVEN

A most exciting tale

THE BOYS were busy hammering and sawing and the girls sat and waited till the noise died down. Snippet was there, leaping about ridiculously with little bits of wood in his mouth, and Nosey the jackdaw had suddenly taken a fancy to the shavings that now covered the floor, and ran about chacking and picking them up.

Outside the hens clucked and squawked, and not far off the ducks quacked loudly. 'Those are the kind of noises I like to hear,' said Anne, settling herself on a sack in a corner. She raised her voice and shouted above the hammering to Dick. 'WANT ANY HELP, DICK?'

'No thanks,' said Dick. 'We'll just finish this job, then sit down and have a rest, and listen to what you have to say. You sit and watch our wonderful carpentering! Honestly, I'd make pounds a week if I took it up!'

'Look out – Nosey has got your nails again!' shouted George. Timmy leapt up as if he was going to chase Nosey, and the jackdaw promptly flew up to a crossbeam, and sat there chacking with laughter. Timmy thought him a very exasperating bird indeed. He lay down again with a thump.

At last the boys had finished the job they were on, and sat down, rubbing their hands over their wet foreheads. 'Well, now you can tell us your news,' said Dick. 'Good thing we got rid of that little pest of a Junior – I might have hammered a few nails into him by mistake if he'd come worrying us this afternoon.' He imitated Junior's whining drawl. 'Aw shucks, Pop, lemme come with you!'

Outside, his ear to the hole, Junior clenched his fists. He would willingly have stuck a few nails into Dick at that moment!

George and Anne began to tell the four listening children what old Mr Finniston had told them that morning. 'It's about Finniston Castle,' said Anne. 'The old castle that gave the village its name – and the farm as well. The old fellow who told us about it is called Finniston, too – and will you believe it, he's a descendant of the Finnistons who lived in the castle centuries ago!'

'He seems to have spent most of his life trying to discover everything possible about the old castle,' said George. 'He said he'd delved into old libraries – and into the church records here – anywhere that might help him to piece together the castle's history!'

Outside the hen-house, Junior held his breath so as not to miss a single word. Why – his Pop had told him that he couldn't get *anything* out of that old Mr Finniston at the antique shop – not a word about the castle, and its history, or even where the site was. Then why had he told Anne, and the horrible boy George? Junior felt angry, and listened even more keenly.

'The story goes that the twelfth-century enemies came to attack the castle one night – and there were traitors already inside it who set it on fire, so that the castle folk would be busy trying to put out the fire, and wouldn't be prepared for a fight,' said George. 'The inside of it was burnt down to the ground – and then the great stone walls outside collapsed inwards, and lay in enormous heaps there, covering the place where the castle had stood.'

255

'Whew!' said Dick, visualising it all. 'What a night that must have been! Everybody killed or burnt, I suppose?'

'No, the Lady of the castle wasn't killed and it is said that she took her children to the little chapel near the farmhouse – we really must go and see that, twins – and they stayed there in safety. Anyway, *some* of the family must have escaped, because it is one of their descendants who keeps that little antique shop – old Mr Finniston!'

'This is tremendously interesting,' said Julian. 'Where's the site of the castle? It should easily be known, because of the great mass of stones that fell there when the walls collapsed.'

'No, they're *not* there now,' said George. 'Mr Finniston said he thought that when the wind and weather had broken them up small enough to be lugged away by the farmers and peasants living nearby, they were taken to build field-walls, or to line wells. He said there were some on this farm. He didn't know himself where the castle once stood because the site would be all grown over, and with no stones left to mark it, it wouldn't be easy to find.'

'But oh, Julian, I *wish* we could find it!' cried Anne, her voice rising in excitement. 'Because, so Mr Finniston says, the cellars and dungeons are probably still there, quite untouched. You see, no one could uncover them for years, because of the heavy stones there – and when the stones were taken away, people had forgotten about the castle and the dungeons!'

'Gosh! So they may *still* be there – with whatever was stored in them hundreds of years ago,' said Dick, thrilled. 'My *word* – there might be priceless things there, as old as the hills! I mean, even an old broken sword would be worth its weight in gold, because it would be so very, very old. I say – don't say a word of all this in front of that American, or he'd dig up the whole farm!'

'We shouldn't *dream* of it,' said George. 'He shan't get to hear a word of this.'

Alas! George little knew that every single word had been overheard by Junior, whose left ear was still pinned to the knot-hole in the wood! His face was red with surprise and delight. WHAT A SECRET! Whatever would his pop say? Dungeons! Perhaps full of gold and jewels and all kinds of things! He rubbed his hands together in delight, thinking that he would soon get even with those annoying children now – as soon as Pop came home, he'd spill everything to him. GEE!

Timmy heard the small sound of Junior rubbing his hands together and sat up, growling, his ears pricked. Snippet growled too, a miniature little sound that nobody took seriously. Timmy then heard Junior creeping away, afraid because he had heard the big dog growling. Timmy growled again and then barked sharply, running to the shut door of the hen-house, scraping at it with his foot.

'Somebody's outside – quick! If it's Junior, I'll throw him on to the muck-heap!' yelled Dick, and flung open the door. They all trooped out and looked round – but there was nobody there! Junior had shot off at top speed, and was now safely behind the nearest hedge.

'What was it, Tim?' said George. She turned to the others. 'He may have heard those hens scratching near the door,' she said. 'There's no one about. Gosh, I was so afraid that it was that little sneak of a Junior! He'd tell his pop every single thing!'

'Twins, listen – Mr Finniston told us that one of the things that *was* saved from the castle – or found afterwards, perhaps – was a great old oak door, iron-studded,' said Anne, suddenly remembering. 'Is that one of your kitchen doors?'

'Yes – that must be the door leading into the dark little

258

passage,' said Harry. 'You wouldn't have noticed it particularly because it's usually kept open, and it's very dark just there. Gosh, I suppose it *could* have come from the castle. It's enormously thick and strong. I wonder if Dad knows.'

'We'll tell him,' said Harriet. 'I say – shall we go and look for the site of the castle sometime? If only we could find it! Do you suppose that if we found the cellars and dungeons, full of chests and things, they'd belong to *us*? The farm belongs to our family, of course, and all the land around.'

'Does it? Well then, perhaps anything found on this land would be yours!' said Julian.

'We might be able to buy a new tractor!' said the twins, both together, in the same excited voice.

'Let's go and look for the castle site *now*,' said George, her voice sounding so excited that Timmy sat up and barked.

'No. We must finish this job,' said Julian. 'We promised we would. There's plenty of time to hunt around, because nobody knows about this except us.'

Julian was wrong, of course. Junior knew – and Junior meant to tell the whole secret to his father as soon as ever he could! He could hardly wait for him to come home.

'Well, we'd better be getting back to the house,' said George. 'We told Mrs Philpot we'd pick some raspberries for supper tonight, so we'd better fetch baskets, and begin. Oh, I do HOPE we find that castle site. I shall dream about it tonight, I know I shall.'

'Well, try and dream where it *is*,' said Julian, with a laugh. 'Then you can lead us straight to it tomorrow morning. I suppose *you* haven't any idea where it might be, have you, twins?'

'No,' they said together, frowning. 'No idea at all!' And Harriet added, 'You see, the farm's so big – and I suppose it might have been built *any*where on our land.'

'Yes – but probably near the top of a hill,' said Julian. 'Castles used to overlook surrounding land, you know, so that approaching enemies could easily be seen. And then again, George said Mr Finniston told them that the Lady of the castle escaped with her children and took them in safety to the chapel, which wouldn't be very far away. I should guess that the castle site must be not further than a quarter of a mile from the chapel, so that narrows the search down a bit. By the way, we really must look at the chapel – it sounds interesting, even though it has been used as a storehouse for years!'

The girls picked raspberries for the rest of the afternoon, and the boys finished their jobs. They went back to the farmhouse for tea, feeling pleasantly tired. The girls were already there, laying the table. They pounced on the twins, and George spoke excitedly.

'Twins! We've been looking at the old studded door. It's MAGNIFICENT! Come and see it, Julian and Dick. If it isn't from the old castle, I'll eat my hat – *and* my shoes as well!'

She took them to the great door that opened from the kitchen into the passage that led to the yard. With much difficulty she swung it shut. They all gazed at it. It had been almost too heavy for George to move! Great iron studs had been driven into it, so deeply and firmly that only by destroying the door itself could they ever be removed. There was a curious iron handle in the middle of the outer side, and George raised it and brought it down smartly. A loud bang resounded through the kitchen, and made the others jump.

'The knocker that visitors used when they came to the castle, I suppose!' said George, laughing at their surprised faces. 'Noise enough to rouse everyone, and alert any guard at once. Do you suppose it was the *front* door of the castle – it's big enough! It must be worth an enormous sum of money!'

'Look out – there's Junior!' said Anne, in a low voice. 'He's grinning all over his face. What do you suppose he's been up to? I wish I knew!'

CHAPTER TWELVE

Really very thrilling

AT TEATIME Julian spoke to Mrs Philpot about the old kitchen door. 'That's a fine old door,' he said. 'Did it come from the castle, do you suppose?'

'Yes – so it's said,' answered Mrs Philpot. 'Great-Grandad here knows more about it than I do, though.'

Great-Grandad was not at the table. He was sitting in his enormous old chair in the window, with Snippet at his feet. He was pulling contentedly at his pipe, a cup of tea on the windowsill beside him.

'What's that?' called the old man. 'Speak up!' Julian repeated what Mrs Philpot had said, and the old fellow nodded.

'Oh ay! That door's from the castle all right. Made of the same oak as the beams in the barns, and the floors of the bedrooms above! Ay, and that American fellow's been at me about it, too! Hoo! Offered me fifty pounds for it. FIFTY POUNDS. I wouldn't take a thousand. What – have that old door hanging in some newfangled house out in that American country, wherever it is? NO. I say NO, and I'll say it till I'm blue in the face!'

'All right, Grandad – don't upset yourself,' said Mrs Philpot. She spoke to Julian in a low voice. 'Change the subject, quickly, or Grandad will go on and on, poor old fellow!'

Julian racked his brain for a change of subject, and

262

fortunately remembered the hen-houses. He at once began
to tell Great-Grandad all they had done that afternoon, and
the old fellow calmed down at once, and listened with
pleasure. Snippet, who had run in fright to the twins as
soon as Great-Grandad had begun to shout, ran back to
him, and settled on his feet. Timmy also decided to join
them, and soon Great-Grandad was completely happy
again, drawing on his old pipe, with one dog at his feet,
the other resting a great head on his knee. Timmy certainly
did love Great-Grandad!

Mr Henning did not come back that night, much to
everyone's relief, but arrived next day just before lunch,
bringing with him a dried-up fellow wearing thick glasses,
whom he introduced as Mr Richard Durleston.

'The *great* Mr Durleston!' he said proudly. 'Knows
more about old houses in England than anyone else in
the country. I'd like him to see that old door after lunch,
Mrs Philpot – and the strange opening in the wall of the

bedroom upstairs, which was used to heat embers and bricks for warming beds years ago.'

Fortunately Great-Grandad was not there to object, and after they had had dinner, Mrs Philpot took Mr Durleston to the old studded door. 'Ah, yes,' he said. 'Quite genuine. Very fine specimen. I should offer four thousand pounds, Mr Henning.'

How Mrs Philpot longed to accept such an offer! What a difference it would make to her housekeeping! She shook her head. 'You'd have to talk to old Great-Grandad,' she said. 'But I'm afraid he'll say no. Now I'll take you to see the strange old opening up in one of the bedrooms.'

She took Mr Henning and Mr Durleston upstairs, and the four followed, with Timmy. It was indeed a strange opening in the wall! It had a wrought-iron door rather like an old oven door. Mrs Philpot opened it. Inside was a big cavity, which had obviously been used as a kind of oven to heat bricks for placing into cold beds; some of the old bricks were actually still there, blackened with long-ago heating! Mrs Philpot took out what looked like a heavy iron tray with an ornamental raised edge. On it were old, old embers!

'This tray was used for heating and holding the embers before they were put into warming-pans,' she said. 'We still have one old warming-pan left – there on the wall, look.'

The four, just as interested as the two men, looked at the copper warming-pan, glowing red-gold on the wall. 'The red-hot embers were emptied into that,' Mrs Philpot told the children, 'and then the pan was carried by its long handle into all the bedrooms, and thrust into each bed for a few minutes to warm it. And that funny little opening in the wall is, as I said, where people years and years ago heated the embers – and the bricks too, which were wrapped in flannel and left in each bed.'

'Hmmmmm. Very interesting. Quite rare to see one in such a well-preserved state,' said Mr Durleston, peering into the opening through thick glasses. 'You could make an offer for this too, Mr Henning. Interesting old place. We'll have a look at the barns too, I think, and the outbuildings. Might be a few things there you could pick up with advantage.'

George thought it was a good thing the twins were not with them to hear all this. They seemed to share with their great-grandad a hatred of parting with any of the treasures belonging to the old farmhouse!

Mrs Philpot took the two men downstairs again, and the four followed.

'I'll just take Mr Durleston to the old chapel, ma'am,' said Mr Henning, and Mrs Philpot nodded. She left them and hurried back into the kitchen, where she had a cake baking. The four looked at one another, and Julian nodded his head towards the two men, now making their way out of doors. 'Shall we go too?' he said. 'We haven't seen this chapel yet, either!'

So they followed the two men, and soon came to a tall, quaint old building with small and beautifully arched windows set high up in the wall. They went in at the door, a few paces behind the two men, and stared in wonder.

'Yes – you can see it was once a chapel!' said Julian, instinctively speaking in a low voice. 'Those lovely old windows – that arch there . . .'

'And the *feel* of it!' said Anne. 'I know now what old

265

Mr Finniston down at that little shop meant, when he said that though it was now a storehouse, it was still full of prayer! You can *feel* that people have been here to pray, can't you? What a lovely little chapel. Oh, I do wish it wasn't used as a storehouse!'

'I was told by an old fellow down in the village antique shop that a Lady Phillippa, who was once the Lady of the castle, brought each of her fifteen children here to learn their prayers,' said Mr Durleston, surprisingly. 'Hmm, hmm – nice old story. Probably true. Chapels were often built near to castles. Wonder which path they took from the castle to the chapel. All gone now, no castle, nothing! Hmm, hmm.'

'I'd like to buy this chapel, knock it down, and take it stone by stone to my place in the States,' said the American enthusiastically. 'Fine specimen, isn't it? It would look wonderful in my place.'

'Can't advise that,' said Mr Durleston, shaking his head. 'Not in good taste. Let's go to those outbuildings over there. Might see something in the old junk there.'

They went off, and the children stayed behind, entranced with the little chapel. Sacks upon sacks of grain and what looked like fertiliser were arranged in rows all over the floor. A cat had three kittens cuddled together on one sack, and a dove cooed somewhere high up in the arched roof. It was a very peaceful sound, somehow just right for the silent little place. The children trooped out quietly, not feeling inclined to follow the brash Mr Henning round any more.

'At least the other man stopped him from his mad idea of removing the chapel stone by stone,' said Anne. 'I couldn't *bear* that beautiful old place to be torn up by its roots and replanted somewhere else.'

'You sound quite angry, Anne – almost as fierce as old Great-Grandad!' said Julian, slipping his arm through his sister's. 'I don't somehow think the old chapel will be sold to Mr Henning – even if he offered a million dollars for it!'

'Well, I like most Americans very much,' said Anne. 'But not Mr Henning. He – he wants to buy history just as if it were chocolate or toffee!'

That made the others laugh. 'I say!' said Julian, 'what about having a snoop round, now we're out, and just see if we can decide where to hunt for the site of the castle? I presume we all agree that it can't be *very* far away from the chapel?'

'Yes – that's agreed,' said Dick. 'And it's also agreed that the site is probably on a hill. The snag is that there are rather a lot of hills on this undulating farmland!'

'Let's make our way over there – up the nearest slope,' said George. 'Hallo, here are the twins. We'll call them. They might like to come.'

The twins soon joined them, and said yes, they would certainly like to hunt for the castle site. 'But it might take years!' said Harry. 'It might be anywhere on the farm!'

'Well, we plan to examine this slope first,' said Julian. 'Heel, Tim, heel, Snippet. Oh gosh, here's Nosey the jackdaw too. NOT on my shoulder, if you don't mind, Nosey. I rather value my ears!'

'Chack!' said the jackdaw, and flew to the twins.

They made their way up the slope. There was, however, absolutely nothing to be seen except grass, grass, grass! They came to a big mound and stood looking at it.

'A very *large* mole must have made that!' said Dick,

which made them all laugh, for the mound was as high as their shoulders. Rabbit holes could be seen at the bottom, though it was probable that very few burrowed there now – the great rabbit disease, myxomatosis, had wiped them practically out of existence on Finniston Farm.

REALLY VERY THRILLING

Timmy couldn't see a rabbit hole without scraping at it, and soon he and Snippet were scattering earth over everyone. Snippet was small enough to disappear into one hole, and came out carrying – of all things – an oyster shell! Julian took it out of his mouth in amazement.

'Look here – an *oyster* shell – and we're miles from the sea. How did it get there? Go in again, Snippet. Scrape hard, Timmy. Buck up! An idea is glimmering in my brain!'

Before long, what with Timmy's excited scraping and Snippet's explorations deep into the burrow, quite a collection of oyster shells, and small and large bones lay on the grass!

'Bones!' said Anne. 'Not bones of *people* surely. Don't tell me this is a mound covering an old grave or something. Ju.'

'No. But it *is* something rather exciting!' said Julian. 'I'm pretty sure it's an old kitchen-midden.'

'A *kitchen-midden*? What on earth's that?' said George. 'Oh look – Timmy's got another mouthful of oyster shells!'

'A kitchen-midden is what you might call the rubbish-heap of the old days,' explained Julian, picking up some oyster shells. 'It was often very big, when it comprised the rubbish thrown out from large houses – or castles! Things like bones and shells wouldn't rot away like other rubbish – and I do believe we've found the kitchen-midden of the old castle. My word – what a find! Now we know something very important!'

'What?' asked everyone, in excitement.

'Well – we know now that the site of the castle must be

269

somewhere on this slope!' said Julian. 'The kitchen-midden was probably not far from its walls. We're on the scent, scouts, we're on the scent! Come on – let's go further on. Spread out, examine every inch of the ground!'

CHAPTER THIRTEEN

Junior springs a surprise

THE SIX children felt a sudden surge of excitement, and
Timmy felt it too and barked loudly. Snippet joined in,
and the jackdaw danced up and down on Harry's
shoulder, chacking hoarsely. Junior, who had seen them
start out and was tracking them, stared in surprise from
behind a bush in a nearby hedge. NOW what was all the
excitement about? What had Timmy and Snippet found?

He saw the six children spread out and begin to go
slowly up the great slope of the hill. Timmy followed
them, rather puzzled. He wished he knew what they were
looking for – then he could hunt too! Junior kept safely
behind the bush. He knew that if he followed too closely
after the children, Timmy would hear him, and bark.

Suddenly the Harries gave a shout. 'Hey!' the others
looked up from their search, and saw them beckoning in
excitement. 'What about THIS? Come and look!'

Everyone hurried over to the twins, who were standing
on a little ridge about two hundred metres below the top
of the gently sloping hill. 'Look!' said Harry, sweeping his
arm in a circle. 'Would *this* be a likely place for the castle
site?'

The four looked at the great shallow depression that the
twins pointed to. In shape it was like a very shallow soup
plate, certainly big enough for a castle to have been built
there! It was covered with thick, closely growing grass,
which was a little darker in colour than the grass around.

Julian clapped Harry on the shoulder. 'Yes! I bet this is where the castle once stood! Why should the ground here suddenly have this great depression in it, as if it had sunk down for some reason? The *only* reason could be that some enormously heavy building once stood here – and it *must* have been the castle!'

'It's not too far from the kitchen-midden, where they threw their rubbish, is it?' asked Anne, anxiously, looking back to see how far away that was.

'No – just about right,' said Julian. 'They would be sure to have it some distance away because it would smell, especially in the hot weather. Yes, twins – I think you really have hit on the castle site – and I bet if we had the machinery to excavate here, we'd come across dungeons, cellars, underground passages – and all they contain!'

The twins went red with excitement, and stared solemnly at the great basin-like circle, green with grass. 'What *will* our mother say?' they said, both together.

'Plenty!' said Dick. 'This might be the saving of your farm! But look – let's not say a word about it yet, in case it gets round to Mr Henning. Let's get Bill and ask him if he'll lend us spades and things. We'll tell him we've found some interesting old shells and bones on the hill and want to do a little digging. We'll soon know if this really *is* the site of the castle.'

'Good idea,' said Julian, excited at the thought of being one of the first to dig down into the old dungeons! 'Let's pace round this old site and see how big it is.'

They walked round and round it and decided it was more than big enough for even a large castle. They thought it was strange that the grass should be a different colour there.

'But it does sometimes happen that grass marks out where old buildings once stood,' said Julian. 'I say – this is just about the most exciting thing that ever happened to us – and I'm so glad it was the twins who first recognised the site! After all, it's on their farm!'

'Isn't that Junior running over there?' said George suddenly, as she saw Timmy prick up his ears, and turn his nose to the wind. 'Yes, it is. He's been spying on us, the little beast! There he goes, look!'

'Well, he can't know *much*,' said Julian, gazing after the running figure. 'I don't expect he even knows that a castle was once built here, at the top of this hill – and he certainly wouldn't know we were looking for the site. He's just snooping, that's all.'

But Junior *did* know all about the old castle, for he had overheard the children talking in the hen-house! And he *did* know what they had been looking for. He had followed them as closely as he dared, listening to their shouts – and now he felt that he must get back to his father and tell him what he knew!

He found his father still with Mr Durleston, examining an old fireplace. 'Now that's worth buying,' Mr Durleston was saying. 'You could rip that out, and use it in your own house – a beautiful thing. Very old! And . . .'

'Pop! I say, Pop! Listen!' cried Junior, bursting in. Mr Durleston looked annoyed. That boy again! But Junior took no notice of the old man's annoyance, and pulled urgently at his father's arm. 'Dad! I know where the place is that the castle once stood on! And there's dungeons and cellars underneath, full of treasure, I know there are. Pop, those kids found the place, but they don't know I saw them!'

'What *is* all this, Junior?' said his father, half-annoyed too. 'Silly talk! You don't know anything about castle sites and dungeons and the rest!'

'I do, I do! I heard them all talking in the hen-house – I told you I did!' cried Junior, tugging at his father's sleeve again. 'Pop, they've found an old rubbish-heap too, that belonged to the castle – they called it – a – let me see now – a . . .'

'A midden?' asked Mr Durleston, suddenly taking an interest.

'Yes! That's it. A kitchen-midden!' said Junior triumphantly. 'With bones and shells. And then they looked for where the old castle might have been built – they said it couldn't have been far away, and . . .'

'Well, they were right,' said Mr Durleston. 'A kitchen-midden would certainly pinpoint the castle area! Mr Henning, this is extremely interesting. If you could get permission to excavate, it would be a . . .'

'Oh BOY!' said Mr Henning, interrupting, his eyes almost staring out of his head. 'Can't you see the papers – "American discovers old castle site – unknown for centuries! Excavates dungeons – finds bones of long-ago prisoners – chests of gold coins . . ."'

'Not so fast, not so fast,' said Mr Durleston, disapprovingly. 'There may be nothing at all there. Let us not count our chickens before they're hatched. And mind – not a word to the newspapers, Henning. We don't want a crowd of people rushing to pry over the farm, sending up its price!'

'I didn't think of that,' said Mr Henning, a little cast down. 'All right – we'll go carefully. What do you advise?'

'I should advise you to approach Mr Philpot – *not* the old great-grandad, but the farmer himself – and offer to put down, say, £5,000 for the right to excavate up on the hill there,' said Mr Durleston. 'Then if you strike anything interesting, you can offer a further sum for whatever's down there – say another £5,000. If there *is* anything there, it will be *extremely* valuable – so very, very old. Hmmm. Hmmm. Yes, that is my advice to you.'

'And it sounds pretty good to me,' said Mr Henning, excitement flooding him again. 'You'll stay here and advise me, won't you, Durleston?'

'Certainly, certainly, if you are prepared to pay my fee,' said Durleston. 'I think it would perhaps be advisable if *I* approached Mr Philpot, Mr Henning, not you. You might – er – well – give something away in your excitement. You will come with me, of course – but let me do the talking.'

'Right, old man, you do everything!' said Mr Henning, feeling friendly with the whole world. He clapped the

275

listening Junior on the back. 'Well done, son! You may have let us into something good. Now don't you breathe a word to ANYONE, see?'

'Aw shucks!' said Junior. 'What do you think I am? My mouth's sewn up from now on! Think I'd split, Pop, when there's a chance of getting even with those snooty kids? You go on up that hill when they've gone, and have a look yourself. Mr Durleston will know if it's the real thing or not!'

So, when the six children and dogs were safely out of sight, gone to help with various jobs of work on the farm, Mr Henning and Mr Durleston went with Junior to see the kitchen-midden and the supposed site of the old castle. Mr Henning became very excited indeed, and even the weary-looking Mr Durleston brightened up and nodded his head several times.

'*Looks* the real thing!' he said. 'Yes, we'll get going this evening – after that fierce old fellow – the old great-grandad – has gone to bed. He might put a spoke in our wheels. He's as old as the hills, but as quick as a jackdaw!'

And so, that evening, when Great-Grandad was safely in bed, Mr Henning and Mr Durleston had a private, very private talk with Mr and Mrs Philpot together. The farmer and his wife listened, amazed. When they heard that Mr Henning proposed to hand them a cheque for £5,000 merely for the right to do a little digging, Mrs Philpot almost cried!

'And I have advised Mr Henning that he should offer you further sums, if he finds anything he would like to take back to the States with him, as – er – as mementos of a very pleasant stay here,' finished Mr Durleston.

'It sounds too good to be true,' said Mrs Philpot. 'We could certainly do with the money, couldn't we Trevor?'

Mr Henning took out his cheque book and produced his pen before Mr Philpot could say anything else. He wrote out the sum of £5,000, and signed the cheque with a flourish. He then presented it to Mr Philpot.

'And I hope there'll be more cheques to come,' he said. 'Thank you, sir. I'll get men along tomorrow to start digging.'

'I'll have a formal agreement drawn up,' put in Mr Durleston, thinking that he saw a rather doubtful look coming over Mr Philpot's face as he took the cheque. 'But you can cash the cheque straight away. Well, we'll leave you to talk it over!'

When the twins and the four heard of this the next morning, they were astounded. Mrs Philpot told the twins first, and Harry and Harriet ran at once to find the others. They listened, amazed and angry.

'How did they know all that? How did they guess where to find the castle site?' said Dick, fiercely. 'I bet it's that snoopy little Junior who put them on to this! I bet he spied on us! I *thought* I saw two people up on that hill after tea yesterday. It must have been Mr Henning and that friend of his – with Junior. Gosh, I could pull that kid's hair out!'

'Well, I suppose there's absolutely nothing we can do now!' said George, angrily. 'The next thing we'll see is lorries rolling up with men inside, and spades and drills and goodness knows what!'

She was quite right! That very morning the hill became quite a busy place! Four men had already been hired by Mr Henning, and they all went up the hill in their lorry, bumping slowly along, past the kitchen-midden mound,

277

and on up to the shallow basin-like depression near the summit of the hill. Spades, forks and drills rattled in the lorry. Junior was mad with joy, and danced about at a safe distance, yelling defiance at the six children.

'You thought I didn't know anything, didn't you! I heard *everything*! Serves you right! Yah!'

'Timmy – chase him!' ordered George, in a furious voice. 'But don't hurt him, mind. Go on!'

And off went Timmy at a gallop, and if Junior hadn't leapt into the lorry and picked up a spade, Timmy would certainly have rolled him over and over on the ground!

Now what was to be done? The children almost gave up – but not quite! There *might* be something they could do – there might! *Why* was Julian suddenly looking so excited?

CHAPTER FOURTEEN

Snippet and Nosey are very helpful

'LISTEN!' SAID JULIAN, lowering his voice, and looking all about to make sure that no one was near. 'Do you remember what you told us, George, about a secret passage from the castle to the old chapel?'

'Yes! Yes! I do!' said George, and Anne nodded, her eyes bright. 'You mean the story that old Mr Finniston told us, down at the little antique shop, about the Lady of the castle taking her children in safety from the burning castle, by way of an underground passage to the old chapel? Gosh, I'd forgotten that!'

'Oh, Julian! Yes, George is right!' said Anne. 'Are you thinking that the passage might still be there, hidden underground?'

'What I think is this,' said Julian. 'If the Lady and her children escaped *underground*, they must first have fled down into the cellars of the castle – and so the passage or tunnel must have *started* from there. They couldn't have escaped in any other way because the castle was itself surrounded by enemies. So she must have gone with her children to hide in the cellars – and then, when the castle fell, she took them safely down the secret passage that led to the old chapel. So *that* means . . .'

'That means that if we can find the secret passage, we can get into the cellars ourselves – perhaps before the workmen do!' cried George, almost shouting with excitement.

'Exactly,' said Julian, his eyes shining. 'Now don't let's lose our heads and get too excited. Let's talk about it quietly – and for GOODNESS sake keep a watch for Junior.'

'Timmy – on guard!' said George, and Timmy at once went some paces away, and stood up straight, looking now in this direction, and now in that. Nobody could come within sight now, without Timmy giving a warning bark!

The children settled down beside a hedge. 'What's the plan?' asked Dick.

'I vote we go to the old chapel, take a line from there to the castle site, and walk slowly up that line,' said Julian. 'We might *possibly* see something that would guide us as to where the secret passage is. I don't know what – maybe the grass might be slightly different in colour – a bit darker than the surrounding grass, just as it was on the castle site. Anyway, it's worth trying. If we *do* see a line of darker grass, or something like that, we'll dig down underground ourselves, hoping the secret passage is underneath!'

'Oh *Ju*! What a wonderful idea!' said Anne. 'Come on, let's go down to the chapel straight away!'

So off they all went, Timmy, Snippet and Nosey the jackdaw too. He loved being with Snippet, though he teased him unmercifully. They arrived quickly at the chapel door and went in. 'I always feel as if there ought to be an organ playing when I'm inside,' said Anne, looking round the stacked sacks of grain.

'Never mind about organs,' said Julian, standing at the open door, and pointing up the hill. 'Now, see, there's the place where the old castle stood – where the men are already at work – and if we take a fairly straight line to it, we *should* be more or less walking over the old passage. I should think the men who made it would drive as straight a tunnel as they could, to save themselves work. A winding one would take a long time.'

'I can't see that the grass is any different in colour, along the line I'm looking,' said Dick, squinting, and everyone agreed, very disappointed.

'So there's nothing to help us!' said George, mournfully. 'All we can do is to work in a straight line up the hill, and hope to find something that will tell us if we're over a tunnel. Hollow-sounding footsteps, perhaps!'

'That's very doubtful, I'm afraid,' said Julian. 'Still, I can't see that we can do anything else. Come on, then. All right, Tim, you can come back to us. Look at Nosey, on Snippet's back again! That's right, Snippet, roll over and get him off.'

'Chack!' said Nosey, crossly, as he flew up in the air. 'Chack!'

The six children walked up the slope in as straight a line as they could. They came right up to where the men were digging, without having seen or heard anything of any help at all. It was most disappointing. Junior saw them, and yelled loudly.

'Children not allowed here! Keep off! My dad's bought this place!'

'Liar!' shouted back the two Harries at once. 'You've got the right to dig and that's all!'

'Yah!' yelled Junior. 'You wait! Now don't you set that great dog on me again! I'll tell my pop, see?'

Timmy barked loudly, and Junior disappeared in a hurry. George laughed. 'Silly little idiot! Why doesn't somebody box his ears? I bet one of the men will before he's many hours older. Look at him trying to use that drill!'

Junior was certainly not at all popular. He made himself a great nuisance, and in the end his father put him roughly into a lorry and told him to stay there. He howled dismally, but as no one paid any attention, he soon stopped!

The six children went slowly back down the gentle slope of the hill, taking a slightly different line, still hopeful. The jackdaw flew down to Harry's shoulder, chacking loudly, bored with all this walking! He suddenly saw Snippet sitting down to scratch his neck, and at once launched himself at him. He knew that the poodle always shut his eyes when he scratched himself, and that that was a very good time to give him a well-placed peck!

But, unfortunately for Nosey, the poodle opened his eyes too soon, and saw the jackdaw just about to perch on him! He snapped at him – and got him by the wing! 'Chack-chack-CHACK!' cried the jackdaw, urgently calling for help. 'CHACK!'

Harry ran to Snippet, shouting, 'Drop him, Snippet, drop him! You'll break his wing!' Before he could reach the pair, the jackdaw managed to free himself by giving Snippet a sudden peck on his nose, which made him bark in pain. As soon as he opened his mouth to bark, the jackdaw dropped on the ground, and scuttled away, his wing drooping, unable to fly.

The poodle was after him in a second! The twins yelled in vain. He meant to catch that exasperating jackdaw if it was the last thing he did! The squawking bird looked anxiously for a hiding place – and saw one! A rabbit hole – just the thing to hop down in a trice! In he went with another loud squawk, and disappeared from sight.

'He's gone down that rabbit hole!' said Dick, with a

shout of laughter. 'Clever old bird. You're outwitted, Snippet!'

But no – Snippet wasn't! He disappeared down the hole too! He was as small as a rabbit, and could easily run down a burrow. He had never done more than sniff at one before, being rather scared of dark tunnels – but if Nosey had gone down, well, he would too!

The children stared in surprise. First the jackdaw – now Snippet! The twins bent down by the hole and yelled. 'Come back, Snippet, you idiot! The hill's honey combed with old warrens – you'll get lost for ever. Come back! Snippet. Snip-Snip-Snippet, can you hear us! COME HERE!'

There was silence down the rabbit-hole. No chack, no bark. 'They must have gone deep down,' said Harry, anxiously. 'There's a perfect maze of burrows in this hill. Dad said there used to be thousands of rabbits here at one time. Hey, Snippet – COME HERE!'

'Well, we'd better sit down till they come back,' said Anne, feeling suddenly tired with excitement and with climbing up hill and down.

'Right,' said Julian. 'Anyone got any sweets?'

'I have,' said George, as usual, and took out a rather grimy packet of peppermints. 'Here you are; have one, twins?'

'Thanks,' they said. 'We really ought to be getting back – we've plenty of work to do!'

They sat sucking their peppermints, wondering what in the world the jackdaw and Snippet were up to. At last Timmy pricked up his ears and gave a small bark, looking at the entrance of the burrow as he did so. 'They're coming,' said George. 'Timmy knows!'

Sure enough, Timmy was right. Out came first Snippet, and then Nosey, apparently quite good friends again.

Snippet rushed to the twins and flung himself on them as if he hadn't seen them for days. He put something down at their feet. 'What's this you've found?' said Harry, picking it up. 'Some dirty old bone?'

Julian suddenly took it from him, almost snatching it. 'Bone? No – that's not a bone. It's a small carved dagger with a broken handle – old as the hills! SNIPPET! Where did you find it?'

'The jackdaw's got something too!' cried Anne, pointing to him. 'Look – in his beak!'

Harriet caught the jackdaw easily, for he still could not fly. 'It's a ring!' she said. 'With a red stone in it – look!'

All six children gazed at the two strange articles. An old carved knife, black with age – and an old ring, with a stone still set in it! They could have come from only one place! George said what everyone was thinking.

'Snippet and the jackdaw have been to the cellars of the castle! They must have! That burrow must have led *straight* into the tunnel that goes to the dungeons and the cellars – and they've been there! Oh, Snippet – you clever, clever dog – you've told us JUST what we want to know!'

'George is right!' said Dick, jubilantly. 'We know quite a lot of things now, because of Snippet and Nosey. We know there must be plenty of things still in those castle cellars – and we know that *some*where near the end of this burrow is the secret passage – because that's the only way they could have got into the cellars – by using the passage! The burrow led into the passage! Don't you agree, Julian?'

'You bet!' said Julian, flushed with excitement. 'My word, this *is* a bit of good luck! Hurray for Snippet and Nosey. Look, the jackdaw's trying to fly, his wing isn't badly hurt – just bruised, I expect. Good old Nosey – little did he know what his bit of mischief would lead to!'

'What happens now?' said George, her eyes shining. 'Do *we* dig, too – now that we know where the passage is? It can't be very far; and once we've got down to it, we can easily get into the cellars – before that American does!'

WHAT an excitement! Timmy really thought everyone had gone completely mad!

CHAPTER FIFTEEN

Digging for the secret tunnel

'How CAN we get permission to dig?' asked Anne. 'I mean
– will we be allowed to?'

'I don't see why not – Mr Henning has only been given
permission to dig in one place,' said Julian. 'I bet we'd get
permission to dig just here – it's a pretty good way from
the castle site, anyway.'

'Why shouldn't we just dig and see if anyone stops
us?' said George. 'If Mr Philpot stops us, we could tell
him what we're *really* doing. He'd probably let us,
then. But whatever happens, we don't want
Mr Henning to know what we've discovered – or *think*
we've discovered!'

'Well, what shall we say then, if he asks why we're
digging?' said Anne.

'Say silly things – joke about it!' said Dick. 'Twins, have
you work to do this morning? Can you find us spades, do
you think?'

'Yes – you can have our spades, and Dad's old ones,
too!' said Harry. 'We wish we could help – but we've tons
to do, and we're very late already.'

'Oh dear – and I promised that George and I would help
in the kitchen!' said Anne. 'And pick peas for dinner and
pod them – and get more raspberries! Can you and Dick
dig all on your own, Ju?'

'Good heavens, yes!' said Julian. 'It'll be slower with
just two of us digging, but we'll soon get deep down, you'll

287

see! Anyway, we could all take turns this afternoon, perhaps, if the twins finish their work.'

'We will! We'll do it at top speed!' said Harry and Harriet together. 'Now we'll get some spades for you.'

They raced off, with Snippet beside them, and the two girls went down the hill more slowly, feeling very thrilled. If only, only they could dig down and find the secret passage from the chapel to the cellars of the old castle! Timmy felt the excitement and wagged his tail happily. He was always happy when George was thrilled about anything.

Harriet soon brought two big spades and two smaller ones to the boys. They were heavy, and she panted as she carried them up the hill.

'Good girl – or is it good boy?' asked Dick, as he took the spades. 'Wait – it's Harriet, isn't it? You've no scar on your hand!'

Harriet grinned and ran off swiftly to join her brother in the farm work that was their task. Julian gazed after her. 'They're good kids,' he said, as he turned to drive his spade into the earth. 'Worth a hundred Juniors! Funny how some children are made of such good stuff, and others aren't worth a penny. Well, Dick – go to it! This earth is pretty hard. I wish we could borrow one of those machines the men are using up there!'

They dug hard, and were soon very hot indeed. They stripped themselves to their shorts, but were still far too hot. They greeted Anne with joy when she laboured up the slope, carrying a jug of cool lemonade and some buns.

'I say! You've made quite a hole already!' she said. 'How far down do you think the tunnel will be?'

'Well, not too far down, really,' said Dick, taking a long drink of the lemonade. 'This is super, Anne. Thanks a lot.

We've dug into the burrow, and we're following it at the moment – hoping it will enter the secret tunnel before we're too tired to dig any more!'

'I say – here comes Junior!' said Anne suddenly, looking up the slope. Sure enough, it was the American boy, feeling quite brave now that neither Timmy nor Snippet was about.

He stopped a little way away and shouted: 'What do you think you're doing, digging in our hill?'

'Go away and lose yourself!' shouted back Dick. 'This isn't your hill! If you can dig, so can we!'

'Copy-cats!' shouted Junior. 'My pop's laughing his head off about you!'

'Well, tell him to pick it up before it rolls down the hill!' yelled Dick. 'Clear off!'

Junior watched them for a little while, puzzled, and then

went off up the hill, presumably to report to his father. Anne laughed and went back to the farmhouse.

'As his pop doesn't know a thing about the secret passage, he must think we're off our heads, digging here,' said Julian, with a chuckle. 'Well, let him think so. He'll be off *his* head with rage when he finds out what we're really doing – and he won't know that till we're in the cellars!'

Dick laughed, and wiped his forehead again. 'I wish this burrow would come to an end. And I hope to goodness it *does* lead into the side of the tunnel. I don't want to have to dig up half the hillside. The ground's so hard and dry.'

'Well, thank goodness it's getting sandy here,' said Julian, driving his spade deeper down. He suddenly gave a cry. 'I say! My spade went right down by itself, then! I believe I've come to the secret passage! The burrow must go right through one side of it!'

He was right! The rabbit hole ran sideways and down – and into a passage! The boys dug feverishly now, panting, their hair falling over their foreheads, perspiration dripping off their faces.

Soon they had a deep hole, fairly wide – and at the bottom of it a way into the tunnel beneath! They lay down and peered into it. 'It's just over a metre below the surface,' said Dick. 'We might have had to do much more digging than this! Whew, I'm hot!'

'It must be dinner-time,' said Julian. 'I don't really like to leave our hole, now that we've got down to the tunnel. And yet we simply MUST have something to eat. I'm ravenous!'

'So am I. But if we leave the hole unguarded, that pest of a Junior might come along and climb down and find the passage!' said Dick. 'Look – here comes George – with old Tim. I wonder if she'd leave him here to guard the hole.'

George was delighted to hear their news. She gazed down the hole in great excitement. 'How deeply you've dug!' she said. 'No wonder you're hot. My word – if Mr Henning knew what you've found, he'd be down here in two shakes of a duck's tail!'

'He certainly would,' said Julian, soberly. 'That's what we're afraid of. Or that snoopy Junior might climb down into the hole, if he came along. He's been here already to see what we're doing.'

'We're scared of going in to dinner, in case one of them comes along and investigates the hole while it's un-guarded,' said Dick. 'And we wondered if . . .'

But George interrupted him, almost as if she knew what he was going to say. 'I'll leave Timmy here on guard, while you come down to dinner,' she said. 'He won't let anyone come within metres of it!'

'Thanks, old thing,' said the boys gratefully, and went off down the hill with George, leaving Timmy behind. 'On guard, Timmy,' said George. 'On guard. Don't let *anyone* come near that hole.'

'Woof,' said Timmy, understanding at once, and look-ing fiercely all round and about him. He lay down with a small growl. Let anyone come near the boys' hole, if they dare!

They did dare – but when they saw Timmy leaping to his feet, the hackles on his neck thick and upright, and heard his deep, continuous growl, Junior and his father thought better of it, and went on down the hill to have dinner at the farmhouse. Poor Mr Durleston trailed behind them, al-most knocked out by the heat of the sun.

'Silly kids,' said Mr Henning to Junior. 'Thinking it's clever to dig just because *we're* digging? What do they suppose they'll find down there? Another kitchen-midden?'

Junior sent a stone scudding along towards Timmy – and then fled for his life as the dog came bounding angrily down the slope. Even Mr Henning hurried. He didn't like Timmy either!

That afternoon the twins, Julian, Dick, George, Anne and Snippet all climbed the hill to the hole, where Tim still lay watching for intruders. They brought him two fine bones, and a jug of water. He was very pleased indeed. Snippet danced round, hoping for a bite at a bone, and the jackdaw, his wing apparently quite recovered now, dared to go and peck at the bigger bone, even though Timmy growled warningly!

The twins were thrilled to see the deep hole. 'Can't we go down now?' they said eagerly, both together.

'Yes – it would be a jolly good time to let ourselves slide into the tunnel,' said Julian. 'All the men working on the castle site have gone off to have dinner at the little village pub, and haven't yet come back – and the Hennings and Mr Durleston are safely at the farmhouse.'

'I'll go first,' said Dick, and lowered himself into the hole. He held on to the grassy edges and poked hard with his feet, to widen the opening into the tunnel. Then he let himself slide down until his legs were out of the rabbit hole, and dangled through the wall of the tunnel.

'Here we go!' he said, and let himself drop. Whooooosh! He slid right into a dark, musty tunnel, and landed on soft earth. 'Chuck me down a torch,' he shouted. 'It's pitch-dark in here. Did you remember to bring our torches, George?'

DIGGING FOR THE SECRET TUNNEL

Yes, George had four! 'Look out!' she said. 'Here comes one!' And she dropped it down the hole. She had already switched it on, so Dick saw it coming and caught it neatly. He shone it into the dark place around him.

'Yes! It *is* a tunnel!' he shouted. 'The secret passage, no doubt about it! I say – isn't this great? Come on down, all of you, let's share in the find together. Let's walk right up to the castle cellars. Come on, everybody! Come on!'

CHAPTER SIXTEEN

Up the tunnel and into the cellars

DICK HELD up his torch to the hole, so that the others might see their way. One by one they slid into the dark tunnel, too excited for words. Timmy came too, and so did Snippet, but the jackdaw thought better of it, and remained at the enlarged opening of the burrow, chacking loudly.

The children swung their torches to and fro. 'That must be the way down to the old chapel,' said Julian, his torch shining down the dark tunnel. No one could stand upright just there except Timmy, for the roof was low. He sniffed suspiciously here and there, and kept close to George.

'Well – come on!' said Julian, his voice shaking a little with excitement. 'We'll go straight up, and see where the passage ends. My word – I can hardly wait to see what's at the top!'

They made their way slowly up the passage. There had been roof-falls here and there, but not enough to matter. Tree roots, withered and twining, sometimes caught their feet. 'Funny!' said Harry, in astonishment. 'There aren't any trees growing on the hillside here – why the roots, then?'

'They may be the remains of the roots of long-ago trees that did once grow on the hill,' said Julian, shining his torch up the passage, hoping against hope that there would be no serious obstacle to their journey. 'Hallo – what's this at my feet? *Two feathers!* Now how in the world did *they* get here!'

It was a puzzle! The children examined them earnestly by the light of their torches. Feathers – looking quite new too – how *did* they get there? Was there any other way into the passage – and had the birds found it?

Dick gave a shout of laughter that made everyone jump. 'We're idiots! They're two of the *jackdaw's* feathers – they must have dropped out of his bitten wing when he went down the burrow and up this passage with Snippet after him!'

'Of *course*! Why on earth didn't I think of that?' said Julian. They went on upwards once more, and then Julian suddenly stopped again. A curious humming noise had come down the dark, low tunnel, a throbbing that seemed to get right inside their heads.

'What's that?' said Anne, in great alarm. 'I don't like it.'

They all stood there, and felt, like Anne, that the noise was indeed inside their heads. They shook them, put their fingers into their ears – but it was no good. The strange throbbing went on and on.

'This is a bit too mysterious for me,' said Anne, scared. 'I don't think I want to go on.'

The noise stopped, and they all felt better at once – but almost immediately it started again. To everyone's surprise, George began to laugh.

'It's all right! It's only those men at work on the castle site. It's their drills we can hear – throbbing through the hillside, and down this passage right into our ears. They must be back from lunch. Cheer up, everybody!'

They all smiled in relief, though Anne's hands were still shaking a little as she held up her torch to shine through the black darkness. 'There's not an awful lot of air here,' she said. 'I hope we soon get into the cellars!'

'They can't be far,' said Julian. 'This tunnel goes in a

pretty straight line, just as we thought it would. Where it curves, it's probable that the men of long ago who made it were forced to burrow round tree roots that blocked their way. Anyway, as we can hear the drills so loudly now, we can't be far from the castle site.'

UP THE TUNNEL AND INTO THE CELLARS

They were nearer than they thought! Julian's torch suddenly shone on the remains of a great door, lying on the ground before him – the door that once shut off the cellars from the passage! The tunnel ceased just there, and the torches shone on a vast underground place, silent, full of shadows.

'We're there!' said Julian, in a whisper that went scurrying round in the darkness and came back as a strange echo that said: 'There-there-there-there-there.'

'That fallen door must have been one made all those years gone by!' said Anne, in awe. She touched a corner of it with her foot, and the wood crumbled into dust with a strange little sigh.

Snippet pushed in front of them and ran into the cellars. He gave a short bark as if to say, 'Come on – don't be afraid. *I've* been here before.'

'Oh, Snippet, be careful!' said Anne, half-afraid that everything would crumble away at the sound of Snippet's pattering feet!

'Let's go on – but carefully,' said Julian. 'Everything will be ready to crumble into dust – unless it's made of metal! It's a marvel that door was preserved like that – it looks good enough – but I'm sure if any of us sneezed it would be gone.'

'Don't make me laugh, please, Ju,' said Dick, stepping carefully round the fallen door. 'Even a laugh might do damage down here!'

Soon they were all in the blackness of the underground cellars. They flashed their torches around. 'What a vast place!' said Julian. 'Can't see any dungeons, though!'

'Thank goodness!' said Harriet and Anne together. They had both dreaded coming across old bones of long-forgotten prisoners!

'Look – there's an archway,' said George, shining her torch to the right. 'A fine, semicircular arch it is, too, made of stone – and there's another, look. They must lead into a main underground chamber, I should think. There's nothing much to see just here, except heaps of dirt. It all smells so musty, too!'

'Well, follow me carefully,' said Julian, and led the way towards the stone archways, his torch shining brightly. They came to one of the beautiful rounded arches and stood there, all four torches shining brightly into a large underground room.

'No cellars here – but just one great underground storeroom,' said Julian. 'The roof was shored up with great beams – see, some of them have fallen. And those stone arches must have borne much of the weight, too. Not one of those has fallen! They must have stood there for centuries – what wonderful workmanship!'

Dick and the twins were more interested in the great mass of jumble scattered about round the walls. It was covered with dust that rose lightly into the air when Timmy brushed against anything. Snippet ran round happily, sniffing everywhere, and sneezing every now and again as the fine dust went up his nose.

'Any treasures, do you think?' whispered Anne, and the echo came back weirdly, whispering too.

'Whispers seem to echo back more than our ordinary voices!' said Julian. 'Hallo – what's this?'

They shone their torches on to the floor where lay what looked like a heap of blackened metal. Julian bent down and then gave a loud exclamation. 'Do you see what this is? A suit of armour! Almost perfect still. Look, though, it must be ages old – and here's another – and another! Were

298

they old ones, thrown out – or spare ones? Look at this helmet – *grand*!'

He kicked it gently with his foot, and it gave out a metallic sound and rolled away a little. 'Would that be valuable now?' asked Harry, anxiously.

'Valuable! Worth its weight in gold, I should think!' said Julian, such excitement in his voice that everyone felt even more thrilled. Harriet called to him urgently.

'Julian – here's a chest of some sort. Quick!'

They went slowly over to where she stood, for they had already learnt that any quick movement raised clouds of fine, choking dust. She pointed to a great dark chest, its corners bound with iron, and with iron strapping all round it.

It was made of wood, as black with age as the iron itself. 'What's inside, do you think?' whispered Harriet, and at once her whisper echoed from every corner: 'You think, you think, you think . . .'

Timmy went to sniff at the chest – and to his amazement it disintegrated at once! Slowly, softly, the sides and the great lid fell into dust that settled gently on the ground around. Only the iron corners and strapping were left. It was strange to watch something crumble away before their eyes. Like magic! thought Anne.

As the wooden sides of the chest crumbled, something shone out brightly in the light of the torches – something that moved and slid out of the chest, as the sides fell away – fell with a jingling, clinking, sound, curious to hear in that silent darkness.

The children stared in astonishment, hardly believing their eyes. Anne clutched Julian and made him jump. 'Ju! What is it? Is it gold?'

299

Julian bent to pick up one of the rolling pieces. 'Yes! It's *gold*. No doubt about it. Gold never tarnishes, it keeps bright for ever. These are gold coins of some sort, treasured and hidden away. There couldn't have been time to take them, when the Lady fled with her children – and no one else would be able to get them, for the castle was burnt down and buried by the falling walls! This hoard of gold must have lain here untouched all these long years.'

'Waiting for *us* to come!' said George. 'Twins – your mother and father needn't worry about their farm any more! With the proceeds from the treasures down here they will be able to buy all the tractors and equipment they could possibly need! Julian, there's another chest, look – like this one, but smaller, and beginning to fall to pieces. Let's see what's inside that! More gold, I hope.'

But the second chest did not hold gold pieces – it held a different kind of treasure! One side had burst open, and its contents had dribbled out.

'Rings!' said Anne, picking up two from the dust in which they lay.

'A golden belt!' said George. 'And look – these tarnished chains must be necklaces, because they're set with blue stones. This must be where the jackdaw found that ring!'

'*We've* found something else, too!' called Harry, his excited voice making everyone jump. 'Look – racks of swords and daggers! Some are beautifully carved, too!'

Clamped to the wall were iron racks, held in place by great iron rods driven deep into the hard earth of the wall. Some had loosened and the racks hung crooked, their knives and swords askew, or lay on the floor. Snippet ran to pick one up – just as he had done before when he and Nosey first went into the cellars by themselves!

'What wonderful swords!' said Julian, picking one up. 'My word, this one's heavy! I can hardly hold it! Good gracious – what's that?'

301

Something had fallen from the roof of the cellar in which they were standing – a great piece of old wood, that had originally been placed there as part of the roofing. At the same time the continual hum of the drilling above rose to a roar that made the children jump.

Julian gave a shout. 'Out of here, quickly!' he yelled. 'Those men will soon be through the roof, and it may suddenly fall and bury us! We'll have to go at once!'

He snatched a dagger from the rack, and, still with the sword in his hand, ran back to the entrance of the secret passage, pulling Anne with him. The twins were last of all, for they had run to get a handful of the gold, and two of the necklaces and rings. They *must* show their mother a few of the treasures, they must!

Just as they reached the entrance, more of the roof fell. 'We'll have to stop this excavating,' panted Julian, looking back. 'If the roof falls in, it may destroy many of the old treasures there!'

They hurried into the dark, low tunnel, feeling more excited than they had ever felt in their lives! Timmy led the way, glad to think they were going out into the open air once more!

'What will Mother say?' the twins kept saying to one another. 'WhatEVER will she say!'

CHAPTER SEVENTEEN

Trapped!

THE SIX children stumbled down the tunnel, still hearing the far-off sound of the drills, and fearing that at any moment the cellars would be discovered by Mr Henning, who, no doubt, would be anxiously watching from above!

They came to where they thought the burrow must be, that Dick had dug through – but instead, there was nothing but a great mass of earth, some of it seeping into the tunnel! Julian gazed at it by the light of his torch, dismayed.

'The burrow's fallen in!' he said, his voice shaking. 'What are we to do?' We've no spades to dig ourselves out!'

'We can use our hands,' said Dick, and began to scrabble at the fallen earth, sweeping it into the tunnel. But as he scrabbled, more and more earth fell into the widened burrow, and Julian stopped Dick at once. 'No more of that, Dick – you might start an earthfall, and we'd all be buried alive. Oh gosh – this is awful! We'll have to go back up the passage and try to make the men hear us shouting. BLOW! That means Mr Henning will know what we're up to.'

'I don't believe the men will be there much longer,' said Dick, looking at his watch. 'They pack up at five, and it's almost that now. My word, we've been ages – Mrs Philpot will wonder where we all are.'

'The drilling has just stopped,' said Anne. 'I haven't got that awful noise inside my ears any longer.'

303

'In that case, it's certainly no good going back up the tunnel,' said Julian. 'They'd be gone before we got there. I say, you know – this is serious. I ought to have thought of this – any idiot knows that ground entrances to passages should be strengthened, if they're newly dug!'

'Well, we can always go back to the cellars and wait for the men to come tomorrow,' said George, sounding more cheerful than she felt.

'How do we know they'll be there tomorrow?' said Dick. 'Henning may have paid them off today, if he's disappointed in his hopes!'

'Don't be such a dismal Jimmy!' said George, sensing that the twins were getting panicky. They certainly *were* worried – but more because they were certain that their mother would be scared to death if they didn't come home, than for their own safety.

Timmy had been standing patiently beside George, waiting to get out of the hole. At last, tired of waiting, he trotted away – but *down* the tunnel – not up!

'Timmy! Where are you going?' cried George, and shone her torch on him. He turned his head and looked at her, showing quite clearly by his manner that he was tired of standing about, and intended to find out where the tunnel led!

'Ju, look at Timmy! He wants us to go *down* the tunnel!' cried George. 'Why didn't we think of that?'

'I don't know! I'm afraid I thought it would be a sort of blind alley!' said Julian. 'I fear it will, too. Nobody knows where the chapel entrance to the tunnel is, do they, twins?'

'No,' they said, both together. 'It's never been discovered, as far as *we* know.'

'Anyway, it's worth trying,' said George, her voice sounding muffled as she went down the passage after the impatient Timmy. 'I'm getting suffocated in here!'

The others followed, Snippet dancing along behind, thinking the whole thing was a huge joke. The tunnel, as the children had imagined, went downwards in more or less a straight line. It had fallen in slightly here and there, but by bending their heads and crouching low, they managed to get through. Finally they came to a bad fall of earth from the roof, and had to crawl through on hands and knees. Anne didn't like that part at all!

They came at last into a strange little place, where the tunnel ended abruptly. It was like a stone vault – a little chamber about one and a half metres high and two metres square. Julian looked up fearfully at its low roof. Was it of stone? If so, they were trapped. They would never be able to lift a heavy stone slab!

No – not all the roof was made of stone. A piece in the middle about a metre square was made of strong stout wood, which rested on ledges cut in the stone.

'It looks like a trap-door,' said Julian, examining it by the light of his torch. 'I wonder if we are just below the floor of the old chapel? Dick, if you and I and Harry all heave at the same time, we might be able to move this trap-door.'

So they all heaved, George, too – but although the door did lift a little at one corner, it simply could *not* be moved upwards.

'I know why we can't move it,' said Harry, red in the face with heaving. 'There are sacks of grain and fertiliser and all kinds of stuff spread over the floor of the old chapel! They're heavy as lead! We'd never be able to move that trap-door if two or three sacks are on it!'

'Gosh – I didn't think of that,' said Julian, his heart sinking. 'Didn't you know of this entrance into the tunnel, twins?'

'Of course not!' said Harry. 'Nobody did. I can't think

why it wasn't known, though. Except, of course, that a storehouse like this has its floor always covered with sacks of something, and with the spillings out of those sacks! It may not have been cleaned out or swept for hundreds of years!'

'Well, what are we to do now?' demanded Dick. 'We can't stay here in this stuffy little place!'

'Listen – I can hear something!' said George suddenly. 'Noises overhead.'

They listened intently, and, through the tightly fitting oak trap-door above them, they heard a loud voice shouting. 'GIVE US A HAND, BILL WILL YOU?'

'It's Jamie – the men are working overtime this week!' said Harry. 'He's come to get something out of the chapel. Quick, let's all yell and hammer on the trap-door with whatever we've got that'll make a noise!'

At once there was a riot of sound from the little vault – yells, shouts, barks, and the hammering of sword handles and fists on the wooden slab overhead. Then the children ceased their hammering, and fell silent, listening. They heard Jamie's voice, lifted in wonder.

'Bill! What in the name of goodness was that? A rat-fight, do you suppose?'

'They heard us,' said Julian, excited. 'Come on – once again. And bark the place down, Timmy!'

Timmy was only too ready to oblige, for he was very tired of tunnels and dark, echoing places by now! He barked long and fiercely, frightening Snippet so much that the little poodle actually ran back up the tunnel! What with Tim's barking, and everyone's yelling, and the constant hammering, the noise was even louder than before, and Bill and Jamie listened in amazement.

307

'Comes from over there,' said Bill. 'Something's going on there. Beats me what it is though. If it were night-time, I'd think it were ghosties having a game! Come on – we'll have a look.'

The place was so full of sacks that the two men had to clamber over the rows, disturbing the cat and her kittens. She had curled herself round them, scared of the unexpected noise.

'This corner, Bill,' said Jamie, standing on top of two layers of sacks. He put his hands to his mouth and bellowed like a bull.

'ANYONE ABOUT?'

The six below answered frantically at the tops of their voices, Timmy barking too.

'There's a dog barking down there,' said Bill, scratching his head, puzzled, looking down at the sacks as if he thought there might be a dog in one of them.

'A dog! There're folks as well,' said Jamie, astounded. 'Where are they? Can't be under these sacks!'

'Maybe they're in that little old store place we found one day, in the floor,' suggested Bill. 'Remember? Under an old trap-door, it were, that were covered by a great slab of stone. You remember, man!'

'Oh ay,' said Jamie, and then the clamour began again, for the children were now getting near despair. 'Come on, Bill,' said Jamie, hearing the note of urgency, though he couldn't make out a word from below. 'Heave over these here sacks. We've got to get to the bottom of this!'

They heaved a dozen sacks away, and then at last the trap-door was uncovered. The stone slab that had once hidden it had been taken up some years ago by the two men and now stood against the wall. They had not bothered to replace it, not guessing that the 'little old store place' as they had thought it, was really an entrance to a secret, long-forgotten passage. It was fortunate indeed for the children that only the old wooden trap-door was between them and the men, for if the stone slab had been there too, no sound of their shouting would have been heard in the old chapel above!

'Now for this here trap-door,' said Bill. He tapped on it with his great boot. 'Who's down here?' he demanded, wondering what the answer would be.

'US!' shrieked the twins, and the others joined in, with Timmy barking frantically again.

'Bless us all – that's the twins' voices I heard!' said Jamie. 'How did they climb into the storeroom without moving these here sacks?'

With a great heave the two men pulled up the heavy wooden slab, and looked down in the greatest astonishment at the little crowd below! They couldn't believe their eyes! Timmy was the first out. He leapt upwards and landed beside the men, wagging his great tail and licking them lavishly.

'Oh, thanks, Bill, thanks, Jamie,' cried the twins as the two men pulled them up. 'Gosh, I'm thankful you were working overtime – and happened to come in here!'

'Your ma's been hollering for you,' said Bill, disapprovingly. 'And didn't you say you were going to help me with those poles?'

'How did you get down there?' demanded Jamie, pulling up the others one by one. Julian was the last, and he handed up poor scared little Snippet, who really felt he had had quite enough adventures for one day!

'Oh – it's too long a story to tell you just now,' said Harry. 'But thanks again most awfully, Bill and Jamie. Can you put that slab back? Don't tell anyone we were down there till we tell you how it happened, see? Now we'll have to rush and tell Mother we're all right!'

And away they all went, longing for tea, tired out, full of thankfulness at their escape from the little stone room under the chapel floor. What *would* everyone say when they displayed the treasures they had brought back with them?

CHAPTER EIGHTEEN

A great story to tell!

THE TWINS tore down to the farmhouse, and saw their mother still looking for them. They flung themselves on her, and she gave them a loving shake.

'Where have you been? You're an hour late for tea, all of you. I've been so worried. Mr Henning told me some story about you digging up on the hillside!'

'Mother! We're ravenous, so let's have tea and we'll tell you some great news,' said the twins, both together. 'Mother, you *will* be astonished. Where's Dad – and Great-Grandad too?'

'They're still at the tea-table – they were late too,' said Mrs Philpot. 'They've been out looking for you all! Great-Grandad isn't very pleased. What in the world have you brought with you? Surely those are not *swords*?'

'Mother, let's have tea first and we'll tell you EVERY-THING!' said the twins. '*Must* we wash? Oh blow – all right, come on, everyone, let's wash. And we'll put our treasures down in the darkest corner, so that Dad and Great-Grandad won't see them till we're ready to show them!'

Soon they were all sitting down at the tea-table, glad to see a wonderful spread! Great slices of thickly buttered bread, home-made jam, home-made cheese, a fat ginger cake, a fruit cake, a dish of ripe plums, and even a home-cooked ham if anyone wanted something more substantial!

Mr Philpot and old Great-Grandad were still at the table, drinking a last cup of tea. Mrs Philpot had told them that the children had to wash, but would tell all that had happened when they came to their tea.

'Hoo!' said Great-Grandad, frowning till his great bushy eyebrows almost covered his nose. 'When I was a boy I daren't come in one minute late for my meals! You twins have worried your mother – that's bad!'

'We're awfully sorry, Great-Grandad,' said the twins, in unison. 'But just wait till you hear our story. Julian – you tell it!'

And so, between great munches of bread and butter, ham sandwiches, and slices of cake, the story was told, all the children joining in now and again.

Great-Grandad already knew that Mr Henning had been given permission to excavate, and that a cheque for £5,000 had been given to Mr Philpot. He had flown into a terrible temper, and only when Mrs Philpot had sobbed and said that she would give it back, though she could hardly bear to part with it, had Great-Grandad given in. Now ready to fly into another rage, he listened to the children's story. He forgot to drink his cooling tea. He forgot to fill his pipe. He even forgot to ask a single question! Never had he heard such a wonderful, glorious tale in his life!

Julian told the story well, and the others filled in any bits he left out. Mrs Philpot's eyes almost fell out of her head when she heard how Snippet and Nosey had gone into the rabbit burrow and come out with a broken dagger and a ring!

'But – but where did . . .' she began, and listened again, to hear how Dick and Julian had enlarged the burrow, crawled right through it, and slid down into the long-lost secret tunnel!

'HA!' said Great-Grandad, getting out his great red handkerchief, and dabbing his forehead with it. 'HA! Wish I'd been there. Go on, go on!'

Julian had stopped to drink his tea. He laughed and went on, describing how they had all gone up the tunnel with their torches, the dogs with them.

'It was dark and smelly, and suddenly we heard a terrific noise!' he said.

'It got right inside our heads!' put in Anne.

'What was it, what was it?' said Great-Grandad, his eyes almost as big as the saucer in front of him.

'The noise of the men drilling up on the old castle site,' said Julian, and Great-Grandad exploded in wrath. He pointed his pipe at his grandson, the farmer. 'Didn't I tell you I wouldn't have those men on my farm?' he began, and then calmed down as Mrs Philpot patted his arm, shushing him. 'Go on, Julian,' she said.

And then came the really exciting part, the story of how they came into the actual cellars of the castle – the stone archways – the age-old dust . . .

'And the echoes!' said Anne. 'When we whispered, a hundred other whispers came back!'

When Julian described their finds – the old armour, still good, but black with age – the rack of swords and knives and daggers – the chest of gold . . .

'GOLD! I don't believe you!' shouted Great-Grandad. 'You're making that up, young man. Don't you pile up your tale too much, now. Stick to the truth.'

The twins promptly took some of the gold coins out of their pockets, still brilliant and shining. They laid them on the table in front of the three amazed grown-ups.

313

'There you are! *They* will tell you if we are making up all this or not – these gold coins! They will speak more loudly than words!'

In awe Mr Philpot picked them up, and passed them one by one to the old man, and to his wife. Great-Grandad was dumbfounded and dumbstruck. He simply could not say a single word. He could only grunt and puff as he turned the coins over in his great horny hand.

'Are they really gold?' said Mrs Philpot, quite overcome at the sudden appearance of the shining coins. 'Trevor – will they belong to *us*? Does it mean – does it mean that we'll be well enough off to buy a new tractor for you – and . . .'

'Depends how much of this stuff there is, up in those old cellars,' said Mr Philpot, trying to keep calm. 'And depends on how much we're allowed to keep, of course. Might belong to the Crown by now.'

'THE CROWN!' roared Great-Grandad, standing up sud-

denly. 'The CROWN!' No, SIR! It's mine! Ours! Found on
my land, put there by our ancestors. Yes – and I'll give old
Mr Finniston down in the village a share, so I will. He's
been a good friend of mine for years!'

The children thought that was quite a good idea! They
then showed the jewellery they had brought, and
Mrs Philpot marvelled at it, tarnished though it was.

But the swords and dagger brought the greatest excitement to old Great-Grandad and his grandson, Mr Philpot!
As soon as they heard that the children had actually
brought back some of the old weapons, the two men
got up and went to get them. Great-Grandad picked up
the biggest and heaviest of the swords, and swung it
dangerously round his head, looking like a reincarnation
of some fearsome old warrior, with his great beard and
blazing eyes.

'No, no Grandad!' said Mrs Philpot in fright. 'Oh,
you'll knock down the things on the dresser – there, I
knew you would! Bang goes my meat dish!'

And down it went, CRASH! Timmy and Snippet almost
jumped out of their skins, and began to bark frantically.

'Sit DOWN, all of you!' cried Mrs Philpot to the excited
dogs and the men. 'Let Julian finish his story! Great-
Grandad, SIT DOWN!'

'Ha,' said Great-Grandad, a broad smile on his face,
sitting down in his chair. 'HA! Did me good to swing that
sword. Where's that American? I might try it out on him!'

The children roared with delight. It was great to see the
old man so delighted. 'Go on with that tale of yours,' he
said to Julian. 'You tell it well, boy. Go on! Now, Ma,
don't you take my sword away. I'm keeping it here,
between my legs, in case I want to use it. HA!'

Julian quickly finished his tale, and told how they had walked back down the passage and found their burrow entrance fallen in – and then gone right down the rest of the tunnel and come at last into the little stone-walled room.

'And we couldn't get out,' said Julian. 'There was a great wooden trap-door over our heads, and on it lay a dozen or so sacks – heavy as lead! We couldn't lift it. So we yelled!'

'So *that's* where the secret passage led to!' said Mr Philpot. 'How did you get out?'

'We yelled and hammered, and Bill and Jamie heard us, and pulled off the sacks, and lifted up the old trapdoor,' said Julian. 'Gosh, we were glad to see them! We thought we might be lost for ever! Jamie knew about the little stone vault down under the chapel floor – but he thought it was just an old storeroom!'

'I've never heard of it before,' said Mrs Philpot, and old Great-Grandad nodded his head in agreement.

'No more have I,' he said. 'For as long as I can remember the floor of that old chapel has been piled with sacks, and what bits I could see of the floor were covered with thick dust. Yes, even when I was a boy, playing hide and seek in the old place, it was full of sacks – and that's every bit of eighty-five years ago now! Well, well – seems like yesterday I was playing in there with a cat and her kittens!'

'There's a cat and her kittens there now,' said Anne.

'Ay, little lass – and there'll be a cat and her kittens there when you're an old, old woman!' said Great-Grandad. 'There's some things never change, thanks be to the Lord. Well, well – I can sleep easy of a night now – I reckon you and the farm will be all right Trevor, with the money you'll make out of those old finds – and I'll live to see the twins growing up and handling the finest farm in Dorset, so I shall – with everything newfangled they want, bless their bonny faces! And now I'll just have one more swing with that sword!'

The children fled! Great-Grandad looked years younger already – and goodness knows *what* damage he would do with that great sword! What an afternoon it had been – one they would never forget!

CHAPTER NINETEEN

'The most exciting adventure we've ever had!'

AFTER ALL the excitement of the afternoon the children felt lazy. The twins went off to feed the chickens. 'Better late than never!' they said, together.

'Where are Mr Henning and Mr Durleston and that awful Junior, Mrs Philpot?' asked George, getting up to help with the washing of the tea things.

'Oh, Mr Henning came in to say he and Mr Durleston were going to a meal at a hotel, and taking Junior too,' said Mrs Philpot. 'He seemed very pleased with himself indeed. He said that they had broken through to the cellars of the old castle, and expected great things – and that maybe a second cheque of £5,000 would be coming soon!'

'You won't take it, though, will you, Mrs Philpot?' said Julian quickly, overhearing what was being said. 'The things down in that cellar will be worth much more than any money Mr Henning is likely to offer you. He'd only take them to America and sell them for vast sums and make a huge profit. Why should you let him do that?'

'That nice old man, Mr Finniston, down in the little antique shop, would know what everything was worth,' said George. 'And he's a descendant of the long-ago Finnistons of Finniston Castle, isn't he – he'll be thrilled to bits when he hears what's been happening!'

'We'll send word for him to come up tomorrow,' decided Mrs Philpot. 'After all, Mr Henning has *his* adviser – that surly Mr Durleston. We'll have Mr Finniston for ours. Great-Grandad would be pleased about that – they're great friends, those two.'

There was however, no need to send for Mr Finniston, for Great-Grandad had himself gone down straight away to tell the great news to his old crony. What a talk they had together!

'Gold coins – jewellery – suits of armour – swords – and goodness knows what else!' said Great-Grandad for the twentieth time, and old Mr Finniston listened gravely, nodding his head. 'That splendid big sword!' went on Grandad, remembering. 'Just right for me, William! Look, if ever I've lived before, that old sword once belonged to me! I feel it! That's one thing I won't sell, mind! I'll keep it just for the sake of swinging it round my head, when I lose my temper!'

'Yes, yes – but I hope you'll be sure to stand in the

middle of an empty room if you do that,' said
Mr Finniston, a little alarmed at the fierce look in the
old man's eye. 'You won't be allowed to keep all the gold,
I'm afraid – there's such a thing as treasure trove, you
know – some finds go to the Crown, and I fear that will be
one of them. And the jewellery too perhaps. But you'll get
the value back; and the suits of armour and the swords –
you'll be able to make a mint of money on those!'

'Enough for *two* new tractors?' said Great-Grandad.
'Enough for a new Land Rover? That one my grandson
has, it jolts every bone in my body! Look now, William –
we've got to get men digging on that site – uncovering all
those cellars. What say we keep on the men that fellow
Henning's got? We shan't let *him* excavicate, or whatever
it's called, any more. HA! That fellow gets under my skin,
and sets me itching all over. Now I can scratch him out!
And see here, William, you'll shut up this shop of yours
and be my adviser, won't you? I won't have that American
talking me down – or that fellow Durleston!'

'*You'd* better stop talking for a bit, Grandad, you're
getting too red in the face,' said Mr Finniston. 'You'll go
pop if you excite yourself much more! Go home now, and
I'll be up tomorrow morning. I'll arrange about the workmen too. And don't you play about with that old sword
too much – you might cut off somebody's head by mistake!'

'So I might, so I might,' said Great-Grandad, with a sly
look in his eye. 'Now, if that Junior got in the way when I
was swinging my sword . . . it's all right, William, it's all
right! Just my joke, you know, just my joke!'

And chuckling deep down in his long beard, Great-
Grandad strode off, turned up the little lane, and walked

back to the farmhouse, feeling very pleased indeed with life!

Mr Henning, Mr Durleston and Junior did not come back that night. Apparently they were all so excited over the excavations they had made in the drilling down through the cellar roof, that they stayed too long at the hotel and decided to spend the night there, much to Mrs Philpot's relief.

'Most farm people like to go to bed about nine o'clock,' said Mr Henning, 'and it's already gone that now. We'll go over tomorrow morning and we'll get them to sign that agreement you've drawn up, Durleston. They're so short of money they'd sign anything. And mind you cry down what we think we've found, so that they won't expect any *more* than £5,000. We're going to make our fortunes over this!'

So, next morning, the two men, with an excited Junior whom Mr Durleston found most annoying, arrived at the farmhouse at about ten o'clock. They had telephoned to say they would be there then, and would bring the agreement with them, '. . . and the cheque, Mrs Philpot, the cheque!' purred Mr Henning down the phone.

When they arrived there was quite a company there to greet them! There was old Great-Grandad, his grandson Mr Philpot and his wife, the twins, of course, and old Mr Finniston, sniffing a fight, his dull eyes bright this morning for the first time in years! He sat at the back, wondering what was going to happen.

All the Five were there too, Timmy wondering what the excitement was. He kept as close to George as he could, and growled at Snippet every time the excited little poodle came near. Snippet didn't mind! He could always growl back!

A car purred up the drive, and in came Mr Henning, Mr Durleston and Junior, whose face was one big grin.

'Hallo, folks!' said Junior, in his usual jaunty manner. 'How's tricks?'

Nobody answered except Timmy, and he gave a small growl, which made Junior skip out of the way quickly. 'You shut up,' he said to Timmy.

'Did you have your breakfast in bed at the hotel, little boy?' said George suddenly. 'Do you remember the last time you had it in bed here, and Timmy pulled . . .'

'Aw shucks!' said Junior, sulkily. 'Skip it, sister!' He subsided after that, and sat down by his father. Then began a short, sharp and satisfactory meeting – from Mr Philpot's point of view!

'Er – Mr Philpot – it's my very great pleasure to say that I have been advised by Mr Durleston to offer you a further cheque for £5,000,' said Mr Henning smoothly. 'While we are rather *disappointed* in what appears to be in the cellars of the castle, we feel it would only be fair to offer you the sum we suggested before. Is that right, Mr Durleston?'

'Absolutely,' said Mr Durleston in a business-like voice, and glared round through his horn-rimmed glasses. 'I've the agreement here. Mr Henning is being very generous. Very. The cellars are *most* disappointing.'

'I'm sorry about that,' said Mr Philpot. 'I hold a different opinion – and my adviser, Mr Finniston, upholds me in this. We are going to excavate the site ourselves, Mr Henning – and then, if any disappointment lies in wait, *we* shall be the ones to suffer, not you.'

'What's all this?' said Mr Henning, glaring round. 'Durleston, what do you say to that? Bit of double-crossing, isn't it?'

322

'Offer him £10,000,' said Mr Durleston, looking startled at this unexpected set-back.

'You can offer me a hundred thousand if you like, but I tell you, I prefer to do the excavation myself on my own land,' said Mr Philpot. 'What is more, I will return the cheque you gave me yesterday – and as I intend to keep on the men you engaged, I will pay them myself for their work. So do not trouble to dismiss them. They will now be working for *me*.'

'But this is MONSTROUS!' shouted Mr Henning, losing his temper, and jumping to his feet. He banged on the table, and glared at Mr and Mrs Philpot. 'What do you expect to find in those derelict old cellars? We drilled right through yesterday, and there's practically *nothing* there! I made you a very generous offer. I'll raise it to £10,000!'

'No,' said Mr Philpot, quietly. But Great-Grandad had had enough of Mr Henning's shouting and raging. He stood up too, and bellowed so loudly that everyone jumped, and Timmy began to bark. Snippet at once fled to the kitchen cupboard and hid there.

'HA! NOW YOU LISTEN TO ME!' bellowed Great-Grandad. 'This farm belongs to ME, and my GRANDSON, and it'll go to my GREAT GRANDSON, sitting yonder. A finer farm there never was, and my family's had it for hundreds of years – and sad it's been for me to see it go downhill for lack of money! But now I see money, much money – down in those cellars! HA! All the money we want for tractors and bailers and combines and the Lord knows what! We don't want *your* money. No, SIR! You keep your dollars, you keep them. Offer me a *hundred* thousand if you like, and see what I'll say!'

Mr Henning turned swiftly and looked at Mr Durleston,

who at once nodded. 'Right!' said the American to Great-Grandad. 'A hundred thousand! Done?'

'NO!' bawled Great-Grandad, enjoying himself more than he had done for years. 'There's *gold* down in those cellars – jewels – suits of armour – swords, daggers, knives – all of them centuries old . . . and . . .'

324

'Don't hand *me* stories like that,' said Mr Henning, sneeringly. 'You old liar!'

Great-Grandad banged his clenched fist down on the table and made everyone almost fall off their chairs. 'TWINS!' he roared. 'Fetch those things you got yesterday – go on, fetch them here. I'll show this American I'm no liar!'

And then, before the astounded eyes of Mr Henning and Mr Durleston, and of Junior, too, the twins laid the gold coins, the jewellery, and the swords and knives on the table. Mr Durleston stared as if he couldn't believe his eyes.

'Well – what do you say to *that*?' demanded Great-Grandad, banging on the table again.

Mr Durleston sat back and said one word. 'Junk!'

Then it was old Mr Finniston's turn to stand up and say a few words! Mr Durleston, who hadn't noticed the quiet old man sitting at the back, was horrified to see him there. He knew he was learned and knowledgeable, for he himself had tried to pick his brains about the old castle site.

'Ladies and gentlemen,' said Mr Finniston, just as if he were addressing a well-conducted meeting, 'I regret to say that, speaking as well-known antiquarian, I do not consider that Mr Durleston knows what he is talking about if he calls these articles junk! The things on the table are worth a small fortune to any genuine collector. I could myself sell them in London tomorrow, for far more than any sum Mr Durleston has advised Mr Henning to offer. Thank you, ladies and gentlemen!'

And he sat down, bowing courteously to the assembled company. Anne felt as if she wanted to clap him!

'Well, I don't think there's any more to say,' said Mr Philpot, getting up. 'If you'll tell me what hotel you'll be staying at, Mr Henning, I'll have your things sent there. You will certainly not wish to stay here any longer!'

'Pop, I don't *wanna* go, I wanna stay here!' howled Junior, most surprisingly. 'I wanna see the cellars exca-exculpated! I wanna dig down! I wanna STAY!'

'Well, we don't *want* you!' said Harry, fiercely. 'You and your peeping and prying and listening and boasting and tale-bearing. Cissy-boy! Breakfast in bed! Can't clean his shoes! Howls when he can't get his own way! Screams when . . .'

'That's enough, Harry,' said his mother sternly, looking quite shocked. 'I don't mind Junior staying on if he'll behave himself. It's not his fault that all this has happened.'

'I wanna *stay*!' wept Junior, and kicked out peevishly under the table. He unfortunately caught Timmy on the nose, and the dog rose in anger, growling and showing his teeth. Junior fled for his life.

'Do you *wanna* stay now?' shouted George, as he went, and the answer came back at once.

'NO!'

'Well, thanks, Timmy, for helping him to make up his mind,' said George, and patted the big dog.

Mr Henning looked as if he were about to burst. 'If that dog bites my boy, I'll have him put to sleep,' he said. 'I'll sue you, I'll . . .'

'Please go,' said Mrs Philpot, suddenly looking tired out. 'I have a lot of baking to do.'

'I shall take my time,' said Mr Henning, pompously. 'I will *not* be turned out suddenly, as if I hadn't paid my bills.'

'Seen this sword, Henning?' said old Great-Grandad, suddenly, and snatched from the table the big sword that he so much liked. 'Beauty, isn't it? The men of old knew how to deal with their enemies, didn't they? They swung at them like this – and like THAT – and . . .'

'Here, stop! You're dangerous! That sword nearly cut me!' cried Mr Henning, in a sudden panic. 'WILL you put it down?'

'No. It's mine. I'm not selling this,' said Great-Grandad, swinging the sword again. It hit the light-bulb above his head, and the glass fell with a clatter. Mr Durleston deserted Mr Henning and fled out of the kitchen at top speed, colliding violently with Bill, who was just coming in.

'Look out – he's mad – that old man's mad!' shouted Mr Durleston. 'Henning, come along before he cuts off your head!'

Mr Henning fled too. Great-Grandad pursued him to the door, breathing blood and thunder, and the two dogs barked in delight. Everyone began to laugh helplessly.

'Grandad – what's got into you?' said Mr Philpot, as the old fellow swung the sword again, his eyes bright, a broad grin on his wrinkled old face.

'Nothing! I just thought that only this sword would get rid of those fellows. Do you know what *I* call them? JUNK! Ha – wish I'd thought of that when they were here! JUNK! William Finniston, did you hear that?'

'Now you put that sword down before you damage it,' said Mr Finniston, who knew how to manage Great-Grandad, 'and you and I will go down to the old inn and talk over what we're going to do about all this treasure trove. You just put that sword down first –

NO, Grandad, I am NOT going to take you into the inn carrying that sword!'

Mrs Philpot heaved a sigh of relief when the two old fellows went off down the lane, leaving the sword safely behind. She sat down, and, to the children's horror, began to cry!

'Now, now – don't take any notice of me!' she said, when the twins ran to her in dismay. 'I'm crying for joy – to have got rid of them – and to know I've not got to pinch and scrape any more – or to take in visitors. To think that your dad can buy the farm machinery he wants – and . . . oh dear, what a baby I am, acting like this!'

'I say, Mrs Philpot – would you like *us* to leave too?' asked Anne, suddenly realising that she and the others were ranked as 'visitors', and must have been an added burden for poor Mrs Philpot.

'Oh no, my dear, no – you're not really visitors, you're *friends*!' said Mrs Philpot, smiling through her tears. 'And what's more I shan't charge your mothers a single penny for having you here – see what good fortune you've brought us!'

'All right – we'll stay. We'd love to,' said Anne. 'We wouldn't miss seeing what else is down in those castle cellars for anything. Would we, George?'

'Gosh, no!' said George. 'We want to be in on everything. This is just about the most exciting adventure we've ever had!'

'We always say that!' said Anne. 'But the nice part about this one is – it isn't finished yet! We'll be able to go and watch the workmen and their drills. We'll be able to help in moving all the exciting old things out of their hiding places – we'll hear what prices you get for them –

and see the new tractor! Honestly, I really do believe the *second* part of this adventure will be better than the first! Don't you think so, Timmy?'

'WOOF!' said Timmy, and wagged his tail so hard that he knocked Snippet right over.

Well, goodbye, Five! Enjoy the rest of your adventures, and have a good time – and DO make sure that Grandad is careful with that great old sword!

FIVE ARE TOGETHER AGAIN

CONTENTS

CHAPTER ONE

Back for the holidays

'GEORGE, CAN'T you sit still for even a minute!' said Julian. 'It's bad enough to have the train rocking about all over the place, without you falling over my feet all the time, going to look out of first one window and then the other.'

'Well, we're nearly at Kirrin – almost home!' said George. 'I can't *help* feeling excited. I've missed old Timmy so *much* this term, and I just can't *wait* to see him! I love to look out of the window and see how much nearer we are to Kirrin. Do you think Timmy will be on the station to meet us, barking madly?'

'Don't be an idiot,' said Dick. 'He's a clever dog, but not clever enough to read railway timetables.'

'He doesn't need to,' said George. 'He *always* knows when I'm coming home.'

'I really believe he does,' said Anne, seriously. 'Your mother always says how excited he is on the day you are arriving home from school – can't keep still – keeps going to the front gate and looking down the road.'

'Dear, dear Timmy!' said George, falling over Julian's feet again, as she scrambled once more to the window. 'We're nearly there. Look, there's the signal-box, and the signal is down. HURRAH!'

Her three cousins looked at her in amusement. George was always like this on the way home from school. Her thoughts were full of very little else but her beloved Timmy all the way home. Julian thought how much she looked like a restless boy just then, with her short, curly hair, and her determined expression. George had always longed to be a boy, but as she wasn't, she made up for it by trying to speak and act like one, and would never answer to her full name of Georgina.

'We're coming into Kirrin station!' yelled George, almost falling out of the window. 'I can see Peter, the guard. Hey, we're back again. WE'RE BACK AGAIN!'

The train slid into Kirrin station, and Peter waved and grinned. He had known George since she was a baby. George opened the door and leapt out of the carriage.

'Home again! Back at Kirrin! Oh, I do hope Timmy will be at the station!' she said.

But there was no Timmy there. 'He must have forgotten you were coming,' said Dick, with a grin, and at once got a scowl from George. Peter came up, smiling all over his face, and gave them his usual welcome. Everyone in Kirrin village knew the Five – which, of course, included Timmy the dog.

Peter helped the children with their luggage, and wheeled it down the platform on his trolley. 'Had a good term?' he asked.

'Fantastic!' said Dick. 'But it seemed very long, as Easter is so late this year. Gosh – look at the primroses on the railway banks.'

But George had no eyes for anything just then. She was still looking out for Timmy. Where was he? WHY hadn't he come to the station to meet them? He came last time and the time before! She turned a troubled face to Dick.

'Do you think he's ill? she asked. 'Or has he forgotten me? Or . . .?'

'Oh, don't be silly, George,' said Dick. 'He is probably

336

in the house somewhere and can't get out. Look out – the trolley nearly ran you over then.'

George skipped out of the way, glaring. WHERE was Timmy? She was sure he was ill – or had had an accident – or was tied up and couldn't get away. Perhaps Joanna, who helped her mother in the house, had forgotten to let him loose.

'I'm going to take a taxi home, if I've enough money,' she said, taking out her purse. 'You others can walk. I must see if anything's happened to Timmy – he's *never* missed meeting our train before.'

'But George, it's such a lovely walk to Kirrin Cottage!' said Anne. 'You know how you love to see your island – dear old Kirrin Island – as we walk to your mother's house – and the bay – and hear the waves crashing on the rocks.'

'I'm taking the station taxi,' said George, obstinately, counting the money in her purse. 'If you'd like to come with me, you can. It's Timmy I want to see, not islands and waves and things! I'm SURE he's ill or has had an accident or something!'

'All right, George, do as you please,' said Julian. 'Hope you find dear old Timmy is perfectly well – and has only forgotten the time of the train. See you later.'

The two brothers and their sister Anne set off together, looking forward to the walk to Kirrin Cottage. How lovely to see Kirrin Bay again, and George's island!

'Isn't she lucky to have a real island of her very own!' said Anne. 'Fancy it belonging to her family for years and years – and then one day her mother suddenly gives it to George! I bet she worried and worried dear Aunt Fanny until she gave in to old George. I do so hope Timmy is all right; we shan't enjoy our holidays with George's mother if there's anything wrong with Timmy.'

'Oh, George will probably go and live in Timmy's kennel with him,' said Dick, with a chuckle. 'Ha – look! The sea – and Kirrin Bay – AND the little old island as lovely as ever!'

'With its gulls circling round, and mewing like cats,' said Julian. 'And the old ruined castle there, just exactly the same as usual. Not a single stone fallen out of it, as far as I can see.'

'You can't *possibly* see that at this distance,' said Anne, screwing up her eyes. 'Oh, isn't the first day of the hols heavenly? We seem to have all the time in the world in front of us!'

'Yes. But, after a few days, the holidays *rush* by,' said Julian. 'I wonder if George is home by now.'

'Well, her taxi passed us going at a tremendous pace!' said Dick. 'I bet old George was shouting at the driver to go as fast as possible!'

'Look – there's Kirrin Cottage – I can just see the chimneys in the distance,' said Dick. 'Smoke is coming from one of them.'

'Funny – why only one?' said Julian. 'They usually have the kitchen fire going, and a fire in Uncle Quentin's study. He's such a cold mortal when he's working out all his wonderful figures for his inventions.'

'Perhaps he's away,' said Anne, hopefully. She was rather afraid of George's hasty-tempered father. 'I should think Uncle Quentin could do with a holiday at times – he's always buried in rows and rows of figures.'

'Well, let's hope we don't disturb him too much,' said Julian. 'It's hard on Aunt Fanny if he keeps yelling at everyone. We'll try and be out of doors most of the time.'

They were nearly at Kirrin Cottage now. As they came near to the front gate, they saw George come running down the garden path. To Julian's horror, she was crying bitterly.

'I say – it does look as if something has happened to old Timmy,' he said. 'It's not like George to cry – she *never* cries! What *can* have happened?'

In great alarm they began to run, and Anne shouted as she ran, 'George! George, what's the matter? Is something wrong with Timmy? What's happened?'

'We can't stay at home,' wept George. 'We've got to go away somewhere. Something awful's happened!'

'What is it? Tell us, you idiot!' said Dick, in alarm. 'For goodness' sake, what's happened? Is Timmy run over, or something?'

'No – it isn't Timmy,' said George, wiping her eyes with her hand, because, as usual, she had no handkerchief. 'It's Joanna – Joanna, our dear, darling Joanna!'

'What's the matter with her?' asked Julian, thinking of all kinds of dreadful things. 'GEORGE, will you please TELL US!'

'Joanna's got scarlet fever,' said George, sniffing dolefully. 'So we can't be at Kirrin Cottage.'

'Why not?' demanded Dick. 'Joanna will have to go to hospital – and we can all stay at Kirrin Cottage and help your mother. Poor old Joanna! But cheer up, George, scarlet fever isn't much of a thing to have nowadays. Come on – let's go in and see if we can comfort your mother. Poor old Aunt Fanny, she *will* be in a stew – with all of us four cousins at Kirrin Cottage too! Never mind, we can . . .'

'Stop jabbering, Dick,' said George, exasperated. 'We *can't* stay at Kirrin Cottage. Mother wouldn't even let me go in at the front door! She shooed me away, and said I was to wait in the garden, the doctor was coming in a minute or two.'

Someone called to them from a window of Kirrin Cottage. 'Are you all there, children? Julian, come here, will you?'

They all went into the garden, and saw their Aunt Fanny, George's mother, leaning out of a bedroom window.

'Listen, dears,' she said. 'Joanna has scarlet fever, and is waiting for an ambulance to take her to the hospital, and . . .'

'Aunt Fanny – don't worry. We'll all turn to and help,' called back Julian, cheerfully.

'Dear Julian – you still don't understand,' said his aunt. 'You see, neither your uncle nor I have had scarlet fever – so we are in quarantine, and mustn't have anyone near us, in case we get it, and give it to them – and that might mean we'd give it to all you four.'

'Would Timmy get it?' asked George, still sniffing dolefully.

'No, of course not. Don't be silly, George,' said her mother. 'Did you ever hear of dogs getting measles or whooping-cough or any of *our* illnesses? Timmy isn't in quarantine. You can get him out of his kennel as soon as you like.'

George's face lit up immediately, and she shot round the back of the house, yelling Timmy's name. At once there came a volley of barks!

'Aunt Fanny – what do you want us to do?' asked Julian. 'We can't go to my home, because Mummy and Daddy are still in Germany. Should we go to a hotel?'

'No, dear, I'll think of somewhere you can all go,' said his aunt. 'Good gracious, what a row Timmy is making! Poor Joanna – she has such a splitting headache.'

'Here's the ambulance,' cried Anne, as a big hospital van drew up outside the gate. Aunt Fanny disappeared from the window at once to tell Joanna. The ambulance man went up to the front door, his mate behind him carrying a stretcher. The four children watched in surprise. 'He's gone to fetch dear old Joanna,' said Julian. And sure enough the stretcher was soon carried out with Joanna lying on it, wrapped round in blankets. She waved to the children as the men carried her out.

'Soon be back!' she said, in rather a croaky voice. 'Help Mrs Kirrin if you can. So sorry about this!'

'Poor Joanna,' said Anne, with tears in her eyes. 'Get better quickly, Joanna. We shall miss you so!'

The ambulance door closed and the van went off very smoothly and quietly.

'Whatever shall we do?' said Dick, turning to Julian. 'Can't go home – can't stay here! Oh, here's TIMMY! How are you, Tim, old thing? Thank goodness *you* can't get scarlet fever. Don't knock me over, old boy. Down! Gosh, what a licky dog you are!'

Timmy was the only one in high spirits. The others felt really down in the dumps. Oh dear – what was to be done? Where could they go? What a horrid beginning to a holiday! Down, Timmy, DOWN! What a dog! Anyone would think he had never even *heard* of scarlet fever! WILL you get down, Timmy!

CHAPTER TWO

Plans for the Five

GEORGE WAS still looking upset. What with her fears that Timmy might be ill or hurt, and now her distress at Joanna being carried off in the ambulance, she wasn't much help to anyone.

'Do stop sniffing, George,' said Anne. 'We've just got to be sensible and think of some way out of this.'

'I'm going to find Mother,' said George. 'I don't care if she's in quarantine or not.'

'Oh no you're not,' said Julian, taking her firmly by the arm. 'You jolly well know what quarantine means. When you had whooping-cough *you* weren't allowed to come near any of us, in case we caught it too. You were infectious, and that meant that you didn't have close contact with anybody for at least a few weeks. I think it's only two weeks for scarlet fever, so it won't be too bad.'

George went on sniffing, trying to pull away from Julian's hand. Julian winked at Dick, and said something that made George pull herself together at once.

'Well, REALLY, George!' he said. 'You're acting *just* like a weepy girl. Poor Georgina! Poor little old Georgina!'

George stopped sniffing immediately and glared at Julian in fury. If there was one thing she really hated it was to be told she was acting like a silly *girl*! And how *awful* to be called by her real name, Georgina! She gave Julian a hefty punch, and he grinned at her, warding her off.

344

'That's better,' he said. 'Cheer up! Just look at Timmy staring at you in amazement. He's hardly ever heard you crying before.'

'I'm NOT crying!' said George. 'I'm – well, I'm upset about Joanna. And it's awful to have nowhere to go.'

'I can hear Aunt Fanny telephoning,' said Anne, who had very sharp ears. She fondled Timmy's head, and he licked her hand. He had already given everyone a wonderful welcome, whining with pleasure, and licking lavishly. He had been mad with joy to see George again, and was surprised and sad to find her looking so miserable now. Dear Timmy – he certainly belonged to the Five!

'Let's sit down and wait for Aunt Fanny,' said Julian, settling himself on the grass. 'We look a bit silly standing staring at Kirrin Cottage like this. Aunt Fanny will come to the window in a minute. She is sure to have thought of a good idea for us. TIMMY! I shan't stay sitting down for long if you keep licking my neck like that. I shall send you for a towel in a minute, so that I can wipe it dry!'

The little joke made everyone feel better. They were all sitting on the grass now, and Timmy went lovingly from one to the other. All his family back again – it was too good to be true! He settled down at last, his head on George's knee, George's hand caressing his ears.

'Aunt Fanny's put down the telephone,' said Anne. 'Now she'll come to the window.'

'You've got ears like a dog – just as good as Timmy's,' said Dick. '*I* couldn't hear a thing!'

'Here's Mother!' said George, and leapt to her feet as Aunt Fanny came to the window and leaned out.

'It's all right, dears,' she called. 'I've been able to

arrange something for you. I have been telephoning the scientist that your father has been working with, George – Professor Hayling. He was coming here for a day or two, and when I told him he couldn't, because we're in quarantine, he at once said that *you* must all go *there* – and that Tinker, his son – you remember him, don't you – would be delighted to have your company!'

'Tinker! Goodness, yes, I shall never forget him – or his monkey either!' said Julian. 'He's the boy who owns that old lighthouse at Demon's Rocks, isn't he? We went to stay there with him, and had a marvellous time.'

'Well – you're not staying at the lighthouse, I'm afraid,' said his aunt, from the window. 'Apparently a storm blew up one night and damaged it, and it's not safe to live in any more.'

Groans from all the Five, of course, Timmy joining in as usual! 'Where are we to go then? To Tinker's *home*?' said Dick.

'Yes. You can get a bus from here, at Little Hollow, that will take you almost to Big Hollow, where Professor Hayling lives,' said Aunt Fanny. 'You're to go today. I'm so very sorry about this, dears, but it's just one of those things we have to put up with. I'm sure you'll have a good time with Tinker, and that monkey of his. What was it called now?'

'Mischief,' said everyone together, and Anne smiled in delight to think of being with the naughty little creature, and watching its wicked ways.

'The bus will pass in ten minutes,' said her aunt. 'And have a good time, dears, and send me a card or two. I'll let you know how we get on – but I really don't think that either your uncle or I will catch scarlet fever, so don't worry. And I'll send you some money to spend. You'd better run for the bus now.'

'Right, Aunt Fanny, and thank you!' called Julian. 'I'll look after everyone and keep them in order – especially old George. Don't worry at all – and I do hope you or Uncle don't go down with the fever. Goodbye.'

They all went to the front gate where the luggage still stood. 'Anne, go out into the road and stop the bus when it comes,' ordered Julian. 'Then Dick and I will heave our bags aboard. Gosh, I wonder what it will be like with old Tinker at Big Hollow. I've a feeling it might be rather exciting!'

'*I* don't think so,' said George, mournfully. 'I like Tinker all right – he's funny – and that little monkey is a darling – such a *naughty* little thing too. But oh dear, don't you remember what it was like when Tinker's *father* came to stay with us? It was *awful*! He never remembered to come to meals, and was always losing his coat or his hanky or his money, and losing his temper too. I got very tired of him.'

'Well, he'll probably get very tired of *us*!' said Julian. 'He won't find it very funny to have four kids parked on him, especially if he's in the middle of difficult work – to say nothing of a rather large, licky dog leaping round the house as well.'

'Timmy isn't likely to lick *him*,' said George, at once, and put on one of her scowls. '*I* didn't like Tinker's father at all.'

'Well, don't look like a thunderstorm,' said Julian. 'I don't expect he'll like any of *us* either. But it's kind of him to let us come and stay at Big Hollow, and we're jolly well going to behave ourselves, see? There's to be no back-chat

347

from *you*, George – even if he dares to disapprove of Timmy!'

'He'd better *not*,' said George. 'In fact, I've a good mind not to go. I think I'll live in the summer-house with Timmy, at the bottom of the garden!'

'You will NOT!' said Julian, taking firm hold of her arm. 'You'll play fair, come with us, and behave properly! Listen, there's the bus. Come on, we'll all wave, and hope there are a few empty seats.'

Anne had already stopped the bus, and run round to ask the driver if he would help with the bags. He knew the children very well, and leapt down at once.

'You're going back to school pretty quick!' he said. 'I thought the schools had only just broken up.'

'They have,' said Julian, 'but we're off to stay at Big Hollow. The bus goes there, doesn't it?'

'Yes, we go right through the village of Big Hollow,' said the driver, carrying three bags at once, much to Julian's envy. 'Whereabouts are you staying there?'

'At Professor Hayling's house,' said Julian. 'I think that's called Big Hollow too, like the village.'

'Ah, we pass it,' said the driver, 'I'll stop the bus just outside and give you a hand with your things again. My word – you'll have to mind your ps and qs there – old Professor Hayling's a bit peculiar, you know. Goes off the handle properly if things don't go his way! Once a horse got into his garden and believe it or not he chased that horse for two miles, shouting at it all the way. And bless me, when he got back home, tired out, there was that horse, chewing up his garden again. The horse was cute – he'd taken a short cut back. Yes – you be careful how you behave at Big Hollow. The old man might get cross and pop you into one of his strange machines and grind you up into little pieces!'

The four children laughed. 'Oh, the old Professor is all right,' said Julian. 'A bit forgetful, like most people who work with their brains all the time. My brain goes fairly slowly – but my Uncle Quentin's goes about a hundred miles an hour, and I bet the Professor's does too! *We'll* be all right!'

Away went the bus, bumping over the road from Kirrin and Little Hollow, and on to Big Hollow. The four children gazed out of the windows as they passed alongside the shore, where the sea shone as blue as cornflowers, and once more saw Kirrin Island out in the big bay.

'Wish we were going *there*!' sighed George. 'We'll have to take a picnic meal there sometime, and enjoy ourselves. I'd like old Tinker to visit my island. He may have a lighthouse of his own, but having an island is MUCH *better*!'

'I think I agree with you,' said Julian. 'Tinker's lighthouse is certainly lovely and all on its own, and the view from it is amazing – but there's something about Kirrin Island that I *love*. Islands are quite different from anything else!'

'Yes. They are,' said Anne. '*I'd* like one too. A very little one, so that I could see all round it at one glance. And I'd like one little cave to sleep in – just big enough for *me*.'

'You'd soon be lonely, Anne,' said Dick, giving his sister a friendly pat. 'You love to have people round you, you like to be friendly!'

'So does Timmy!' said Julian, as Timmy left his place by George's knee and went to sniff at a string bag held by an old man, who at once fondled the big dog, and fumbled for a biscuit out of a paper bag. 'Timmy doesn't mind how many people there are around, so long as one or two of them have a biscuit or a bone to hand out!'

'Come to heel, Timmy,' said George. 'You're not to go round begging, telling people you are half-starved! I should think you eat more than any other dog in Kirrin. Who eats the cat's dinner whenever he can, I should like to know?'

Timmy gave George a loving lick and settled down beside her, his head on her toes. He got up politely every time someone entered or left the bus. The driver was most impressed.

'I wish all dogs were as good on my bus as yours,' he told George. 'You'd better get ready to jump out. Our next stop is supposed to be a little way beyond Big Hollow, but I'll stop for a moment, and you can get out.'

'Thanks a lot,' said Julian, gratefully, and when the bus stopped with a jerk a minute later, all the Five were ready to jump out.

The bus went on, and left them standing outside a large wooden gate. The drive from it led steeply downwards, and a large house could just be seen hidden in a hollow by great trees.

'Big Hollow!' said Julian. 'Well – here we are. What a strange place – sort of mysterious and brooding. Now to find old Tinker! I bet he'll be pleased to see us all, especially Timmy! Help me with the bags, Dick!'

CHAPTER THREE

Big Hollow – and Tinker and Mischief again!

THE FOUR children and Timmy went through the big heavy gate, which groaned loudly. Timmy was very startled to hear the mournful creak, and barked sharply.

'Sh!' said George. 'You'll get into trouble with the Professor, Timmy, if you raise your voice like that. I expect we'll have to talk in whispers, so as not to disturb the Professor – so just see if you can whisper too.'

Timmy gave a small whine. He knew he couldn't whisper! He trotted at George's heel as they all went down the steep drive to the house. It was a curious house, built sideways to the drive and had astonishingly few windows.

'I expect Professor Hayling is afraid of people peering in at his work,' said Anne. 'It's very, very secret, isn't it?'

'I know he uses miles and miles of figures,' said Dick. 'Tinker told me one day that his monkey Mischief once chewed up a page of figures when he was very small – and Professor Hayling chased him for a whole hour, hoping to catch him and find even a *few* bits of paper still in his mouth, so that he could rescue at least part of his figures. But Mischief fled down a rabbit hole and didn't come up for two days, so it wasn't any good.'

Everyone smiled at the thought of poor Mischief hiding down a rabbit hole. '*You* couldn't do that, Timmy old thing!' said Julian. 'So just be careful of any paper *you* eat.'

'He wouldn't be so silly,' said George, at once. 'He knows perfectly well what's eatable and what's not.'

'Ha! *Does* he!' said Anne. 'Well, I'd just like to know what kind of food he thought my blue slipper was that he chewed up last hols!'

'Don't tell tales on him,' said George. 'He only chewed it because someone shut him in your bedroom and he hadn't anything else to do.'

'Woof,' said Timmy, quite agreeing. He gave Anne's hand a little lick, as if to say, 'Very sorry, Anne – but I was so *bored*!'

'*Dear* Timmy! I wouldn't mind if you chewed up *all* my slippers!' said Anne. 'But it would be nice if you chose the very *oldest* ones!'

Timmy suddenly stopped and looked into the bushes. He gave a low growl! George put her hand on his collar at once. She was always afraid of snakes in the springtime.

'It might be an adder!' she said. 'The dog next door trod on one last year, so I heard, and his leg swelled up terribly, and he was in great pain. Come away now, Timmy – it's an adder, with poison in its fangs!'

But Timmy went on growling. Then he suddenly stood still and sniffed hard. He gave an excited whimper and pulled away from George, jumping into the bushes – and out came, not a snake, but Mischief, Tinker's bright-eyed little monkey!

He at once leapt on to the dog's broad back, put his little monkey fingers under Timmy's collar, and chattered in delight. Timmy nearly dislocated his neck to twist his head round to lick him!

'Mischief!' cried everyone at once, in real delight. 'You've come to welcome us!'

And the little monkey, jabbering away excitedly in monkey language, leapt first on to George's shoulder, and then on to Julian's. He pulled Julian's hair, twisted his right ear round, and then leapt from him to Dick, and on to Anne's shoulder. He cuddled into her neck, his eyes bright and brown, looking very happy.

'Oh! *Isn't* he pleased to see us again!' said Anne, delighted. 'Mischief, where's Tinker?'

Mischief jumped off Anne's shoulder and scampered down the drive as if he quite understood all that Anne had said. The children raced after him – and then a loud voice suddenly roared at them from one side of the drive.

'What are you doing here? Clear out! This is private ground. I'll fetch the police. Clear OUT!'

The Five stopped still in fright – and then Julian saw who it was – Professor Hayling! He stepped forward at once. 'Good afternoon,' he said. 'I hope we didn't disturb you, but you did tell my aunt we could come here.'

'Your aunt? Who's your aunt? I don't know any aunt!' roared the Professor. 'You're sightseers, that's what you are! Come to pry into my work, just because there was a piece about it in some silly paper! You're the third lot today. Clear out, I tell you – and take that dog too. How DARE you!'

'But – don't you *really* know us?' said Julian very startled. 'You came to stay at our house, you know, and . . .'

'Stuff and nonsense! I haven't been away for years!' shouted the Professor. Mischief, the monkey, was so frightened that he leapt away into the bushes, making a funny little crying noise.

'I hope he fetches Tinker,' said Julian, in a low voice to Dick. 'The Professor has forgotten who we are, and why we've come. Let's retreat a bit.'

But as they went cautiously back up the steep path, followed by the angry Professor, a loud voice hailed them, and Tinker came racing up with Mischief on his shoulder, clinging to his hair. So the little monkey had gone to fetch him. Good for *him*! thought Julian, pleased.

'Dad! Don't yell at our friends like that!' cried Tinker, dancing about in front of his angry father. 'You asked them here yourself, you know you did!'

'I DID NOT!' said the Professor. 'Who are they?'

'Well, George, that girl, is the daughter of Mr Kirrin, and the others are his niece and nephews. And that's their dog, Timmy. And you asked them all here because Mr and Mrs Kirrin are in quarantine for scarlet fever,' shouted Tinker, still dancing about in front of his father.

'Stop jigging about like that,' said the Professor, crossly. '*I* don't remember asking them. I would have told Jenny the housekeeper if I had.'

'You did tell her!' shouted Tinker, still jigging about, with Mischief the monkey jigging too in delight. 'She's angry because you left your breakfast and now it's almost dinner time. She's cleared it away.'

'Bless us – so *that*'s why I feel so hungry and cross!' said Professor Hayling, and he began to laugh. He had a tremendous laugh, and the children couldn't help laughing too. What an odd fellow – so brainy, such a fine scientist – with the most enormous amount of knowledge in his head – and yet no memory for such ordinary things as breakfast and visitors and telephone calls.

'It was just a misunderstanding,' said Julian, politely. 'It was very, very kind of you to invite us here when we can't be at home because of the scarlet fever. We'll try not to be a nuisance, and if there's anything we can do to help you, please ask us. We'll make as little noise as possible, and keep out of your way, of course.'

'You hear that, Tinker?' said Professor Hayling, suddenly swinging round on the startled Tinker. 'Why can't you do the same – make very little noise, and keep out of

my way? You know I'm very busy now – on a MOST IM-
PORTANT project.' He turned to Julian. 'You'll be very
welcome if you keep Tinker out of my way. And NOBODY –
absolutely NOBODY – is to go up into that tower. Understand?'

They all looked up to where he was pointing, and saw a
tall, slender tower rising up amid the trees. It had curious
tentacle-like rods sticking out at the top, and these shook
slightly in the breeze.

'And don't ask me questions about it,' went on the
Professor, looking fiercely at George. 'Your father's the
only other man who knows what it's for, and *he* knows
how to keep his mouth shut.'

'None of us would *dream* of prying,' said Julian. 'It's
very, very kind of you to offer to have us here, and do
believe me when I say we shan't be any trouble to you at
all – but a help if you'll allow us.'

'Ah well, you sound a sensible fellow, I must say,' said
the Professor, who had now calmed down, and looked
quite peaceable. 'Well, I'll say goodbye for now and go
and have my breakfast. I hope it's fried eggs and bacon.
I'm very hungry.'

'Dad – Jenny's cleared your breakfast AWAY! I told you
that before!' said Tinker in despair. 'It's almost dinner-
time, now.'

'Ah good – good!' said the Professor. 'I'll come at once.'

And he led the way indoors, followed by the five
children, with Timmy and Mischief, all looking rather
worried. Really, nobody *ever* knew what the Professor was
going to do or say next!

Jenny certainly had a good dinner for them all. There
was a large and delicious stew with carrots, onions and

peas swimming in the gravy, and plenty of potatoes. Everyone tucked in well, and Mischief, who loved the peas, took quite a few from Tinker's plate, his little paw creeping up, and neatly snatching a pea from the gravy.

The girls went out to help bring in the next course, which was a big steamed pudding with plenty of raisins in it. Mischief at once jigged up and down in delight, for he loved raisins. He leapt on to the table, and received a sharp smack from the Professor, who unfortunately smacked the pudding dish at the same time, making the pudding jump in the air.

'Good gracious, Dad – we nearly lost the pudding!' cried Tinker. 'And it's my favourite. Oh, don't give us such *small* pieces! Mischief, get off the table. You are NOT to put your paw into the sauce!'

So Mischief disappeared under the table, where he received quite a lot of raisins from various kindly hands, unseen by the Professor. Timmy felt rather left out. He was under the table too, having been rather scared by the Professor's angry voice, but as he didn't very much like raisins, he wasn't as lucky as Mischief.

'Ha – I enjoyed that!' said the Professor, having cleaned his plate thoroughly. 'Nothing like a good breakfast!'

'It was midday dinner, Dad!' said Tinker. 'You don't have pudding at breakfast.'

'Dear me, of course not – that was pudding!' said his father, and laughed his great laugh. 'Now you can all do exactly what you like, so long as you do NOT go into my study, or my workroom, or that tower. AND DON'T MEDDLE WITH ANYTHING! Mischief, get off the water jug, you'll upset it. Can't you teach that monkey some table manners, Tinker?'

And with that he marched out of the room, and disappeared into some mysterious passage that apparently led to his study or workroom. Everyone heaved a sigh of relief.

'We'll clear away and then I'll show you your rooms,' said Tinker. 'I do hope you won't find it too dull here.'

Dull, Tinker! You needn't worry! There is far too much excitement waiting for the Five – and you too! Just wait a bit, and see!

CHAPTER FOUR

Jenny has a very good idea

TINKER RACED out to the kitchen to fetch a tray or two. He made a most peculiar noise as he went, and for a moment Timmy looked extremely startled.

'Goodness – don't say that Tinker *still* has that awful habit of pretending to be some kind of car!' groaned Julian. 'How on earth does his father put up with it? What's he think he is now? A motorbike by the sound of it.'

There was a sudden crash and a loud yell. The Five raced down the kitchen passage to find out what had happened, Timmy at the front.

'Accident!' bellowed Tinker, scrambling up from the floor. 'I took the bend too quickly, and my front wheel skidded, and I went bang into a wall! I've bent my mudguard.'

'Tinker – do you mean to say you're *still* being silly enough to pretend to be cars and motorbikes and tractors and lorries?' demanded Julian. 'You nearly drove us all mad, driving about all over the house, when you stayed with us. Have you *got* to be a machine of some sort?'

'Yes,' said Tinker, rubbing one of his arms. 'It sort of comes over me, and away I go. You should have heard me yesterday, being a lorry absolutely *loaded* with new cars for delivery. Dad *really* thought it was a great lorry and he rushed out into the drive to send it away. But it was only me. I hooted too – like this!'

And the sound of a loud and a deep hooter immediately

360

filled the passage! Julian shoved Tinker into the kitchen and shut the door.

'I should have thought that your father would have been driven completely mad by now!' he said. 'Now, you just shut up. Can't you grow up a bit?'

'No,' said Tinker, sullenly. 'I don't want to grow up. I might be like my father and forget to eat my meals, and go out with one sock on and one off. And I'd hate to forget my meals. Just think how *awful* it would be! I'd always be hungry.'

Julian couldn't help laughing. 'Pick up your tray, and help to clear away!' he said. 'And if you simply can't HELP being a car sometimes, for goodness' sake go outside! It sounds terrible in the house. You're much too good at awful noises.'

'Oh, am I *really* good?' said Tinker, pleased. 'I suppose you wouldn't like to hear me being one of those new planes that go over here sometimes, making a funny droning noise?'

'No, I WOULD NOT!' said Julian, firmly. 'Now will you PLEASE get that tray, Tinker. And tell Mischief to get off my right foot. He seems to think it's a chair.'

But Mischief clung to Julian's ankle and refused to move. 'All right, all right,' said Julian. 'I shall just have to walk about all day with you riding on my foot.'

'If you *stamp* as you walk, he soon gets off,' remarked Tinker.

'Why didn't you tell me that just now?' asked Julian, and stamped a few steps round the room. Mischief leapt off his foot at once and sat on a table, making an angry noise.

'He sits on Dad's foot for ages, even when he walks about,' said Tinker. 'But Dad doesn't even notice him there! He even sat on Dad's head once, and Dad thought he was wearing his hat indoors and tried to take it off. But it was only Mischief there!'

That made everyone laugh. 'Now come on,' said Julian, briskly. 'We really must clear away the dinner things. We

362

three boys will carry out the loaded trays and you girls can wash up. And DON'T let Mischief think he can carry teapots or milk jugs.'

Jenny was very pleased with their help. She was short and fat, and waddled rather than walked, but managed to get here and there remarkably quickly.

'I'll show your visitors their bedrooms after we've cleared,' she said. 'But, you know, Tinker, those mattresses we sent to be remade haven't come back yet. I've told your father a dozen times to telephone about them, but I'm sure he hasn't remembered.'

'Oh JENNY!' said Tinker, in dismay. 'That means that the two beds for visitors can't be slept in! What ever are we to do?'

'Well, your Dad will have to ring up for new mattresses to be sent today,' said Jenny. 'Maybe they would send them out by van.'

Tinker immediately became a furniture van and rushed down the passage, into the dining-room and back again, Mischief following him in delight. He made a noise exactly like a slow-moving van, and the children couldn't help laughing.

The Professor shot out of his study, his hands to his ears. 'TINKER! COME HERE!'

'No thanks,' said Tinker, warily. 'Sorry, Father. I was a van bringing the mattresses you forgot to order for the beds for visitors.'

But the Professor didn't seem to hear. He advanced on Tinker, who fled upstairs with Mischief leaping after him. Professor Hayling turned on Jenny.

'Can't you keep the children quiet? What do I pay you for?'

'Cleaning, cooking and washing,' she said, briskly. 'But I'm not a nurse for children. That Tinker of yours could do with half a dozen nurses, and he'd still be a nuisance to you while he was in the house. Why don't you let him take his tent and camp out in the field with his friends? It's hot weather and those new mattresses haven't come, and they'd all love it. I can cook for the children and take them out meals – or they could come and fetch them.'

The Professor looked as if he could give Jenny a big hug. The children waited eagerly to see what he would say. Camping out – that would be fun in this weather – and honestly, living in the same house as the Professor wasn't going to be much fun. Timmy gave a little whine as if to say 'Fine idea! Let's go at once!'

'Good idea, Jenny, VERY good idea!' said Professor Hayling. 'But that monkey's to camp out too. Then perhaps he won't jump in at my workroom window and fiddle about with my models!'

He marched back into his study and slammed the door so hard that the whole house shook. Timmy was startled and gave a yelp. Mischief the monkey leapt up the stairs again, howling in fright. Tinker began to dance round in joy, and very firmly Jenny took hold of him and propelled him into her big, clean kitchen.

'Wait, Jenny, I've remembered something. We've only one tent, and that's mine, a small one. I'll have to ask Dad if I can get two big ones!' And before anyone could stop him he was banging at the Professor's door, then flung it open, and shouted out his request.

'WE WANT TWO MORE TENTS, DAD. CAN I BUY THEM?'

'For goodness sake, Tinker, clear out and leave me

alone!' shouted his father. 'Buy SIX tents if you want them, but GET OUT!'

'Ooh, thanks, Dad!' said Tinker, and was just slipping out of the door when his father yelled again.

'But what on earth do you want TENTS for?'

Tinker slammed the door and grinned at the others. 'I'd better buy Dad a new memory. He's only *just* told us we can camp out, and he knows there's only my very small tent – almost a toy one.'

'I'm glad we shan't be in the house,' said Anne. 'I know what a nuisance it is to *George's* father to have us around, playing about. We'll be better out of the way.'

'Camping out again!' said George, very pleased. 'Let's catch the bus back home and get our own tents. I've got them all stored away in the garden shed. We can just ask Jim the carrier to take them in his van, when we've found them.'

'He's calling here today – I'll give him the message for you, if you like,' said Jenny. 'The sooner you get the tents, the better. It was a kind thought of the Professor's to ask you all here, but I just knew it wouldn't work! You'll be all right out in the field at the back of the house – he won't hear a thing, not even if you all yell together! So you get your tents and put them up, and I'll see what I can find in the way of ground-sheets and rugs.'

'Don't bother, Jenny,' said Julian. 'We've got all those things – we've often camped out before.'

'I only hope there aren't any cows in the field,' said Anne. 'Last time we camped, a cow put its head into my tent opening, and mooed. I woke up with such a jump, and I was too scared to move.'

'I don't think there are any cows,' said Jenny, laughing. 'Now I MUST get on with the washing-up, so will you bring out the dinner things please – but don't let that monkey carry anything breakable, for goodness sake! He tried to balance the teapot on his head last week – and that was the end of the teapot!'

Soon everyone was hard at work, clearing away, and helping Jenny with the washing-up.

'I shall like camping out,' Anne told her. 'I'd be scared of staying here in the house. Professor Hayling is a bit like my Uncle Quentin, you know – forgetful, and quick-tempered and a bit shouty.'

'Oh, you don't want to be scared of him,' said Jenny, handing Anne a dish to dry. 'He's kind, for all his cross-ness when he's upset. Why, when my mother was ill, he paid for her to go into a really good nursing-home – and believe it or not, he gave me money to buy her fruit and flowers!'

'Oh goodness – that reminds me – we MUST send Joanna some flowers,' said George. 'She has scarlet fever, you know. That's why we're here.'

'Well, you go and telephone the florist,' said Jenny. 'I'll finish this job.'

But George was rather afraid that Professor Hayling might rush out to see who was using the telephone!

'I'm sure we can buy flowers in Kirrin village, and have them sent,' she said. 'We've got to go and get our things ready for Jim, and I can order the flowers then. We might as well come back on our bicycles – they'd be useful here.'

'Well, you'd better go now,' said Jenny, 'or you won't be back in time for tea, and *then* there'd be trouble.'

'*I'll* bring back Anne's bicycle,' said Julian. 'I can easily manage it beside mine as I ride back.'

'Look, George,' said Dick, 'you needn't come. I'll order the flowers and I can bring your bike back too. So you stay with Anne.' Reluctantly George agreed.

Off went Julian and Dick, leaving Tinker and the girls to help Jenny. But Jenny soon sent Tinker off, afraid that he would drop things and break them.

'You go and be a nice, quiet, purring Rolls-Royce at the bottom of the garden,' she said. 'And when you think you've done thirty miles or so, come back for petrol.'

'Lemonade, you mean!' said Tinker, with a grin. 'All right. I haven't been a Rolls-Royce for a long time. Dad won't hear me right at the bottom of the garden!'

Off he went, and Jenny and the girls finished the washing-up. Mischief was a nuisance and went off with the teaspoons. He leapt to the top of a high cupboard, and dropped them there.

Tinker suddenly put his head in at the window. 'Come on out to the field where we're going to put up our tents,' he called to Anne and George. 'We'll choose a nice sheltered spot. Buck up! You must have finished washing-up by now. I'm tired of being a Rolls-Royce!'

'You go with him, Anne,' said George. 'I don't feel like it just now.'

So down the garden went the two children and out through a gate at the bottom into a big field.

'Good gracious!' said Tinker, staring. 'Look at all those caravans coming in at the gate the other end of the field. I'll soon send them off. It's OUR field!' And away he marched to the gate in the distance.

'Come BACK, Tinker,' shouted Anne. 'You'll get into trouble if you interfere. COME BACK!'

But Tinker marched on, his head held high. Ha – he'd soon tell the caravan folk it was HIS field!

CHAPTER FIVE

The travelling circus

ANNE WATCHED anxiously as Tinker went on and on over the field. There were now four caravans trundling in the far gate, and behind them, in the lane, were vans – enormous vans – all with enormously large words painted on them.

TAPPER'S TRAVELLING CIRCUS

'Hoo! I'll tell Mr Tapper what I think of him, coming into *my* field!' said Tinker to himself. Mischief the monkey was on his shoulder, jogging up and down as Tinker marched along, muttering furiously.

Four or five children from the caravans looked at him curiously as he marched along. One small boy rushed up to him, shouting in delight to see the monkey.

'A monkey, look, a monkey!' he cried. 'Much smaller than our chimp. What's he called, boy?'

'Mind your own business,' said Tinker. 'Where's Mr Tapper?'

'Mr Tapper? Oh, you mean our grandad!' said the boy. 'He's over there, look, beside that big van. Better not talk to him now. He's busy!'

Tinker walked over to the van and addressed the man there. He was rather fierce-looking and had a long, bushy beard, enormous eyebrows that hung down over his eyes, a rather small nose, and only one ear. He

369

looked inquiringly down at Tinker, and put out his hand to Mischief.

'My monkey might bite you,' said Tinker, at once. 'He doesn't like strangers.'

'I'm no stranger to *any* monkey,' said the man, in a deep-down voice. 'There's isn't a monkey in the world, nor a chimp either, that wouldn't come to me if I called it. Nor a gorilla, see?'

'Well, *my* monkey won't come to you,' said Tinker, angrily. 'But what I've come to say is . . .'

Before he could finish his sentence, the man made a curious noise in his throat – rather like Mischief did when he was pleased about anything. Mischief looked at the man in surprised delight – and then leapt straight from Tinker's shoulder to his, nuzzling against his neck, making little crooning noises. Tinker was so amazed that he stared without saying a word.

'See?' said the man. 'He's my little friend already. Don't gawp so, little fellow. I've trained the monkey family all my life. You lend me this little chap and I'll teach him to ride a small tricycle in two days.'

'Come here, Mischief!' said Tinker, amazed and angry at the monkey's behaviour. But Mischief cuddled down still farther into the big man's neck. The man hauled him out and handed him to Tinker.

'There you are,' he said. 'Nice little fellow he is. What is it you wanted to say to me?'

'I've come to say that this field belongs to my father, Professor Hayling,' said Tinker. 'And you've no right to bring your caravans here. So please take them all out. My friends and I are planning to camp out here.'

'Well, I've no objection to that,' said the big man, good-temperedly. 'You choose your own corner, young man. If you don't interfere with us, we shan't interfere with you!'

A boy of about Tinker's age came sidling up, and looked at Tinker and Mischief with interest. 'Is he selling you that monkey, Grandad?' he asked.

'No I'm NOT!' almost shouted Tinker. 'I came to tell you and your caravans to clear out. This field belongs to my family.'

'Ah, but we've an old licence to come here every ten years, and show our circus,' said the bearded man. 'And believe it or not, there's been a Tapper's circus in this field every ten years since the year 1648. So you just run home and make no silly fuss, young man.'

'You're a fibber!' cried Tinker, losing his temper. 'I'll tell the police! I'll tell my father! I'll . . .'

'Don't you talk to my grandad like that!' shouted the boy, standing beside the old man. 'I'll hit you if you do!'

'I'll say what I like!' shouted Tinker, his temper now quite lost. 'And just you shut up!'

The very next moment Tinker found himself flat on his back on the grass. The boy had shot out his fist and hit Tinker hard in the chest! He struggled to his feet, red in the face, quite furious.

The old man fended him away. 'Don't you be silly now, boy,' he said. 'This youngster is a Tapper, like me, and he'll never give in. You go home and be sensible. We're not going to take notice of a hot-headed little kid like you. Our circus is coming in this here field, just like it has for years and years!'

He turned and walked to the nearest caravan. It was drawn by horses, and he clicked to them. They strained forward and the caravan followed. Others behind began to move too. The circus boy put his tongue out at Tinker. 'Sucks to you!' he said. 'Nobody gets the better of my grandad – or of me either! Still – it was plucky of you to go for him. I enjoyed it.'

'Shut up!' said Tinker, alarmed to find himself very near to tears. 'You just wait till my dad tells the police! You'll all go out much quicker than you came in – and one of these days I'll knock *you* down!'

He turned and ran back to the gate. He wondered what to do. He had so often heard his father say that the field

372

behind their house belonged to him, and that he had let this or that farmer have the grazing rights for his horses and cattle. How DARE the travelling circus come into his father's field?

'I'll tell Dad,' he said to Anne, who was waiting at the gate. '*He* ought to turn them out! It's *our* field and I love it, especially just now when it's so green and beautiful, and the hedges are just going to be covered in white may. I'll tell Dad the boy knocked me down – shot out his fist just like *that* – and down I went. I'd like to do the same to *him*!'

He went into the house, followed by a puzzled Anne.

He looked into the sitting-room and saw George there.

'Tinker! That boy knocked you down!' said Anne, in a horrified voice. 'Why did he do that?'

'Oh – just because I told his grandad to take his caravans away,' said Tinker, feeling rather grand. 'He didn't hurt me at all – just punched me on the chest. Still – I said what I had gone to say.'

'But *will* they take the caravans away out of the field?' asked Anne.

'I told them I'd tell the police,' said Tinker. 'So I bet they'll skedaddle. They haven't any right to be there. It's *our* field!'

'*Are* you going to the police?' asked George, disbelievingly. 'I really don't see why you have to make such a fuss about it all, Tinker. They might make it difficult for *us* to go camping there.'

'But I tell you it's *my* field – Dad's always said so!' said Tinker. 'He said it wasn't any use to him, so I could consider it my own. And I do. AND we're going to camp in it, whatever anyone says! It's a travelling circus that's coming there, so the old man said.'

'Oh TINKER! How marvellous to have a circus at the bottom of the garden!' said George, her eyes shining, and Anne nodded too. Tinker glared at them.

'JUST like girls to say a thing like that!' he said. 'Would *you* want people trespassing all over a field that belonged to you, with horses neighing and tigers and lions roaring, and bears grunting, and chimpanzees stealing things – and nasty circus boys being rude all the time, ready to knock you down?'

'Oh Tinker! You *do* make it sound so exciting!' said George. 'Will there really be lions and tigers? Suppose one escaped – what a thrill!'

'Well – *I* shouldn't like that,' said Anne, at once. 'I don't particularly want a lion peering in at my window, or a bear clomping round my bedroom!'

'Neither do I,' said Tinker, in a most decided voice. 'That's why I'm going to tell Dad about it. He's got the old document that sets out our rights to that field. He showed me it one day. I'll ask him about it, and if he'll let me see it, I'll take it straight to the police and let them turn out that rude old man and his horrible circus.'

'How do you *know* it's horrible?' asked George. 'It might be really good. I'm sure they'd let us camp in the corner nearest the garden, and we'd get a great view of what's going on all the time. Look – there's your father strolling down the path, smoking a pipe. He never does that if he's busy. It would be a good time to go and ask him about the document. He might even show it to us.'

'All right,' said Tinker, rather sulkily. 'But you'll see I'm right. Come on.'

However, Tinker proved to be quite, quite wrong! His father went to fetch the old, yellowed piece of parchment at once. 'Ha! Here it is!' he said. 'It's pretty valuable too, because it's so old. It dates back quite a few centuries.'

He undid the rather dirty piece of ribbon round it and unrolled it. Neither the girls nor Tinker could read the old-fashioned lettering.

'What does it all say?' asked Anne, with great interest.

'It says that the field known as "Cromwell's Corner" is to be held by the Hayling Family for always,' said Professor Hayling. 'It was given to them by Cromwell because our family allowed them to camp in that field when they sorely needed a rest after battle. It's been ours ever since.'

'So NOBODY else is allowed to camp in it, or use it for grazing or anything, unless we say so!' said Tinker, triumphantly.

'Quite right,' said his father. 'But wait a minute – I seem to remember an odd clause that said something about a travelling show – a show that had rights to camp in the field since about 1066. Not even Cromwell could alter that – it was in the original deeds, long before Cromwell battled in that district. Now let's see – that piece would come about the end, I expect.'

The two girls and Tinker waited while the Professor pored over the old and beautiful lettering. He jabbed his finger on to three lines towards the end.

'Yes. There it is. I'll quote it. Listen! "And let it be known that Ye Travelling Show so-named 'Tapper's Travelling Show', which has always had camping rights, shall still have the right to claim these once every ten years so long as the show travels the country ways – Given under my hand . . ." and so on and so on. Well – I don't expect that Tapper's Travelling Show is going now, all these years and years after the document was drawn up and signed in the year 1648. See – here's the date – if you can read the old figures!'

The children stared at the date, and then glanced up at Tinker. He looked angry and very red in the face. 'You might have told me all that before, Dad,' he said.

'Why?' asked his father, astonished. 'What possible interest can it have for you children?'

'Only that there's a circus called Tapper's Travelling Circus in that field this very minute,' said Anne. 'And the old man with it is called Tapper – and he said it was his right to be there, and . . .'

'He was rude to me and I want you to turn out this circus this very day!' said Tinker. '*We* want to camp there.'

'I'm sure Mr Tapper would have no objection to you camping there,' said his father. 'Aren't you being rather silly, Tinker? *You* weren't rude to any of the circus folk, were you?'

Tinker went very red, turned his back and stalked out of the room, Mischief clinging to his neck. He rubbed his chest where the circus boy had punched him. 'Just you wait!' he said in a whisper. 'I'll punch *you* one day!'

'Anne, if you and the others want to camp in the field, I'll go and speak to Mr Tapper,' said the Professor, puzzled by Tinker's behaviour.

'Oh no – it's all right,' said Anne, hastily. 'He has already said that it didn't matter if we camped there. Oh – there are the boys back again. I'll just go and see if they have brought back all our bicycles safely. Thank you for showing us that marvellous old document, Professor!'

And away she went looking rather hot and bothered!

CHAPTER SIX

Getting ready for camping out

DICK AND Julian were most interested to hear about Tinker and the travelling circus – and the old, old document.

'You made a bit of a fool of yourself,' said Julian, looking at Tinker. 'Still, there's no harm done, apparently. I vote we go and see where we can put up our tents. Personally, I shall be thrilled to see a bit of circus life so close to me! I wonder how they'll manage to put on a show. I suppose they've everything with them, and can put up a circus ring and a tent and anything else necessary.'

'There are a lot of big vans,' said Anne. 'I went down to have a look about half an hour ago. The field is almost full now, except for one corner near our hedge that I suppose they have left for our tents.'

'I saw the posters about the circus as we cycled back,' said Dick. 'Dead-Shot Dick – Chimpanzee that plays Cricket – the Boneless Man – Madelon and her Beautiful Horses – Monty and Winks, the Clowns – the Dancing Donkey – Mr Wooh, the Wonder Wizard – gosh, it sounded *quite* a circus. I'm glad we can camp in the same field – we shall really see behind the scenes, then.'

'Don't forget there was Charlie the Chimp, and the Bonzo Band,' said Julian. 'What fun if the chimp got loose and peeped in at the kitchen window!'

'It wouldn't be at *all* funny,' said Anne. 'Jenny would run for miles! So would Tinker's monkey!'

378

'What about putting up our own tents after tea?' said Dick. 'Jim said he'd have them here by tea time. It's hotter than ever today. I don't feel I can do much at the moment. I just want to laze.'

'Woof,' said Timmy, who was lying down with his head on his paws, panting.

'You feel the same, old chap, don't you?' said Julian, poking him with his toe. 'You're tired out with your long run back from Kirrin, aren't you?'

'The roads were so *dusty*!' said Dick. 'He kept sneezing whenever a car passed us, because the dust got up his nose. Poor old Tim. You really are tired out with that long, long run!'

'Woof!' said Tim, suddenly sitting up straight and pawing vigorously at George. Everyone laughed.

'He says he's not at *all* tired, he wants a walk,' chuckled Dick.

'Well, if he's not tired, I *am*,' said Julian. 'It really was a job sorting out all our things at Kirrin – and cycling all the way back. NO, Timmy – I am NOT going to take you for a walk!'

Timmy whined, and at once Mischief the monkey leapt down from Tinker's shoulder and went to cuddle against the big dog, making small comforting noises. He even put his thin little arms round Timmy's neck!

'You're being just a *little* soppy, Mischief,' said Tinker, but Mischief didn't care. His big friend was sad about something, or he wouldn't have whined. Timmy put out a big red tongue and licked the little creature delicately on his nose. Then he suddenly pricked up his ears, and sat straight up. He had heard a noise from somewhere. So had all the others.

'It's music of some kind,' said Anne. 'Oh – I believe I know what it is!'

'What?' said the others.

'It must be Tapper's Travelling Circus Band practising for opening night,' said Anne.

'Well, that's tomorrow,' yawned George. 'Yes – it does sound like a band. Maybe we shall see the bandsmen after tea, when we put up our tents. I'd like to see the Boneless Man, wouldn't you?'

'NO!' said Anne. 'He'd be all limp and wriggly and horrid – like a worm or a jellyfish! I shan't go and see him. But I'd love to see the horses and the Dancing Donkey. Does he dance to the band, do you think?'

'We'll find out when we go,' said Dick, 'as it opens tomorrow. If Mr Tapper isn't annoyed about Tinker trying to turn them out, he might let us wander round.'

'I don't think I want to come,' said Tinker. 'Mr Tapper was rude – and that boy knocked me flat.'

'Well, I expect I'd do the same if I thought you were being rude to *my* grandad,' said Julian, lazily. 'Now – it's settled, is it, that we go down with our things to the field after tea, and see if we can put up our tents in some sheltered corner?'

'Yes,' said everyone. Dick idly tickled Mischief's nose with a thin blade of grass. The monkey sneezed at once, and then again. He rubbed his little paw across his nose and stared disapprovingly at Dick. Then he sneezed once more.

'Borrow a hanky, old thing,' said Julian. And, to everyone's intense amusement, Mischief leapt across to Dick and neatly pulled his handkerchief out of his pocket! Then he pretended to blow his nose.

Everyone roared with laughter, and Mischief was delighted. 'You'll be stolen to act in a circus one day, if you behave like that!' said Dick, snatching back his hanky. 'The Pickpocket Monkey!'

'He'd be very good in a circus,' said Julian.

'I'd *never* let him join a circus!' said Tinker at once. 'He might have a dreadful life.'

'No. I don't think he would,' said Julian. 'Circus folk love their animals and are proud of them. And after all, if they treated them unkindly, the animals wouldn't be happy or healthy, and couldn't enjoy their acts. *Most* circus people treat their animals like one of the family.'

'What! Even a chimpanzee!' said Anne, in horror.

'They're nice creatures – and very clever,' said Julian. 'Mischief, do *not* remove my handkerchief, please. It was funny the first time, but *not* a second time. Look at him now, trying to undo Timmy's collar.'

'Come and sit quietly by me, Mischief,' ordered Tinker, and the little creature obediently went to him and cuddled on to his knee, making a soft, crooning noise.

'You're a humbug,' said Tinker, fondling him. 'You be careful I don't give you away to the circus, and get an elephant in exchange!'

'Idiot!' said Dick, and everyone laughed at the thought of Tinker and an elephant. What in the world would he do with it?

A voice called from the house. 'Tinker! Jim's here with all the camping things. He's put them in the hall, *just* where your father will fall over them. You'd better come and see to them now.'

'In a few minutes, Jenny!' called back Tinker. 'We're busy.'

'You're a real fibber, Tinker,' said Dick. 'We are *not* busy. You could easily go to find out where the things are, and see if they're all there. There are quite a lot.'

'We'll go in twenty minutes or so,' said Anne, yawning.

'I bet Tinker's father is asleep this hot afternoon. He won't stir out of his study.'

But she was wrong. Professor Hayling was wide awake, and when he had finished his work, he wanted a drink of very cold water. He threw open his study door, strode out towards the kitchen – and fell over a pile of all kinds of camping gear, bringing them down with a tremendous noise.

Jenny rushed out of the kitchen with loud screams of fright, and the Professor bellowed in anger as he took a ground-sheet off his head, and a tent-pole off his back. 'WHAT ARE THESE THINGS? I WILL NOT HAVE THEM IN THE HALL! JENNY! JENNY! Take them down to the bonfire and burn the lot!'

'Our camping things!' cried George, listening in horror. 'Quick! We must get them! Oh, I do hope Tinker's father hasn't hurt himself. Bother, bother, bother!'

While Julian and Dick deftly removed everything that had fallen on to the angry Professor and took it all down the garden, Anne and George comforted him, and made such a fuss of him that he began to feel decidedly less angry. He sat down in a chair and wiped his forehead. 'I hope you've taken all those things down to the bottom of the garden,' he said after a while.

'Yes,' said Tinker, truthfully. 'Er – they're all by the bonfire, but it's not lit yet.'

'I light it myself tomorrow,' said his father, and Tinker heaved a sigh of relief. His father would forget, of course – and anyhow, everything was going to be taken into the camping field after tea.

'Have a cup of nice hot tea,' said Jenny, appearing with a tray of tea things. 'Sit down and drink this. It's

y made. Best thing to have after a fall and a
k.'

he turned and whispered crossly to Tinker, 'Didn't I
call to you and tell you the Professor would trip over those
things, the poor man? Now you just get your own tea,
while I take him into the dining-room and comfort him
with a nice hot scone, and a cup of tea!'

'I'll get *our* tea,' said Anne. 'Then we'll set up the tents
down in the field, and enjoy ourselves. And Tinker, don't
you get into any more trouble with the circus folk.'

'I'll see he doesn't,' said George, firmly. 'Come on – let's
go down to the field while Anne gets the tea. I could do
with a bun or two!'

Between them, Dick and Julian had lugged all the things
down the garden – two tents, ground-sheets, blankets,
tent-pegs and all the rest. Timmy ran with them in
excitement, wondering what all the fuss was about. Mischief, of course, leapt to the top of whatever was being
carried, and chattered excitedly all the way down the
garden.

He got into trouble when he ran off with a tent-peg, but
Timmy managed to catch him and make him drop it. Then,
very solemnly, Timmy carried the tent-peg to Julian.

'Good dog!' said Julian. 'Just keep an eye on that
wicked little monkey, Tim, will you? There are all sorts
of things he might run off with!'

So Timmy kept an eye on Mischief, nosing him away
whenever he thought the monkey was going to pick up
something he shouldn't. Finally Mischief became tired of
Timmy's nose and leapt on his back, where, clinging to the
dog's collar, he rode just as if he were on horseback. 'Only
it's dogback, not horseback,' said George, with a laugh.

'They would make quite a good pair for the circus,' said Dick. 'I bet Mischief could hold on to reins, if Timmy had any!'

'Well, he's not *going* to have any,' said George. 'The next thing would be a whip! Whew! What a lot of things we've got – is that the lot?'

It was, thank goodness. A bell rang out from the house at that moment, and everyone heaved a sigh of relief.

'Tea at last!' said Dick. 'I could drink a whole potful. Come on – we've finished piling up all the things. We'll get busy after tea with them, I can't do a thing more. Don't you agree, Timmy?'

'Woof!' said Timmy, heartily, and galloped up the garden path at top speed, with Mischief scampering after him.

'Talk about a circus!' said Dick. 'We've a ready-made one here! All right, Anne – we're coming! We're coming!'

CHAPTER SEVEN

In the circus field

NOBODY WANTED to spend a long time over tea. They all longed to go down to the field and set up their little camp.

'We shall have a wonderful look-in at what goes on in a circus camp,' said Dick. 'We shall be living so near the circus folk! I do hope Mischief won't get too friendly with the people there. They might take him away with them when they leave.'

'*Indeed* they won't!' said Tinker, fiercely. 'What a thing to say! As if Mischief would go with them, anyhow! I don't expect he'll mix with the circus crowd at all.'

'You wait and see!' grinned Dick. 'Now buck up with your tea – I'm longing to go and set our camp in the field, and see what's going on there.'

It wasn't long before they were ready. They were soon down by the fence, and gazed over it in amazement. Great vans were in the field, all with Mr Tapper's name on and all painted in bright colours. There were caravans too, much smaller than the great vans, and these had windows, each with neat lace curtains. The circus folk lived in the caravans, of course, and George found herself wishing that she herself could go about in one, instead of living in a house that couldn't move anywhere!

'Look at the horses!' cried Dick, as a bunch of them appeared with tossing heads and beautiful long thick tails. The boy who had knocked Tinker down was with them, whistling. They were all coming from a big horse-van, and were delighted to be in a field with lush green grass.

'Is that gate properly shut?' yelled an enormous voice, and the boy yelled back, 'Yes, Grandad. I shut it. There's nowhere the horses can get out. Don't they like this grass!'

Then he saw Julian and the others all looking over the fence, and waved to them. 'See our horses? Aren't they a great lot?'

And, just to show off a little, he leapt on to the back of the nearest one, and went all round the edge of the field with it. George watched him enviously. If only *she* could have a horse like that!

'Well, let's take our camp things into the field,' said Tinker. 'The nearer we are to the circus the better. We ought to have some fun.'

He climbed over the fence and Dick followed. 'I'll hand everything over,' said Julian. 'George can help me – she's a strong old thing!'

George grinned. She loved to hear anyone say that! It was quite a job getting some of the things over the fence. The tents, neatly wrapped though they were, were heavy, awkward things to handle, but at last everything was safely over, lying on the grass.

Then Julian, Anne and George climbed over the fence too, and stood in the field, looking round for a good corner to set up their things.

'What about near those bushes over there?' said Julian. 'There's that big tree behind as well to protect us from the wind – and we aren't *too* near the circus folk – they might not like us right on top of them – and yet we're near enough to see what's going on.'

'Oh, it's going to be FUN!' said Anne, her eyes shining.

'I think I'd better go and find the old grandad – Mr Tapper,' said Julian. 'Just to tell him we're here, in case he thinks we're intruders and have no right to be here.'

'You haven't got to ask his permission for us to be in MY field!' said Tinker, at once.

'Now don't keep flying off the handle like that, Tinker,' said Julian. 'This is merely a question of good manners – something you don't seem to know much about! How do we know that the circus folk won't resent us camping so near them? Much better to show ourselves friendly from the start.'

'All right, all right,' said Tinker, sulkily. 'But it is *my* field, after all! You'll be telling me to be friends with that nasty circus boy next!'

'Well, you'd better be – else he might knock you flat again!' said George. 'Anyway, be sensible, Tinker – it's not often people have a circus just at the bottom of their garden, and can pop over the fence and mix with the circus folk.'

Julian walked over to the nearest caravan. It was empty – no one answered his knock.

'What you want, mister?' called a high little voice, and a small girl with tangled, untidy hair came running up:

'Where's Mr Tapper?' asked Julian, smiling at the bright-eyed little thing.

'He's with one of the horses,' said the small girl. 'Who are you?'

'We're your neighbours,' said Julian. 'Will you take us to Mr Tapper?'

'Old Grandad's this way,' said the child, and slipped a dirty little hand into Julian's. 'I'll show you. I like you.'

She led the children to the middle of the camp. A mournful howl came from somewhere behind them and George stopped suddenly. 'That's Timmy! He must have found out that we've got out of the garden. I'll go back for him.'

'Better not,' said Julian. 'There might be ructions if he met the chimpanzee. A big chimp would make mincemeat of him!'

'It *wouldn't*!' said George, but all the same she didn't go back to fetch Timmy. Julian hoped that the dog wouldn't jump over the fence and come to find them.

'There's old Grandad Tapper on those steps,' said the little girl, smiling up at Julian, whose hand she still held. 'I like you, mister.' Then she shouted loudly to the old fellow sitting on the steps of a nearby caravan. 'Grandad! Here's folks to see you!'

Grandad was looking at a beautiful chestnut-brown horse, tethered close to him. He had one of the horse's hooves in his hand. The children stood and gazed at him – black beard, frowning eyebrows – and, oh dear! thought Anne, only one ear, poor man. What *could* have happened to the missing one?

'GRANDAD!' called the girl again. 'SOME FOLKS TO SEE YOU!'

Mr Tapper looked round, his eyes very bright under his black eyebrows. He set the horse's hoof down, and gave the lovely creature a pat. 'You don't need to limp any more, my beauty,' he said. 'I've taken out the stone that was in your hoof. You can dance again!'

The horse lifted up its magnificent head and neighed as if it were saying thank you. Tinker almost jumped out of his skin, and Mischief slipped from his shoulder and cuddled under his arm in terror.

389

'Now, now, little monkey, don't you know a horse's voice when you hear one?' said Grandad, and Mischief poked his head out from under Tinker's arm to listen.

'Does that horse *really* dance?' said Anne, longing to stroke its long, smooth nose.

'Dance! It's one of the finest dancing horses in the world!' said Grandad, and began to whistle a lively little tune. The horse pricked up its ears, gazed at Grandad, and then began to dance! The children watched in astonishment.

There it went, round and round, nodding its head to the tune, its feet tapping the grass in perfect time to Grandad's whistling.

'Oh, the lovely thing!' said George. 'Do *all* your horses dance as well as this one?'

'Yes. Some a good deal better,' said Grandad. 'This one has a fair ear for music, but not as good an ear as some. You wait till you see them dressed up, with feathery plumes nodding on their heads. Horses – there's nothing in the world as beautiful as a good horse.'

'Mr Tapper – we come from the house over the fence there,' said Julian, feeling that it was time to explain their visit. 'As you probably know, Tinker's father owns this field, and . . .'

'Yes, yes – but we have an old right to come every so often,' said the old man, raising his voice. 'Now don't you start arg . . .'

'I haven't come to argue with you,' said Julian, politely. 'I've only just come to say that we – that is my friends here and I – would like to come and camp in this field, but we shouldn't annoy you in any way, and . . .'

'Oh well – if that's what you want, you're more than welcome!' said the old man. 'More than welcome! I thought maybe you'd think you could turn us out – like that youngster there would like to do!' And he nodded at Tinker.

Tinker went red and said nothing. The old man

laughed. 'Ha! My grandson didn't think much of that idea, did he, youngster? He hit out, and down you went on your back. He's got a temper, he has, young Jeremy. But another time maybe he'll find himself on *his* back, eh?'

'Yes. He will,' said Tinker, at once.

'Right. Well, you'll be even with one another then, and you can shake hands like gentlemen,' said the old man, his eyes twinkling. 'Now – what about you bringing your gear right into the field, and setting up your tents? I'll get old Charlie the Chimp to help you. He's as strong as ten men!'

'The *chimpanzee*! Is he tame enough to help us to put up our *tents*?' said Anne, disbelievingly.

'Old Charlie is cleverer than all of you put together, and as tame as you are!' said Grandad. 'And he could beat you three boys at cricket any day! You bring your bat along one morning and watch him. I'll call him to help you. CHARLIE! CHARLIE! Where are you? Snoozing I suppose!'

But no Charlie came. 'You go and fetch him,' said the old man, pointing to a corner of the field where stood a big, strong cage, with a tarpaulin roof to keep out the rain. 'He'll do anything you want him to do, so long as you give him a word of praise now and again!'

'Let's get him, Ju,' said Dick, eagerly. 'Fancy having a chimpanzee to help us!'

And off they all went to the great cage. CHARLIE! CHARLIE! Wake up, you're wanted! CHARLIE!

CHAPTER EIGHT

Charlie the Chimp is a help!

TINKER CAME to the big cage first. He peered inside. Charlie the Chimp was there all right, sitting at the back of his cage, his brown eyes looking at the children with curiosity. He got up and went over to where Tinker was peering in and pressed his nose against the strong wire, almost against Tinker's. Then he blew hard and Tinker backed away, surprised and cross.

'He *blew* at me!' he said to the others, who were laughing at Tinker's disgust. The chimp made a funny noise that Mischief the monkey immediately tried to imitate. The chimpanzee stared at Mischief, then he grew very excited. He rattled his cage, jumped up and down, and made some very odd noises indeed.

A boy came running up at once. It was the boy who had knocked Tinker down. 'Hey – what are you doing to the chimp?' he called. 'Oh – aren't you the boy who shouted at my grandad – the one I knocked down?'

'Yes. And don't you dare try that on again, or you'll be sorry!' said Tinker in a fierce voice.

'Shut up, Tinker,' said Julian. He turned to the boy. 'Your name's Jeremy, isn't it?' he said. 'Well, we've just been talking to your grandad over there, and he said we could get the chimpanzee to help us with our camping gear. It's all right for him to come out of his cage, isn't it?'

'Oh yes – I take him out two or three times a day,' said Jeremy. 'He gets bored in his cage. He'd love to help put

393

up your tents – he's always helping us with things like that. He's as strong as a lion.'

'Is he – er – is he safe?' asked Dick, eyeing the big animal doubtfully.

'Safe? What do you mean – safe?' asked Jeremy, surprised. 'He's as safe as I am! Charlie, come on out! Go on, you can undo your cage perfectly well, you know you can!'

The chimpanzee made a funny little chuckling noise, put his hand through the wire, reached the bolt, pulled it, took his hand back – and pushed open the cage door.

'See! Easy, isn't it?' said Jeremy, grinning. 'Charlie boy, come along. Your help's wanted!'

Charlie lumbered out of his cage, and went with the children to where they had left their tents and groundsheets and the rest. He walked with his fists on the ground in a most inelegant manner, making a funny little groaning noise all the time. Mischief was rather afraid of him, and kept well to the back – but the chimpanzee suddenly turned round, caught hold of Mischief, and sat him up on his shoulder! Mischief held on, not knowing whether to be scared or jubilant!

'I wish I had my camera here,' said Anne to George. 'Just look at them – Mischief is as pleased as can be!'

They arrived at the pile of camping gear. 'Carry this, Charlie, and follow us,' ordered Jeremy. The chimp grabbed at this, that and the other, and, with his great arms full, followed the children to where they thought they could camp, with the great tree to shelter them from the wind.

'Drop those things, Charlie,' said Jeremy, 'and go back for the rest. Buck up. Don't stand there staring! You've got work to do!'

But Charlie still crouched there, staring straight at Mischief. 'Oh! He wants Mischief the monkey to go with him!' cried George. 'Go on, Mischief, have a ride again!'

Mischief leapt up on to the chimpanzee's shoulders. Charlie put up a great paw to steady him and then lumbered off to fetch the rest of the things. One of the ground-sheets came undone and slithered over his head like a tent, so that he couldn't see where he was going. In a rage he leapt on it and began to jump up and down, up and down, growling most terrifyingly. The children felt rather scared.

'Charlie, don't be silly!' said Jeremy, and pulled it away from him, rolling it up swiftly. The chimpanzee could manage it then, and his good temper immediately came back again.

Everything was soon piled up in one place, and Julian and Dick began to put up the tents. Charlie watched them with the greatest interest, and helped most intelligently when he saw that he could.

'He's a good sort, isn't he?' said Jeremy, proud that his friend the chimpanzee could show off like this. 'Did you see him put that tent-pole in exactly the right place? And you ought to see him fetch the pails of water for the horses each day. He carries a full pail in each hand!'

'He ought to get wages,' said Tinker.

'He does!' said Jeremy. 'He gets eight bananas a day and as many oranges as he likes. And he LOVES sweets!'

'Oh! I think I've got some!' said Tinker and delved into one of his pockets. He brought up a peculiar mixture of things, among which was a screwed-up sweet bag. Inside was a mass of half-melted boiled sweets.

'You can't give him *those*!' said Anne. 'They're old and sticky and messy!'

But Charlie thought differently. He took the paper bag straight out of Tinker's hand, sniffed it – and then put the whole thing into his mouth at once!

'He'll choke!' said Julian.

'Not Charlie!' said Jeremy. 'Let him be. He'll go straight back to his cage, get in, shoot the bolt and sit there sucking sweets till they're gone. He'll be as happy as can be.'

'Well – he certainly deserved a reward,' said George. 'He did all the heavy work! Come on, let's finish putting everything straight. Hey – won't it be fun sleeping out in tents tonight! We'd better have supper first.'

'You can come and join *us*, if you like,' said Jeremy. 'We don't have posh food like you, of course – but it's good food, all the same. Old Grandma cooks it in her pot. She's two hundred years old.'

The children laughed in disbelief. 'Two hundred! Nobody lives as long as that!' said George.

'Well, that's what she tells everyone,' said Jeremy. 'And she looks it, too! But her eyes are as sharp as needles still! Shall I tell her you'll be here to supper?'

'Well – would there be enough for so many extra?' said Julian. 'We meant to bring our own meal. Should we bring that and share everything with you? We've more than enough. Jenny said she would have it all ready for us to bring down tonight – a meat pie, cold sausages, and apples and bananas.'

'Sh! Don't say bananas in front of Charlie,' said Jeremy. 'He'll worry you for them all the time. All right – you bring your food and we'll share with you round our campfire. I'll tell old Grandma. We're having a sing-song tonight, and Fred the Fiddler's playing his fiddle. Ah, that fiddle! Its tunes get into your feet and away you go!'

This all sounded very exciting. Julian thought they ought to go back home before anyone began to be worried about their complete disappearance, and pack up the food for supper that night.

'We'll be back as soon as we can,' said he. 'And thanks a lot for all your help. Come on, Mischief. Say goodbye to Charlie for the moment, and don't look so gloomy. We're coming back here tonight!'

They all went back over the fence, feeling a little tired

now, but full of their plans for the evening. 'It's almost like *belonging* to the circus, going back to sit round a camp fire and eat supper from that old black stewpot on the fire,' said Tinker. 'I bet the supper will taste delicious. I hope Dad won't mind us popping off to the circus camp.'

'I don't expect he'll even notice that we've gone,' said George. 'My father never notices things like that. Sometimes he doesn't even notice when people are there, in front of his nose!'

'Well, that must be useful at times if they're people he doesn't like,' said Tinker. 'Now – let's see what Jenny's got that we can take back with us.'

Jenny listened wide-eyed to all they had to say. 'Well, well, well!' she said. 'Camping out with the circus folk! Whatever next? I'd like to know what your parents would think of *that*!'

'We'll ask them, next time we see them,' said Julian, with a grin. 'What do you have for our supper? We're taking it down to our camp.'

'I thought maybe you'd do that,' said Jenny. 'It's all cold. A meat pie, cold sausages, a cucumber and lettuce hearts and tomatoes, rolls, and apples and bananas. Will that be enough?'

'Gosh, yes,' said Tinker, thrilled. 'What about something to drink?'

'You can take lemonade or orangeade with you, whichever you like,' said Jenny. 'But listen now – don't go bursting into your father's workroom. He's worked hard all day, and he's tired.'

'And cross, I expect,' said Tinker. 'People are always cross when they're tired. Except you, dear, dear Jenny.'

'Ha! You want something else out of my cupboard, calling me your dear, dear Jenny,' she said with a twinkle.

'Could we have some sugar lumps?' asked Tinker. 'Oh, Jenny, there are the loveliest horses you ever saw down in the circus field. I want to give them a sugar lump each.'

'And yourself a few as well!' said Jenny. 'All right. I'll pack up everything for you, and give you a few enamel plates and mugs and knives. What about Timmy? Doesn't he want a meal too?'

'Wuff!' said Timmy, glad that someone had remembered him. Jenny patted his big head. 'It's all ready in the larder for you,' she said. 'George, you go and get it. He must be hungry.'

George fetched a plate of meat and biscuits from the larder and Timmy fell on it with happy little barks. Yes – he was very, VERY hungry!

At last all the food was ready, packed to take down the garden to the field. What a lot there seemed! Well, they would certainly have plenty to spare for their circus friends. They said good night to Jenny, and set off down the garden again. They thought they had better not disturb Professor Hayling.

'He might be cross and forbid us to go and eat with the circus folk,' said Tinker. 'Mischief, come off that basket, and don't pretend you weren't fishing in it for a banana. And please put on your best table manners tonight, or Charlie the Chimp will be ashamed of you!'

It was fun going back down the garden and over the fence into the field again. The sun was sinking fast and soon the shadows would fall. How lovely to sit round a fire and eat supper with the kindly circus folk – and perhaps to sing old songs with them – and hear Fred the Fiddler fiddle his old, old tunes! What fun to creep into a tent, and sleep with the cries of owls around, and stars shining in at the tent opening!

There they go, over the fence, handing the food one to another. Take your paw out of that basket, Mischief! That's right, Timmy, nibble his ear if he's as mischievous as his name! You're all going to have some fun tonight!

CHAPTER NINE

A wonderful evening

As SOON as Jeremy saw the visitors climbing over the fence, he ran to help them. He was very excited at the thought of having guests. He took them over to old Grandad first, to be welcomed.

'Now I expect your friends will like to see round a bit,' said Grandad. 'Charlie the Chimp can go with you. We've a rehearsal on tonight, so the ring has been set up. You can watch some of the show.'

This was great news. The children saw that curved pieces of painted wood had been set together to make a great ring in the field, and as they went across the grass, the Musical Horses began to troop into the ring, the leading one ridden by Madelon, a lovely girl dressed in shimmering gold.

How beautiful they are! thought Anne, as she watched. Look at their great feathery plumes, nodding on their magnificent heads.

The Bonzo Band struck up just then, and the horses at once trotted in perfect time to the music. The band looked a little peculiar as the bandsmen had not put on their smart uniforms. They were saving those for the opening night!

The horses trotted prettily out of the ring after two or three rounds, the beautiful Madelon on the leading horse. Then in came Fred the Fiddler and played his violin for a few minutes. First the music was slow and solemn, then

Fred began to play quickly, and the children found themselves jigging about, up and down and round about. 'I can't keep still!' panted Anne. 'The tune's got into my feet.'

Charlie the Chimp came up just then, walking on hind legs, and looking unexpectedly tall. He usually walked on all fours. He began to jig about too, looking very funny. He ran right into the ring and put his arms round Fred the Fiddler's legs. 'He loves Fred,' said Jeremy. 'Now he's going to rehearse his cricket act. I must go and bowl to him.'

And off went Jeremy into the ring. The chimpanzee rushed over to him and hugged him. A bat was thrown into the ring, and Charlie picked it up and made a few swipes into the air with it, making delighted noises all the time.

Then a cricket ball was thrown to Jeremy, who caught it deftly. A small girl appeared from somewhere and set up three stumps for a wicket. 'Can't find the bails, Jeremy!' she called. 'Have you got them in your pocket?'

'No,' said Jeremy. 'Never mind, I'll knock the stumps right over!'

But that wasn't so easy with Charlie the Chimp at the wicket! He took a terrific swipe at the ball and it went right over Jeremy's head, too high to catch. The chimp lost his balance and sat down on the wicket, knocking the stumps out of the ground.

'OUT!' yelled Jeremy, but the chimp wasn't having that. He carefully put up the stumps again, and then set himself in front once more, waggling the bat.

It was the funniest cricket that the children had ever seen! The chimpanzee was very, very clever with the bat, and sent poor Jeremy running all over the place. Then he chased the boy all round the ring with the bat, making curious chortling noises. The children didn't know if he was amused or angry! Finally he threw the bat at Jeremy and walked off, scratching himself under one arm.

The children roared with laughter at him. 'He's as good as any clown!' said Dick. 'Jeremy, does he do this cricket act every night when the circus is open?'

'Oh yes – and sometimes he hits the ball into the audience,' said Jeremy. 'There's great excitement then. Sometimes, for a treat, we let one of the boys in the audience come down and bowl to Charlie. One bowled him right out once, and Charlie was so cross that he chased him all round the ring three times – just as he chased *me* just now. The boy didn't like it much!'

Charlie came up to Jeremy and put his great arms round him, trying to swing him off the ground. 'Stop that, Charlie,' said Jeremy, wriggling free. 'Look out – here comes the Dancing Donkey! Better get out of the ring – goodness knows what antics *he'll* be up to!'

In came the Dancing Donkey. He was dark grey, and tossed his head as he came galloping in. He stood and looked round at everyone. Then he sat down, lifted up a leg and scratched his nose. The children stared in astonishment. They had never in their lives seen a donkey do *that* before! Then, when the band suddenly began to play, the donkey stood up and listened, flapping his ears first one way and then another, and nodding his head in time to the music.

The band changed its tune to a march. The donkey listened again, and then began to march round the ring in perfect time – clip-clop-clip-clop-clip-clop. Then it apparently felt tired, and sat down heavily on its back legs. The children couldn't help laughing. The donkey got up, and somehow its back legs became entangled with its front ones and it fell down, looking most ridiculous.

'Has it hurt itself?' asked Anne, anxiously. 'Oh dear – it will break one of its legs if it goes on like this. Look, it can't untangle them, Jeremy.'

The donkey gave a mournful bray, tried to get up, and flopped down again. The band changed its tune, and the donkey leapt up at once, and began to do a kind of tap dance – clickety-click, clickety-click, clickety-click – it was marvellous!

'I shouldn't have thought that a donkey could possibly have been taught to tap dance,' said George.

Soon the donkey seemed to feel tired again. It stopped dancing, but the band still went on playing. The donkey ran towards it and stamped a foot.

A weird voice suddenly came from it. 'Too fast! TOO FAST!' But the band took no notice and went on playing. The donkey bent down, wriggled hard – and its head fell off on to the grass in the ring! Anne gave a shriek of fright.

'Don't be an idiot, Anne,' said Dick. 'You didn't think the donkey was a *real* one, did you?'

'*Isn't* it?' said Anne, relieved. 'It looks *just* like that donkey that used to give rides to children on Kirrin beach.'

The donkey now split in half and a small man climbed out of each half, both taking their legs carefully out of the donkey's legs. The donkey-skin fell to the ground and lay there, flat and collapsed.

'Wish *I* had a donkey-skin like that,' said Tinker. 'I've got a friend at school who could be the back legs and I'd be the front legs. The things we'd do!'

'Well, I must say you'd make a first-class donkey, the way you behave sometimes,' said George. 'Look, this must be Dead-Shot Dick coming on.'

But before Dead-Shot Dick could do any of his shooting tricks, the two donkey-men had run to the band and begun a loud argument with them.

'Why play so fast? You *know* we can't do our tricks at top speed. Are you trying to mess up our turn?'

The bandleader shouted something back. It must have been rude, because one of the donkey-men shook his fist and began to run towards the band.

A loud voice crashed in on the argument and made everyone jump. It was Mr Tapper, old Grandad, giving his orders in an enormous voice.

'ENOUGH! You, Pat, and you, Jim, get out of the ring. I give the orders, not you. ENOUGH, I SAY!'

The two donkey-men glared at him, but did not dare to say a word more. They stalked out of the ring, taking the donkey-skin with them.

Dead-Shot Dick looked very ordinary, dressed in a rather untidy flannel suit. 'He's not going to go all through his act,' said Jeremy. 'You'll see him another night, when the show's on for the public – he shoots at all kinds of things – even a five-pence piece dangling on a long string from the roof – and never misses! He's got a smashing rig-

out too – sequins sewn all over his trousers and jersey –
and his little horse is a wonder – goes round and round the
ring and never turns a hair when Dead-Shot Dick fires his
gun! Look – there he is, peeping in to see if Dick's coming
back to him.'

A small white horse was looking anxiously at the ring, its
eyes fixed on Dead-Shot Dick. It pawed the ground as if to
say 'Buck up! I'm waiting for you! Am I to come on or not?'

'All right, Dick – you can go off now,' shouted Grandad. 'I hear your horse has hurt a foot – give him a good
rest tonight. We'll want him on tomorrow.'

'Right, sir!' said Dead-Shot Dick. He saluted smartly,
and ran off to his little horse.

'What's next, Jeremy?' asked George, who was enjoying
everything very much.

'Don't know. Let's see – there's the acrobats – but the
trapeze-swings aren't put up yet, so they won't come on
tonight. And there's the Boneless Man – look, there he is.
Good old Boney! I like him. He's free with his money, he
is, not like some of the other folk!'

The Boneless Man looked very peculiar. He was remarkably thin, and remarkably tall. He walked in, looking
quite extraordinary. 'He can't be boneless!' said Dick. 'He
couldn't walk if he was!'

But the Boneless Man soon began to seem absolutely
boneless. His legs gave way at the knees, and his ankles
turned over so that he sank down to the ground, unable to
walk. He could bend his arms all kinds of different ways,
and turned his head almost completely round on his neck.
He did a few peculiar things with his apparently boneless
body, and finally wriggled along the ground exactly like a
snake!

'He'll be dressed in a sort of snake-skin when he does his act properly,' said Jeremy. 'Funny, isn't he?'

'How on earth does he do it?' wondered Julian amazed. 'He bends his arms and legs all the wrong ways! Mine would break if I did that!'

'Oh, it's easy for *him*!' said Jeremy. 'It's just that he's completely double-jointed – he can bend his arms both ways, and his legs both ways, and make them seem so loose that it looks as if he really *is* boneless. He's a nice chap. You'd like him.'

Anne felt a bit doubtful. What strange people made up a circus! It was a world of its own. She jumped suddenly as there came the sound of a trumpet blowing loudly.

'That's for supper,' said Jeremy, gleefully. 'Come on – let's go to old Grandma and her pot! Buck up, all of you!'

CHAPTER TEN

Round the camp fire

JEREMY LED the way out of the circus ring. It had been well-lit, and the night seemed very dark outside the ring. They went over the field to where a large fire was burning, cleverly set about with stones. An enormous cooking pot was hung over it, and a very, very nice smell came to their noses as they went near.

Old Grandma was there, of course, and she began stirring the pot when she saw them. 'You've been a long time in the ring,' she grumbled to Grandad. 'Anything gone wrong?'

'No,' said Grandad, and sniffed the air. 'I'm hungry. That smells good. Jeremy, help your grandma.'

'Yes, Grandad,' said Jeremy, and took a pile of plates to the old lady, who at once began ladling out pieces of meat and potatoes and vegetables from the steaming pot. Old Grandad turned to Julian.

'Well – did you like our little rehearsal?' he asked.

'Oh *yes*!' said Julian. 'I'm only sorry you didn't rehearse *all* the turns. I badly wanted to see the acrobats and the clowns. Are they here? I can't see them.'

'Oh yes – there's one clown over there – look – with Madelon, who had the horses,' said Grandad.

The children looked – and were very disappointed. 'Is he a *clown*?' said Dick, disbelievingly. 'He doesn't look a bit funny. He looks miserable.'

'That's Monty all right,' said Grandad. 'He always

looks like that out of the ring. He'll make you double up with laughter when the circus is on, he's a born clown – but a lot of clowns are like Monty when they're not performing – not much to say for themselves, and looking miserable. Winks is a bit livelier – that's him, pulling Madelon's hair. He'll get a smacked face in a minute, he's a real tease. There – I knew he'd get a clip on the ear!'

Winks went howling over to the children, boohooing most realistically. 'She smacked me!' he said. 'And she's got such p-p-p-pretty hair!'

The children couldn't help laughing. Mischief ran to the clown, jumped up on his shoulder and chattered comforting monkey words into his ear. Charlie the Chimp let himself out of his cage, and came to put his great paw into Winks' hand. They both thought that Winks really was hurt.

'That's enough, Winks,' said Grandad. 'You'll have the horses comforting you next! You do that in the ring tomorrow when we open, and you'll bring the house down. Sit down and have your supper.'

'Mr Tapper,' said Julian. 'There's another member of your circus we didn't see at the rehearsal – and that's Mr Wooh, the Wonder Magician. Why wasn't he there?'

'Oh, he never rehearses,' said Mr Tapper. 'He keeps himself to himself, does Mr Wooh. He may come and join us for supper, and he may not. As we're opening the circus tomorrow night, maybe he'll turn up tonight. I'm a bit scared of him, to tell you the truth.'

'But he's not a *real* wizard, is he?' asked Tinker.

'Well, when I talk to Mr Wooh I feel as if he is,' said Mr Tapper. 'There isn't a thing he doesn't know about figures, there isn't a thing he can't do with them. Ask him to multiply any number by any other number, running into dozens of figures, and he'll tell you in a second. He shouldn't be in a circus. He should be an inventor of some sort – an inventor whose invention needs pages and pages of figures. He'd be happy then.'

'He sounds a bit like my father,' said Tinker. '*He's* an inventor, you know, and sometimes when I creep into his study I see papers FULL of millions of tiny figures and plans and diagrams with tiny figures all over them too.'

'Very interesting,' said Grandad. 'Your father and Mr Wooh ought to meet. They would probably talk figures all day long! My word – what's that you're handing round, young lady?'

'Some of the food *we* brought,' said Anne. 'Have a sausage or two, Mr Tapper – and a roll – and a tomato.'

'Well, thanks,' said Mr Tapper, pleased. 'Very kind of you. Nice to have met you all. You might be able to teach Jeremy a few manners!'

'Grandad – here's Mr Wooh!' said Jeremy, suddenly, and got up. Everyone turned round. *So this* was Mr Wooh, the Wonder Magician. Well, he certainly looked the part.

He stood there, with a half-smile on his face, tall, commanding and handsome. His hair was thick and black as soot, his eyes gleamed in the firelight, half hidden by great eyebrows, and he wore a thin, pointed beard. He had a curiously deep voice, and spoke with a foreign accent.

'So we have visitors this night?' he said, and showed a row of gleaming white teeth in a quick smile. 'May I join you?'

'Oh do, Mr Wooh,' said Anne, delighted to have the chance of talking to a Wonder Magician. 'We've brought plenty of food. Do you like cold sausage – and tomato – and a roll?'

'Most deelicious!' said the magician, and sat down cross-legged to join the group.

'We were disappointed not to see you at the rehearsal,' said Dick. 'I'd have liked to hear you doing all kinds of wizard sums in your head, as quick as lightning!'

'My father can do that too,' said Tinker proudly. 'He's a wizard at figures as well. He's an inventor.'

'Ha! An inventor? And what does he invent?' asked Mr Wooh, eating his roll.

That was enough to set Tinker describing at once how wonderful his father was. 'He can invent *any*thing he's asked for,' said the boy, proudly. 'He invented a wonderful thing for keeping aeroplanes dead straight in the right direction – better than any idea before. He invented the sko-wheel, if you know what that is – and the electric trosymon, if you've ever heard of that. I don't suppose you have, though. They're too . . .'

'Wait, boy!' said Mr Wooh, sounding most interested. 'These things I have heard of, yes. I do not know them, but I have certainly heard of them. Your father must be a very, very clever man, with a most unusual brain.'

Tinker swelled with pride. 'Something got into the papers about his inventions a little while ago,' he said, 'and reporters came down to see Dad, and his name was in the papers – but Dad was awfully cross about it. You see, he's in the middle of the biggest idea he's ever thought of and it messed up his work to have people coming to interview him – some of them even peered through the window, and went to see his wonderful tower, with its . . .'

'Tower? He has a tower?' said Mr Wooh, full of surprise. Before Tinker could answer, he received a hard poke from Julian's finger. He turned crossly, to see Julian frowning fiercely at him. So was George. He went suddenly red in the face. Of course – he had been told never to talk about his father's work. It was secret work, very secret.

He pretended to choke over a piece of meat, hoping that Julian would take the chance of changing the subject – and Julian did, of course!

'Mr Wooh, could you do a bit of magic reckoning with figures?' he asked. 'I've heard that you can give the answers to any sum as quick as lightning.'

'That is true,' said Mr Wooh. 'There is nothing that I cannot do with figures. Ask me anything you like, and I will give you the answer at once!'

'Well, Mr Wooh, answer this then,' cried Tinker. 'Multiply sixty-three thousand, three hundred and forty-two by eighty thousand, nine hundred and fifty-three! Ha – you can't do that in a hurry!'

'The answer is, in figures, 5127724926,' said Mr Wooh at once, with a slight bow. 'That is an easy question, my boy.'

'Crumbs!' said Tinker, astounded. He turned to Julian. 'Is that right, Ju?'

Julian worked out the sum on paper. 'Yes. Absolutely correct. Whew!' he said. 'You said that as quick as lightning!'

'Let *me* give him a sum to do!' cried George. 'What do you get if you multiply 602491 by 352, Mr Magician?'

'I get the figures 2–1–2–0–7–6–8–3–2,' said Mr Wooh, immediately. And once more Julian worked out the sum on paper. He raised his head and grinned. 'Yes – correct. How do you do it so quickly?'

'Magic – just a little elementary magic!' answered Mr Wooh. 'Try it sometime yourself. I am sure that this boy's father would be as quick as I am!' He looked at Tinker. 'I should much like to meet your clever father, my boy,' he said in his deep voice. 'We would have much, so much to talk about. I have heard about his wonderful tower. A monument to his genius! Ah, you see, even we foreigners know of your father's great work. Surely he is afraid of having his secrets stolen?'

'Oh, I don't think so,' said Tinker. 'The tower is a pretty good hiding place, and . . .' He stopped suddenly, and went red again as he received an even harder kick from Julian. How *could* he be so stupid as to give away the fact that his father's secret plans and models were hidden in the tower!

Julian thought it was time to take Tinker firmly away from Mr Wooh and give him a good lecture on keeping his mouth shut. He looked at his watch, and pretended to be horrified at the time. 'Look. Do you know what the time is? Jenny will be ringing up the police if we don't get back straight away. Come on, Tinker, and you others, we *must* go. Thanks a lot, Grandad, for letting us share your supper.'

'But we haven't yet finished!' said Grandad. 'You haven't had enough to eat.'

'We really couldn't eat any more,' said Dick, following Julian's determined lead. 'See you tomorrow, Grandad. Good night, Grandma. Thanks very much indeed.'

'We've still got bananas and apples to eat,' said Tinker, feeling obstinate.

'Oh, we brought those for Charlie the Chimp,' said Dick, not quite truthfully. He could have boxed Tinker's ears! Silly little idiot, couldn't he realise that Julian wanted to get him away from this cunning Mr Wooh? Wait till he got Tinker by himself!

Tinker found himself hustled on all sides, and felt a bit scared. Julian sounded rather fierce, he thought. Old Grandad was most astonished at the sudden departure of his guests – but Charlie the Chimp didn't mind! The guests had left behind a generous supply of fruit!

Over the fence they all went, with Julian hustling Tinker in front of him. Once over the fence and out of Mr Wooh's hearing, Julian and George rounded on the boy angrily.

'Are you mad, Tinker?' demanded Julian. 'Didn't you guess that that man was trying to pump you about your father's hush-hush job?'

'He wasn't,' said Tinker, almost in tears. 'You're just exaggerating!'

'Well, I hope *I* never try to give away *my* father's secret work!' said George, in a tone of such disgust that Tinker could have howled.

'I don't like him and I don't trust him,' said Julian, sounding suddenly very grown up. 'But there you sat lapping up everything he said, ready to pour out all he wanted to know. I'm ashamed of you. You'd get a jolly good thrashing if your father had heard you. I only hope you haven't already said too much. You know how angry your father was when a report of his latest ideas got into the papers, and swarms of people came prying round the house . . .'

Tinker could stand it no longer. He gave a forlorn howl that made Mischief jump, and fled up the garden to the house, the little monkey running swiftly behind him. He wanted to comfort Tinker. What was the matter? Poor little Mischief felt bewildered, and tried his best to catch up with the sobbing Tinker. He caught him up at last, leapt to the boy's shoulder and put his little furry arms round Tinker's neck, making a funny comforting noise.

'Oh Mischief,' said Tinker. 'I'm glad *you're* still my friend. The others won't be now, I know. Aren't I an *idiot*, Mischief? But I was only being proud of my father, I was, really!'

Mischief clung to Tinker, puzzled and upset. Tinker stopped outside the tall tower. There was a light at the top. His father must still be working there. A faint humming noise came to his ears. He wondered if it was those strange, spindly tentacles right at the very top of the tower that made the noise.

Suddenly the light at the top of the tower went out.

Dad must have finished his work for tonight, thought
Tinker. He'll be coming to the house. I'd better go. He
might wonder why I'm all upset. Gosh, I never heard
Julian be so angry before. He sounded as if he absolutely
despised me!

He crept up the path that led to the house, and in at the
garden door. Better not go and see Jenny. She might worm
everything out of him, and be as disgusted with him as
Julian was. She would wonder why he wasn't camping out
with them! He'd go upstairs and sleep in his own bed
tonight!

'Come on, Mischief,' he said, in a mournful voice. 'We'll
go to bed, and you can cuddle down with me. You'd never
be mean to me, would you? You'd always be my friend.'

Mischief jabbered away, and the funny little monkey
voice comforted Tinker all the time he undressed. He flung
himself into bed, and Mischief lay at the bottom, on his
feet. 'I shall never be able to get to sleep tonight,' said
Tinker, still miserable. 'Never!'

But he fell asleep at once – which was a great pity,
really. He might have shared in quite a bit of excitement, if
he hadn't slept so soundly! Poor Tinker!

CHAPTER ELEVEN

In the dark of the night

JULIAN AND the others made no attempt to follow Tinker. 'Let him go, the little idiot!' said Julian. 'Come into one of the tents and have a low pow-wow before we get undressed and go to sleep.'

'I'm sorry poor old Tinker isn't going to camp out with us, our first night in the field,' said Anne. 'I don't think he *meant* to give anything away.'

'That's no excuse, Anne,' said George. 'He can be really stupid at times, and he's got to learn not to be. Let's go to our tent. I feel quite tired. Come along, Timmy!'

She yawned and Dick yawned too. Then Julian found himself yawning. 'Awfully catching, this yawning business!' he said. 'Well, it's turned out to be a lovely night as regards weather – warm and dry – and there's a nice little half-moon to look at. Good night, girls, sleep tight! And don't scream if a spider wakes you, because I warn you, I am NOT going to get up to deal with a harmless spider!'

'You wait till one runs all over *your* face!' said Anne, 'and starts making a web from your nose to your chin and catches flies in it!'

'Don't, Anne,' said George. 'I'm not a bit scared of spiders, but that's a horrible idea of yours! Timmy, please watch out for spiders, and give me warning of them!'

Everyone laughed. 'Well, good night, girls,' said Dick. 'Pity about young Tinker. Still, he's got to learn a few things, and keeping his mouth shut is one of them.'

419

They were all quite tired, and it wasn't long before everyone's torch was out, and peace and quiet descended on the little camp. Much farther up the field the circus was also peaceful and quiet, though there were still lights here and there in the tents. Someone belonging to the circus band was strumming a banjo, but not loudly, and the sound was pleasant to hear – strum-a-strum – strum-a-strum – strummmm . . .

A few clouds blew up and slid across the moon. One by one the lights went out in the circus tents. The wind blew softly through the trees, and an owl hooted.

Anne was still awake. She lay listening to the wind, and to the owl's 'Too-whoo-too-whit', and then she, too, fell asleep. Nobody heard someone stirring in the circus camp. Nobody saw a shadowy figure creep out when the moon was safely behind a cloud. It was late, very late, and the two camps were lost in dreams.

Timmy was fast asleep too – but in his sleep he heard a faint sound, and at once he was awake. He didn't move, except for his ears which switched themselves to listen. He gave a little growl, but not enough to wake George. So long as the person who was moving about in the circus camp did not come near to George's tent, or the boys' tent, Timmy did not mean to bark. He heard a tiny grunt and recognised it at once. Charlie the Chimp! Well, that was all right! Timmy fell asleep again.

Tinker, too, was fast asleep in his bed up at the house, Mischief at his feet. He had thought he would be too miserable to sleep, but found himself half-dreaming in no time. He didn't hear a small noise outside, a very small noise indeed – a little scrape, as if someone's foot had caught against a stone. Then there came other very small noises – and a whisper of a voice – and more noises again.

Nobody heard anything at all until Jenny woke up thirsty, and stretched out her hand to get a glass of water from her bed table. She didn't switch her light on, and was about to lie down again when her quick ears caught a little sound.

She sat up. That can't be the children, she thought. They're camping down in the field. Oh my goodness me, I hope it's not a burglar – or someone trying to steal the Professor's secrets. He's got papers all over the place. Thank goodness he keeps most of them in that tower of his!

She listened, and then lay down again. But soon she heard another little noise, and sat up, scared. It sounds as if it comes from the tower, she thought, and got out of bed. No – there was no light in the tower – no light anywhere, that she could see. The moon was behind a cloud. She'd just wait till it slid out and lit up the court-yard below, and the tower. There! That was another little noise. Could it be the wind? No, it couldn't. And now, what was *that*? It sounded just like someone whispering down there in the courtyard. Jenny felt really frightened, and began to shake. She must go and wake the Professor! Suppose it was someone after his precious papers? Or his wonderful new invention!

The moon swung out from behind the cloud and Jenny peered cautiously out of the window again. She gave a loud scream, and staggered back into her room, still screaming. 'There's a man! Help! Help! He's climbing up the wall of the tower! Professor! PROFESSOR HAYLING! Come quickly! Thieves, robbers, help, help! Get the police!'

There came a long slithering sound, and before Jenny

dared to look out again, the moon had gone behind another cloud, and she could not see a thing in the sudden darkness. There was a deep silence after the slithering noise, and Jenny couldn't bear it. She rushed out of her bedroom, yelling at the top of her voice. 'THIEVES! ROBBERS! COME QUICKLY!'

The Professor woke with a jump, threw off his bed-clothes and rushed out into the passage, almost colliding with Jenny. He clutched at her, thinking she was the thief, and she screamed again, sure that one of the intruders had got hold of her. They struggled together, and then the Professor realised that he wasn't holding a thief, he was holding poor, plump Jenny!

'JENNY! What on earth are you doing, waking up the whole household!' said the Professor, switching on the passage light. 'Have you had a bad dream – a nightmare?'

'No, no,' panted Jenny, out of breath with her struggle. 'There's robbers about. I saw one climbing up the tower wall – and there must have been others below. I heard them whispering. Oh, I'm scared! What shall we do? Can you telephone for the police?'

'Well,' said the Professor, doubtfully. 'Are you quite sure, Jenny, that you didn't have a nightmare? I mean – if there really *are* robbers, I'll certainly telephone – but it's rather a long way for the police to come out here, and . . .'

'Oh – then won't you just take a torch and look round the place?' begged Jenny. 'You know there's your precious papers in that tower. And isn't there that new invention of yours? Oh yes, I know I'm not supposed to know anything about it, but I do dust your rooms thoroughly, you know, and I see quite a lot, though I keep my mouth shut, and . . .'

'Yes, yes, Jenny, I know,' said poor Professor Hayling, trying to stop Jenny's stream of talk. 'But honestly, every-thing seems quiet now. I've looked out into the courtyard. There's no one there. And you know as well as I do that nobody can get into my tower. It has three different keys – one to unlock the bottom door – one for the middle door, halfway up – and one for the top door. Jenny, be sensible. Nobody could have used my three keys. Look, there they are on my dressing-table.'

Jenny began to calm down, but she still wasn't satisfied. 'I *did* hear whispering, and I *did* see someone halfway up the wall of the tower. Please do come down with me, and let's look around. I daren't go on my own. But I shan't sleep again tonight till I know nobody's forced the tower door, or taken a ladder to go up the tower.'

'All right, Jenny,' said the Professor, with a sigh. 'Put on your dressing gown, and I'll put mine on too – we'll try the doors, and we'll look for a ladder – though, mind you, it would have to be an absolutely colossal one to reach the top of that tower. Nobody could possibly bring one that size and length into our small courtyard! All right, all right – we'll go.'

And so, a few minutes later, Jenny and the Professor were down in the courtyard. There was no sign of any ladder at all – no sign of anyone climbing up the wall – and the downstairs tower door was safely locked! 'You unlock the door, and go up to the top room and see if that door's locked too,' begged Jenny.

'I think you're being rather silly now, Jenny,' said the Professor impatiently. 'Here, take the keys yourself. This one's locked, of course – and if the middle door is still locked, you'll know nobody could have got into my top room. Hurry, Jenny.'

So Jenny, still trembling, slid a key into the bottom lock, opened the door, and began to climb the spiral stair that led upwards. Halfway was another door, also safely locked. She unlocked this too. She began to feel rather silly. Nobody could have gone through locked doors. And there now – the top one was well and truly locked also! She gave a sigh of relief and ran down the spiral stairway, locking the middle door, and then the bottom one. She gave the keys to the Professor, who by now was feeling rather chilly!

'All locked,' said Jenny. 'But I'm still sure someone was about. I could have sworn I saw someone up that tower wall, and heard somebody else whispering below.'

'I expect you were so scared that you imagined things, Jenny,' said the Professor, yawning. 'I think you'll agree with me that the wall is far too steep for anyone to climb – and I'm pretty certain I'd have heard it if a ladder had been dragged about the courtyard!'

'Well, I'm sure I'm very sorry,' said poor Jenny. 'It's a good thing we didn't wake Tinker – though I'm surprised Mischief didn't hear something and come running down the stairs.'

'But Mischief is surely with Tinker, camping out in the field!' said the Professor in surprise.

'No – Tinker and Mischief are back. I found them asleep in bed – but not the others!' said Jenny. 'Maybe Tinker had quarrelled with them. Funny that Mischief didn't come running out to see what was up – he must have heard us!'

'Mischief is clever – but not clever enough to open Tinker's bedroom door,' said the Professor, yawning again. 'Good night, Jenny. Don't worry. You'll feel all right in the morning, and that will be that!'

The Professor went sleepily to his room. He looked out of the window down into the courtyard and then across at the tower, and smiled. Dear Jenny! She did rather let her imagination run away with her! As if anyone in the world could get up into that tower room without a ladder! And HOW could a long, long ladder be brought into that small courtyard without either being seen or heard? The Professor yawned once more and climbed into bed.

But someone *had* been in the tower room! Someone very clever, someone very light-fingered! What a shock for poor Professor Hayling next morning when he crossed the courtyard, unlocked the bottom door of the tower – walked up the spiral stairway – unlocked the middle door, and went on up the stairway again – and finally unlocked the top door and opened it wide.

He stood and stared in horror. The place was upside down! All his papers were scattered everywhere. He crouched down at once to see if any were missing. Yes – quite a lot! But they seemed to have been taken quite haphazardly – a few pages from this notebook – a few pages from that – some letters he had written and left on his desk to post – and good gracious, the ink was spilt all over the place – and the little clock was gone from the mantelpiece. So Jenny was right – a thief *had* been about last night. A thief that could apparently get through three locked doors – or else could climb up a long, long ladder that he had put outside without being seen – and taken away again!

I'll have to ring the police, he thought. But I must say it's a mystery! I wonder if Tinker heard anything in the night? No, he couldn't have, or he would have run to fetch me. It's a mystery – a real puzzle of a MYSTERY!

CHAPTER TWELVE

A shock for Tinker

TINKER WAS horrified when Jenny told him the next morning what had happened. 'Your father's in a rare old state,' she said. 'He came down early this morning because he wanted to finish some work up in the tower – and as soon as he unlocked the top door into the tower room, he saw the whole room upside down and some of his precious papers gone, and . . .'

'JENNY! How awful!' said Tinker. 'Dad kept his most precious papers there – with all the figures for that new electric thing of his. It's a wonderful thing, too marvellous for words, Jenny, it's for . . .'

'Now don't you give away any of your father's plans, not even to *me*, said Jenny. 'You've been told that before. Maybe you've been talking too much already, and somebody's ears took it all in!'

Tinker suddenly felt sick. *Was* it because of something he had been silly enough to say in public? In the bus, perhaps? Or in the circus field? What would the others say – especially Julian – when they heard that someone had come in the night and stolen precious papers containing figures and diagrams for some of his father's inventions? Julian would be sure to say that it was *his* fault for not keeping his mouth shut! Oh dear – would *this* be in the papers – and would hordes of people come visiting the place again, staring and whispering and exclaiming in awe at his father's curious tower with its waving tentacles?

427

He dressed quickly and ran downstairs. Jenny had told him that she was sure she had heard whispering down in the courtyard the night before, and had seen someone climbing up the tower. 'Your father says nobody could have brought a long ladder into that courtyard,' she said. 'Not without us seeing it, anyway, or hearing some kind of noise when it was dragged in. But it might have been a sliding ladder, mightn't it? That would be a smallish thing, with ropes to pull out the sliding part.'

'Yes. Like the window cleaner uses,' said Tinker. '*It* couldn't have been the window cleaner, could it?'

'No. He's a really decent fellow,' said Jenny. 'I've known him for twenty years. So put *that* out of your head. But the ladder could certainly have been the sort that window cleaners use. We'll go out into the courtyard as soon as I've finished washing-up, and see if we can find the marks where the ladder was dragged over the court-yard. Though I must say I didn't hear any *dragging* noises.

I heard whispering – and a kind of slithery noise – but that's all.'

'The slithery noise *might* have been made by the ladder when it was dragged along!' said Tinker. 'Hey – look at old Mischief. He's listening as if he understood every word. Mischief, why didn't you wake me up last night when all this was going on? You usually wake if anything unusual happens, or you hear a strange noise.'

Mischief leapt into Tinker's arms and cuddled there. He didn't like it when Tinker was upset about anything; he knew by the boy's voice that he was worried. He made small comforting noises, and rubbed his monkey nose against the boy's chin.

'You'd better go to your father,' said Jenny. 'You might be able to comfort him a little. He's very upset indeed. He's up in the tower room, trying to sort out his papers. My word, they were left in a state – scattered all over the room!'

Tinker stood up to go, and was astonished to find that he was shaky at the knees. Would his father ask him if he had been talking about the work he was doing? Oh dear – he had even boasted about it just the day before, and talked about his father's sko-wheel, and the wonderful new machine, the electric trosymon! Tinker's knees became shakier than ever.

But, fortunately, his father was far too upset about his muddled room and missing papers to worry about anything Tinker had said or done. He was up in the tower room, trying to discover which of his papers were missing.

'Ah, Tinker,' he said, when the boy came into the tower room. 'Just give me a hand, will you? The thief who came last night must have knocked the whole bunch of papers

429

off the table, down on the floor – and fortunately he seems not to have seen some that went under the table. So I doubt very much if the papers he *did* take away with him will be of any use. He'd need to be quite a scientist to understand them, without having the ones he left behind.'

'Will he come back for the others, then?' asked Tinker.

'Probably,' said his father. 'But I shall hide them somewhere. Can you think of a good hiding place, Tinker?'

'Dad – don't *you* hide them,' begged Tinker. 'Not unless you tell *me* where they are! You know how you forget things! You might forget where you'd put this bunch of papers, and then you wouldn't be able to go on with your inventions. Have you copies of the stolen sheets of figures and diagrams?'

'No. But they're all in my head as well as on paper,' said his father. 'It will take me a bit of time to work them all out again, but it can be done. It's a nuisance – especially as I'm working to a date. Now run along, Tinker, please. I've work to do.'

Tinker went down the spiral staircase of the tower. He'd have to make sure that his father *did* hide away those papers very carefully indeed – in some really good place. Oh dear – I hope he won't do what he did with the last lot of papers he wanted to hide, he thought. He stuffed them up the chimney – and they nearly went up in flames because Jenny thought she'd light the fire the next night, it was unexpectedly so cold. Good thing they fell down when she laid the fire and she rescued them before they got burnt! Why are brainy people like Dad so silly about ordinary things! I BET he'll either forget where he puts them – or go and hide them in some easy place where anyone could find them!

He went to talk to Jenny. 'Jenny – Dad says that the thief only took *some* of his papers – and that he can't make much use of the ones he took, unless he has the whole lot. And Dad says he thinks that when the thief finds this out, he'll try to steal the rest of the papers.'

'Well, let him try!' said Jenny. '*I* could hide them in a place where no thief would find them – if your Dad would let *me* have them. I shan't tell you where!'

'*I'm* afraid he might hide them up a chimney again, or some silly place like that,' said Tinker, looking so worried that Jenny felt really worried too! 'They've got to be hidden somewhere NOBODY would think of looking. And if Dad finds a place like that he'll promptly forget all about it, and never be able to find them again! But a thief might find them – he'd know ALL the places to look in.'

'Let's go up to the tower room and clear up the mess that the spilt ink made, and see if your father has taken his precious papers and hidden them somewhere there,' said Jenny. 'It would be just like him to hide them in the very room that the thief went to last night! Up the ladder, in at the window – left wide open, I've no doubt – snatched up every paper he could see, the rogue, and then raced down the ladder again!'

'Come on up to the tower, then,' said Tinker. 'I only hope Dad isn't there!'

'He's just crossing the courtyard, look,' said Jenny, leaning out of the window. 'See, there he is – carrying something under his arm.'

'His morning newspapers,' said Tinker. 'It looks as if he's going to have a jolly good read, doesn't it? Oh dear, I do hope all this won't be printed in the newspapers – it would bring hordes of people down here again. Do you remember how awful it was last time, Jenny – people even walked over the flower-beds!'

'Hoo – some people like to poke their noses into everything!' said Jenny. 'I don't mind telling you that I emptied my dirty washing water out of the window on to a few of them – quite by mistake, of course – how was *I* to know they were out there, staring up and down?'

Tinker gave a shout of laughter. 'I wish I'd seen that!' he said. 'Oh Jenny – if people come poking their noses into Dad's business again, DO let's empty water on their silly heads! Come on, Jenny – let's go up to the tower room now Dad's out of the way. Quick!'

They were soon out in the courtyard and, as they crossed it, Jenny stopped and looked hard at the ground.

'What are you looking for?' asked Tinker.

'Just to see if there are any marks that might have been made by someone dragging a ladder across,' said Jenny. 'I heard a funny slithering sound, you know but it didn't *sound* like a ladder being dragged across.'

The two of them looked all over the courtyard, but could see no marks there that could possibly have been made by a ladder.

'Funny,' said Jenny. 'It worries me, that slithery sound.' She looked up at the tall, steep wall of the tower. It was made of flint-stones of all shapes and sizes, the kind found in the countryside round about Kirrin and Big Hollow.

'Well, I suppose a *cat* might climb up,' said Jenny, doubtfully. 'But not a *man*. He'd slip sooner or later. It would be far too dangerous. I doubt if even a cat would get far.'

'And yet you say you thought you saw someone up the

tower wall!' said Tinker. 'Go on, Jenny – it must have been the shadow of a passing cloud that you saw! Look up this wall – now can you imagine ANYONE climbing up it at night, when it was dark?'

Jenny stared up. 'No – you're right. Only a madman would even try. Well, my eyes must have played me up, then, when I looked out last night – but I really *did* think I saw a dark shadow climbing up the tower wall. Still, it's easy to be mistaken at night. And I don't believe there was a ladder, either! There *would* be marks on the paving-stones of the courtyard if there had been a ladder. Oh well – let's hurry on up to the tower room before your Dad decides to go back to it again!'

They went up the spiral stairway. All the doors were unlocked, as it was plain that the Professor was going to come back again after he had read his papers.

'All the same – he shouldn't leave the doors unlocked, even for a minute!' said Jenny. 'Well, here we are – just look at the ink splashes everywhere – and that dear little clock that kept such good time is gone. Now what would the thief want with a clock, I'd like to know?'

'It would be small and neat enough to pop into his pocket,' said Tinker. 'If he was dishonest enough to steal Dad's papers, he would certainly not say no to a nice little clock like that! He's probably taken other things too!'

They went right into the room, and Jenny at once gave a loud exclamation. 'LOOK! Aren't those some of the papers your father was working on – on the table there? All covered with tiny figures?'

Tinker looked closely at them. 'Yes – they're his very latest papers. He showed me them the other day. I remember this diagram. Jenny – how COULD he leave them on the table with the door unlocked this morning – when only last night the thief was here! How could he? He *said* he was going to hide them away so carefully, because, if the thief found them, he could use them with the other papers that were stolen – but as long as the thief only had half of them, they wouldn't be much use – and now he's forgotten all about hiding them, after all!'

'Look now, Tinker – let's hide them away ourselves,' said Jenny, 'and not tell him where they are. These thieves will have another try for them, no doubt about that. Let's think of some place where they'd be absolutely safe.'

'*I* know!' said Tinker. 'We could hide them on Kirrin Island! Somewhere in the old ruined castle! NOBODY would guess they were there.'

'Now that's a *fine* idea!' said Jenny. 'I'd be glad to think they were out of the house.' She gathered up the papers quickly. 'Here you are. You'd better tell Julian and the others, and go across to the island with them as soon as you can. My, what a relief to think they'll be well away from here. I'll be able to sleep soundly in my bed at nights then!'

Tinker stuffed the precious papers under his jersey, and he and Jenny ran at top speed down the spiral stairway. They saw the Professor not far off, and he turned and hailed them. 'Tinker! Jenny! I know what you're going to ask me! You want to know where I've hidden those papers of mine. Come here and I'll whisper!'

Not knowing quite what to say, the two went rather guiltily over to Tinker's father. He whispered loudly, 'I've wrapped them up, and put them under the coal at the back of the coal-cellar – right at the *very* back!'

'And a fine mess you've made of your trousers,' said Jenny, disgusted. 'And good gracious – you must have sat down in the coal yourself! You look a right mess. Come along and let me brush you down. Not indoors, though, or the place will be thick with coal-dust!'

'Don't you think it was a good hiding place, Jenny?'

asked the Professor. 'Ha – you thought I'd forget to hide them, didn't you?'

He went off, looking very pleased with himself. Jenny chuckled in delight. 'Dear old Professor! He's hidden all his *newspapers* there, but not a single one of his own precious papers. And now whatever shall we tell him when he wants the morning papers? Tinker, you cycle out to the paper shop and get another lot. My goodness – what it is to have a brainy man in the house! Whatever will he do next?'

CHAPTER THIRTEEN

Quite a lot of plans!

AFTER TINKER had fetched a new supply of morning papers, he decided to go down to the camp in the field and tell the others all that had happened that morning. He still felt angry about being ticked off by Julian the night before – but he simply couldn't wait to tell the others about the robbery – and about the grand idea he, Tinker, had of hiding the rest of his father's papers on Kirrin Island.

So off he went, with Mischief happily on his shoulder, holding tightly to his hair. The others were all there in the field. They had just come back from a shopping expedition, and Tinker's eyes gleamed when he saw the various tinned meats and tinned fruits, fresh rolls, tomatoes and apples and bananas that had been brought back from the shops at Big Hollow.

Julian was glad to see that Tinker looked bright and cheerful. He was afraid that the boy might have sulked, and that would have spoilt things for the others.

'Hi!' said Tinker. 'I've got news!' And he proceeded to tell the others all about the happenings of the night before, ending up with his father solemnly going off to hide his morning newspapers under the coal at the back of the coal-cellar, under the impression that he was hiding the rest of his precious papers.

'But why on earth didn't you tell him he had left his valuable papers behind and hidden his newspapers?' asked George.

'Because, if he knew that, he'd go and hide the *precious* papers somewhere, and forget where he'd put them – and they might be lost for ever!' said Tinker.

'Well, what are *you* going to do with them?' asked Dick.

'I've had rather a brainwave,' said Tinker, as modestly as he could. 'Er – I thought that *we'd* hide them away ourselves, where nobody could *possibly* find them.'

'And where is this wonderful hiding place?' asked Dick.

'On Kirrin Island!' said Tinker, triumphantly. 'Who'd think of looking *there*? And as we shall *all* know the hiding place, we can't possibly forget it. The papers will be absolutely safe. Dad can get on with the rest of his ideas without worrying about anything?'

'Have you told him all this?' asked Julian.

'Well, no,' said Tinker. 'Jenny thought we'd better just keep it to ourselves. She's pretty certain the thieves will try their hand at breaking in to get the rest of the papers, though.'

'Ha! Well, I vote we scribble some papers ourselves,' said Dick. 'Complete with wonderful diagrams, and all kinds of peculiar figurings and numberings. I feel I could do that very well! And we'd leave them up in the tower room for the thieves to take – they'd think they were the ones they'd missed!'

Everyone chuckled. 'Idiot!' said Julian. 'Still – it's not a bad idea to leave something behind for the thieves that isn't worth a moment's look – and hide the genuine figures where they'd never dream of finding them – on Kirrin Island!'

'When shall we go?' asked George. 'It's ages since I've visited my island – and will you believe it, last time I rowed over *trippers* had been there and left their beastly mess everywhere! Paper bags, broken glass, lettuce leaves, orange peel, ugh!'

'Why DO people do that?' asked Anne. 'They'd hate to have to sit in the midst of *other* people's mess – so why in the world can't they clear up their own?'

'Oh, they're probably just like that in their own homes,' said Dick. 'All mess and litter – and yet it takes so little time to clear up a picnic mess, and leave the place decent for the next comers.'

'What did you do with all the mess left on Kirrin Island?' asked Julian.

'I buried it deep in the sand at the back of one of the beaches,' said George. 'Where the tide can't turn it all up again. And with every dig of my spade I said "Blow you, you awful trippers without manners, blow you – and next time you go anywhere, may you find someone else's litter to make you feel sick. Blow you!"'

George looked and sounded so very fierce that everyone

burst out laughing. Timmy sat there with his tongue lolling out, looking as if he were laughing too, and Mischief made a funny little noise rather like a giggle.

'Good old George. She always says straight out what she thinks!' said Julian.

They sat and talked over their plans for some time. 'Dick and Julian had better make the fake plans and figures,' said George. 'They'd be better at that kind of thing than anyone else. And Tinker can plant them somewhere in his father's tower room for the thief to take if he goes there again – and I bet he will. He found it easy enough last night!'

'And George could take Tinker's father's papers with the *correct* figures and plans over to Kirrin Island,' said Anne.

'Not till night time, though,' said Dick. 'If anyone were on the watch, and saw George rowing over there, they might guess she was taking something important to hide. They might be watching her father too. By the way – where *are* these papers? You did not leave them behind at home, did you, Tinker?'

'I didn't dare to,' said Tinker. 'I felt as if there might be eyes peeping at me, watching and hoping I'd go out and leave the papers behind. I've got them under my jersey, just here!' And he patted the top of his stomach.

'Oh – so *that*'s why you look as if you've had too much breakfast!' said George. 'Well – what shall our plans be?'

'We'd better make out the false papers straight away, with figures and diagrams,' said Julian. 'Just in case thieves come sooner than we think. Tinker, we'd better go into *your* house to do those. If we go to George's her father might spot us and wonder what on earth we were doing. We'd probably be sent off, anyway, because of the scarlet fever business.'

'Well, what about *my* father?' said Tinker. '*He* might spot us too. Anyway, he's not keen on my having anyone there this week, because he's so busy with his new invention. It's awfully good, and . . .'

'*Tinker* – don't start spilling beans again!' said Julian, warningly. 'I say it would be best to go to your house.'

'What about *me* going indoors and bringing out Dad's big drawing-board, and some of his paper, and his mapping pens and ink, and doing the diagrams and things out here in the tent?' said Tinker. 'Honestly, I never know when Dad is going to come into my room. He'd wonder what on *earth* we were doing if he found us all there! We can have a good look at the papers I've got under my jersey, and do a whole lot in the same style – not the *same* figures, naturally – and we could do some diagrams too.'

'All right,' said Julian, giving way, as he saw that Tinker was genuinely afraid that his father might see them making the false papers. 'Go and get the drawing-board and come back with it, and anything else we'll need. You go with him, George.'

'Right,' said George, and she and Tinker went up Tinker's garden to the house. Tinker scouted round to see if his father was anywhere about, but couldn't see him. He found a large drawing-board, some big sheets of paper used by his father for working out his figures, and a book of odd but easy-to-copy diagrams. He also brought mapping pens, Indian ink and blotting-paper, and even remembered drawing-pins to pin the sheets of paper to the board. George carried half the things, and kept a sharp lookout for Tinker's father.

'It's all right. He's asleep somewhere – can't you hear that noise?' asked Tinker; and sure enough George could – a gentle snoring from some room not far off!

They went back down the garden and over the fence, handing everything to the others before they climbed over. 'Good!' said Julian. 'Now we can produce some beautiful charts of figures that mean absolutely nothing at all – and diagrams that will look perfect and not mean a thing either!'

'Better come into the tent,' said George. 'If anyone wanders down from the circus camp, they might ask us what we're doing.'

So they all went into the boys' tent, which was the bigger one, Timmy too, and Mischief, who was delighted to be with the big dog. Julian soon set to work, though he found the space rather cramped. They were all watching him in admiration as he set out rows of beautiful, meaningless, figures when Timmy suddenly gave a deep growl, and all his hackles rose up on his neck.

Julian turned the drawing-board over at once, and sat on it. The canvas doorway of the tent was pulled aside and in poked the grinning face of Charlie the Chimp!

'Oh, it's *you*, Charlie!' said Julian. 'Well, well, well, and how are you today?'

The chimpanzee grinned even more widely, and held out his hand. Julian shook it solemnly, and the chimpanzee went carefully all round the tent, shaking hands with everyone.

'Sit down, Charlie,' said Dick. 'I suppose you've let yourself out of your cage as usual, and come to see what we've got for our dinner. Well, you'll be glad to hear we've got enough for you as well as ourselves.'

Charlie squashed himself between Timmy and Tinker, and with much interest watched Julian at work with his pen and ink. 'I bet that chimp could draw, if you gave him a piece of paper and a pencil,' said Anne.

So, to keep him quiet, he was given a pencil, and a notebook. He at once began to scribble in it very earnestly.

'Goodness – he's doing a whole lot of funny figures!' said Anne. 'He's trying to copy *you*, Ju!'

'If he's not careful, I'll hand the whole job over to him!' said Julian, with a chuckle. 'George, let's talk about your plans for tonight. I think, if you are going over to Kirrin Island to hide those papers, you must take Timmy with you.'

'Oh, I will!' said George. 'Not that there will be a single soul on the island, but I'd like old Tim just for company. I'll take the papers straight to the island, land, and hide them.'

'Where?' asked Julian.

'Oh, I'll decide that when I'm there,' said George. 'Somewhere cunning! I know my own little island from top to bottom. And there those papers will stay until all danger is past. We'll let Professor Hayling think he has hidden them somewhere himself, and forgotten where! It will be fun to row across to my island at night, with Timmy.'

'The thieves can make do with *my* figures and diagrams if they come to the tower room again,' said Julian. 'Don't they look professional?'

They certainly did! Everyone looked at the neat figures and carefully drawn diagrams with admiration.

Timmy suddenly sat up and gave a deep growl again. Charlie the Chimp patted him as if to say 'What's wrong, old boy?' but Timmy took no notice and went on growling. He suddenly shot out of the tent, and there was a shout from someone outside. 'Get off! Get down! GET DOWN!'

George swung back the tent opening. Mr Wooh was there, looking extremely frightened as Timmy growled menacingly round his ankles. Charlie the Chimp ran up to him on all fours and, angry because Timmy was snarling at his friend, showed his teeth suddenly at the big dog. George was terrified. 'Don't let them fight!' she cried, afraid that Timmy would get decidedly the worst of it. Charlie was jumping up and down in a most alarming way.

'Charleee!' said Mr Wooh in his deep voice. 'Charleee!'

And Charlie stopped jumping up and down and making horrible noises, and leapt straight on to Mr Wooh's back, putting his arms round his neck.

Mr Wooh bowed courteously to them all. 'I trust I have not disturbed you, my friends,' he said, with his strong accent. 'I'll now take a little walk with my friend Charleee. You come again to see our show, I hope. Yes? No?'

'Probably,' said Dick, noticing that the magician had taken a quick and interested look at Julian's figures and diagrams. Julian covered them up immediately, as if he didn't want the magician to see them. He had seen something in the man's eyes that puzzled him. Could Mr Wooh possibly have had anything to do with the theft of the papers the night before? After all, he was a wizard at figures himself – he might be able to read the Professor's figures and diagrams and understand them perfectly. Well – he wouldn't gather much from the ones Julian was now doing – they were more or less nonsense made up by Julian himself to deceive anyone interested in the real ones.

'I interrupt you? Pardon me!' said Mr Wooh, and bowed himself politely away from the group in the tent. Charlie the Chimp followed him, hoping that Mischief would too, so that they could have a game. But Mischief didn't want to. He didn't like Mr Wooh.

'Well, I didn't realise that anyone from the circus would

445

walk down the field so quietly, and be able to hear what we were saying inside the tent,' said Julian, worried. 'I didn't like the look in his eyes. Dick – you don't suppose he heard anything we were saying, do you?'

'Would it matter?' said Dick.

'It might,' said Julian. 'Do you think he heard what George said about going over to Kirrin Island with the other papers – the valuable ones that the thieves didn't see in the tower room last night? I wouldn't let George go if I thought he had heard. In fact, I think she'd better *not* go. She might run into danger.'

'Don't be silly, Ju,' said George. 'I *am* going. And Timmy will be with me.'

'You heard what I said, George. You are *not* to go!' said Julian. '*I'll* take the papers and hide them on the island. I'll get them when it's dark, fairly late. I'll cycle over to Kirrin and untie the boat you keep there, and row over to the island.'

'All right, Julian,' said George, astonishingly meekly. 'Shall we have a meal now? We've only to open the tins, and empty the tomatoes and lettuces out of the basket there. And the drinks are in that cool corner over there.'

'Right,' said Julian, glad that George had given way to him so easily. *He* would go across in George's boat and find a good hiding place. If danger was about, he reckoned he could deal with it better than George could.

Yes, Julian, you may be right. But don't be too sure about tonight!

CHAPTER FOURTEEN

Ladders – and a lot of fun!

THE CHILDREN stared after Mr Wooh and the chimpanzee. They saw Charlie pick up two empty buckets, one in each strong paw, and race off to the right with them.

'Where's he going?' said Anne, astonished at the rate he was running along.

'I bet he's going to get some water from the stream in those pails, and take them to whoever washes down the horses,' said George. She was right! Charlie soon came back again, walking this time, holding a heavy pail of water in each hand!

'Well, I must say that chimpanzee is jolly useful!' said Dick. 'Look – there's Madelon who trains those beautiful

447

horses that paraded round the ring last night – she's wearing old trousers this morning, she looks quite different. There – Charlie has set the pails of water down beside her. I bet that as soon as she wants any more water, he'll be off again to the stream!'

'I rather like old Charlie,' said Anne. 'I didn't at first – but now I do. I wish he didn't belong to Mr Wooh.'

Julian stood up, looking down at the paper on which he had so carefully written lines of small figures and drawn many peculiar diagrams. 'I somehow feel this isn't much good now,' he said. 'I think Mr Wooh must have guessed it was all a make-up as soon as he saw it. He gave himself away a bit, though – I saw him looking at the paper in a rather startled way, as if he'd seen something very like it very recently indeed!'

'So he had, the wretch, if he'd sent someone up to get my dad's papers out of the tower room!' said Tinker. 'Hey! What about having a look round the circus to see if we can spot a ladder anywhere – one tall enough to reach the tower room!'

'Good idea!' said Dick. 'Come on – we'll go now. Chuck that drawing-board and diagram paper over our fence, Ju. I hardly think it's worth your while to finish it.'

The Five, with Tinker and Mischief, wandered down the field to where the circus was encamped. Dick spotted a ladder lying in the grass, and nudged Julian.

'Julian! See that? Would it reach the tower?' Julian walked over to it. It certainly was very, very long – but *would* it be long enough? No – he didn't think it would. Still – he might as well find out who owned it. At that moment up came the Boneless Man, walking perfectly. He grinned at the children – and then suddenly put all his double-joints to work, bent his knees into peculiar positions, twisted his head round so that he was looking over his own back, and then bent his double-jointed arms the wrong way, so that he looked very odd indeed!

'Don't! I don't like it!' said Anne. 'You look so peculiar and strange! Why are you called the *Boneless* Man? You aren't boneless – you just make yourself *look* as if you were, with all those funny double-joints of yours!'

The Boneless Man seemed suddenly to lose all his bones, and crumpled up on the grass in a funny heap. The children couldn't help laughing. He didn't look as if he had any bones at all then!

'Er – can you climb ladders if you're double-jointed?' asked Julian, suddenly.

'Of course!' said the Boneless Man. 'Run up them backwards, forwards, sideways – any way you like.'

'Is that *your* ladder, then?' asked Dick, nodding his head towards the ladder in the grass.

'Well – I use it, but so does everyone else!' said the Boneless Man, turning his head the wrong way round, so that it seemed as if it was put on back to front. It was odd to speak to someone whose head did that – one minute they were talking to his face, the next to the back of his head!

'I *wish* you wouldn't do that,' said Anne. 'It makes me feel giddy.'

'Do you use that ladder to put the flag on the top of the circus tent?' asked Dick. 'It doesn't look long enough for that.'

'It isn't,' said the Boneless Man, turning his head the right way round, much to Anne's relief. 'There's a much

449

longer one over there – it takes three men to carry it, it's so heavy – but the centre circus pole is very tall, as you see. One man couldn't *possibly* carry the long ladder.'

The children looked at one another. That ruled out the very long ladder too, then. If it needed three men to carry it, Jenny would certainly have heard a lot more noise last night!

'Are there any more ladders in the circus camp?'

'No – just the two. Why? Thinking of buying one?' said the Boneless Man. 'I must go. The Boss is beckoning to me.' Off he went, walking in a most peculiar fashion, using his double-joints for all he was worth!

'What about the acrobats?' said Julian. '*They* must be used to climbing and clambering everywhere. I wonder if any of *them* could have climbed the wall?'

'I don't think so,' said Tinker. 'I had a good look at it this morning – and although there *is* a kind of creeper climbing up the wall, it stops halfway – and above that there's just the stone wall. Even an acrobat would have to have some help up the tower wall!'

'Could the *clowns* have found a way?' said George. 'No – I suppose they're not as good even as the acrobats at climbing. I don't believe the thief *could* have been anyone from the circus after all. Look – what's that on the ground over there – outside that tent?'

They all went over to see. It looked like a pile of dark-grey fur. George touched it with her toe. 'Oh – *I* know what it is – the donkey-skin!'

'Golly – so it is!' cried Tinker in delight, and picked it up – or tried to. It was much too heavy for him to hold up all of it.

In a trice Dick and George were inside that donkey-skin! Dick had the head, and found that he *could* see quite well where he was going, for the donkey neck had neat eye-holes in it – the head itself was stuffed with paper. George was the back legs, and kicked up her feet and made the donkey look extremely lively. The others roared with laughter.

Someone shouted loudly. 'Hey – you leave that donkey-skin alone!'

It was Jeremy. He came running up, looking furious. He had a stick in his hand, and hit out at the donkey's hind parts, giving poor George a good old whack, and making her yell.

'Hey! Stop that, it hurt!'

Tinker looked furiously at Jeremy. 'How dare you do that?' he shouted. 'Dick and George are in the donkey-skin. Put down that stick!'

But Jeremy gave the donkey's hind legs another whack and George yelled again. Tinker gave a shout too, and flung himself on Jeremy, trying to get the stick out of his hand. The boy struggled, holding on to the stick, but Tinker gave him a straight blow on the chest, and down he went!

'Ha! I *said* I'd knock you down sometime, and I have!' yelled Tinker. 'Get up and fight. *I'll* teach you not to hit animals!'

'Now stop it, Tinker,' said Julian. 'Come out of the skin, you two idiots, before old Grandad comes up. He looks as if he's on his way now!'

Jeremy was up now, and danced round Tinker with doubled fists. Before either boy could exchange a blow, Grandad's great voice came to them.

'NOW THEN! STOP IT!'

451

Jeremy swung his fist at Tinker, who dodged, and then in his turn hit out at Jeremy, who ran back – straight into old Grandad, who at once clutched him.

By this time George and Dick were out of the donkey-skin, looking rather ashamed of themselves. Old Grandad grinned at them, still holding on to the furious Jeremy.

'Fight's off,' said Grandad to Tinker and Jeremy. 'If you want to go on, either of you, you can fight *me*, not each other.'

However, neither of the boys wanted to take on old Grandad. He might be old, but he could still give some mighty slaps, as Jeremy very well knew. They stood staring at one another, looking rather sheepish.

'Go on – shake hands and be friends,' said Grandad. 'Quick, now, or I'll do a little fighting myself!'

Tinker held out his hand just as Jeremy held out his. They shook, grinning at one another. 'That's right!' said old Grandad. 'No harm done. No bones broken. You're quits now, so no more knocking each other about.'

'Right, Grandad,' said Jeremy, giving him a friendly punch. The old man turned to Dick and George. 'And if *you* want to borrow that donkey-skin, you're welcome,' said old Grandad. 'But it's manners to ask the owner's permission first.'

'Yes. Sorry,' said Dick, grinning. He wondered what Professor Hayling and Jenny would say if he and George did borrow it, and galloped into Hollow House at top speed. But no – he decided reluctantly that Jenny might be scared stiff and give notice, and that would never do. She wouldn't at all like being chased by an apparently mad donkey, nor would Professor Hayling.

Grandad went off, and Julian spoke to Jeremy, who wasn't quite sure whether to go or to stay. 'We saw old Charlie carrying pails of water for the horses,' he said. 'Isn't he strong!'

Jeremy grinned, glad to be friends again, and to be able to stay with the Five and Tinker. They wandered all round the field together, looking at the magnificent horses and at

FIVE ARE TOGETHER AGAIN

Dead-Shot Dick doing a little practising at shooting and then watched one small acrobat practising amazing jumps and somersaults.

Mischief the monkey came with them. He was absolutely at home with everyone in the circus now, man, woman or animal. He leapt on to the horses' backs, and they didn't mind! He pretended to help Charlie the Chimp to carry one of the pails of water – he ran off with Dead-Shot Dick's cap. He went into the chimp's cage and cuddled up in the straw with him, scrabbling about as if the cage belonged to him. He even went into Grandad's tent and came out with a small bottle of lemonade! He couldn't get the top off, and took it to Charlie, who was watching nearby! Charlie promptly forced it off with his strong front paws – and then, to Mischief's disgust, tipped up the bottle and drank the lot!

Mischief was very angry indeed. He ran to Charlie's cage, which was open, and sent the straw flying everywhere. Charlie sat outside his cage and enjoyed the fun, grinning happily.

'Come out, Mischief!' called Tinker. 'You're making a nuisance of yourself!'

'Let him be,' said one of the acrobats, who was standing nearby. 'Old Charlie enjoys a bit of temper – when it's someone else's! Look at him sitting grinning there.'

They watched for a few seconds more, to make sure that Mischief wasn't annoying the big chimpanzee, and then turned to watch Monty and Winks, the clowns, having an argument, which ended in Monty throwing water over Winks, and Winks emptying a basket of rubbish over Monty. What a pair!

When they turned to see if Mischief was still annoying

454

Charlie, they saw that the little monkey had left the cage, and was tearing down the field to the fence. He leapt up, and over, and disappeared.

'He must think it's dinner time,' said Tinker, looking at his watch. 'And gosh, so it is. Come on everyone, Jenny will be in a fine old fury if we're really late – it's hot dinner today.'

Away they all went in a hurry. Hot dinner! Over the fence, then, and up the garden at top speed. They mustn't keep a hot dinner waiting – or Jenny either!

CHAPTER FIFTEEN

A happy day – and a shock for Julian

TINKER AND the Five were two minutes late for their dinner. Jenny was just taking it in, looking a little grim, as she had not been able to find the children anywhere. 'Ah – here you are at last!' she said. 'I looked down the garden but you were nowhere to be seen. It's a good thing you came in when you did – five minutes more and I'd have taken the dinner back again.'

'*Dear* Jenny, you know you wouldn't,' said Tinker, giving her a sudden squeeze that made her squeal. 'Oh, how good it smells! Mmmmm-mmmmm!'

'You and your mmmmms!' said Jenny, pushing Tinker away. 'And I've told you before, that I don't mind a gentle hug, but those *squeezes* of yours take all my breath away. *No*, Tinker, keep away from me – another squeeze like that and I'll feel like a lemon!'

Everyone laughed at that. Jenny did say the most amusing things. Anne felt sorry that she hadn't offered to stay and help her with the dinner. Oh dear – the time went so quickly, once they were all out together.

The talk at dinner time was very lively. So was Mischief the monkey! He took bits from everyone's plate and handed some of them down to Timmy, who was lying under the table as usual. Timmy appreciated these titbits very much!

'Well! *I* didn't see a single ladder in the circus camp that was tall enough to reach up to the tower room,' said George.

'No. If there was one, it was jolly well hidden,' said Dick. 'Pass the mustard, someone!'

'In front of you, idiot,' said Julian. 'You know I'm beginning to wonder if Mr Wooh had anything to do with the stealing of your father's papers, Tinker. I can't somehow see him climbing high ladders – he's so – so . . .'

'Polite and proper,' said Anne. 'Actually, I can't think of *any*one in the circus who would either *want* the papers, or is nasty enough to steal them. They're all so nice.'

'I still think Mr Wooh is the most *likely* one,' said Julian. 'He's interested in complicated figures and clever inventions. But all the same, I'm beginning to think I'm wrong. He could NOT have got up to the tower room as there is no ladder long enough – and I really doubt if he'd *dare* to take a ladder into the courtyard and risk putting it up to the tower. He might so easily be caught.'

'Right. We'll rule him out,' said Tinker. 'But if nobody went up the spiral stairway, because all doors were locked, and nobody used a ladder, I don't see HOW those papers disappeared.'

'Wind took them out of the window, perhaps?' suggested Anne. 'Would that be possible?'

'No. For two reasons,' said Julian. 'One is that the window wasn't wide enough open for the wind to blow in with enough strength to blow papers *out*. And secondly, we'd have been sure to have found some of them down in the courtyard if they'd been blown out. But we didn't find a single one there.'

'Well – if nobody got through the three locked doors, and nobody got through the window, HOW did those papers get stolen?' demanded George. 'It would have been a miracle for those papers to have hopped away by themselves – and I don't believe in that kind of miracle!'

There was a long silence. What a mystery it was! 'I suppose Tinker's father couldn't *possibly* have gone walking in his sleep, and taken them, could he?' asked Anne.

'Well – I don't know if a sleep-walker can unlock doors with the right keys, and steal his own papers, leaving some on the floor, and then walk carefully down the spiral stairway still fast asleep, locking all the doors behind him, and then go to his own bedroom, get into bed, and then wake up in the morning without remembering a single moment of the whole thing!' said Julian.

'No. It can't be possible,' said Dick. 'Have you ever known your father to walk in his sleep, Tinker?'

Tinker considered. 'No, I can't say I have,' he said. 'He's a very light sleeper, usually. No. I don't believe Dad did all that in his sleep. It was somebody else.'

'It must have been some sort of miracle man, then,' said George. 'No *ordinary* person could do it. And whoever planned it wanted those papers very, very badly, or he would never have risked getting them against so many odds.'

'And if he wanted them so VERY badly, he'll certainly make an effort to get the ones he left behind under the table,' said Julian. 'Good thing we've got those! He will probably try to get up into the tower the same way as he did before – but goodness knows what it was!'

'Well – those papers will be safely out of his way, tonight!' said George. 'On my island!'

'Yes,' said Julian. 'I'll find a most unlikely hiding place – somewhere about the ruined castle, I think. By the way – I hope you haven't *still* got them under your jersey,

Tinker. No – you don't look fat any more. What have you done with them?'

'George said I'd better give them to her to keep, in case they slipped out of my jersey,' said Tinker. 'You took them, didn't you, George?'

'Yes,' said George. 'Don't let's talk about it any more.'

'Why not? The thief's not here. He can't be listening to us!' said Tinker. 'I believe you're cross, George, because Julian won't let you take the papers yourself!'

'Oh, do shut up, Tinker,' said George. 'I shall be jolly cross with *you* in a minute, if you let Mischief upset your glass of lemonade again, all over my bread. Take him off the table! His manners are getting worse!'

'They aren't – but your temper is!' said Tinker and promptly received a kick under the table from Julian. He was about to kick back but thought better of it. Julian could kick very much harder than he could! He decided to take Mischief off the table in case George smacked him. He put the little monkey under the table where Timmy was sitting quietly. Mischief immediately cuddled up to him, putting his little furry arms round the big dog's neck. Timmy sniffed him all over, and then gave him two or three licks. He was very fond of the naughty little monkey.

'What shall we do this afternoon?' asked Dick, when they had all helped Jenny to clear away and wash up. 'What about a bathe in the sea? Is it warm enough?'

'Not really. But that doesn't matter, we always feel warm when we come out of the water and run about and then rub ourselves down,' said Anne. 'Jenny – do *you* feel like a bathe?'

'Good gracious, no!' said Jenny, shivering at the thought. 'I'm a cold mortal, I am. The thought of going into that cold sea makes me shudder. If you want your towels, they are all in the airing cupboard. And don't you be late for tea, if you want any, because I've a lot of ironing to do afterwards.'

'Right, Jenny,' said Tinker, about to give her one of his 'squeezes' but thinking better of it when he saw her warning look. 'Julian, may I come with you to Kirrin Island tonight? I'd like a bit of fun.'

'You may not,' said Julian. 'Anyway, there won't be any fun.'

'There might be if Mr Wooh did hear George say she was taking those papers over,' said Tinker. 'He'd be waiting on the island – and you might be glad to have me with you!'

'I should *not* be glad to have you with me,' said Julian. 'You'd just be in the way. It would be much easier to look after myself than to see what *you* were up to all the time. I am going by myself. Please don't scowl at me like that, George.'

He got up from the table and went to look out of the window. 'Wind's died down a bit,' he said. 'I think I'll have a bathe in an hour's time. If any of you others want to come, we'll go down together.'

They all went down to the beach after a while and bathed, except Mischief, who put one small paw into the water, gave a howl and scampered back up the beach as fast as ever he could, afraid that Tinker might catch him and make him go in! Timmy went in, of course. He swam marvellously, and even gave Tinker a ride on his back, diving down when the boy felt heavy, so that Tinker suddenly found himself sprawling in the water! 'You wretch, Timmy!' yelled the boy. 'The water's gone up my nose. Wait till I catch you! I'll put *you* under!'

But he couldn't possibly catch old Timmy, who really enjoyed the joke. The big dog gave a joyful bark, and swam after George. How he loved being with them all!

The rest of the day went quickly. Jenny had a fine tea for them, with slices of ham, and salad, and fruit to end with, and said afterwards that she had time to play a game of Scrabble with them if they liked. Mischief sat on the table to watch.

'I don't mind you *watching*,' said Anne. 'But you are NOT to scrabble, Mischief. You sent all my little ivory tiles on the floor last time we played, and I lost the game.'

Timmy watched gravely, sitting on a chair beside George. He simply could NOT understand what made the children play games like this when they could go for a nice long walk with him. They took pity on him when the game was over and went out for a two-mile walk along by the sea. How Timmy loved that!

'I shall cycle to Kirrin Village as soon as it's dark,' announced Julian. 'I suppose your boat is tied up in the usual place, George? I'm sorry I can't take you with me, but there *might* be a bit of danger, as we said. However I won't run into any if I can help it. I shan't feel comfortable until those secret papers are safely out of the way! You can give them to me just before I go, George.'

Anne suddenly yawned. 'Don't start too late or I shall fall asleep!' she said. 'It's getting dark already. All that swimming has made me feel tired!'

Dick yawned too. 'I'm jolly sleepy as well,' he said. 'I shall bed down in our tent as soon as you've gone, Ju. I'll see you off safely first, papers and all! You'd better go to your tent, too, girls – you look tired.'

'Right!' said Anne. 'You coming, George?'

'We'll all go,' said George. 'Come on, Tinker. Bet you I get over the fence and down to our tents first! Good night, Jenny. We're off!'

She and Anne and Tinker, with Timmy running behind, went off down the darkening garden. Dick and Julian helped Jenny to tidy up, and to draw all the curtains. 'Well, good night, Jenny,' said Dick. 'All you have to do is to lock the door behind us and go safely up to bed. We'll go down to our tents now. Sleep well!'

'Oh, I always do,' said Jenny. 'Look after yourselves now and don't get into any mischief! Hide those papers well, where nobody can find them!'

Julian and Dick went off down the garden, having heard Jenny carefully locking the door behind them.

Tinker and the girls were already over the fence, Mis-

462

chief on Tinker's shoulder. Anne spoke anxiously to George. 'I do hope Julian will be all right going over to Kirrin Island,' she said. 'I wish he'd take Dick with him.'

'If he took anyone it should be *me*!' burst out George. 'It's *my* island!'

'Oh, don't be silly, George. The papers would be much safer with Julian,' said Anne. 'It would be an awful business for you, cycling by yourself to Kirrin, getting your boat into the water, and rowing over in the dark!'

'It would not!' said George. 'If Julian can do it, then so could I. You go into our tent, Anne, and get ready for bed. I'll come in a minute, after I've taken Timmy for a run.'

She waited till Anne had disappeared through the tent opening. Then she went quietly off by herself in the dark, Timmy trotting beside her, rather surprised.

Soon there came the sound of voices, as Julian and Dick reached the fence and leapt over it. They went to their tent and found Tinker there, yawning and getting ready for bed.

Soon the three boys were all rolled up in their rugs, Mischief cuddled up to Tinker. After some time Julian sat up and looked at his watch, and then peeped out of the tent opening. 'Quite dark!' he said. 'But the moon's coming up, I see. I think I'll get the papers from George now, and set off on my bicycle to Kirrin. I can easily get it out of the shed.'

'You know where George keeps her boat,' said Dick. 'You won't have any difficulty in finding it. Got your torch, Ju?'

'Yes – and a new battery,' said Julian. 'Look!'

He switched on his torch. It gave a good, powerful beam. 'Shan't miss the island if I put *this* on!' he said.

'Now – I'll get those papers. Hey, George – I'm coming to your tent for the papers!'

He went over to the girls' tent. Anne was there, only half-awake. She blinked as Julian's torch shone into her eyes.

'George!' said Julian. 'Give me those papers now, please – hallo – *Hey*, Anne – where is George?'

Anne started looking all round the tent. George's rugs were there, piled in an untidy heap; but there was no George – and no Timmy either!

'Oh, Ju! Do you know what George has done – she's slipped out with the precious papers – and taken Timmy too! She must have gone to fetch her bike, and ridden off to Kirrin to get her boat – and row over to Kirrin Island! Julian, whatever will happen if she rows over and finds somebody waiting to grab those papers from her?' Poor Anne was very near to tears.

'I could *shake* her!' said Julian, very angry indeed. 'Going off alone like that in the dark – cycling to Kirrin – rowing over to the island – and back! She must be mad! Suppose Mr Wooh and his friends are waiting there for her! The – silly – little – idiot!'

'Oh, Julian, quick! You and Dick get your cycles and try to catch her,' begged Anne. 'Oh please do! Anything might happen to her! Dear, silly old George! Thank goodness Timmy's gone with her.'

'Well, that's a blessing, anyway,' said Julian, still angry. 'He'll look after her as much as he can. Oh, I could shake George till her teeth rattled! I *thought* she was rather quiet tonight. Thinking out this plan, I suppose!'

He went up to the house with Dick and Tinker to tell Jenny about George, and then he and Dick at once went to get their bicycles. This was serious. George had no right to be out alone at night like this – and go rowing over to Kirrin Island – ESPECIALLY if there was any chance of someone lying in wait for her!

Jenny was very worried indeed. She watched the two boys cycling off in the dark. Tinker begged her to let him go too, but she wouldn't. 'You and Mischief would just be nuisances,' she said. 'Oh, won't I shake that rascal of a George when she gets back. What a girl! Well, well – thank goodness Timmy's with her. That dog's as good as half a dozen policemen!'

CHAPTER SIXTEEN

Night on Kirrin Island

IT WAS certainly very dark when the half-moon went
behind the clouds. George was glad that her bicycle lamp
shone so brightly. The shadows in the hedges were deep
and mysterious – 'as if they hid people ready to jump out
at us,' she said to Timmy. 'But you'd go for them at once,
wouldn't you, Timmy!'

Timmy was too much out of breath to bark an answer.
George was going pretty fast, and he didn't mean to let her
get out of sight. He was sure she shouldn't be out by
herself on a dark night like this. He couldn't *imagine* why
she had suddenly taken it into her head to go for a long
night ride! He raced along, panting.

They met cars with dazzling headlamps, and George had to keep pulling to the side. She was terribly afraid that Timmy might be hit by one of the cars. Oh dear – I'd never, never forgive myself if anything happened to Timmy, she thought. I half wish I hadn't set out now. But I'm NOT going to let Julian hide anything on *my* island. That's my job, not his. 'Timmy darling, PLEASE keep on my left side. You'll be safe then.'

So Timmy kept on her left, still mystified by this sudden journey out into the night. They came at last to Kirrin village, where windows were still lit here and there. Through the village and on to Kirrin Bay – ah, there was the bay! The half-moon slid out from behind a cloud and George saw the dark sea, shining here and there as the moonlight caught the crests of the waves.

'There's my island, look Timmy,' said George, feeling a swelling of pride as she looked over the dark heaving sea to a darker stretch, which she knew was Kirrin Island. 'My very *own* island. Waiting for me tonight!'

'Woof,' said Timmy, rather quietly, because he really hadn't any breath to waste. *Now* what was George going to do? Why had she come out on this lonely ride without the others? Timmy was puzzled.

They came to the stretch of beach where boats were kept. George rode down a ramp to the beach, jumped off her bicycle, and put it by a bathing-hut in the deep shadows. No one would see it there. Then she went to stare over the sea at her island.

She had only looked for a moment or two when she clutched Timmy's collar, and gave an exclamation.

'TIMMY! There's a *light* on my island! Look, to the right

467

there. Can you see it? Timmy, there's somebody camping there. How DARE they? It's *my* island and I don't allow *any*one on it unless they have my permission.'

Timmy looked – and yes, he could see the light too. Was it made by a camp fire – or a lantern? He couldn't tell. All he knew was that he didn't want George to go over there now. He pawed at her, trying to make her understand that he wanted her to go back home with him.

'No, Timmy. I'm *not* going back till I've found out who's there!' she said. 'It would be cowardly to turn back now. And if it's somebody waiting for me to turn up with the papers, they can think again. Look – I'm hiding them here under the tarpaulin in this boat. It would be idiotic to try and hide them on the island if there's someone there who *might* rob me of anything I've got – it might be one of the thieves who climbed into the tower room, and left some of the papers behind. If *he*'s waiting for me, he won't get any papers!'

George stuffed the parcel of papers under the tarpaulin as she spoke. 'It's Fisherman Connell's boat, called *Gypsy*,' she said, reading the name on the boat by the light of her torch. '*He* won't mind me hiding something in it!'

She covered up the papers with the tarpaulin, and then looked over to the island again. Yes – that light was still there. Anger welled up in George again, and she went to look for her own boat, which should be somewhere near where they were.

'Here it is,' she said to Timmy, who leapt in at once. She ordered him out for she had to pull the boat down to the water. Fortunately it was a small, light boat and as the tide was almost fully in, she didn't have very far to drag it. Timmy took hold of the rope with his teeth and helped too. At last it was on the water, bobbing gently about in

the dim light of the half-moon. Timmy leapt in, and soon
George was in too, though with very wet feet!

She took the oars and began to pull away from the
shore. 'Tide's almost on the turn,' she told Timmy. 'It
won't be too hard a row. Now we can find those campers
and tell them what we think of them. You're to bark your

very loudest and scare them, Timmy – in fact, you can chase them to their boat, if you like.'

Timmy answered with a small bark. He knew quite well that George didn't want him to make much noise. He thought it was odd that she was going over to her island tonight, all by herself. Why hadn't she taken the others? He was sure that Julian would be very cross!

'Now don't bark or whine, Timmy,' she said, in a whisper. 'We're almost at my landing place – but I'm going under those trees there, not landing here. I want to hide my boat.'

She guided the boat towards some trees whose branches overhung a tiny creek that ran a little way inland. She leapt out, and flung the mooring rope round the trunk of the nearest tree, and made it fast.

'There, little boat,' she said. 'You'll be safe there. No one will see you. Come on, Tim – we'll tackle those campers now.'

She turned to go, and then stopped. 'I wonder where *their* boat is,' she said. 'Let's have a look round, Timmy. It must be here somewhere.'

She soon found the boat lying on the sands, its rope thrown round a nearby rock. The tide was almost up to it. She grinned to herself. 'Timmy!' she whispered. 'I'm going to untie this boat and set it loose on the tide. It will soon be far away. Ha – what will those awful campers say?'

And, to Timmy's amazement, she undid the rope from the rock, rolled it up, and threw the coil inside the boat. Then she gave the boat a push – but it was still embedded in the wet sand.

'Never mind,' she said. 'Another ten minutes and the tide will be right under it – and then it will turn and take the boat with it!'

She began to make her way up the beach, Timmy close to her side. 'Now let's go after those campers, whoever they are,' she said. 'Where's their light gone? I can't see it now.'

But in a minute or two she saw it again. 'It's not from a camp fire – it's from a lantern of some sort,' she whispered to Timmy. 'We'll have to be careful now. Let's see if we can creep up behind them.'

The two of them made their way silently towards the middle of the little island. Here there was an old ruined castle – and there, in the courtyard of the castle, sitting in the midst of thick, overgrown weeds, were two men. George had her hand on Timmy's collar, and tugged it gently. He knew that meant, 'No barking, no growling, Tim,' and he stood perfectly still, the hackles on his neck rising fast.

The two men were playing cards by the light of a fairly powerful lantern, which they had set on a ruined stone wall. Timmy couldn't help giving a surprised growl when he saw one of them, but George hushed him at once.

Mr Wooh, the magician from the circus, was there, dealing out the cards! The other man she didn't know. He was well-dressed, and seemed bored. He flung down his cards as Timmy and George watched from a dark corner of the old castle, and spoke to his companion in an irritated voice.

'Well, whoever it is you said was bringing the rest of those papers here to the island doesn't seem to be turning up. The papers you've given me are good – very good – but

471

of no use without the others. This scientist fellow you've stolen them from is a genius. If we get the complete set of papers, they will be worth a tremendous sum of money, which I can get for you – but without the other papers, there will be no money for you – the first set would be useless!'

'I tell you, someone will be here with them. I heard them say so,' said Mr Wooh in his stately voice.

'Who stole them – you?' asked the other man, shuffling the cards quickly.

'No. I did not steal them,' said Mr Wooh. 'Me, I keep my hands clean – I do not steal.'

The second man laughed. 'No. You let other people do your dirty work for you, don't you! Mr Wooh, the World's Most Wonderful Magician, does not soil his hands! He merely uses the hands of others – and charges enormous prices for the goods they steal. You're a cunning one, Mr Wooh. I wouldn't like you for an enemy! How did you manage to get the papers?'

'By using my eyes and my ears and my cunning,' answered Mr Wooh. 'They are better than most people's. So many people are stupid, my good friend.'

'I'm not your good friend,' said the other man. 'I've *got* to do business with you, Mr Wooh, but I wouldn't like to have you for a friend. I'd rather have that chimpanzee of yours! I don't even like playing cards with you! *WHY* doesn't this fellow come?'

George put her mouth to one of Timmy's ears. 'Timmy, I'm going to tell them to clear off my island,' she whispered furiously to the listening dog. 'Fancy fellows like *that* daring to set foot here – rascals and rogues! Don't come with me – wait till I call you, then if you have to rescue me, come at once!'

Leaving a most unwilling Timmy standing beside part of the old castle wall, she suddenly appeared before the two astonished men by the light of their lantern.

They leapt to their feet at once. 'It's the girl who's come – I shouldn't have thought that the boys would have let her,' said Mr Wooh, astonished. 'I am . . .'

'WHAT ARE YOU DOING ON MY ISLAND?' demanded George, angrily. 'It belongs to *me*. I saw your light and came over with my dog. Be careful of him – he's big and strong and fierce. Clear off at once, or I'll report you to the police!'

'Easy, easy, now!' said Mr Wooh, standing very straight and looking immensely tall. 'So the boys sent *you* to hide the papers instead of daring to come themselves. How cowardly of them! Where are the papers? Give them to me.'

'I've hidden them,' said George. 'They're not very far away. You didn't think I'd be silly enough to come along

473

to you with them in my hands when I saw your light and knew that people were here, did you? No – I've hidden them somewhere on the shore – where *you* won't find them. Now you just clear off, both of you!'

'A very brave and determined young lady!' said Mr Wooh, bowing solemnly to George.

'Do you mean to tell me that's a *girl*!' said the other man, amazed. 'Well! She's a plucky kid, I must say! Look here, kid, if you've got those papers, hand them over, and I'll give you a whole lot of money which you can give to Professor Hayling with my best wishes.'

'Come and get them,' said George, turning as if to go. The two men looked at one another, eyebrows raised. Mr Wooh nodded, and then winked. If George had seen his face she would have known what that wink meant. It meant let's humour this silly kid, follow her – see the hiding place, snatch the papers and clear off in our boat without paying a penny! But LOOK OUT for the dog!

George led the way, Timmy walking between her and the two men. He was growling all the time, deep down in his throat, as if to say 'Just you lay a finger on George and I'll bite it off!' The men took care not to go too near him! They shone the lantern on him all the time, making sure that he was not going to leap at them.

George led them to the shore, to the place where they had left their boat. Mr Wooh gave a cry. 'Where's our boat? It was tied to that rock!'

'Is this it over this ridge?' called George climbing up a steep bank that overhung the water, which was now quite deep with the surging tide.

The men went to look – and then George gave them the

474

surprise of their lives! She ran at Mr Wooh and gave him such a push that he fell right over the high bank into the sea below, landing with a yell and a terrific splash. George shouted a command to Timmy, who was now very excited, and the big dog did the same to the other man, leaping at him and pushing him over. He, too, shot over the ridge and fell into the sea with a splash. Timmy stood on the little cliff and barked madly, as excited as George.

'You'll have to swim to the shore of the mainland if you want to escape!' yelled George. 'The tide has taken away your boat – I set it loose! You'd better not get back on my island yet – Timmy's on the watch for you – and he'll fly at either of you if you try to set a foot on it again!'

Both men could swim, though not very well, and both were exceedingly angry and very frightened. They were sure they could never swim to the mainland – but how to get on the island to safety, they didn't know. That great, fierce dog was there, barking as if he wanted to bite them into small bits. Their boat had been set loose, there was no way to escape. They swam round in circles, not knowing what to do!

'I'm going back to the mainland now!' yelled George, climbing into her boat. 'I'll send the police to rescue you in the morning. You can get on my island now – but you're in for a VERY cold night! Goodbye!'

And off went George in her boat, with Timmy standing at the back, watching to make sure those men didn't swim after them. He gave George an admiring lick. She wasn't afraid of ANYTHING! He'd rather belong to *her* than to anyone else in the world. WOOF, WOOF, W-O-O-F!

CHAPTER SEVENTEEN

And at last the mystery is solved!

GEORGE COULDN'T help singing loudly as she rowed back to the shore in her boat. Timmy joined in with a bark now and again. He was glad that George was so happy. He stood in the prow of the boat, wishing it was not night time, so that he could see clearly where he was going. The moon clouded over, and the sea looked endless in the dark. Very few lights showed on the mainland at that time of night – just one or two from houses where people were still up.

Wait, though – what was that bright light suddenly shining out from the mainland? Was it someone trying to pick out their boat? Timmy barked at the light, and George, who, of course, was rowing with her back to the shore, shipped her oars for a moment and looked round.

'It's someone on the quay,' she said. 'Maybe a late fisherman. Good! He'll be able to help me drag my boat up out of the way of the tide!'

But it wasn't a fisherman. It was Julian and Dick. They had arrived about five minutes ago, and had looked at once for George's boat and hadn't found it. 'Bother! We're too late to stop her, then. She's gone over to the island!' said Julian and began to examine all the other tied-up boats to see if he could find one that he could borrow, belonging to a friend. *Somehow* they must get over to Kirrin Island, and rescue George. He felt sure she would be in danger of some kind.

477

Then suddenly the two boys heard the sounds of oars splashing not far out to sea. Well, if that was a fisherman coming home, maybe Julian could ask *him* to lend him his boat to go to Kirrin Island in. He could tell him that he was afraid his cousin might be in need of help.

Timmy, in George's boat, suddenly recognised the two boys when the moon swam out from a cloud, and gave a delighted volley of barks. George, wondering if it *was* Julian and Dick, rowed as quickly as she could. She came into shore, jumped out and began to drag in her boat. The boys were beside her at once, and the boat was soon in its usual place, carefully made safe in case the tide was a high one.

'George!' said Julian, so overjoyed to see his cousin safe and sound that he couldn't help giving her a bear hug. 'You wicked girl! You went to the island – just what I said you *weren't* to do. You might have found the thieves on the island, and *then* you would have been in trouble!'

'I *did* find them – but it's *they* who are in trouble, not me!' said George. 'I saw a light over there, took my boat and went over to the island – and there they were – Mr Wooh the Magician and another man – ON MY IS-LAND! Did you ever hear such cheek? They asked me for the papers at once!'

'Oh, George – did you give them to the men?' asked Dick.

'Of *course* not! I'd already hidden them where those men couldn't possibly find them. I wasn't idiotic enough to take them over to hide on the *island* when I saw somebody was there – probably waiting for me – *and* for the papers!' said George.

'But, George – if you knew somebody was there, why on

478

earth did you risk going over to Kirrin Island then?' asked Julian, puzzled. 'It was a very dangerous thing to do.'

'I wanted to turn off whoever it was, of course,' said George. 'As if I'd allow just *anyone* on my island! It's mine, my very own, and I only allow people on it that I like. You know that.'

'I just NEVER know what you'll do next, George,' said Julian, patting Timmy on the head. 'How did you *dare* to go and tackle those men? Oh, I know Timmy was with you, but even so . . . why in the world didn't the men row after you, and ram your boat?'

'Well, you see, they couldn't,' said George. 'I found their boat, untied it, and set it adrift on the tide. It's probably half a mile away by now!'

The boys were so astonished that they couldn't even laugh at first. But then, when they thought of the two men marooned on Kirrin Island, their boat gone goodness knows where, they laughed till tears came into their eyes!

'George, I don't know how you can *think* of doing such things!' said Julian. 'Weren't the men furious?'

'I don't know,' said George. 'I didn't tell them about their boat. I pretended that I'd take them to where I'd hidden the papers – and then when we got on to a nice high ridge overlooking the sea, they looked over it to see if their boat was all right, and I gave Mr Wooh a jolly good push, and Timmy leapt at the man with him – and in they went – SPLASH! SPLASH!'

Julian really *had* to sit down and have another bout of laughing till the stitch in his side grew so bad that he was forced to get up and walk about. George suddenly saw the funny side of it all too, and she began to laugh as heartily as Julian. Dick joined in as well, and Timmy barked madly, enjoying the fun.

'Oh dear!' said Julian, feeling weak with laughter, 'and then I suppose you said a polite farewell and left them to their fate?'

'Well, actually I yelled out to tell them I'd send the police to rescue them in the morning,' said George. 'I'm afraid they'll both spend a very uncomfortable night – they were soaking wet, you see!'

'George – I'm beginning to think it was a good thing *you* went with the papers to the island, and not me, after all,' said Julian. 'I should *never* have thought of doing all the things you did – pushing the men into the sea – really, how *could* you and Timmy dare to do such things? And setting their boat loose! What on earth will the police say when we tell them?'

'I don't think we'd better tell them, had we?' said George. 'I mean – they might think I'd gone too far. Anyway, why not let the two men kick their heels on the island all night, and we'll decide what to do about the police in the morning. It's funny – I suddenly feel awfully tired.'

'I bet you do!' said Dick. 'Come on, let's get our bikes. Oh, and those precious papers – where are they?'

'Under the tarpaulin in Fisherman Connell's boat,' said George, and suddenly gave the most enormous yawn. 'I hid them there.'

'I'll get them,' said Julian. 'Then off we go back to Big Hollow House. The others will be getting awfully worried by now!'

He found the papers in the fishing boat and then the three of them rode off quickly along the road from Kirrin to Big Hollow, Timmy running behind them. Julian kept laughing to himself. George was amazing! Fancy tackling those two fellows like that – pushing them into the water, and setting their boat adrift. Julian was sure he would never have thought of doing such daring things himself.

At last they were back at the tents, and the others crowded round them to hear what had happened. Anne looked very white. Jenny was with her, comforting her – she had *just* made up her mind to telephone the police, and was *most* relieved to see George again.

'We'll tell you all the details in the morning,' said Julian. 'But all I'll say now is that the papers are safe all right, here in my pocket – the thieves were probably Mr Wooh and another man. They were on the island tonight, waiting for George. They *had* overheard what she said in the tent! However, George and Timmy pushed them both into the water and set their boat adrift, so things are settling down nicely! They will have to spend the night on the island, cold and wet through!'

'*George* did all that!' said Jenny, amazed. 'Well! I never knew she was so *dangerous*! Good gracious! I feel right-down scared of her! Settle down to sleep in your tent, dear – you look tired out!'

George was glad to flop down on her rugs. Now that the excitement was all over she felt too sleepy for words! She fell asleep at once – but Julian and Dick didn't. They lay awake for some time, chuckling over George's deeds of daring. What a cousin to have!

When they were up at the house at breakfast next morning, Jeremy came up the garden and put his head in at the dining-room window. 'Hey!' he said. 'Mr Wooh's not in his tent this morning! He's disappeared! And poor old Charlie the Chimp is too miserable for words.'

481

'Ah – we can tell you *exactly* where Mr Wooh is,' said Julian. 'But – wait a bit, Tinker, where are you going? You haven't finished your . . .'

But Tinker had gone off with Jeremy at top speed! He was very fond of Charlie. Oh dear, would the chimpanzee weep for his master and refuse to take his food? Tinker called Mischief and they both ran down to the fence with Jeremy and climbed over it. Tinker went straight to Charlie's cage. The chimpanzee sat with his head in his hands, rocking himself to and fro, making sad, crying noises.

'Let's get into the cage with him,' said Tinker. 'He'll like to be comforted. He must be missing Mr Wooh very, very much.'

They crawled into the cage and sat down in the straw, each putting an arm round the sad chimpanzee. Old Grandad was very surprised to see them both there.

'Don't know what's happened to Mr Wooh,' he said. 'Didn't come home last night! Here, Jeremy, you come on out. I can't spare you to cry over Charlie all morning. He'll soon perk up. *You* can stay with him, Tinker, if you like.'

Jeremy crawled out of the cage and went off crossly. Tinker sat with his arm round Charlie, wishing he didn't look so terribly sad. As he sat there, he heard a funny little noise going on all the time. Tick-tick-tick-ticka-ticka-tick-tick-tick-tick-ticka-ticka-tick. 'Sounds like a watch or something,' said Tinker, and scrabbled about in the straw. Perhaps Mr Wooh's big gold watch had fallen into Charlie's cage?

His hand felt something small and round and smooth at

the bottom of the cage. He riffled away the thick straw, and drew out the object underneath it. He stared and stared at it in the utmost surprise. Charlie saw him looking at it, snatched it away and hid it in the straw again. He made a few growly noises as if he were angry.

'Charlie, *where* did you get that little clock?' said Tinker. 'Oh, CHARLIE! Well, as you're so sad this morning, I'll give it to you for your very own. Just to cheer you up. But oh, Charlie, I *am* surprised at you!'

He slid out of the cage and went back over the fence and into his own garden. Up the path he ran and burst into the dining-room, where the others were still finishing their breakfast.

'What's up?' said Dick.

'Listen! I know who the thief was who climbed in at the tower window . . . I KNOW WHO HE WAS!' cried Tinker, almost shouting in his excitement.

'WHO?' said everyone, in amazement.

'It was CHARLIE THE CHIMP!' said Tinker. 'Why didn't we think of him before? He can climb anything! It would be quite easy for *him* to swing himself up that rough-stoned wall, hanging on to the bits of creeper here and there – and to the uneven stones – and climb through the window into the tower room, collect all the papers he could hold – and climb down again – *slither* down again, probably . . .'

'THAT must have been the slithering sound I heard!' said Jenny. 'I *told* you I heard a queer slithering noise!'

'And the whispering you heard must have been Mr Wooh trying to make him go up the tower wall and into the window!' said Julian. 'Gosh – I bet poor old Charlie's been taught to get into all sorts of windows and take whatever he sees. Mr Wooh must have known Tinker's father worked out all his ideas up in the tower.'

'Wooh could easily teach him to take papers,' said Julian. 'But there were, of course, too many for old Charlie in the tower room. He wouldn't be able to carry them *all* in his front paws, for he needed *all* his paws to climb down that steep wall – so he must have crammed as many as he could into his mouth – and dropped the rest under the table! Charlie the Chimp – well! Who would have thought *he* could be the thief!'

'Wait a bit – how on earth do you know it was Charlie?' said Dick. 'Nobody saw him. It was at night.'

'Well, I *do* know it was Charlie,' said Tinker. 'You remember that dear little clock on the tower room mantelpiece? Well, it disappeared on the night when those papers were stolen – and *I* found it hidden in the straw in Charlie's cage this morning! He snatched it away from me, and almost cried – so I let him keep it! It was ticking loudly just like it always did. It was the loud ticking that told me it was there in the cage!'

'Who wound it up at nights, to keep it going?' said Julian, at once, most astonished.

'Charlie, I suppose,' said Tinker. 'He's very clever with his paws! The clock was quite safe, hidden in his cage. Nobody would be likely to get into the chimp's cage and sit there with him – but *I* did this morning, and that's how I found it. I heard it ticking, you see. I bet old Charlie was clever enough to pop his precious clock into his mouth when he saw any of the men coming to clean out his cage!'

'Well, I'm blessed!' said Jenny. 'How was it that Mr Wooh never saw him bringing it along with the papers that night, when he stole them?'

'Well, as Tinker told you – my guess is that old Charlie must have put the little clock in his mouth then, along with the papers,' said Dick. 'He needed all his four paws, climbing – or rather *slithering* down that wall – and he's

485

got a jolly big mouth! You should see what a lot of food he can stuff into it!'

'Yes. And Mr Wooh would take the papers, of course – Charlie would just take them from his mouth and hand them to him – but he'd be crafty enough to keep his precious new toy hidden in his mouth! Poor old Charlie! Can't you see him listening to the clock, and cuddling it – like a child with a new toy!' said George.

'He sounded exactly as if he were crying this morning,' said Tinker. 'I couldn't bear it. Poor old Charlie! He couldn't understand *why* Mr Wooh didn't go and see him today. He was *so* miserable!'

'I think we'll *have* to get the police along now,' said Julian. 'Not only to catch Mr Wooh and his friend, left so conveniently marooned by George on her island – but also because Mr Wooh should be charged with stealing your father's irreplaceable charts and diagrams, Tinker. Goodness knows what else he has taught poor old Charlie to steal. I bet he's sent the chimp into a lot of houses, and up many walls, and into many windows.'

'Yes. There's probably been a trail of robberies wherever the circus went,' said Jenny. 'And many innocent people must have been suspected.'

'What a shame!' said Anne. 'But, oh dear – if Mr Wooh goes to prison, whatever will become of poor old Charlie the Chimp?'

'I bet Jeremy will take him,' said Tinker. 'He loves him, and old Charlie adores Jeremy! He'll be all right with Jeremy and old Grandad!'

'Well, Tinker, I think you'd better go and tell your father all this,' said Jenny. 'I know he's busy – he always is – but this is a thing *he* ought to deal with and nobody else.

AND AT LAST THE MYSTERY IS SOLVED!

If you'd like to fetch him, George could tell him the whole story – and then I rather guess *he'll* ring up the police – and Mr Wooh will find himself in a whole lot of trouble.'

So there goes Tinker, with Mischief on his shoulder, to find his father, down the hall – up the stairs – along the landing – into his father's bedroom . . . R-r-r-r-r-r-r-r-r-r-r! Tinker, you sound like a motor-scooter going up a steep hill! PARP-PARP! *Don't* hoot like that, you'll make your father so angry that he won't listen to a word you say!

But the Professor *did* listen – and soon Jenny heard him telephoning the police. They're coming straight away, and that means that Mr Wooh the Magician is in for a most unpleasant time, and his magic won't help him at all! He'll have to give back the papers that he made Charlie steal – and plenty of other things, too! There he is, marooned on the island, quite unable to escape, waiting fearfully with his companion, for the police!

'Another adventure over!' said George, with a regretful sigh. 'And a jolly exciting one too! I'm glad you solved the mystery, Tinker – it was clever of you to find the little tower room clock. I bet Mr Wooh wouldn't have let Charlie keep it, if he'd known he'd taken it from the tower room! Poor old Charlie the Chimp!'

'I'm just wondering if Dad would let me keep Charlie here, while Mr Wooh is in prison,' began Tinker, and stopped as Jenny gave a horrified shriek.

'*Tinker*! If you so much as *mention* that idea to your father, I'll walk straight out of this house and NEVER COME BACK!' said Jenny. 'That chimp would be in my kitchen all day long – oh yes, he would – and things would be disappearing out of my larder, and my cupboards, and my drawers, and he'd dance up and down and scream at me if I so much as said a word, and . . .'

'All right, dear, dear Jenny, I won't ask for Charlie, honest I won't,' said Tinker. 'I do love you a *bit* more than I'd love a chimp – but think what a companion he would be for Mischief!'

'I'm not thinking anything of the sort!' said Jenny. 'And what about you taking a bit of notice of that monkey of yours – bless us all if he hasn't helped himself to half that jar of jam – just *look* at his sticky face! Oh, what a week this has been, what with chimps and monkeys and children and robberies, and George disappearing, and all!'

'Dear old Jenny,' said George, laughing as she went off into the kitchen. 'What an exciting time we've had! I really did enjoy every minute of it!'

So did we, George. Hurry up and fall into another adventure. We are longing to hear what you and the others will be up to next. How we wish we could join you! Goodbye for now – and take care of yourselves, Five. Good luck!